Samantha Dooley gasped aloud as the vehicle lurched forward.

Not the steady acceleration of a fixed-wing plane, or the nose-dipping surge of a helicopter, this motion was . . . something else. It was discontinuous, jerky, jolting.

My God, this is real! For the first time, as the vehicle lurched forward, true and total conviction penetrated and took hold of her emotions. This isn't a simulation. This can't be a simulation. I'm . . . somewhere else, I've been "translocated." All of her hypotheses fell apart in an instant, revealed for what they really were: facile justifications and evasions, denials of reality. She heard a sound that was a cross between a bitter laugh and a whimper—realized it came from her own throat. Viscerally she knew, at last. She'd been physically translocated to another place (another time?).

"Dooley One, come in. . . ."

NO LIMITS

VIRTUAL GEOGRAPHIC LEAGUE

NO LIMITS

Nigel D. Findley

A ROC BOOK

ROC
Published by the Penguin Group
Penguin Books USA Inc., 375 Hudson Street,
New York, New York 10014, U.S.A.
Penguin Books Ltd, 27 Wrights Lane,
London W8 5TZ, England
Penguin Books Australia Ltd, Ringwood,
Victoria, Australia
Penguin Books Canada Ltd, 10 Alcorn Avenue,
Toronto, Ontario, Canada M4V 3B2
Penguin Books (N.Z.) Ltd, 182–190 Wairau Road,
Auckland 10, New Zealand

Penguin Books Ltd, Registered Offices:
Harmondsworth, Middlesex, England

First published by Roc, an imprint of Dutton Signet,
a division of Penguin Books USA Inc.

First Printing, May, 1996
10 9 8 7 6 5 4 3 2 1

Virtual Geographic League created by Jordan Weisman, Dave McCoy, and Bruce Boyer
Developmental Editor: Jordan Weisman
Series Editor: Sharon Turner Mulvihill

Printed in the United States of America

To my brother Rod—
maybe you'll have the time to read *this* one . . .

No limits but the sky.

—*Don Quixote de la Mancha,*
Miguel de Cervantes (1547–1616)

1

Some self-styled expert once said, "For an aggressive pilot, a MiG at your six is better than no MiG at all." Sam Dooley was starting to have serious doubts about the truth of that little gem of wisdom.

Goddamn it . . . Yeah, the MiG–25 "Foxbat" was still on Dooley's tail—"solidly trapped at six"—firmly in the slot, about three nautical miles back. The MiG's radar was lashing Dooley's F–16 Fighting Falcon, trying to lock onto the smaller plane for a missile shot. Warning buzzers sounded in Dooley's ear, and lights flashed across the Falcon's annunciator panel. No lock-on and no indication of missile launch yet, but it was just a matter of time unless Dooley did something. Unfortunately, Dooley had no idea of just what that "something" should be.

Dooley's eyes scanned the Falcon's instruments. Altitude a hair short of seventeen thousand feet, air speed dropping to 400 knots. Without conscious thought, Dooley eased the throttle through the détente, punching up stage three afterburner. As the speed display on the HUD crept back up to 450—optimal "corner speed" for the Falcon—Dooley threw the plane into a hard turn to the right, muscles tensing to fight the anticipated gee-forces.

Another glance at the MiG. The twin-engine fighter was drifting out of the slot, the enemy pilot an instant slow in reacting to Dooley's break. Drifting, but not enough. Dooley could imagine the MiG jockey punching his own Tumansky R–31 turbojets into burner and loading on the gees to correct. *Damn it to hell!*

"Rogue Two, where the hell are you?" Dooley snapped.

The voice of Dooley's wingman sounded in the helmet's earphone—tight, tortured, as though an elephant were sitting on his chest. "Rogue One, I'm engaged with two MiGs, totally defensive. Things are delta sierra here."

Despite the situation, Dooley had to grin. Delta sierra—

pilot jargon for "dogshit." *Well, things are delta sierra here, too. . . .*

What was that line from *Top Gun*? "I'll hit the brakes and he'll fly right by. . . ." It was to laugh. Only in the movies. Out here in the real world—"out on the pointy end"—it wasn't that easy to orchestrate an overshoot, Dooley knew. *I'll hit the brakes and he'll blow me out of the sky. . . .*

A raucous tone jolted Dooley like an electric shock. *Launch indication.* The Foxbat was hosing off an AA–7 Apex radar-guided missile, and delta sierra just didn't seem to cover the situation anymore. Performance figures flashed through Dooley's head. The Apex had a top speed of Mach 3.5, well over 2,000 knots, and could pull gees that would pulp a flesh-and-blood pilot. Dooley's only hope was that the MiG jockey was too close—within the minimum effective radius of the missile. Optimum range for an Apex engagement was ten nautical miles or more, out to the 25-mile maximum range of the missile. At three miles separation, would the Apex have enough time to correct after the launch and lock on tight?

With a silent prayer, Dooley reversed the turn, hauling the Falcon back around to the left, simultaneously punching out four packages of chaff. The strips of metal-coated Mylar, cut to lengths designed to confuse a missile's guidance radar, spread out beyond the edge of Dooley's peripheral vision. Throttle to the firewall—the Falcon's Pratt & Whitney F100 turbofan wailed. Forward on the stick, pointing the nose at the ground three miles below, straining for every iota of speed the F–16 could extract from the unyielding laws of physics. . . .

Something flashed past the Falcon beyond the bubble canopy, so close that Dooley could almost have touched it. It was the Apex, blazing by at three times the speed of sound, confused by the chaff and the F–16's desperate maneuver. There and gone so fast that Dooley's brain barely registered it. Dooley rolled hard, imagining the stresses in the plane's small wings, vectors of force like shifting lines of light on a computer screen.

"Rogue One." The voice of Dooley's wingman was sharp, high-pitched—*Fear?* "Rogue One, I've got three on me."

Dooley scanned the sky for Rogue Two as the Falcon completed its turn and its nose came up again. *There, four miles out.* The other F–16's blue-gray paint scheme normally made it hard to pick out against the high cirrus clouds, but now a trail of black smoke pointed to it like an arrow. The three MiGs on its tail showed up clearly, deadly-looking darts dark against the sky. MiG–29 Fulcrums, faster and more maneuverable than the Foxbat, maybe even as nimble as the F–16 Falcon itself. As Dooley watched, smoke burst from under the wing of the lead Fulcrum. A finger of white, tipped by a point of fire, reached out toward Rogue Two.

"Rogue One . . . ah, hell, Atoll inbound, I'm in trouble. . . ."

Rogue Two's Falcon snap-rolled, but it was way too late. Dooley couldn't make out the details, but then seeing it wasn't really necessary, was it? Proximity fuse. Warhead detonation. Secondary explosions. The F–16 was blotted from the sky by a chain of dirty-red puffballs as the Atoll missile's thirteen-pound warhead lanced hot fragments into the fighter's wing tanks and the fuel ignited. The voice in Dooley's ear cut off in mid-cry.

Something burned in Dooley's gut. *Fury? Is that what this is?* Part of the pilot's mind flagged the emotion as inappropriate . . . but that wasn't the part of Dooley's brain in control of the plane. With a growl, Dooley snapped the Falcon into a tight, climbing turn, simultaneously pulling the throttle out of burner to shorten the turning radius. *Where's that goddamn MiG . . . ?*

There it was, drifted well off line. Dooley smiled grimly. *You blew it. You figured you had me dead to rights with that missile shot, and you hung back to watch the fun.*

Make him pay, a voice in Dooley's brain murmured. *Make him pay.* Again, Dooley pulled back on the stick, loading on all the gees the Falcon could give.

The MiG jockey knew he'd made a mistake. Desperate not to make another, he tried to bring his big interceptor around to counter Dooley's maneuver. But he was too late and Dooley knew it, deep down in the gut where you feel true knowledge. The Foxbat was fast, almost half as fast again as the Falcon in level flight, driven by its two powerful turbojets. But it was big and heavy, 44,000 pounds with no load, more than twice the weight of the F–16. A lot of mass, a lot of momentum to wrestle around the sky. By hanging back, he'd lost his position of advantage—and if Dooley did things right, he'd soon be losing a lot more than that.

The three MiG–29s were already closing after splashing Rogue Two, eating up the distance to Rogue One. They'd be on Dooley in moments, and were probably already setting up for heat-seeker shots. To counter—for what little good it might do—Dooley punched out a string of five flares, hot-burning targets to confuse the IR seeker heads. That was the only option at the moment. *I'll get to you soon enough,* Dooley silently promised the Fulcrums.

Dooley's tight maneuver was doing its job. The Falcon was turning inside the pursuing MiG, bringing the enemy plane around toward the F–16's twelve o'clock. To increase his turn rate, the Foxbat pilot had punched up his own afterburners, and the twin engines were trailing black smoke. In Dooley's ear, the seeker tone of the Falcon's Sidewinder missiles started singing its funeral dirge. The F–16's HUD—its head-up display—showed the seeker head drifting toward the target designator box that marked the MiG. Seeker head and designator met and began to flash; the Sidewinder's growl became a high-pitched tone in Dooley's earpiece.

The missile was off before Dooley was even aware of squeezing the trigger, lancing toward the MiG at the apex of its white smoke-trail. Dooley snarled with satisfaction. The tiny, sun-bright points of flares trailed behind the Foxbat, the pilot's desperate attempt to throw the Sidewinder off track. But, in burner, the MiG was the strongest IR-source in the sky; a blind man could have *felt* its heat at a hundred paces. Dooley eyeballed the missile all the way in, watched it bore straight past the flares to detonate in the Foxbat's right engine. Again, secondary explosions as the target's fuel lit off. Dooley crowed in triumph.

The Falcon jolted like a car hitting a pothole at highway speed. Lights flashed around the annunciator panels, warning buzzers sounded. Dooley automatically checked six, already knowing what was there.

Yup, one of the Fulcrums had saddled up, gotten into a good attack position a little less than a mile back. Much too close for missiles, but ideal range for the Fulcrum's

30mm cannon . . . which was already ripping the crap out of Dooley's plane.

Dooley silenced the alarms, simultaneously checking the caution light panel to the right of the console. Annunciators burned over NAV and WEP ARM. *Shit.* NAV meant the Falcon's inertial navigation system was gone—no stress there, at least not immediately. But WEP ARM meant the central mechanism that armed the F-16's weapons systems had taken damage and was now useless. Even though the hardpoints still carried three air-to-air missiles, Dooley couldn't fire them. *Time to draw my gun.*

A flick of the thumb brought the Falcon's M61A1 cannon online. *So you want to play, huh?* Dooley asked silently. *Let's see if you're up for a knife fight.*

But that made no sense. Dooley was outnumbered three to one—four, if the dead Foxbat had a wingman waiting to put in an appearance. One-against-many air combat maneuvering was a fool's game, a sure ticket to slaughter, no matter how good you were. The only logical move was to extend, punch up full burner and head for the horizon and hope the MiG jockeys weren't in the mood to give chase.

Not that the Fulcrums were giving Dooley much chance to cut and run. The Falcon jerked again as another burst of 30mm fire tore into its fuselage. The warning buzzers screamed again, and red lights bloomed across the annunciator panels. The HUD's symbology vanished from the half-mirrored panel mounted atop the console. *Smoke?* Dooley thought, as fire warnings hooted. *Or is that just my imagination?*

Dooley drove the stick forward, pointing the Falcon's nose at the distant ground, simultaneously firewalling the throttle. The F-16 leapt forward. . . .

Too late. The back of the pilot's chair slammed into Dooley's kidneys like the kick of a mule. The cockpit slewed sideways, bouncing Dooley's helmet against the canopy with stunning force. Every warning light on every panel flashed. *"Caution! Caution!"* crowed the plane's synthesized voice-warning system—"Bitching Betty," the pilots called it—then fell silent.

Missile hit, what else could it be? The Falcon was out of control, yawing rapidly as the force of the explosion threw it into a wild spin. The view beyond the canopy whirled madly—sky, then ground, then sky again. Dooley fought with the stick, trying to force the Falcon back under control. Airspeed was dropping, the engine had flamed out. The stall-warning klaxon sounded once, then it too died as the plane's electrical system failed.

Instinct took over. Dooley's hands flashed to the ejection handles, pulled firmly. Nothing happened.

. . . Of course. *"Shit!"* As the world spun hypnotically beyond the canopy, Samantha Dooley unsnapped the chin strap of her helmet, pulled the acrylic shell from her head and shook out her long, brown hair.

"Shit!" she said out loud. Then, "Okay, already," she snapped.

The lights on the consoles flicked off, the sound of the air rushing by the canopy fell silent. A moment later, the outside world itself—still cartwheeling around her—vanished, showing the plain gray of the simulator's dome screen. With a faint whir, the cockpit shifted a final time on its hydraulic struts, returning to an even keel.

Dooley reached out and unlocked the bubble canopy, pushing it up and out of the way. She took a moment to detach the pressure feeds and telemetry lines from her gee-suit—*simulators at Edwards don't miss a trick,* she thought wryly—and clambered out of the cockpit, down the metal ladder to the floor a dozen feet below.

Lt. Benjamin Katt waited for her to leave the simulator dome, sprawled back in his chair, feet up on the corner of the computer console. He was grinning like a bandit, looking indecently smug and relaxed, Sam thought grimly. "Have fun?"

"And just what the hell was *that*?" she demanded.

Katt shrugged. "You said you wanted challenging," he pointed out, his grin growing even broader, if that was possible.

"Challenging?" Sam carefully placed her helmet on the console next to his booted feet, resisting the urge to throw it at him. "*Challenging?* Two Falcons against a Foxbat and three Fulcrums? *Three?* Challenging isn't what *I'd* call it."

"I didn't hear Rogue Two complain."

She snorted. "No, you programmed him to be such a twinkie that he didn't even bitch about it."

Katt shrugged again. "Twinkie or not, you didn't last much longer than he did."

Sam's body was starting to filter the adrenaline out of her bloodstream, and her anger was fading with it. She knew the adrenaline hangover was just a few minutes away, that emotionally sluggish feeling that always followed heavy stress. But for the moment she was feeling pretty good—tired, wrung out like a wet rag, but pretty good. Her lips quirked in a half-smile. "Yeah, yeah." She pulled off a glove, combed her fingers through her sweat-matted hair. "Okay. I *did* say I wanted a challenge. But, jeez, Ben, *three* Fulcrums? Is that fair?"

He gestured eloquently. "Hey, whoever said life was fair? Shit happens."

Sam laughed. "That wasn't shit—that was the runs."

"A bet's a bet."

"I know it."

"My choice of restaurant, right?"

Sam shook her head in mock despair. "I have the feeling this is going to hurt."

"Hey, I promise—no more than a couple of weeks' salary." Katt linked his hands behind his head. "Tonight?"

"Can't do it tonight, sorry." She smiled sweetly. "Prior engagement."

"*Uh*-uh," Katt replied vehemently. "That's not the way it works. Business before pleasure. Pay your dues; *then* you can meet your date."

She stepped forward and patted him on the cheek. "Ah, Ben," she cooed. "You *know* you're my first choice." She struggled to keep a straight face, but his expression told her he wasn't buying it. *Yeah, right,* his eyes said. "Seriously, I've got to go out of town for a few days."

"Business or pleasure?"

She hesitated. "Not business," she said slowly. *But not pleasure, either.*

For a moment, she thought he was going to ask what she meant, but then he nodded. *Not too insensitive,* she thought . . . *for a pilot.* "Have it your way," he agreed. "Next week's okay"—his predatory grin was back—"but we're going to have to talk some about interest on late payments."

She patted his cheek again, this time hard enough to sting a little. "Keep it in your pants, soldier," she told him, mock-sternly. "Or . . ." She paused, her expression one of deep thought. "Or maybe . . ." She stepped back and flowed into a jujitsu defensive stance. ". . . How about double or nothing, right here, right now? Two falls out of three. What d'ya say, *lieutenant*?"

Katt was on his feet in an instant, backing away in mock horror, empty palms raised in a warding gesture. "Hey now, hey now," he said, "you know I do my fighting the civilized way—with missiles and cannons."

Sam chuckled. Still in a fighting stance, she licked her lips lasciviously. "Sure you don't want to get up close and personal with me, big boy?"

"Good pilots learn from their mistakes."

"Which means . . . ?"

"Never again," Katt pronounced reverently. "One drubbing is more than enough for *this* boy. Now get the hell out of here before the brass sees you."

Sam laughed. "Catch ya later." She flipped him a jaunty salute and headed for the door.

"Hey, Dooley!"

She turned back. "Yeah?"

"You done good, Dooley," Katt said, and for the first time that day his expression was completely serious. "Good flying." And with that, he turned back to his computer console.

Samantha Dooley buttoned her blouse. The crisp cotton felt good against her skin after her shower. *A welcome change after the gee-suit.* Why couldn't the aerospace industry—the same military-industrial complex that could build a plane that flew faster than a bullet from a rifle—develop a comfortable gee-suit, one that didn't make you feel like you'd been jogging in a neoprene wet suit?

She tossed her bottle of shampoo and her towel into her carry bag, then shut the locker Benjamin Katt, known—predictably—to his colleagues by the call sign "Kit," had loaned her. The simulator building was starting to come alive. She could hear voices in the hallway outside the locker room, pilots and technicians exchanging a few words before they got on with their day. Sam zipped up her bag and headed for the fire door that led out the back of the building. While it was an open secret that pilots and simulator techs brought friends onto the site outside standard operating hours, no one wanted to rub the commanding officers' noses in the fact. Aggravating though Ben Katt could be, she didn't want to get him in trouble—at least, not *too* much trouble. She slipped out the fire door, shutting it quietly behind her.

The sun was just rising over the Cady Mountains to the east, but already the breeze was warm, carrying with it the distinctive sweet smell that Dooley always associated with the desert. It was going to be another hot one, she knew. She could imagine the shimmers of heat rising from the hard surface of dry Rogers Lake, creating thermals strong enough to throw an unwary jet-jockey out of control.

Around her, Edwards Air Force Base was starting its day. In the distance, out on the flight line, she could hear the scream of jet engines running up, counterpointed by the distinctive thudding of a helicopter's rotor. Three thousand feet above her, a flight of four F–15 Eagles split the morning air with a ripping sound that made her think of a giant tearing an enormous canvas. She watched the eggshell-blue fighters hurtle by, relishing the roar of their engines as the sound resonated in her chest. *The sound of power,* she thought. Multiple pounding concussions shook her to her core as the Eagle pilots pushed their engines into afterburner and stood the planes on their tails. Climbing vertically, the Eagles continued to accelerate, quickly becoming dots against the sky, then vanishing completely.

A group of flight-suit-clad pilots emerged from the building across the parking lot. Sam recognized two of them, John "Chopstick" Lui and Lincoln "Cerberus" Brown, two of Ben Katt's closest friends. The other four she didn't know by name, but figured she knew them anyway. *They're fighter pilots, aren't they?* she thought with a smile. *Self-anointed members of that warrior fraternity.* It still amazed her, sometimes, how similar pilots were, as though they'd all been pressed out of the same mold. Oh, there were differences; fighter jocks were individuals, after all. But it was strange: those differences served mostly to exaggerate the similarities. *How does it happen?* she asked herself. *Is it flight training that does it to them, that shapes them all into the archetype, the* stereotype, *of the fighter pilot? Or is it that the only people attracted to fast jets who don't wash out of the training already match that archetype?* She chuckled. It was like the old joke, "Are all fishermen liars, or do only liars fish?" Which came first . . . ?

Chopstick and Cerberus shot her smiles and a quick wave. The others just stared in unabashed admiration as she walked by. Sam smiled to herself. She knew she looked good: tall, slender and self-possessed in her white blouse and tan five-pocket slacks, and that was just the way she liked it. She saw one of the pilots—a short, stocky guy with sandy hair—nudge his buddy with an elbow and mutter something to him, all without taking his eyes off Dooley. *I wonder what they're saying about me?* she thought. *They've got to know Ben's sneaking me into the simulator. They probably think I'm sleeping with him.* Ben wouldn't have told anyone he was—she knew him that well, at least—but he sure wouldn't have gone out of his way to stop any speculation on the subject.

She chuckled again. Sex had certainly been at the top of Ben Katt's to-do list when she'd first met him. He'd been aggressive and self-confident, but not pushy or arrogant—the way men can be when they're truly secure in who and what they are. Any number of other women would have succumbed to his charms. *And probably have,* Sam thought wryly. But Sam Dooley had long ago learned how to deal with young men in rut without bruising their sometimes delicate male egos. She'd made it perfectly clear from the outset that she liked Benjamin Katt and enjoyed his company as a friend, but nothing more. Not in the immediate future, at least. *And judging by my record,* she admitted, *the day I let a friendship cross that line is the first day of the end.*

Ben had accepted her parameters—more proof, if she needed it, that his apparent self-confidence wasn't an empty act—though he hadn't given up on the double-entendre comments and sometimes risqué remarks. Probably because it was expected of him more than because he thought it would work, she figured. They fit well as friends, and it certainly didn't hurt that they both could provide something the other wanted.

For Sam, of course, it was access to Edwards Air Force Base's extensive range of simulators. Officially, these multimillion dollar systems were off-limits to civilians—not because they might damage them, but more because some of the "civilians" might be foreign intelligence agents trying to learn more about the performance of American jets than the military wanted them to know. Predictably, of course, reality didn't correspond too closely to the official picture. Nearly every pilot on the base occasionally snuck a friend in for a simulator session, or even for a short flight in a twin-seater jet. The brass usually turned a blind eye, unless the infringement of the rules was just too blatant. Sam laughed out loud, remembering the pilot who tried to have carnal knowledge of a young groupie in the cockpit of his jet. About the only thing he'd never done there, he'd claimed. Slipped a spinal disk in the process and had to radio for a ground crew to haul him out. Ben had less to worry about on that front than many other pilots, she knew—because Sam was actually a hell of a flier. If an officer wandered into the middle of one of her simulator sessions or checked out the telemetry tapes, he wouldn't see some twinkie blundering around the simulated sky. He'd see someone with an instinct for squeezing performance out of an aircraft. *Hell,* she told herself firmly, *if you didn't hear my voice or see me getting out of the simulator, you couldn't tell I'm not a fighter jock with almost as many hours as Ben.*

And then there was the quid pro quo. For Ben, it was flight time at the controls of a helicopter. He was checked out on jets and just about any other fixed-wing vehicle in existence, and he had often boasted to Sam that if she put wings on a brick, he could fly it. He loved the speed, the exhilaration, the danger. But he also relished the things you could do in a helicopter that you couldn't in a supersonic interceptor: hang motionless in the sky, pivot on the craft's axis, cruise backward or sideways, land on a dime. That was what Sam could provide him. For the last two years, since she was twenty-three, she'd been flying for WestAir, a helicopter sightseeing company that operated from near her home in Venice, California, just south of Santa Monica. The pay wasn't the best, and she sometimes felt heartily sick of flying groups of interchangeable tourists to "ooh" and "ah" over the same landmarks day after day. But at least she was *flying,* and getting paid for it! And she'd cut a deal early on with her employers that allowed her to take the company chopper up on her own time, so long as she picked up all fuel and maintenance costs. *Much better than nothing,* she told herself for the thousandth time.

It was that deal that let her trade stick-time with Ben. At first, she couldn't understand why he was so interested (unless it was all an ongoing ploy to get her into the sack). He picked up all the fuel costs for his joy rides without a murmur, even though there had to be chopper pilots at Edwards who'd be glad to take a fellow air force officer up for a spin. And the choppers he could fly there! Huey Cobras, Apaches—gunships, fast and maneuverable. How could a Bell Jet Ranger—a *sightseeing platform,* for chrissake—possibly compare?

When she finally figured out the answer, she considered it pretty obvious, and highly amusing. It all came back to the "fighter-pilot archetype," and, beyond that, to the good old male ego. Ben *couldn't* ask one of his colleagues to take him up because then he'd have to admit he wasn't the best there was at absolutely everything.

It could still make her laugh, months after she'd reached that realization. Ben Katt was a good fighter jock; she knew that. He was a hell of an intuitive pilot. Considering how few hours he'd spent at the controls of a chopper, he was pretty damn good at that, too. *But he wasn't the best,* that was the point. That was what he couldn't admit, and couldn't reveal, to his comrades on the base.

It was a stupid attitude, of course. Katt's specialty was fast fixed-wings; his interest in rotorcraft wasn't anything more than a hobby. Taking that into consideration, he was doing well—*remarkably well,* she corrected mentally, remembering how much smoother his landings had become over the last several flights. But did that matter to him? No, of course not. Totally irrational.

But then, males are irrational, aren't they?

Well, she allowed, maybe not *all* males. Maybe not even *most* males. But sure as hell, all male fighter pilots. She shook her head, watching the knot of khaki-clad men vanish into the hanger.

Fighter pilots *knew* they were good in the cockpit. That was their job, they did it every day—and every day that they made it back in one piece after a training mission or after hassling with their buddies, they got confirmation of that fact. But they made a big mistake by assuming that they were equally good *outside* the cockpit. Every single fighter pilot Sam had ever met thought of himself as the best driver, the best fighter, the best athlete, the best lover—and it just stood to reason that they were wrong.

Take Benjamin Katt, for example. Early on in their friendship, when he'd learned that Sam trained in the martial arts, he'd suggested that they hit the mat sometime for a practice bout. "Just for the hell of it," he'd said. (*Yeah, right. He just wanted the opportunity to get me down on the ground—anywhere, anyhow.*) He'd had some martial arts training himself, he'd assured her. A couple of years ago, true, so he might be a little rusty—but some things you don't forget, right? Sam had tried to talk him out of it, but now she knew she'd gone about it the wrong way. She'd had a little more than "some" training, she'd explained to him carefully. She still worked out regularly to keep in shape and in practice, and her skills certainly couldn't be described as rusty. That was a mistake, she'd realized quickly. She'd made it so that Ben *couldn't* back down, even if he'd wanted to. He had to prove to her, and to himself, maybe, that he was her equal on the mat, or die trying.

The next evening at Sam's jujitsu club, Ben had come out onto the mat all full of piss and vinegar—the invincible fighter pilot, ready to humor the girl who thought she could take him. He'd been good, granted, surprisingly good. His reflexes were fast, his decision-making quick, and his well-honed killer instinct had certainly stood him in good stead. For a while, at least. It hadn't taken her long to draw him out, to gauge his strengths and weaknesses. He'd been fast and strong, but Sam's experience and training had counted for more in the end—and she had a good measure of killer instinct of her own.

At least Ben had kept his sense of humor about the whole thing. He'd been gracious enough as he admitted defeat when she was helping him to his feet after his twelfth trip to the mat. He'd bowed to her politely as they'd gone to change, and he'd even bought the beers afterward.

But he'd never taken her up on her offer of a return bout, and she still wondered what he'd told the other hot-shot pilots. She couldn't imagine him telling the complete truth, but she noticed that the others all treated her with considerably more respect from that point on. She laughed again, brushing a strand of long, brown hair back from her face. *One of these days, I'll get my foil and mask out of storage and see if Ben wants to try his hand at fencing. . . .*

Grendel was parked in the far corner of the visitors' lot, right up against the fence, gleaming white in the California sun. (Better to walk an extra hundred yards or so than have to touch up dings and nicks in Grendel's paint job made by car doors.) Sam tossed her bag into the backseat, opened the door, and slid into the Mustang convertible. Grendel's powerful five-liter engine caught at once, and she blipped the throttle, enjoying the car's throaty roar.

Some of her acquaintances had given her a hard time when she'd picked up the big convertible the year before. "Buy an import," they'd all told her. "Don't buy a Detroit junker."

But she'd loved the Mustang from the first moment she'd laid eyes on it. Not only because it brought back memories—her father, Jim Dooley, Jr., had bought a Mustang when they'd first come out in 1965, two years before he'd died—but also because of the way it looked, and the way it felt on the road. She loved the straight-ahead power; the 225–horsepower mill could push the car to well over 140 miles per hour if she opened up the throttle. The handling could be better, she had to admit. The car was overpowered and a little temperamental, and it was all too easy to spin the wheels and lose it on a turn. But she'd soon learned the sensitive yet firm touch needed on the steering wheel and throttle, and replacing the standard-equipment Goodyear Eagle tires with low-profile Pirellis also helped.

As the big V–8 warmed up, she clipped her hair back in a barrette and slipped on a pair of Ray-Ban™ aviator-style sunglasses. She rolled down the power windows and settled herself more comfortably in the leather seat. *A good day for driving,* she thought with a smile. Grendel was designed for the highway, and this was a perfect opportunity to let him stretch out. As she accelerated out of the parking lot, the Mustang's roar sang counterpoint to the scream of distant jets.

2

Samantha felt wiped out by the time she rolled into Gold Beach, Oregon. Her face and arms prickled with sunburn, even through the SPF–25 cream she'd slathered on repeatedly during the day, and her nerves felt frayed around the edges.

She'd expected the drive to take twelve or thirteen hours: up I–5 to Redding, then along the winding, scenic route that followed the Trinity River until she hit the coast at Arcata. Then north up 101 across the Oregon state line and into Gold Beach. Eight hundred miles, give or take. Twelve hours seemed reasonable because, though the stretch from Redding to the coast was a winding road through the Trinity National Forest and her average speed would drop to about 40 miles per hour, on the interstate and on Highway 101 she'd expected to be able to let the Mustang run and make up any time she'd lost. She'd left Edwards Air Force Base at about 07:30 (like many pilots, she always thought in military time), which meant she should be rolling into Gold Beach an hour or two before the sun went down.

What's that they say about the plans of mice and men? she asked herself wryly. Everything seemed to have gone wrong. Road crews on I–5 squeezing the traffic down to a single, slow-moving lane. A seemingly endless parade of sluggish sightseers on the Trinity road, creeping at 20 miles an hour around turns Grendel could have taken at 55. A Winnebago overturned outside of Smith River, surrounded by police cars and emergency vehicles. Twelve hours stretched to fourteen, then to sixteen. By the time she finally saw the lights of Gold Beach, it was well after midnight. Her eyes stung like open wounds, and her feet felt swollen in her shoes. She rented a room at the first motel she saw boasting a vacancy sign, which turned out to be the prosaically named Inn at Gold Beach, and slept for nine solid hours, lulled by the susurrus of the surf below the highway.

She rose refreshed, but lingered over repacking Grendel and breakfast at a coffee shop across the road. It had taken her longer to get here than she'd expected; even so, she found herself wishing it would take longer still. *Stupid,* she admonished herself. *Putting it off isn't going to make it any easier.*

It was almost noon by the time she got back on the road, cruising slowly through the six-block "downtown" of Gold Beach. She crossed the concrete bridge over the mouth of the Rogue River, then took the first right. The road passed the dock from which the U.S. mail boats departed, high-speed, minimal-draft hydrojet craft that daily carried tourists and the mail upriver. An osprey, its white chest and dark wings clear against the cloudless sky, hung overhead, riding the thermals like a sailplane. She remembered reading an article about ospreys that described how the birds snatched fish from the water with their powerful talons and carried their prey to the shore or an overhanging tree branch. The thing about those talons was that they couldn't release what they'd grasped until they could set it down on something solid. Elaborating on that point, the author had explained that if an osprey misjudged and grabbed a fish that was too heavy for it to lift out of the water, the bird would drown. *And* that's *full investment for you,* she thought. *Maybe there's a life lesson in there somewhere.*

She glanced at the Mustang's speedometer and realized she was creeping along at 20 miles an hour, even though the road was clear and well-surfaced. *Still postponing the inevitable, is that it?* With a snort of disgust, she hit the gas and power-shifted into second. Grendel leaped forward with a chirp of rubber.

She reached her destination a couple of minutes later. A house nestled in the trees, atop a bluff overlooking the Rogue. Set well back from the road at the end of a winding gravel drive, only a portion of the house was visible to passersby. Sam knew how deceptive that view was, however. The house was larger than it looked, spacious and well appointed. *With a wooden deck at the back, giving a perfect view of the river valley.* She couldn't see the deck from this angle, but she held a vivid picture of it in her mind's eye. *Are the old Cape Cod–style chairs still there, with arms wide enough to safely hold a large mug of hot chocolate on a brisk spring night?*

Slowly she turned in at the open gate and crunched up the gravel drive. Another car was parked in front of the single-car garage, a nondescript gray Chrysler. For a moment she was surprised. *Shouldn't the red Jensen be parked out front, in pride of place?* But no, she realized at once. There had to be space for visitors. The Jensen Interceptor III would be safely inside the garage. *After all, it won't be going for another spin until it has a new owner, will it?*

Sam's eyes stung. She rubbed at them disgustedly. *Damn it, I promised myself I wasn't going to do that.* She parked the Mustang next to the gray car and turned off the motor. For a few seconds she closed her eyes and listened. She tuned out the metallic clicking as the big engine block cooled, until all she could hear was the wind in the trees and the low, steady rushing of the river. Cautiously, she relaxed her mental control, opening herself to the memories that were struggling to flood through her mind.

No childhood memories these; no decades of images. (*And that's where some of the pain comes from,* she knew, *that there's not more of them.*) She'd seen this house for the first time less than seven years ago, and she'd visited it fewer than a dozen times. But they were so intense, some of those memories, more vivid than a lot of the images she recalled from her childhood, the so-called formative years. *What does that tell me?*

She shook her head firmly, opened the car door and climbed out. She climbed the three stone steps to the front door and pressed the button on the intercom mounted nearby on the wall. After a few moments, a voice sounded from the box—tinny, electronic, but still familiar. "Hello?"

"It's me, Pop-Pop," she said around a lump in her throat. "Sam."

She heard the warmth in her grandfather's voice, even through the intercom's distortion. "Come on up, Samantha Rose." She could imagine his smile. "I think you know the way." The door unlocked itself with a faint click.

Samantha slowly climbed the faintly creaking stairs, past the window at the landing that looked out over the side garden, past the grainy black-and-white pictures—framed memories—on the walls. Even now, she felt a measure of comfort, the comfort that this house had always represented for her. The comfort of belonging, of being able to be herself without embarrassment or apology.

Pop-Pop's bedroom, his sickroom, was at the far end of the upstairs hallway, at the back of the house. As she approached it, she passed the closed door of his study and the guest room where she'd slept in the past. (Part of her wished she was staying there again, until all this was over. But the wiser part knew that she couldn't. Not that she wasn't welcome, because she knew she was; but because, for her own reasons, she just wouldn't be able to stand it.)

The door at the end of the hallway was ajar. She could hear the rumble of conversation—two male voices, too soft for her to make out the words. She hesitated, then took a deep breath, squared her shoulders and knocked firmly on the doorjamb.

The conversation inside cut off, then she heard, "Samantha? Come on in, this is no time to start getting formal on me." Her grandfather's voice. . . .

. . . Yet, at the same time, *not.* The tone carried the same dry humor she always associated with Pop-Pop, but there was something missing—vibrancy, energy . . . *life.* The thought came unbidden. *The difference between live music and a recording, all the immediacy gone.* She closed her eyes for a long moment, struggling to bring her emotions under control. Then she pushed open the door and walked in.

Jim Dooley, Sr., was watching her with those bright green eyes she knew so well, those eyes that always seemed able to look inside her mind and her heart. The room's curtains were half-drawn, but even in the dim light those eyes flashed with energy, and with understanding. Samantha forced a smile onto her face and kept her attention on those eyes.

Because that was the only part of Jim Dooley that looked familiar. The cancer he was fighting had ravaged his body as it had sapped his energy. He was a husk of a man, dwarfed by the steel-framed hospital bed that had replaced his cherished oak four-poster. Sunken cheeks, bruise-blue bags under his eyes, sparse strands of hair sweat-pasted across parchment-dry scalp, skin stretched tight over his big-boned frame. She remembered how he'd looked the last time she'd visited: tanned and weathered, a big, bluff outdoorsman who looked two decades younger than his seventy-two years. Now he looked twenty years *older* than his chronological age.

A shell, Sam thought, *that's all he is An empty shell, hollowed out and drained.* He hardly seemed to indent the mattress, as though he were weightless. *If I breathe hard, he'll blow away, like a dried leaf.*

He's like a caricature of himself . . . no, she corrected herself, *a* distillation, *that's what he is.* The cancer ravening through his bones might have dissolved his flesh, melted away his muscles, turned his skin to brittle, ancient paper. *But what are flesh and muscle and skin anyway?* she asked herself silently. *Is that all that makes up a person? Of course not.*

She looked at her grandfather again, and it was as if she were seeing him for the first time. In a way, it was as if the wasting disease had *purified* him, melted away everything but the essentials. *Everything that isn't purely* him, she thought. She could almost imagine that he glowed with an inner light, a light seen not with the eyes but felt with the heart. She imagined she could feel the febrile fire of disease, the fever burning within him, like the heat of a distant bonfire on her face. Yet there was something more, a purer glow rivaling that of the cancer. That fire was the Jim Dooley—the spirit, the energy, the personality—who resided within the withered shell.

Her epiphany took no more than a moment, yet Samantha knew it would stay with her for the rest of her life. Her forced smile became genuine, and the sting of unshed tears receded. She crossed to the bed and took one of the old man's hands—light and fragile, like a small bird—between hers.

"It's good to see you, Samantha. I'm glad you could come."

"You think you could keep me away, Pop-Pop?" she asked softly.

"You're looking good."

"So are you."

Jim Dooley raised an eyebrow and opened his mouth to make a snide comment. But then, as though he'd seen something surprising in Sam's eyes, he didn't speak. After a moment, he nodded wordlessly. She felt him squeeze her hand, the grip a pale shadow of its old strength.

"Are they taking good care of you, Pop-Pop?"

Jim shrugged his fleshless shoulders. "When I let them," he said dryly, and his jade eyes flashed.

"You've got a nurse?"

He nodded. "The reincarnation of Attila the Hun's governess." He grinned nastily. "I gave her the morning off. No doubt she's taking advantage of the unexpected free time to vivisect a few kittens."

Suddenly he made a *tsk* sound with his tongue, and shook his head. "Samantha, I'm forgetting my manners. I want you to meet Ernest Macintyre, an old friend of mine. Mac, I want you to meet my granddaughter."

Sam turned. She'd momentarily forgotten that anyone else was in the room.

The other man had his back to the corner, as far from the bed as he could stand and still be inside the room. Behind his wire-rimmed glasses, his eyes widened as she approached him, and for a moment Sam wondered if he'd try to run past her and out of the room. But then he smiled—*An* innocent smile, she couldn't help thinking, *almost childlike*—and held out his hand. "Ms. Dooley," he said politely.

She raised an eyebrow at his formality. "Mr. Macintyre." As she shook his proffered hand, she looked him over. Medium build, average height—actually, she realized on second inspection, he was quite tall, at least six feet. But there was something about his build, or maybe the way he carried himself, that made him seem somehow shorter. Sandy-brown hair, conservative cut. Pale complexion, eyes of clear cornflower blue. *Not handsome,* Sam caught herself thinking, *but attractive, in a guileless sort of way.*

"You're a friend of Pop-Pop's, then?" she asked as he released her hand.

Macintyre opened his mouth to speak, but nothing came out. Sam saw him flash a quick look toward the man on the bed.

"An old colleague," Jim Dooley replied smoothly. "Recently *become* a friend, I suppose you could say." Sam blinked. *Old colleague?* This Macintyre didn't look more than a few years older than she was—she thought thirty, maybe.

Jim shifted his gaze from Sam to Macintyre. "And I don't want to impose on that new friendship any longer, Mac," he went on, with a kindly smile. "I know you've got work to do, and that's more important than waiting attendance on an old man."

Again, Macintyre's mouth worked silently. Then he visibly swallowed, and bobbed his head. "If you're sure there's nothing I can get for you . . . ?" Jim shook his head. "All right, then. I'll . . . I'll visit again."

"When you can," Jim agreed calmly.

Macintyre swallowed once more, and stuck his hand out toward Sam. She took it, amused but also mildly puzzled.

"Maybe I'll see you again, Mr. Macintyre," she suggested.

The slender man hesitated, as if he didn't know quite how to take that. Then, "A pleasure meeting you," he mumbled. He released her hand and headed for the door, stopping in the hall to look back at her. Then he was gone. Sam heard footsteps on the stairs, then the front door opened and clicked shut. She turned back to her grandfather, a question on her lips.

Jim was chuckling quietly. His eyes sparkled with amusement. "The good Mr. Macintyre makes his usual first impression," he said gleefully.

Sam couldn't help but mirror his smile. "Who *is* he?"

"As I said, an old colleague." Then his smile faded. "A long story, and not a particularly happy one. You can think of him as"—he paused—"as an air force brat, more or less. Troubled childhood, early loss . . ." He shot her a meaningful look. "Familiar?"

"Familiar," she echoed.

"He was . . . *adopted,* really . . . by some old colleagues of mine. Aviators, flight-test engineers, most of them. They were his family for many years." He shrugged. "And I suppose they still are.

"I first knew Mac when he was a child," he went on, closing his eyes—*As though he's watching movies of those days on his eyelids,* Sam thought. "We took turns being in loco parentis for him, as it were. Some were more involved than others, but over the years I think everyone spent some time with him." Jim Dooley smiled gently. "A quiet child. If you had the sensitivity God gave a barnacle, you could *feel* the aura of tragedy that followed him like a little black cloud. He never said much, and if you didn't know him, you'd probably think he wasn't all there, as they used to say. But the people who knew him, we knew differently."

The old man's face relaxed even further. Only now that it was gone did Sam see how much tension Pop-Pop had been holding in his face, in his movements. Her heart went out to him. *It hurts, doesn't it, Pop-Pop? But you'll never admit it to me . . . or to anyone.* "Go on," she said softly.

Jim smiled again and, not for the first time, Sam had the feeling that he could almost hear her thoughts. "We got on well, Mac and I," he continued. "We had things to teach each other, it turned out. I taught him about the way the world works. He taught me the way it *should* work, the way things *should* be." His eyes sprang open and his ice-green gaze fixed on Sam's face. "You've heard the expression, a 'sense of wonder'?" She nodded. "That's what Mac had to teach," he stated. "And he *would* teach it, to anyone who spent any time with him. I spent the time.

"He's an engineer, these days. Aeronautical engineering, and other disciplines, too. If you asked him about our relationship, him and me, he'd probably say I'm his mentor." Jim shrugged eloquently. "It's the right term, but I'm not sure if I agree with the direction, if you know what I mean."

Sam didn't answer right away. Unshed tears sprang to her eyes. *Why?* she asked herself. *Why now? What was it about hearing Pop-Pop talk about Mac that made her feel so sad?*

With an effort, she pushed the muddled, confused emotions aside. *I'll think about that later,* she told herself firmly. She forced the smile back onto her face.

If Jim Dooley had noticed her momentary discomfort, he gave no sign. He patted the edge of the bed beside him. "Enough about Mac," he said. "It's you I want to hear about. You're staying with that air-racer friend of yours, aren't you?"

Samantha sat on the bed beside her grandfather and began to talk.

* * *

"How was it, kiddo?"

Sam shrugged, a little uncomfortable. To give herself a moment to order her thoughts, she picked up her glass of whiskey from the end table and took a sip. "Difficult," she said at last. "Difficult, like I expected."

Her friend nodded. Maggie Braslins was curled up in a big armchair, thick legs tucked underneath her. *She looks like a cat,* Sam thought suddenly. *A big, graying cat—boneless, relaxed and totally unaffected by what's going on around her.*

But no, that wasn't true, she corrected at once. Maggie cared; she always had. Her detached, almost aloof manner was a defense mechanism more than anything else. If anything, she cared too much, and her pose of being unaffected by life was an attempt to keep from getting hurt too badly and too often.

Sam smiled as she remembered the first time she'd met Maggie. Back in 1982, it had been, at a get-together put on by the Sacramento Valley chapter of an organization known as the 99s. A month before, Sam had received a personal letter inviting her to the function, signed by someone she'd never heard of, a Margaret Braslins. Samantha had known very little about the organization, assuming it was some kind of club for women pilots, and hadn't really had much desire to drive up from Los Angeles to Sacramento to hobnob with strangers. *Probably some frighteningly intense political action committee to lobby for female combat pilots,* she'd suspected at the time. But, as these things so often worked out, she'd found herself in the Sacramento area for other reasons and couldn't resist the opportunity to check out this "girls' club."

The 99s *was* a kind of lobby group, she'd found out, but it was a lot more than that. It was an organization with a long and distinguished history, not the Johnny-come-lately outfit she'd expected, founded back in 1929 by the premiere female pilots of the day, then known as "aviatrixes," including Amelia Earhart herself. And *that,* of course, had been enough to pique Samantha Dooley's interest right there. When she'd been growing up, if she'd had any role models at all—other than her father, of course, and later Pop-Pop—Amelia had been at the top of that very small pantheon. From the day of its founding, membership in the 99s had been open to any woman with a pilot's license. The organization had chapters across the United States and counted among its members air racers, stunt flyers, airline pilots, air-evac and rescue fliers, air force officers and even astronauts like Sally Ride.

The official purpose of the 99s, as stated by charter member Amelia Earhart, was "good fellowship, jobs and a central office that could maintain files on women in aviation." All very admirable, Sam thought, but it was the *un*official purpose of the organization that really hooked her and reeled her in. At its core, the 99s represented a gathering place for women who loved the delight of being able to fly and wanted to spend time with those of like mind. Even though she'd been a newcomer on that northern California afternoon, almost from the very first minute she'd arrived Samantha Dooley had felt as though she'd *belonged.* For the first time, she'd been surrounded by women who thought the same way she did. Many of them had even had upbringings similar to hers: "military brats" who'd followed in their fathers' footsteps and earned their pilots' licenses at fifteen or sixteen. The 99s had provided the kinship, the camaraderie she'd looked for in the various sororities who'd tried to "rush" her during her college years. The difference was that the other women in the 99s shared the same world view: the belief that the world looked better from a few thousand feet up, and that any time they spent on the ground was, ideally, just a short visit.

Sam had been so enthralled by the all-encompassing *feel* of the gathering that she'd never made any effort to track down Margaret Braslins, the woman who'd invited her. Only several hours into things had she found herself talking to a graying, matronly woman whom everyone called "Mags" . . . and realized that *this* was who'd mailed her the invitation. She'd learned that Maggie Braslins was a twenty-year member of the 99s, a well-known air racer on the Pacific coast.

The two of them had stayed in touch, meeting up whenever they could at 99s chapter meetings and regional conventions. When Maggie had moved north from Red Bluff, California, to Nesika Beach, Oregon, only about five miles north of Gold Beach, Sam had made the effort to stop by whenever she visited Pop-Pop. *Even this final time,* she thought sadly.

Sam looked over at Maggie, curled up in her armchair. Mags didn't look any different now from the way she had five years earlier. And Sam would lay even money that, ten years from now, she *still* wouldn't look much different.

Maggie nodded slowly. "Difficult," she quietly echoed Sam's comment. "And him?"

Sam shook her head. "He's old." Her voice sounded soft to her own ears, little more than a whisper. "Old and tired." She closed her eyes. "And he *hurts,* Mags. He doesn't talk about it, but you can see it in his face when he's not actively hiding it. He hurts . . . and he'll be glad when . . ." She couldn't finish; the words caught in her throat.

Maggie nodded again, averting her eyes from her friend's suffering. She picked up a pack of cigarettes, shook one out and lit it. Sam smiled as she recognized the lighter. Maggie followed the direction of her gaze and grinned in response, holding up the brushed-steel Zippo lighter to display its crest of interlinked nines. "Oklahoma City," she said.

"I remember." That had been the first 99s general convention Sam had attended, held at the organization's international headquarters. Samantha and Maggie had flown out together in Mags's "baby," a restored T–34A trainer. After four years, Sam couldn't remember who the keynote speaker had been, but she had vivid memories of one of the workshop coordinators, a forty-year member by the name of Amy Langland. They'd met in the bar of a restaurant near the site of the convention, "in the holding pattern," Langland had dubbed it, while waiting for dinner, and they'd gotten on famously. Long afterward, Sam had learned that the rake-thin, hawk-faced woman with whom she'd been drinking Jack Daniel's was one of the "elder stateswomen" of the 99s, a past president and one of the most respected members who still held a valid pilot's license. *Those were the days,* she thought glumly.

Sam shook her head to break her mood. She pointed to the pack of cigarettes beside Maggie. "Give me one of those."

Maggie raised an eyebrow. "I thought you quit."

"I did."

Maggie chuckled, a warm, throaty sound. She flipped the pack over to Sam, followed by the well-used Zippo. Samantha lit up and drew the smoke into her lungs. It tasted like the smell of burning camel dung, but she could feel her body respond to the nicotine. *You never really quit, do you?* she thought. *All you do is put off that next butt, sometimes for years.* She closed her eyes and rode the wave of the mild head rush. *Jack Daniel's and a smoke. It's been a while.*

"You've never talked about your family much," Maggie said at last, breaking the companionable silence.

"I talked about Pop-Pop."

The older pilot shrugged. "And that was all, kiddo," she agreed. "Your grandfather. Almost like you didn't have parents."

"I didn't, not really," Sam responded, her face hard. But then she relented. "That's not true," she continued quietly. "My folks died when I was young."

"How young?"

Sam hesitated. Normally she diverted any conversation that strayed into these areas—"the forbidden lands," as she thought of it—but tonight the Jack Daniel's and the nicotine were taking the edge off her defense mechanisms. "Five for my father." It was hard to force the words out, even so. "Six for my mother."

Maggie sighed, shaking her head. "That's tough." Then she chuckled wryly. "Sorry. I *know* you know it's tough. When I drink I get prosaic."

"Don't we all?" Sam raised her drink in a mock toast. Then she stared into the crystal pony glass, focusing on the way the amber contents refracted the light. "They weren't together when it happened," she said at last. "When he died, I mean."

"They'd divorced?"

"Separated," Sam corrected. "The year before. I went with my mother." She snorted. "Not that I had much choice in the matter."

"Oh?"

Samantha looked up and met her friend's gaze. Maggie was keeping her face studiously neutral—*the perfect psychoanalyst,* Sam thought. Her first instinct was to change the subject, to fire off some clever comment and divert the conversation into safer territory. Instead, "She left him," she said quietly. "When I was four."

"What happened?" Maggie's voice was gentle.

Again, Samantha's instinct was to avoid the conversation but she decided, *What the hell anyway?* She sat silently for a few moments, trying to decide where the story really started.

I was four, Samantha began. We were living in one of the tiny cinder-block houses that made up the married officers' quarters for Patuxent River Naval Air Station, "Pax River," in Maryland. Dad—Jim Dooley, Jr.—was with the flight-test group checking out the new generation of jet fighters to follow on from the A3J. The Vindicator, the brass called this next-generation plane; the pilots on the flight line, like my dad, called it "the bathtub" or "the coffin." A real dog of a plane that never amounted to anything, and the navy eventually gave up on it. But before the navy will give up on *anything,* there's a price that has to be paid.

It was the flight-test group that had to pay that price, in blood. It was a bad time for the group, a very bad time. Over a period of four months, three pilots died, all of them burned beyond recognition when they corkscrewed their birds into the ground from a couple of miles up. I didn't realize what was happening at the time, of course. Four-year-olds don't understand much about plane crashes and death. All I knew was that Mom and Mom's friends seemed really quiet and tense about something, while Dad and *his* friends talked more and louder than they usually did. I'd also noticed that the adults got dressed up in dark clothes every few Sundays after church, and went off somewhere for several hours. It was only years later that I understood what it all meant.

Bad time or not, there were certain traditions to be kept up. One of those was the weekly potluck dinners, which test pilots and their wives would take turns hosting. I loved it when the party was at our place. I liked having people around me back then. I liked listening to them talk. I liked the feeling I got from hearing their voices all around me—a feeling of *belonging*—even though I didn't understand most of what they were talking about. More importantly, of course, I'd get to stay up past my regular bedtime on a party night. I'd get to say hello to Dad's fellow pilots and mom's friends: Pete and Maureen, Andy and Catherine and the rest. Sometimes Mom would let me stay up even later, drinking a cup of apple juice while the adults sipped their martinis or their glasses of wine. Eventually I'd be shipped off to bed.

Which didn't mean I went to sleep immediately. The officers' little houses were cheaply built, with thin floors and interior walls. Even upstairs in my room, I could hear the mumble of voices through my floor. I couldn't make out the words, but I could hear enough to know that *they were still having fun* while I'd been banished. Unacceptable!

So most nights I'd take my blanket and creep to the head of the stairs, out of sight of the living room below, and settle myself against the wall. From this vantage point, I could listen in on what was happening below.

Not that I understood most of what the grown-ups were talking about. I didn't get most of the jokes, and the majority of people they talked about were strangers to me. Eventually I'd get bored, and either head back to bed or drop off where I sat. (I realize now that I never asked Dad or Mom how many times they'd had to carry me back to bed after one of their parties.) Even when I *did* understand what they were talking about, it didn't make enough of an impression on my child's mind for me to remember.

Except once.

Once, I could sense that something was different, something was wrong. Dad, Pete and Andy were doing most of the talking. Somebody named Danny had crashed earlier in the day—that's how I reconstructed things later—flaming in while trying to make a crosswind landing. Another death.

"Danny was a good pilot." I'll never forget what Dad said that night, or the almost unconcerned way he said it. "And he was a good man. But"—I can picture him shrugging his broad shoulders—"he didn't have a hell of a lot of experience, did he? And it's not like he was a natural-born stick-and-rudder man. When the controls malfunctioned . . . well, he found himself in a bad corner, and he didn't have the experience to get himself out."

I'd heard those words before, or words like them, I realize that now. It was a kind of litany among the flight-test fraternity, a eulogy for the dead, the standard and accepted response to losing a friend and fellow pilot. One of the survivors would trot out the party line, and everyone else—the pilots and their wives—would nod knowingly. It was a hell of a thing that so-and-so had gotten himself killed, but it wasn't as if he didn't bring it on himself. Denial, of course: that's what it was, pure denial. Excuses, mental games—a technique for separating themselves from the fact that a young man, someone just like them, had lost his life. A technique for denying that the same thing might happen to them, at any time—quite literally, death out of a clear blue sky. In retrospect, it was both comical and pitiful. But it worked for them, as long as everyone played along with the game, followed the script. And, because the alternative was just too terrible to contemplate, everyone played the game.

Except that night. It was my mother's voice that broke the silence, loud and shrill enough to make me jump in alarm. "I don't *believe* you people!"

Shocked silence, that was the only answer she got. Then, after a few moments, I heard a quiet voice—one of the other pilots' wives trying to calm Mom down, trying to stop her before she shattered their comforting little fiction.

But Mom wouldn't be silenced. "I can't *believe* it!" she cried again, and there was so much pain in her voice that I started crying, without even understanding the enormity of what she was doing. "Danny's *dead.* He's dead because the goddamned plane *broke.* That's what a 'control malfunction' means, isn't it? Something *broke*!

"My God!" Her voice was a wail of torment. "What in the name of heaven makes any of you think *you'd* have come out of it any better? It can happen to any one of you—*any time at all.*"

Even today, I can't think of anything Mom could have said that would have hurt them more, that would have more effectively shattered their defense mechanisms. She broke the code—the ultimate crime. That was the end of the party, and it was the end of the marriage.

Nobody mentioned Mom's outburst ever again. The morning after, Mom and Dad were calm, controlled. But two days later, Mom packed up our things, and we left my father behind in that cinder-block house.

* * *

Samantha sighed and lit another cigarette. "He wrote to me often, after the separation," she went on, "a letter every week." She smiled sadly. "Those letters—they were like those brilliant moments when the sun peeks out from behind a storm cloud, reminders that the darkness won't last forever. I'd read them and reread them, imagining that someday he'd come to take me away. We'd be together, him and me, he'd teach me to fly. And it would be wonderful.

"And then he was dead, and a year later so was she."

Unconsciously, her hands tightened around the glass of whiskey. "Sometimes I think that's why I fly," she continued, her voice little more than a whisper, "why I got my pilot's license at fifteen, as soon as the law would allow, using the survivor's benefits the government paid me. I could leave the world behind. The sadness, the memories."

She paused. "It's funny," she said at last. "Even now, twenty years after, I still feel I'm closer to him when I'm flying." Slowly, she raised her eyes from the glass in her hand to the face of her friend, looking for . . . *What?* she asked herself. *Sympathy?* Pity? What she saw there was more valuable than either—*understanding.*

Maggie sighed. "You wanted to go with him, didn't you?"

Sam took another drag on the cigarette, giving herself time to control her response. "Like I said, not that I had much choice," she said, as calmly as she could manage. She shrugged, trying to keep her voice light. "He was a career navy test pilot back when planes were auguring in every other week. She was an elementary school teacher. Who do you *think* got the kid?"

"They never ask the child, do they?"

That was what Sam *thought* Maggie said, but the older woman's voice was so soft that she couldn't be sure. "What was that?" Samantha asked.

Maggie waved it off. "Nothing." She paused. "What happened to him?"

Sam shrugged. She tried to keep her expression, voice and body language light, but she wasn't sure that she was managing it. "The Big Kaboom." Again, she raised her drink in a mock toast. "First flight for a new plane. Turned out they hadn't got all the bugs out yet."

"Hmm. Weren't they working on the X–12 or something about that time?"

"It wasn't military," Sam said with a shake of her head. "He'd gone civilian about six months before." She laughed bitterly. "Said the military was too dangerous."

"General Dynamics?"

"I wish. GD always had a good life insurance plan." Sam sighed. "No, he went with one of those small independents. Generro Aerospace. Ever heard of them?"

"Heard the name," Maggie admitted after a moment, "but no real bells. What have they done?"

"Nothing," Samantha said, and this time the bitterness dripped from her voice. "Nothing relevant. Back then they were playing with hypersonics, but the only thing they were ever good at was making big craters in the desert."

"Hypersonics." Maggie frowned. "Something's starting to come back. Generro . . . the Thunderbolt. Right?"

"Thunder*flash,*" Sam corrected. "The late, unlamented Thunderflash—that's what the marketing wonks called it, at least. A new hypersonic design—the ideal high-speed, high-altitude interceptor. Mach 4 projected top speed, service ceiling supposed to be sixty-three thousand feet, combat radius something like 650 nautical miles."

"Impressive."

Sam nodded. "No question," she agreed. "No operational plane came close to matching those specs for another fifteen years." She sighed. "I saw a picture of the thing later, an old file photograph. It was beautiful, Mags. Everything about it cutting edge. Even primitive LERX—rudimentary versions of that leading-edge root extensions crap the Soviets used in the Su–27 Flanker, damn near twenty years later. Just beautiful. Too bad it was impossible to fly."

"It never became operational, did it?"

Samantha snorted at that. "No, never. It killed my dad, and a few other good pilots too, apparently. According to GA's PR flacks, the project was canceled two years after my dad died—two years too late."

Maggie nodded. After a moment, she pointed to Sam's glass. "Another?"

"No, I'm . . ." Sam stopped. Her whiskey was gone, after

all. She held her glass out toward her friend. "Ah, hell, why not?"

Maggie levered herself out of her chair, took both their glasses and vanished into the kitchen. A minute later she emerged and handed a fresh drink to Sam.

"No ice?"

The older woman's face twisted into an exaggerated mock frown. "What the hell do you think this is?" she demanded. "A bar?" She plopped down in her seat, tucked her legs under her and raised her freshly refilled glass in tribute. "Clear skies!"

"Safe landing," Sam responded. She sipped at the bourbon, and grimaced at the sourness. "Whew! That really bites, doesn't it?"

Maggie flipped her hand, a gesture of dismissal. "Yeah, but only the first bottle." Her smile faded slowly, and after a few moments she asked, "And your mom?"

"Drunk driver." Sam set her whiskey down and took another drag of her cigarette. She tried to blow a smoke ring, but it looked more like a pretzel. "About a year after he died."

"So that's when you went to live with Old Jim, I guess, huh?"

"I never lived with him," Sam pronounced coolly.

Maggie's gray eyes widened in surprise. "But I thought . . ."

"Yeah. Well." Samantha butted out the cigarette violently. "That's what most people think. But he was a pilot too, wasn't he? And my mother's folks, they were your typical salt of the earth—teachers, just like she was. Where do you *think* I ended up, huh?"

"It's not that cut-and-dried," Maggie said, after a moment. "There's always extenuating circumstances. Didn't Jim ask for custody?"

Sam shrugged, as lightly as she could manage. "Don't know."

"Didn't you ask?"

"Why should I?"

Maggie lit another cigarette, and blew a cloud of smoke toward the ceiling. "You're a smart woman, Sam," she said. "Much too smart to say something so damn stupid."

Samantha blinked, startled by the older woman's vehemence. "What . . . ?"

The gray-haired woman gestured with her fresh cigarette. "You *know* what I'm saying to you, Samantha. Geez! It bothers you, doesn't it? Well, why don't you *ask* him, for God's sake?"

"But I *can't,* not now . . ."

"Then *when*?" Maggie didn't relent. "When?" she repeated more quietly. "When you're going to need a Ouija board?"

And then she sighed. "Sorry, kiddo," she said softly. "Maybe I shouldn't drink so much. JD always makes me nosy." She butted out her half-smoked cigarette in the ashtray and rose to her feet. "It's been a long day, I guess. See you in the morning."

After two steps she turned back, and snagged her full glass from the table. "Nightcap," she announced. "Turn off the lights when you go to bed." With that, she left Samantha alone with her thoughts.

3

For the first few moments of wakefulness, Sam couldn't remember where she was. Then memory returned in a rush. She groaned and rolled over, trying to shield her eyes from the bright sunlight streaming through the blinds. The ancient springs of the Hide-A-Bed complained as she moved.

What time is it, anyway? Keeping her eyes shut against the glare, Sam reached out to snag her pilot's watch from the table beside the bed and almost knocked over a glass of water in the attempt. She cursed softly, holding the large watch close to her face with one hand and shading her eyes with the other.

Ten-seventeen. Damn it. With another curse, this one aimed at the state of Tennessee in general and the Jack Daniel's distillery in particular, she flung back the covers and forced herself to a sitting position on the side of the bed.

Her throat felt raw from the whiskey and the cigarettes, and a small, throbbing headache had taken up residence behind her left eye. She drained the glass of water beside the bed, swishing it around in her mouth to wash the fur off her tongue. *This is why I quit smoking in the first place,* she reminded herself grimly.

Maggie was long gone by the time she got downstairs. A note next to the coffeemaker, which the older woman had thoughtfully set up, explained that Maggie was teaching flying lessons all day at the nearby Ophir airstrip, and probably wouldn't be home until late. Sam had the run of the house, the note went on to state, and should do whatever she needed to make herself at home. The scrawled message ended with, "Whiskey loosens the tongue, but it plays merry hell with the memory. If there's anything I should remember from last night, let me know sometime."

Sam smiled as she started the coffee. *In other words,* she translated mentally, "If you want to, we can pretend that nothing at all was said last night." Typical Maggie, she thought warmly. Always gracious, always giving people an out if they wanted one.

Do I want an out? Sam wondered as she sliced a bagel and spread it with cream cheese. *No, I don't think so.* Some of the things Maggie had said the night before had stung, but that didn't make them any less true. *She's right—it still hurts that Pop-Pop didn't take me after Mom died . . . and it hurts even more that I don't know* why. *I* want *to know. And if I don't ask now,* when?

There was a car parked in Pop-Pop's driveway when Sam pulled in, a bright red 1960s-vintage Porsche convertible, immaculately restored and maintained. She gave it a wide berth as she braked Grendel to a stop. *A pilot's car,* she thought with a smile. *What do you bet?*

The car's owner had made himself at home, she saw as she knocked quietly and entered her grandfather's bedroom. He'd pulled an armchair up beside Pop-Pop's bed and was sprawled luxuriously across it, well-worn hiking shoes propped up on the bed's steel foot-rail. To his credit, he was on his feet the instant Sam appeared. He gave her a warm smile, then shot a meaningful look at Pop-Pop. "If this is your nurse, Jim, I think I've got to try this sickroom stuff."

Sam couldn't help but grin; the man's good nature was infectious.

"Samantha, I want you to meet an old flying buddy of mine . . ."

"Hey, not so old," his guest protested.

". . . Sid Warner. Sid, my granddaughter, Samantha Rose."

"Sam," Samantha corrected as she shook the man's extended hand and looked him over. Silver-haired, tall and rangy, he had that kind of loose-limbed look she always associated with athletes. His weather-tanned face marked him as in his late fifties or early sixties, but his gray eyes—surrounded by a complex network of deep wrinkles from squinting into the sun—were clear, and flashed with the energy of a twenty-year-old. "Pleased to meet you, Sid." Sam hesitated. "Sid Warner . . ." she repeated slowly.

"You've heard the name before," Jim Dooley supplied helpfully. "Or read it, at least. Remember that list of altitude record-holders you used to have? Simon Warner, 1965, a hundred thousand feet. Remember?"

"The X–15 flights, that's right." Sam stared at her grandfather. "I didn't know you knew anybody from that program, Pop-Pop."

Dooley chuckled dryly. "The old man's got a lot of secrets yet, child."

"You know what they say," Warner elaborated with a broad smile, "still waters run deep. Either that or they're stagnant.

"Well," the slender man went on, slapping the thigh of his khaki hiking pants, "I'll be heading out, I think, Jimmy-boy, and I'll leave you with your better-looking company."

"Don't let me chase you away, Sid," Samantha said quickly. "You and Pop-Pop were talking." She saw the doubt in the man's gray eyes, and stressed, "*Really.*"

"Well . . ." Warner grinned. "Just so you don't think you *are* chasing me off." He settled himself back down in the armchair. "We were talking about *Yellow Bird,* Jim and me," he said, "about the first time I saw her."

"You know *Yellow Bird*?"

Samantha nodded, but it was Jim Dooley who answered. "Only too well, right, Sam?"

"It was '79, I guess," Warner said, settling back deeper into the armchair. "And *this* reprobate"—he grinned crookedly at Jim—"offered to take me up in his new toy."

The pilot shrugged lightly. "He'd told me about his *Yellow Bird* and I thought I knew what to expect.

"A homebuilt, a kit-plane. A piddly-assed little Glasair taildragger, a real lightweight. Probably running a 160 Lycoming or something equally gutless—200 knots at eight thousand feet, running on *car* fuel, for chrissake. After the kind of stuff we'd flown in the past, Jim and I, that miserable Glasair was going to be a joke. And I'd have to make nice, and tell the old man sweet lies about his new toy." Jim chuckled at that.

"I should have known better, of course," Warner went on wryly. "Hell, it was *Jimmy*'s new toy. Should have told me *something*.

"Man," the pilot sighed, "I remember the first time I laid eyes on her, standing out there on that grass strip. Small, simple-looking—your typical homebuilt. Except for the paint job. *Perfect* it was, burnished like metal. Brilliant yellow, tail numbers standing out crisp and black." He chuckled softly. "The day was overcast, but when I came near to that plane, I could have believed the sun was shining.

"I knew something was different about the plane as soon as we climbed aboard. The control console was more complex than I expected, for one thing. And the layout just didn't seem the same as the other Glasairs I'd seen."

Sam nodded. This might as well have been *her* first exposure to the *Yellow Bird* too.

"And then Old Jim lit up the engine." Warner laughed, a full-throated, *free* sound. "And I said to myself, 'That ain't no gutless Lycoming.' All the other homebuilts I've flown, they sound like sewing machines. Jim's baby—it *roared*.

"Jimmy-boy runs up the engine, and the *Yellow Bird* shifts and shimmies against the brakes, like it's impatient to get up where it wants to be. We finish the checklist, Jimmy gets off the brakes, and he opens the throttle."

Warner sighed, and shook his head with remembered pleasure. "Man, we were up before I knew it. Jimmy points the nose at the sky, and the ground just falls away behind us. Ten thousand feet in . . . well, hell, it felt like less than a minute. And then Jimmy says, 'Your aircraft, captain.'

"I take the stick, put my feet on the pedals, feel out the response in the controls.

"And I was in heaven," the aging pilot said quietly. "I tossed that baby around the sky like it was purpose-built for aerobatics. Snapped it into a spin, then recovered so sharply it felt like we were riding on rails.

"Then I pulled the nose up and opened the throttle all the way. We burst through the cloud-deck and the sun was like a fireball bursting in front of us against the empty blue."

" '. . . To touch the face of God,' " Pop-Pop whispered.

"Yeah." Sid Warner nodded. "Yeah."

For a long moment there was silence in the room—respectful, almost *religious.* Sam stared at Warner, a complex mix of emotions flooding through her. *A kindred spirit*—that was the central impression. *He's someone who understands.*

Warner met her gaze for an instant, and she heard his message as clearly as if he'd spoken aloud: You *know what I'm talking about, don't you?*

Warner broke the spell with a soft chuckle as he climbed to his feet. "Well," he said, "this time I *am* out of here." He patted his flat stomach. "Bingo fuel," he smiled, using the fighter pilot's common term for being dangerously low on fuel. "I'll see you later, Jimmy-boy." He patted Sam's arm. "You too, Sam. I'm a dot." And he was gone.

Sam didn't speak until she heard the Porsche's engine start up and the sports car pull out of the drive. Then she sat down in the armchair vacated by Warner. Jim Dooley was watching the empty doorway, a distant expression on his face.

"I didn't know you knew any of the X–15 pilots, Pop-Pop."

"Hm?" Jim glanced over at her as though surprised. "Oh." He shrugged, and went on lightly, "When you get to be my age you know a lot of people. Even old-time rocket jockeys." His smile faded slowly, replaced by an emptiness in his eyes. "A lot of people," he repeated softly.

Then, with a visible effort, he shook off the momentary funk. "Pilots' associations," he said, "flying clubs like your 99s; I'd wager you know *hundreds* of people through that outfit. That's where I met a lot of them." He smiled wanly. "Take Sid, for example. We were both members of a . . . well, I guess you could call it a kind of special-interest group, back in the 1960s. You'd be surprised who you run into at that kind of thing."

Sam nodded in understanding. *Like Mags, and Amy Langland,* she thought. She leaned back in the armchair and closed her eyes. With her right hand, she reached out and lightly gripped her grandfather's forearm. *So thin, just like a skin-covered skeleton.* Her thoughts began to drift . . .

"Why didn't you come for me, Pop-Pop?" Her eyes sprung open in surprise. The words were out of her mouth before she was even aware she was going to speak.

"What was that?" Jim Dooley turned to her, his hollow eyes fixed on her face.

Sam's skin felt cold, as if a chill breeze had blown across the back of her neck. Desperately she wanted to take the words back, but it was much too late for that. She had no choice but to press on. "When Mom died." It was hard to force the words out through her tight throat. "They sent me to live with Mom's parents. Why didn't *you* take me? Why, Pop-Pop?"

The old man didn't answer at once. When he did, his voice was little more than a whisper, the susurrus of a cold wind blowing through the bare branches of a winter forest. "Why?" He paused again. "Do you think I didn't try, Samantha?"

"I don't know, Pop-Pop. *Did* you try?"

"As hard as I've tried to do anything in my life." He smiled bleakly. "Not that it made any difference."

"What happened?"

"What do you *think* happened?" He sighed. "It was the era of the family, Samantha. *Father Knows Best. Leave It to Beaver. The Donna Reed Show.* What court in the land is going to give custody of a child to a widower—and a pilot at that—in preference to Grandma Ida and Grandpa Steve? A nice, neat nuclear family with a house, a station wagon and a white picket fence?"

"Did you go to court?"

Jim nodded. "Even though a handful of expensive lawyers told me not to even bother."

"There are other options . . ." Sam's voice was almost inaudible, even to her own ears.

Her grandfather turned his green eyes on her. "Don't think I didn't consider it from time to time." He chuckled mirthlessly. "If necessary, we could have dropped off the face of the earth, you and I. No one would have ever found us, you can trust me on that." There was a strange edge to his voice as he spoke, but Sam decided to ignore it for the moment.

"Why didn't you, then?"

Jim closed his eyes again. "Why?" He paused. "I wanted to, Samantha. When your parents died, you were the only real family I had left. But . . . I thought you were happy to live with your mom's folks. Any time we talked, you seemed content."

Content? No, Pop-Pop: reconciled. *There's a big difference.* "You never asked me. You never even talked to me about it."

Her voice was soft, but her grandfather flinched as though she'd screamed at him. "I know, Samantha Rose." He spoke slowly, almost cautiously, as though he were picking carefully through the words, through the thoughts and the feelings they engendered. "Maybe that was a mistake. Maybe I should have handled it differently.

"But like I say, I thought you were happy living with Ida and Steve. You never complained." He smiled, and again there was little humor in it. "And I didn't want to ask you directly, Samantha. I didn't want to put you in that position, where I was forcing you to make a choice—them or me."

"I'd have chosen you, Pop-Pop," she whispered. Her eyes stung. The world blurred around her.

"I know it. *Now* I know it," he corrected. Then, more quietly, he went on, "I probably knew it at the time, too. But maybe I didn't have the courage to risk it. If I hurt you, I'm sorry, Samantha."

She shook her head, momentarily unable to speak. A spear of bittersweet pain pierced her heart.

"Were you really that unhappy?"

Sam blinked back the tears. She clasped her grandfather's hand as it lay on the coverlet. "No, Pop-Pop," she answered. "No. Not actively *un*happy . . ."

"Just not actively *happy,*" he finished for her. "I understand."

"They were never mean to me or anything." She realized she was babbling; Pop-Pop understood what she meant without her having to spell it out, she knew. But part of her *wanted* to talk, to express for the first time the thoughts and feelings she'd kept inside for so long. "They took care of me, they looked after me." She swallowed hard. "I know they loved me, too, in their own way."

"In their own way," Jim echoed softly. "But not *your* way?"

She shrugged, suddenly self-conscious. "I know, it sounds petty, doesn't it? 'I'm upset because they didn't love me precisely the way I wanted to be loved, they didn't say exactly the right things.' But that's the way I felt." She sighed. "Just like Mom."

Pop-Pop turned his head to regard her. His tone was neutral as he said, "What do you mean?"

Again Sam shrugged. "I know you got on well with Mom," she said slowly. "But, you've got to admit, she wasn't the most emotionally giving person in the world."

"Giving?" the dying man mused, as if he were considering the word from all angles. "Giving? Well, no, maybe not. Not by the time you came on the scene, at least."

"What do you mean?"

He smiled sadly. "Everybody reaches their limits sometime, Samantha Rose," he explained gently. "Even your mother." He sighed. "By the time you were around to need her, she'd already given everything she was capable of giving to your father. She was empty, Samantha, all used up. That's why she left him."

"But he didn't ask for . . ."

The level of his voice didn't change, but his words cut her off as effectively as if he'd shouted. "I didn't say he asked," he pointed out. "She gave until she couldn't give any more, your mother did. And then she left."

No, Sam wanted to say, *that's not what happened.*

But maybe it was. Why had her mother "broken the code" that night, so many years ago? Maybe because she'd given all she could. *Couldn't silence also be a gift? And denial, playing her role in the consensual delusion that was "the code," yet another gift? What do you do when your heart's too empty, your* soul*'s too empty, to give someone what they need from you?*

"There *was* another possibility, you know."

She looked over at him, the question on her lips. But then she realized what he meant. She blinked her prickling eyes. "I could have told you, I know," she whispered. "I could have told you I wanted to come live with you." She took a deep breath, willing herself to be calm. "But I didn't want to put *you* in a bad position, either, Pop-Pop. I didn't want to put you on the spot."

He chuckled softly. "And you didn't want to risk me saying no, did you?"

"No." She shook her head, and she let the tears fall. "No, I didn't want to risk that."

Jim Dooley reached across and took her hand between both of his. He squeezed, his grip surprising her with its strength. "If only we had the chance to do it over again . . ."

Sam nodded. With her free hand, she wiped at her tears. *We got to know each other too late, Pop-Pop,* she thought. *I wish we had more time.*

Samantha massaged the back of her neck, feeling the knots in the muscles. With a deep sigh, she let her body relax into the armchair.

Beside her, Jim Dooley was watching her, amusement glinting in his green eyes. "What's the matter with the younger generation?" he asked mock-scornfully. "Why, when *I* was your age, I could sit in a comfortable chair all day without getting tired."

Sam had to chuckle. "You're right, Pop-Pop," she shot back. "You've always been *much* better at sitting on your butt than I have." She reached out to the side table and picked up her glass. She swirled it for a moment, moodily watching the smoky amber liquid. Thirty-year-old single-malt Scotch whiskey, some of Jim's treasured stock of Royal Lochnager "Old Rarity," a whiskey never commercially available in the United States. (She smiled sadly. Jim knew she was a bourbon drinker, but had from time to time lightheartedly tried to "educate" her in the wonders of "civilized" whiskies. *Another opportunity lost,* she thought, as the light but complex aroma filled her head. *There's more to Scotch than I ever imagined, and I've passed up a knowledgeable resource who'd have* loved *to share what he knew.*) She took another sip and set the glass down.

Jim was keeping her company. No whiskey for him, of course—his stomach couldn't handle it. *And God knows how alcohol would potentiate with all the drugs in his system,* she thought. Instead, he had a plastic tumbler of what he called "bug juice," a vaguely fruit-flavored concoction of electrolytes and minerals. He took a sip through the flexible straw that his nurse had thoughtfully provided after Jim had drenched himself trying to drink directly from the cup. (*And if* that *isn't the saddest comment, I don't know what is,* Sam thought, with another heartfelt sigh. *Jim Dooley down-checked to a* straw, *because he doesn't check out on a glass anymore.*)

She saw his hand starting to quiver as he reached out to set the tumbler back down, and she took it from him.

He nodded his thanks. Then his green eyes flashed with devilish humor, and he said ingenuously, "You're going to make some man a wonderful wife someday, Samantha Rose."

She held his tumbler of electrolytes poised to douse him. "What size bug juice do you wear again, Pop-Pop?" she asked sweetly.

Jim laughed aloud at that, a laugh that turned into a dry, aching cough. Sam offered him the bug juice again, but he waved it off. After a moment he had his traitor body under control again, and settled back against the pillow.

"Serious now," he said after a moment. "When do you think you're ever going to get married, Samantha Rose?"

The question took her by surprise, but she answered immediately. "When I find a man stronger than me, Pop-Pop," she told him honestly. "When I find someone who isn't intimidated by me."

He was totally silent for a moment, then he chuckled—*a little ruefully,* she thought. "Then you might have yourself a long wait," he announced softly.

"Oh, I don't know," she said, trying to keep her voice light. "I hope not."

"Hmm." The dying man didn't sound convinced. He was quiet for a long moment, and Sam thought he might have drifted off to sleep again. But then he said, "You've always had a low tolerance for stupidity, haven't you, Samantha Rose? Stupidity and weakness."

Sam blinked, stung by his words. "I don't know that I'd put it like *that,* Pop-Pop."

"Well, maybe not." He paused again. "I've seen that

kind of thing in others, though," he went on thoughtfully. "And I've seen the trouble it can cause. I've seen people who could love and respect whoever they were seeing, or in love with, or sleeping with . . . as long as the other person was strong, and self-confident and centered. But the first moment their lover showed any weakness, or any self-doubt, or any lack of focus . . . well," he shrugged, "they were out of there, emotionally, if not physically. They'd scorn the 'weaklings,' and over time they'd even come to despise them. No matter how much they'd loved them originally." The old man's green eyes fixed on Sam's face. "Do you understand what I'm saying, Samantha Rose?"

"I understand, Pop-Pop." *You could be describing* me.

Jim shrugged his bird-thin shoulders. "People like that, they don't understand something. They don't understand that *everybody*'s weak from time to time. Everybody has moments of doubt, moments when everything gets to feeling just *too big.*" He snorted gently. "Anyone who says he doesn't is either a liar or a psychopath . . . maybe both."

He shook his head, and tried to moisten dry lips with the tip of his tongue. Sam leaned forward and handed him the bug juice. He drew a mouthful and nodded his thanks. "Sometimes I think about the marriage vows," he went on, his voice quiet, contemplative. "The old-style ones, not the new-fangled 'say-whatever-the-hell-you-want' type. The old ones that go, 'In sickness and in health, in poverty or wealth'. . . ." He smiled. "Maybe they should add 'In weakness and in strength,' too.

"Is it reasonable to expect one person, *either* person, in the marriage—or in *any* relationship—to be strong all the time? I don't think so. I think the best you can hope for is that *one* of the partners is able to be strong when there's trouble, and not always the *same* partner." He grinned. "Like wingmen: one's there to cover for the other. The partnership endures; the team makes it through." His smile faded. "A lot of people don't figure that out. Not until it's too late, at least." He looked away.

Sam nodded slowly. *You're talking about yourself, aren't you, Pop-Pop? I wish I'd known your wife, Mary.*

Jim sighed deeply, and then his roguish smile was back. "So," he said, "I repeat my question. When do you think you're ever going to get married, Samantha Rose?"

She looked at the old man, with love, and with respect. *You're telling me I've got something to learn, aren't you? Something to think about.* She clasped her hands demurely in her lap and batted her eyelashes. "Why, I've been waiting for *you* to ask me, Pop-Pop."

Samantha shifted in the armchair, trying to find a more comfortable position. She wanted to sleep—to lose herself, if only for a few minutes—but oblivion eluded her.

Beside her, Pop-Pop snored quietly in his steel-framed bed. The curtains were drawn, but enough late-afternoon sun leaked around the edges for her to see his face, peaceful as a child's. *Sleep's the only place he can escape the pain,* she thought sadly.

The pain had to be bad as the cancer tore at him. She'd known he was hurting. She just hadn't known how much until he asked her to give him four of his pills from the bedside table—"to help me sleep," he'd said. As she was opening the childproof cap—*Stupid to put that kind of cap on a bottle for an old man!*—she'd surreptitiously checked the label. She didn't recognize the brand name, but she *did* notice that the prescription contained 65 milligrams of codeine. *Don't Tylenol 3s have 30 milligrams of codeine in them, less than half as much?* she'd thought. *And two Tylenol 3s are enough to turn my brain to mush.*

I wish there was something I could do for him. It wasn't so much the imminent loss—or, at least, not *only* the loss. What really hurt was the helplessness. *Soon he'll be gone, and the closest I can come to helping him is to hand him the pills that'll make his passing easier. It's not fair.*

Yeah, and what did Ben Katt say when I used that complaint on him? she remembered with a bitter snort. *Whoever told any of us the world was fair?* Sam felt the nape of her neck tingle with the sensation that someone was watching her.

Pop-Pop's eyes were open, his gaze steady on her face. She forced a smile. "Good sleep?"

He shrugged, but didn't answer at once. As she watched him, his face spasmed for a moment before he could control it. His breath caught in his chest with agony. She was on her feet in an instant, reaching for the pain pills, but he waved her off. "I'm all right." His voice told her the words were a lie, but she had to respect them. Grudgingly, she sat down again.

"We've never really talked, have we," he spoke after a long moment. "About afterward."

Sam closed her eyes. *There's not going to be any "afterward." You're going to be fine.* That's what she wanted to say, wanted desperately to be true. *Denial,* she thought grimly. *It runs in the family.*

No, she couldn't deny, couldn't avoid. Her grandfather was dying, they both knew it. False hope, false cheer—that wasn't doing either of them any favors. "You're right, Pop-Pop," she said softly. "We haven't."

"Most of the details are already taken care of." He smiled wanly. "The advantages of having a little time.

"But I want you to help me with something."

She just nodded, not trusting herself to speak.

"I'd like you to deal with my ashes, Samantha Rose. *You.* I'm sure the *professionals*"—he loaded the word with scorn—"will offer to handle things, but I want you to do it, if you're willing."

His eyes were fixed on her face, his expression held carefully neutral. *This means a lot to him,* she knew instinctively. "I'm willing."

Now he smiled, and she could *feel* his relief. "I want you to take the *Yellow Bird,*" he said. "Can you do that?"

He wants me to scatter his ashes. "Of course. Where? Eagle Mountain?" Jim Sr. owned a tract of land near the small town of that name, between Interstate 10 and the boundaries of the Joshua Tree National Monument. He'd intended it as recreational property, the site of a vacation home, but the required zoning had never come through.

Dooley snorted. "Not on your life. I've got better things to do with eternity than spend it getting up your nose and in your hair."

She had to laugh. "You know you'd be welcome, Pop-Pop." She sobered. "Where, then?"

"The mountains." He closed his eyes again. "Around Kings Canyon. The Sierra Nevadas." He laughed softly. "Officially, you've got to get permission from the government. But now's a hell of time to start paying attention to restricted airspace, I figure." His breathing slowed and his face relaxed. For a moment, Sam thought he'd drifted off to sleep again. But then he sighed. "I wish we'd had more time, Samantha Rose. I'd have loved to show you the mountains."

"I've seen them, Pop-Pop, you know that. I've flown over them more times. . . ."

He cut her off. "Not that way." Once more he laughed. "I know you're not going to believe it coming from me, but there are some things you can only appreciate—*really* appreciate—from the ground." He shook his head. "I didn't believe it either, until a good friend dragged me in on foot one year and *showed* me. From then on, it was an annual affair. I wish you could have come along one year."

"Me too, Pop-Pop." Sam shook her head. *An annual hiking trip into the mountains? What else don't I know about him? What else will I* never *know?*

How well do we ever know anyone*?*

The old man's breathing slowed again as he slipped back into sleep. Carefully, so as not to wake him, Sam stroked the back of his hand. His skin seemed almost transparent, the blood vessels showing clearly, intricately branched blue lines like the minor highways on a road map. Samantha settled herself back in the armchair, looking for a comfortable position that let her keep physical contact with her grandfather. She closed her eyes, and worked on slowing her own breathing, letting go of the thoughts that tortured her. Finally, she slept.

It felt like only seconds later that she jolted back to consciousness, but the shift in the sunlight through the window told her it was at least an hour. For an instant she was disoriented. What had wakened her? Her own dreams . . . ?

But then she heard Pop-Pop's labored breathing and she knew. Sudden panic vaulted her to her feet beside his bed. His entire body was tight, every muscle as rigid as an iron bar. His lips were drawn back from his teeth in a rictus of unimaginable agony.

Oh, my God. . . . She fumbled for the vial of pain pills on the bedside table, almost crying with frustration as she struggled with the lid.

May the inventor of the childproof cap burn in Hell . . . !

Finally she had the plastic container open and poured

three of the gritty-feeling tablets into her hand—hesitated, and added a fourth. She leaned over her grandfather . . .

. . . And stood waiting, helpless. His jaws were locked together with the violence of the spasm. There was little chance she could pry his jaws open and no chance whatsoever he could swallow even if she got the pills into his mouth. She had to wait—shifting, agonized, from foot to foot—until the spasm passed naturally.

It seemed to take forever, but the logical, emotionless part of her mind recognized that it could only have been a dozen seconds. The tension drained out of the old man's body and the cadence of his breathing changed as the pain released its steel grip on his nervous system. The flesh of his face sagged, his eyelids fluttered.

"Pop-Pop," Sam whispered fiercely. "*Pop-Pop.* Can you hear me?"

The old man's eyelids fluttered again, then opened. For a few moments his eyes rolled wildly, seemingly unable to focus. Finally they fixed on her face, and then seemed to register what they were seeing. "Samantha Rose . . ." His voice was almost inaudible, the breath of a faint night breeze.

"Here, Pop-Pop, your pills."

His mouth worked silently for a moment, then he nodded. "Help me."

She held his head and slipped the pills into his mouth, then put the water glass to his lips and wiped the spillage from his chin and neck. Once he'd swallowed, she laid him back again. His chest was heaving, his breath laboring as if he'd run a marathon. *Is it going to be now?* she found herself wondering.

But somehow he managed to bring his body back under control. His breathing slowed, the last remnants of tension left his face, the cords in his neck that had stood out with the effort of fighting the pain finally vanished. At last he smiled up at her. "Bad. Very bad." His voice was a little louder, but the words were faintly slurred, as if he couldn't summon the energy to perfectly control his vocal apparatus.

Sam fought back the urge to shiver and forced an answering smile onto her face. "I know, Pop-Pop. I know." She sat down again, and once more took his fragile hand in hers.

She thought he'd slipped back into the blissful oblivion

of sleep, but he surprised her by saying suddenly, "I've told you about my memoirs, haven't I?"

Sam squeezed her grandfather's hand. "Not now, Pop-Pop. Rest now, okay?"

"It's important, Samantha Rose." The slurring in his voice was even more apparent. Maybe it was the spasm of agony that had totally drained him, or maybe it was the strong pain pills that were having their effect. He tried to raise himself up on one elbow, but she gently urged him back, stroked his dry, hot forehead.

"Okay, Pop-Pop."

"I've told you about my memoirs?" he repeated.

"You've told me, Pop-Pop."

"I want you to read them. I want you to . . ."—he hesitated—". . . to *understand* them." He sighed. "To try, at least." His voice faded to a whisper, then a breath, barely audible at all. "And maybe you could try to think kindly of me."

She fought back the tears that threatened to engulf her. "You know I'll always think kindly of you, Pop-Pop. You *know* that."

He shrugged, a minuscule movement of his shoulders against the starched white sheets. "Maybe," he breathed. "Maybe not. My memoirs . . ."

". . . Aren't going to change a thing," she said firmly. With an effort, she injected a note of irony into her voice. "Do they describe your career as a Nazi war criminal? Or a serial killer, maybe?"

He gave her a ghost of a smile and shook his head.

"Then how could they change my feelings toward you, Pop-Pop? *How?*"

Jim Dooley smiled weakly. "Nothing's immutable, Samantha Rose," he said quietly. "Nothing's unchangeable. I learned that a long time ago."

"Even so."

"You will read them, then?"

"Of course I'll read them. You know I'll read them."

Silence for a few moments; then the old man spoke again, with an obvious effort. "Don't wait for the lawyers, Samantha." The slurring was worse, so much so that Sam had to strain to make out some of the words. "Don't wait for the trained seals to jump through all their little legal hoops."

"What do you mean, Pop-Pop? I don't understand."

"Things happen, sometimes," he said darkly. "Don't wait, Samantha. Please. When it's time, just *take* them."

"That's illegal, isn't it?" Then she smiled sadly. "But now's a hell of time to start paying attention to restricted airspace," she added, echoing his own phrase back to him. Her eyes stung as she saw his tired smile. "They're in your study, aren't they? I'll get them right now."

She started to rise, but Pop-Pop's fleshless hand grabbed her wrist, his grip surprisingly strong. *"No,"* he gasped forcefully. "No, not now. Please."

Slowly, Sam sat down again. "Why not, Pop-Pop?" she asked, puzzled.

"Not while I'm still alive. *Please,* Samantha Rose."

She nodded. "Okay, Pop-Pop. Whatever you want."

His grip tightened for an instant, then the pressure vanished almost entirely, as though he'd exhausted his last reserve of energy. "Don't even look at them until I'm gone," he continued. "Please, Samantha."

"I won't. I *said* I wouldn't." She stroked the back of his hand, trying to calm him. "Whatever you want, *really.*"

Jim Dooley hesitated, then he smiled, and his eyes closed. "Thank you, Samantha Rose," he said softly. The tension—the *worry*—that had filled his face just moments before seemed to bleed away. "Thank you," he said again. "I think I'm going to sleep now."

She reached out wordlessly and brushed a strand of hair from his forehead. *Whatever you want, Pop-Pop,* she reassured him silently. *Whatever you want.*

4

Jim Dooley, Sr., declined visibly over the next three days. Samantha thought it was almost as though he had been hanging on to health, even to life, until he'd talked to his granddaughter about the issues that he figured were really important. The flesh that remained on his frame seemed to melt away like a dream with the coming of dawn. His skin shrunk in on itself, stretched across his fragile bones until he reminded her of photos she'd seen of the Holocaust. The familiar brilliance in his eyes faded, their green now shot through with red. He didn't say anything to her—he wouldn't, of course—but Sam was convinced he was almost blind.

It's not fair*!* she silently raged again and again. *He shouldn't have to go out this way.* Jim Sr. was an air-racer, a test pilot. He'd pushed the envelope a thousand times, "tempted the demon" that engineers used to think lurked at the sound barrier. He'd diced with death, the Big Kaboom, a thousand times and won. He'd pushed the old racing birds—nothing but huge radial engines with stubby wings, faster than hell but psychotically temperamental—around the pylon racing circuit, walking away from the kind of pancake landings that had claimed the lives of dozens of his contemporaries. So where was the justice in *this*? He deserved one last challenge, where survival came down to *skill,* not to blind, dumb luck. . . .

Time was precious, she knew. Every minute, every second she could spend with him was valuable—irreplaceable. Maggie had understood, as she'd known her friend would. Sam had returned to Maggie's small house only a couple of times, when she was too tired to keep her eyes open any longer. Each time, she'd considered crawling into the bed in Pop-Pop's spare room, but still the old fears—*the old superstitions,* she admitted—stopped her. Pop-Pop would understand. Sickness was a pilot's nemesis, doctors and nurses the enemy who could ground you on a moment's notice, with no chance for appeal. No, there was no way she could stand to sleep in the same house, for the same reason she couldn't have spent much time in a hospital. The proximity to illness brought out all the old, irrational fears.

She'd met the professional nurse Pop-Pop had hired, Lorna Millington. Firm and no-nonsense, but certainly not "Attila the Hun's governess," as Jim Dooley had described her. They'd talked, Sam and Lorna, when Pop-Pop was asleep. She was Sam's only trustworthy source for how her grandfather was really doing, the real state of his health. She couldn't bring herself to ask Pop-Pop, of course, and even if he had answered her, she worried he'd try to "soften" the truth. The disease was tearing him apart, she'd learned, and the cancerous tissue had spread from his pancreas throughout his lymphatic system, even into his brain. His kidneys were almost ruined by the toxic breakdown his tortured tissues were releasing, and his heart was weakening.

How will he die? Sam had wanted to know, but she hadn't been able to bring herself to put the question into words. Fortunately, Lorna had saved her the pain. Renal shutdown if he was unlucky, the nurse had explained, with all its terrible consequences. But if he was fortunate—*Fortunate! What a damned* hideous *application of that word,* Samantha thought, *but still true for all that*—the cancer in his brain would kill him first, just "turn him off," maybe when he was asleep.

And it wouldn't be long coming. Lorna hadn't had to tell her that, she could see it for herself. See it in her grandfather's dissolving body, and in his blind eyes. Nobody would have to tell Pop-Pop either. A couple more days, at the most.

"Then why isn't he in the hospital, for God's sake?" Samantha had demanded. Lorna hadn't replied, but then she didn't have to. Sam knew the answer the moment she asked the question: *Because Pop-Pop doesn't want to die in an antiseptic, impersonal hospital. He wants to die the way he lived—on* his *terms.*

When she'd planned her last visit to Pop-Pop, Sam had pictured the large house as empty except for herself, her grandfather and some faceless medical personnel. But she should have known it wouldn't be that way. Jim Dooley's friends wouldn't let him die alone. They came through the house in relays—dozens of them, scores of them, one at a time or in small groups. Few of them stayed for long, just short visits—a chance to reminisce one last time before the darkness came. Many were Pop-Pop's vintage, in their sixties and seventies—but there were many younger visitors as well. *Devotees,* she thought sometimes, *supplicants, almost. Pilgrims, hadji, visiting a shrine or a holy place.* They were like the young engineer Macintyre, she realized. Jim Dooley was their mentor; he'd touched their lives in some way, and they were coming from across the continent to thank him in the only way they knew how—with their presence, here at the end.

The faces she recognized surprised her, faces she'd seen in the aviation books she'd read avidly as a child, in documentaries and magazine articles. Pilots, most of them: airjockeys who held speed and altitude records, like Sid Warner, whom she'd already met, and new faces like Jacqueline Cochran. Members of the flight-test fraternity, who'd "wrung out" whole generations of experimental planes on the birds' evaluation and development flights.

Then there were the explorers. Mountain climbers who'd defeated the killer peaks of K2 and Kanchenjunga. Arctic explorers like Will Steger. Adventurers. At first, Sam was puzzled. *What have they got in common with Pop-Pop?* But then she'd figured it out. *The common ground is exploring limits, isn't it, whether it be aerodynamics or geography. It's about pushing back the frontiers.*

And on the morning of the fourth day, a telegram arrived that she took upstairs to Pop-Pop.

Jim, the cable said, *sorry we're going to miss out this year. The Sierra Nevadas aren't going to be the same.* The signature read "Chuck Yeager."

Chuck Yeager*? Was* he *the "good friend" who dragged Pop-Pop into the mountains on foot for the first time?*

Sam generally stayed out of the visitors' way. They weren't here for her, after all, and any time they spent talking with her was time they weren't with Pop-Pop. All of them were friendly and polite, of course, and the majority seemed pleased to meet Jim Dooley's granddaughter. But apart from greetings and unimportant small talk, she had little to say to them, or they to her.

She usually made it back to Maggie's house around 02:00 to catch a couple of hours' restless sleep on the creaking Hide-A-Bed. Then, even before Maggie was up and around, Sam was pointing Grendel south again on Highway 101, with the sun just rising over the Klamath Mountains.

Pop-Pop faded faster every day. His eyes looked like cracked marbles, and his breath sounded painful in his throat. Lorna Millington was there around the clock—no talk of giving her time off now—catching an hour or two of sleep when she could in the downstairs library that she'd converted into her bedroom and office. (With a twinge of guilt, Sam realized that Pop-Pop had kept the guest room vacant for *her,* just in case, rather than giving it over to the nurse.) Between visitors Sam would sit with her grandfather, holding his brittle hand. They'd talk when he was awake—nothing of real import, just "do you remember when . . ." reminiscences. But he tired easily, and the ever-increasing dosage of painkillers often fogged his mind. Still, Sam was content just to sit in silence with him, listening to the river flowing by unceasing and unchanging below the bluff.

James R. Dooley, Sr., died at 03:17 on the morning of July 26, fading away in his sleep.

Sam wasn't there at the time; *predictable,* she told herself bitterly. She'd kissed her grandfather as he lay sleeping at about 02:00 and driven the five miles north to Nesika Beach, struggling to keep her gritty eyes open. Blissfully, she'd slept without dreams until her watch alarm had roused her at 05:00; then she'd been back in Grendel to return to the Rogue River.

She could *feel* it as soon as she opened the door. Deep down in her gut she knew he was gone. The house was silent, no one stirred . . . but there was more to it than that. Something had gone out of the large, comfortable house—left the world itself. She sank down into a crouch in the carpeted hallway, her back against the front door. The upstairs hallway was dark, she saw. There'd always been a dim light at the top of the stairs. But not now. The staircase looked steep, suddenly, a punishing climb. She wiped at her eyes. Her fingers came away dry.

No tears?

No, she realized, the tears would come later. When the reality of this had really penetrated, then she'd cry.

Lorna Millington found her like that, uncounted minutes later. The nurse said nothing—there was nothing to say, after all. Samantha looked up into the older woman's eyes. Yes, there was loss there, too. More than just the loss of a patient? *Yes,* Sam thought, *Jim Dooley touched* her *life, too. . . .*

It took her ultimate effort to force herself to her feet. She took a step toward the stairs.

The nurse's hand on her arm was gentle, but it stopped her as effectively as if it had been a vise.

"I need to see him." In her own ears, Sam's voice sounded bleak, empty.

Lorna hesitated, then, with a sad smile, she nodded. Sam could feel the older woman's eyes on her back as she climbed the faintly creaking stairs.

The curtains in Pop-Pop's bedroom were partially drawn against the dawn. In the half-light, he might almost have been asleep, lying there on the harsh, angular bed. *Almost.* . . . His eyes were closed, his face relaxed and peaceful. Yet she knew he was dead, could feel it. Here was the focus of the emptiness she'd sensed in the front hallway.

Tenderly, she picked up his hand from the coverlet. The skin, stretched over the bones—*like the canvas of an old biplane, drawn tight over the wooden struts*—was cool, but no colder than it had been the night before. She raised it to her lips, kissed it gently.

And then the tears came.

The doctor came and went, completing all the necessary paperwork. And then came the others: young, dark-suited, wearing their professional somberness like a mantle. Samantha followed them into town, Grendel trailing their dark vehicle like a predator on the heels of a sluggish prey-animal. From the parking lot, she watched helplessly as they carried Pop-Pop's sheet-draped body into the funeral home. She couldn't follow them inside, not now. The closing of the heavy mortuary door rang in her mind like a death knell.

The funeral service took place the next day, a Monday. As Pop-Pop had told her, the arrangements had all been made. (In one sense, Sam found this saddening: she'd liked to have been involved in the final process in some way. But another part of her welcomed the peaceful time that allowed her to begin coming to come to terms with her grief.) The service itself was private: Sam, Sid Warner and—to Samantha's surprise—Maggie Braslins. At first Sam was puzzled. Shouldn't someone as well known as Jim Dooley have a larger, more well-attended funeral, so his friends could say one last farewell? But eventually she understood that they'd already said good-bye to him in a way that was much more meaningful to Pop-Pop than any religious service in which he'd never really believed. A wake would have been more in keeping with the way he'd lived his life, she thought: a traditional, Irish-style wake, where his friends could lift a glass of whiskey to his memory. *But if he'd wanted a wake, he'd have arranged for one.* Maybe it was better for his friends to take their leave of him on their own terms, in the ways that suited them, rather than have some structure enforced upon them by someone who could no longer participate.

Samantha and Maggie sat together in the small funeral chapel, the older woman snuffling quietly as the undertaker mouthed his empty platitudes. Simon Warner sat alone at the back, his thatch of silver hair in startling contrast to his black suit. His face was expressionless, his gray eyes guarded, but Sam could sense the grief that he held under unyielding control. His control established a kind of *boundary* around him—that's what it felt like to Sam, at least—a barrier that she felt unwilling to cross. If she hadn't seen him that first day in Pop-Pop's room, she'd have labeled him as emotionless, aloof. Now she knew it to be infinitely more complex than that.

Finally, the curtains draping the far wall parted, and to the cloying strains of mock-angelic choirs, the coffin moved into the crematorium beyond. The curtains hissed back into place, and that was the end. By the time Sam had shaken hands with the undertaker—she hadn't wanted to touch him or listen to his unctuous condolences, but she accepted that there were some forms that must be observed—Sid Warner was gone. She sighed. It was funny: she hardly knew Simon Warner—*I don't know him from a hole in the ground,* she amended wryly—but she couldn't shake that sense of . . . well, *kinship* was still the only word that seemed to fit . . . that she'd felt in Jim Dooley's sickroom a few days before. It would have been nice to speak to the older man again.

If you're going to wish for something, wish for something that counts, she told herself firmly, with one last, wistful look at the closed curtains and the empty bier.

She saw Sid Warner later that same day, however, in the waiting room outside the undertaker's office when Sam returned to pick up Pop-Pop's remains. He rose to his feet as she entered and flashed her a smile that seemed to light up the room.

"Samantha."

"Sam," she corrected automatically. Then, "What are you doing here?" she asked. "I figured you'd be off to . . ."—she shrugged—". . . well, wherever you were going." She saw the crooked smile spreading across the pilot's face, and quickly amended, "Not that I'm unhappy to see you, or anything."

He raised an eyebrow at that. "Thirty years ago, a statement like that would have me running around in circles dragging a wing," he chuckled. "Hell, *twenty* years ago." His smile faded, and he glanced toward the closed door to the undertaker's inner office. "I guess I wasn't quite done with him," he said. He tried to inject a note of humor into the words, but didn't quite pull it off.

Samantha nodded. Wordlessly, she reached out and took the aging pilot's hand. His pale eyes widened in momentary surprise; then his smile returned, and he squeezed her hand in thanks.

The door to the inner office opened, and the undertaker emerged. Cradled in his hands—*with exaggerated care, as if he were carrying a vial of bubonic plague,* Sam thought irreverently—was a brass urn turned on simple, elegant lines. Despite her best intentions, she felt her eyes brim as she saw it. *That's all that's left of him. . . .*

The undertaker nodded to them both. "Ms. Dooley. Mr. Warner." His thin eyebrows raised in a question.

Sam stepped forward and accepted the brass urn.

Beside her, Warner cleared his throat. "Samantha," he began. Then, "Sam," he quickly corrected. "I have a question." He paused, as if struggling to find the right words to express a tricky subject.

"Yes?" she prompted.

"I just wanted to ask . . . well, if you had any *plans.*" He gestured vaguely toward the urn.

Samantha blinked. "Plans?"

Warner nodded. "Yeah. I was wondering if you'd given any thought to where . . . what . . ." He stopped again. *As though unwilling to actually say the words,* Sam thought kindly, *"What are you going to do with his ashes?"*

"If you hadn't," the pilot continued quickly, "I've got a suggestion you might consider."

Samantha looked up into the old man's face, and saw the embarrassment there. *Typical jet-jockey,* she thought warmly. *It's just* not done *to acknowledge death, is it?* Warner's discomfiture was touching, in a way. "He told me where, Sid," she said softly. "Kings Canyon. The Sierra Nevadas."

He smiled. "Of course. He couldn't get enough of that place since Chuck first showed it to him."

Sam nodded. *Chuck Yeager,* she told herself. *I thought so.* "Where were you thinking?" she asked after a moment, curious.

"It doesn't matter. Kings Canyon fits."

"No," she pressed gently, "I'm interested."

Warner shrugged. "Okay. Well, see, there's this . . . *museum,* I guess you might call it. A place to honor the names of people who've pushed the envelope. A couple of the other guys arranged for their ashes to be put there, and I thought. . . ." He shrugged again. "Well, I thought Jimmy might like to wind up among his colleagues and comrades. I hadn't thought of Kings Canyon, but I think I like that idea better." He chuckled. "Jimmy never was one for being cooped up inside, was he?" He patted the top of the urn.

"Where *is* this place?" Samantha asked curiously. "I've never heard of anything like that."

"You wouldn't unless you're a test pilot, I guess. It's not like the flight-test boys turn into household names or anything. Not like those Spam-in-a-can pseudo-pilots who flaked off to join Mercury and Gemini and Apollo."

Sam laughed aloud at the scorn in the man's voice. "I might like to take a look sometime," she said.

"Anytime you're in the area," Warner replied lightly. His smile faded, and he reached out again to touch the polished brass. "I guess it's about that time," he said slowly, and again Sam could see the real pain in his eyes. He started to turn away.

"Sid."

He turned back.

"Sid. Mags and I are having kind of a little wake for Pop-Pop. If you'd like. . . ."

Warner smiled. "A mini-wake, huh? I'd like to, Sam, but

I can't. Places to be, no rest for the wicked, and all the rest of that crap."

"Can I get your phone number?"

His eyebrow shot up. "Oh, really?"

She shrugged. "Seems a shame to lose track of someone who knew Pop-Pop," she pointed out.

He sighed, acting crestfallen. "Ah, well, and I thought it was my manly charm." He patted his pockets, then, "No business cards," he said. He made a long arm and snagged a scrap of paper from a nearby table. Quickly, he scrawled down a number. "Call whenever you like, Sam," he said. "A granddaughter of Jimmy's is a granddaughter of mine . . ." —his face fell comically—". . . and not being interested in either incest or folk dancing, that's the saddest thing I've heard in a long time."

Sam laughed aloud. "Clear skies," she called after him as he left the undertaker's waiting room.

The brass urn rested beside Samantha on the copilot's seat of the *Yellow Bird*, a seatbelt holding it in place. Below were the Sierra Nevada mountains in all their glory, rugged peaks reaching for the sky, bracketing the small plane with their slopes. Snow gleamed an impossible white on the highest peaks, while the lower slopes were girdled with trees. The terrain was fantastic—literally *fantastic*, like something from a dream or a fantasy. She'd flown over the Sierra Nevadas before, but she'd never really *looked* at them, not like this. *What would it be like to be down there?* she asked herself. *On foot, surrounded by those trees, seeing the peaks soaring above you? It must be spectacular.*

She sighed, and once again her eyes misted. She rubbed at them with a knuckle. *Pop-Pop was right*, she thought. This *is the place for him, not the tamer hills of Eagle Mountain. And not Sid Warner's test-pilot museum.*

Carefully she adjusted the throttle and lost a thousand feet of altitude. She flew along a deep, harsh-sloped valley. Several miles ahead, a high mountain lake glinted in the sun. Steadying the stick between her knees, she reached over and released the belt holding the urn in place. The wings rocked slightly as she lifted the brass container onto her lap. For safety's sake, she really should have had a copilot for this flight, someone to take the controls for her while she saw to Pop-Pop's last wishes. She knew that Maggie would willingly have come along; the older woman might even have felt slighted that she hadn't been invited to participate, but it only seemed right that she do this last task alone.

She slid back the small quarter-panel of the window beside her. The slipstream gusted through the plane, carrying with it the clean, pure smell of the mountains, the high desert. Gently, she removed the cap from the urn and raised the metal container to the window.

Careful, now. She had to hold the urn well out the window, below the lip of the fuselage, so the slipstream would pull the contents down and back. She smiled, a little sadly. *Somehow I don't think Pop-Pop would want to spend the rest of eternity blowing around in the back of* Yellow Bird.

Gently, she upended the urn. The slipstream caught the fine, gritty ash and blew it backward in a rapidly dispersing cloud. *Good-bye, Pop-Pop.*

Samantha set the empty urn back on the seat beside her and closed the window. With a last glance at the mountains below, *the mountains where Pop-Pop used to hike with Chuck Yeager,* she pulled the Glasair into a climbing turn and headed back toward the coast.

5

Samantha and Maggie Braslins had their own, very private wake for Jim Dooley the night of his death—just the two of them, some of Maggie's old photo albums, and a bottle of Jack Daniel's. It was Maggie's idea from the start. Sam had been afraid it might turn morbid, but the older woman wasn't going to let that happen. She was very adamant about the old traditions of the wake (Samantha suspected that her friend might have been to many in her time) and claimed that sadness had no place. The purpose of a wake was to *celebrate,* not to mourn: to celebrate the fact that Jim Dooley had lived in the first place, and to honor his achievements and strengths. In fact, Maggie had claimed, the whole concept could be summed up in a phrase she'd heard at a Southern Baptist funeral decades ago, "We thank You, Lord, for loaning this good person to us for a time." Samantha nodded slowly when she heard that. Her mourning wasn't finished, her sadness wasn't gone, but for the moment she could set them aside and be grateful for all the ways Pop-Pop had enriched her life. *We thank You, Lord,* she prayed silently.

Maggie was only in her fifties, and she hadn't taken a serious interest in flying until her mid-twenties. Still, her "career" had overlapped with Jim Dooley's—more than Sam could guess, it turned out. After they'd "christened" the bottle of whiskey, Maggie flipped through the photograph albums until she found the picture she was looking for. It was a typical pilot's photograph, Sam thought: a knot of tousle-haired people clustered in front of a plane on some godforsaken apron somewhere.

"My birthday," Maggie announced, "1965. There I am." With a broad forefinger, she tapped the figure in the center of the grainy, black-and-white photograph. "I was thirty-three."

Sam smiled. It was Maggie, all right. The same smile, the same generous proportions. The only noticeable difference was that the woman in the photograph didn't have any gray in her hair.

Sam found herself momentarily distracted by the plane in the background: a sharp-nosed, delta-winged jet of some type.

"It's a Mirage III." Maggie answered the younger woman's unspoken question. "Dassault-Breguet. French. It's a modified trainer, a two-seater." She smiled broadly. "Quite the birthday present, all in all."

"What?"

Maggie laughed. "Not the plane. *Stick-time* in the plane." She pointed to another figure in the photograph, a broad-shouldered, athletic-looking man with his arm around Braslins' shoulders. "Bobby's idea," she explained. "Bobby Atlow, we were *this close* to being married at the time." She smiled warmly. "Living in sin, actually. Bobby wanted to get me a present I'd always remember: a flight in a fast jet, and a chance to actually take the stick.

"I didn't know anything about it beforehand," she went

on. "I knew Bobby had something cooked up when he took me out to the airport that morning, but I didn't know what. This guy was there"—again she pointed out a figure, a tall, thin-faced man on the other side of Maggie in the photograph—"waiting for me. French air force officer, name of Gilles. He helped me cram myself into a flight suit, and then took me up for an hour of the most fun I've ever had with my clothes on." She traced the angular lines of the fighter with a fingertip. "It was that flight that got me thinking I had to have my own jet, and that's how I eventually ended up with my own T–38."

"All thanks to Bobby," Sam said. "How did he swing it? A French fighter, a French pilot? Hell, in '65, the Dassault Mirage was damn near state of the art, wasn't it?"

"Oh, Bobby knew how to get things done. Well, actually, he knew who to *talk to* when he wanted to get things done. And in this case, who he knew was *this* guy, here." Again she indicated a figure in the back of the group—slightly out of focus, his face shaded by the jet fighter's razor-edged wing.

Sam leaned forward, shifting the book in the light. *Was it?*

Yes, it was. Jim Dooley, Sr.—fit and trim and sunbronzed, in his early fifties. The individual features were blurred, but the way they fit together to create the overall "look" of his face was unmistakable. She looked up wordlessly at her friend.

Maggie nodded confirmation. "Jim Dooley," she confirmed. "One of Bobby's hundreds of contacts." She sighed. "A remarkable man, Bobby Atlow. He attracted people like a magnet attracts iron filings. Too bad most of them were women," she finished with a grin.

"So you knew Pop-Pop, way back then."

"*Met* him, didn't *know* him," Maggie corrected quickly. "He helped Bobby arrange my birthday present, and then he just drifted back to wherever he'd come from. I didn't get to *know* him at all until I learned from you that we were practically neighbors, and even then. . . ." She shrugged. Gently, she took the album back from Sam and closed it. "I don't know why I even showed you that, kiddo," she admitted. "I guess maybe . . . just to show you another facet of his life. I don't know."

Sam reached out and took her friend's hand. "I'm glad you showed me." She raised her whiskey glass in a toast. "We thank You, Lord—whether You exist or not, You secretive bastard—for loaning Jim Dooley to us for a time. Now that You've got him back, I hope You treat him right."

Maggie beamed. "I'll drink to that," she said.

Sam slept late the next morning, and rose slowly. Even so, she was still up and around before Maggie even stirred. Fortunately for her headache, the day was overcast and dark. She wandered downstairs, detouring through the living room on her way to the coffeemaker to check on the mess they'd left the night before.

Maggie's favorite ashtray, a shaft fitting from an old radial aero-engine, was full of butts, and the condition of Sam's throat reminded her that she'd smoked her fair share of them. On the coffee table were two "dead soldiers"—an empty Jack Daniel's bottle, and a wine bottle with a finger of liquid left in the bottom. Sam stared at the wine bottle morosely. *Sour-mash bourbon and white wine. No wonder I'm under the weather.*

She felt a lot better after she ate breakfast, though. Coffee and cornflakes settled her stomach nicely, and the headache diminished from a ugly throbbing to a gentle reprimand somewhere around her sinuses. Once she'd absorbed her third mug of strong coffee, she tidied up a little, including emptying the ashtray. She left the empty bottles in pride of place on the cleared table, though, to remind Maggie of last night's activities when she finally greeted the day.

As she worked, something nagged at her, the unmistakable feeling that she'd forgotten something important, something that she'd let drift past in the turmoil of the day before. *What is it?*

Looking for inspiration, something that might make some internal connection and jar the memory loose, she let her gaze drift around the kitchen. When she saw the notepad by the door, she remembered.

Pop-Pop's memoirs. Damn it!

She forced herself to relax, to breathe deeply for a moment. *No problem,* she told herself. Jim Dooley had said the memoirs were important—important enough that she shouldn't wait for the executors to get them to her through normal channels. But he'd also told her to wait until he was gone before reading them. She hadn't let things go too long, had she?

Whatever, she told herself with a shrug. *I've remembered, so I'll go do something about it now.* She scrawled a short note to her friend on the pad beside the phone, snagged her coat and left the house, shutting the front door quietly behind her.

The cool wind in her hair blew away the last remnants of her headache as she pointed Grendel south and opened up the throttle. By the time she reached the mouth of Pop-Pop's driveway, she was feeling completely human again.

She wasn't sure exactly what to expect at the house. As an adult, she'd never been involved in a death and its aftermath, and she didn't know how people usually handled these matters. She understood that the lawyers would read Pop-Pop's will, probably within a couple of days; she figured it would be simple enough, with no probate problems. Then the executors would take care of making sure the right people got the right bequests. *But before that, what happens?* she wondered. *Is the house just left sitting empty?*

As she rounded the last turn of the winding driveway and pulled to a stop, she saw the answer to her question. Parked in front of the house was a yellow Ford Bronco, a crest and logo on the door proclaiming it to be the property of Curry Private Security. *Private security? Rent-a-cops?* But when she thought about it, it didn't seem so surprising after all. Pop-Pop had a lot of valuable possessions; the Jensen, for one, but a lot of smaller items as well, much easier to carry away, and an empty house might be too much of a temptation for thieves. Obviously, the executors or the lawyers or whoever weren't taking any unnecessary chances.

A slender, blond man wearing a short-sleeved outfit of dark blue appeared around the corner of the house as Sam climbed out of her Mustang. His severely cut uniform made him look like a cop, as did the fact that he carried a lot of *stuff* on his broad belt: small flashlight, handcuffs, walkie-talkie, and other assorted odds and ends. *But no pistol,* she noted. She watched him with some amusement as he approached. He was young, almost baby-faced, and the result of his attempt to grow a "standard-issue" cop mustache was wispy and thin, almost white against his freckled skin. He moved self-consciously, as though he didn't quite know how to carry himself. *He's new at this,* she decided, *and his uniform's too big for him—not physically, but* emotionally.

She hid her thoughts behind a friendly smile. "Hi there," she said lightly.

"Hi, er. . . ." He paused, obviously a little unsure about how he should proceed. "Er, is there anything I can do for you . . . er, ma'am?"

Ma'am, is it? Sam fought the impulse to grin openly. She patted him on the shoulder as she walked past him toward the house's front door. "No, it's okay, thanks."

"Hey. Wait a minute." He sounded alarmed.

Still smiling, Sam turned back to him. "Yes?" she asked.

"You . . . you can't go in there."

Her smile slipped away. "Oh?"

"I'm sorry, ma'am."

Sam drew herself up to her full height and fixed him with a glare of withering scorn. "Look," she enunciated clearly. "My name is Samantha Dooley, granddaughter of Jim Dooley, Sr., the guy who owns this house. My grandfather. Okay?"

The rent-a-cop pulled a small notebook from his back pocket and quickly flipped through it until he found the page he wanted. "Samantha Dooley. . . ." he murmured under his breath. After a few seconds he looked up and shook his head. "Sorry, ma'am. You're not on my list."

This isn't funny any more, Blondie. With an effort, Sam controlled her growing anger. "And what list is that?"

"The list of people I'm to let go into the house. You're not on it."

"Let me see that." Sam snatched the notebook out of the man's hand, ignoring his yelp of, "Hey!" She scanned the short list of names—only six of them, all male. None of them was even vaguely familiar. With a demure, "Thank you," she handed the pad back to the young security guard.

Then, "Look," she said again. "I know you've got a job to do, but the people who gave you that list just weren't thinking. I'm Jim Dooley's granddaughter. I can show you ID if you like. I'm sure your superiors didn't mean for you to keep Jim Dooley's only living relative—and his heir, for that matter—out of his house. What do *you* think?"

He hesitated, but then managed to shore up his sagging resolve. "I don't know nothing about that," he said gruffly. "All I know's you're not on the list." He squared his shoulders. "And I wouldn't let the president of the United States in here if he wasn't on the list," he finished, a little smugly.

"Who hired you to watch the house?"

The guard chewed on his lower lip with a chipped tooth. "I don't think I should tell you that," he said slowly.

It was all Sam could do not to laugh out loud. "You don't know, do you?"

Affronted, the rent-a-cop hooked his thumbs in his equipment belt and puffed out his chest. "I'm sorry, ma'am," he said brusquely, "but I can't let you into the house."

Anger burned in Sam's chest. *I could knock Blondie on his sorry butt and choke him with his belt before he even knows I've moved,* she told herself.

Not smart, Dooley. She concentrated on slowing her breathing and letting go of the anger that twisted inside her. She forced a smile onto her face. "Well," she said as lightly as she could manage, "I suppose I'll be going, then. Have a nice day."

The rent-a-cop held his pose as she climbed into Grendel and fired up the big V8. She drove away slowly, resisting the temptation to spin the wheels and shower him with gravel. She watched the guard in the rearview mirror until a curve in the driveway hid him from view.

Keeping her speed to little more than a crawl, Sam pulled out onto the road and turned left, back toward the coast highway. After a hundred yards or so, she pulled over onto the gravel shoulder and thought for a moment. *Why not?* She smiled as she killed the engine and climbed back out of the car.

Pop-Pop's house was located toward the rear of a large lot, almost triple the size of most land parcels around here. Sam knew that developers had been pestering him for years to sell, or at least to subdivide his property. But Pop-Pop had liked his privacy. There was no way he'd have been comfortable with neighbors only a dozen yards away. Much better to hang on to the whole lot to provide a buffer zone between him and the rest of humanity. When he'd built his house, he'd cleared the area for the foundation and the region immediately around it. The rest of the lot he'd left untouched—more than an acre of century-old trees and thick underbrush.

Samantha strode openly along the road—who knew how the neighbors might react if they saw a stranger "skulking" about?—and turned into Pop-Pop's gate. As soon as she was off the road, she slipped into the shelter of a broad-boled tree and examined the tactical situation. A curve of the driveway concealed the house from the gate . . . and vice-versa. Sam moved deeper into the woods until she was out of sight of anyone passing by on the road.

She crouched in the dry bushes and looked toward the house. Through the trees and the low foliage she could see hints of bright yellow: the rent-a-cop's Ford Bronco. Using that flash of color as a landmark, she made her way silently through the underbrush. As she approached the edge of the woods, she slowed down, then lowered herself to the ground in the shelter of a large bush.

From here she had a perfect view of the entire front of the house. The rent-a-cop—"Blondie," as she'd labeled him—was standing more or less where she'd left him, just at the foot of the steps leading up to the front door. As she watched, he looked around, scanning the surrounding area. Apparently satisfied by what he saw, the security guard fumbled in a pocket and pulled out a pack of cigarettes. Sam smiled wickedly as he lit up and took a deep drag. *Smoking on duty, huh? That's got to be against the rules. He must have been checking to make sure that no one else was around.* As she watched him exhale a stream of smoke, she felt the pang of desire for a cigarette herself. *You never really quit,* she told herself again.

She settled herself more comfortably on the rough ground. For a moment, she questioned what she was doing here. *Why am I bothering? Nothing's going to vanish in the next couple of days.*

She guessed it was the *principle* of the thing. *It's my house now. The lawyers just haven't caught up with that fact. Who the hell do they think they are, keeping me out of my own house?* And then there was Pop-Pop's wishes. For whatever reasons, he'd thought it important that Sam take his memoirs and read them *without* waiting for the legal proceedings to grind to a close.

The rent-a-cop finished his cigarette and, instead of butting it out, flipped it, still burning, into the flower bed to the right of the door. Sam chuckled to herself as he carefully smoothed his wispy mustache with both forefingers. Then he strolled off to Sam's right, vanishing around the corner of the house.

When I first saw Blondie, he came around the house from the left, she remembered. Chances were good that he intended to walk the entire perimeter of the house again. *Time to go.*

Emerging from the cover of the trees, she hurried across the gravel, past the Bronco to the front door. She pulled her keys from her pants pocket, careful that the keys didn't jingle as she looked for the one she wanted. There it was, a large silver Weiser. She fit it into the keyhole and turned, heard the deadbolt *snick* back. She darted through the door, closing it quietly behind her.

A couple of years ago, Jim Dooley had installed a perimeter security system for the house. The control panel, nothing more than a small ten-button keypad with a red and a green status light, was mounted on the wall opposite the door. Sam hurried across the hall to the keypad, reaching out to punch in the code to disarm the system before the thirty-second delay expired. But the system hadn't even been set, she saw immediately. The green, rather than the red, LED was glowing. *Sloppy,* she thought. *Hire a guard, but don't even set the alarm. What kind of security is that?*

She took a deep breath. *Well, I'm in.* The memoirs would be in Pop-Pop's study—at least, she'd *assumed* that's where they would be when she'd talked about them with her grandfather, and he hadn't corrected her. That was where she'd start.

She climbed the first half-flight of stairs, keeping her head below the level of the window on the first landing. Stopping, she cautiously raised her head until she could see the garden beside the house. *There he is.* The security guard's blue uniform stood out clearly against the shrubs and foliage. She waited until he turned the corner around the back of the house and vanished from sight. Then she climbed the rest of the stairs.

The door to Pop-Pop's bedroom, down at the far end of the upstairs hallway, was closed. Sam felt a flash of relief. Even looking into that room would bring up the pain she hadn't yet worked through. The door to Pop-Pop's study, the first room on the right, was ajar. Softly, she pushed it open and stepped inside.

Her throat tightened suddenly and her eyes filled with tears. *He's still here.* The thought came unbidden. Part *of him, at least. He's here, and always will be.* She closed the door behind her and stood with her back against it as she looked around the room.

The blinds were drawn over the single window, opposite the door. It was still light enough for her to pick out the familiar sights, however. Under the window was Pop-Pop's small desk. A two-year-old Macintosh computer sat on one corner under a plastic dust cover. Sam smiled. Her grandfather had bought the machine at her urging, but she was pretty sure he'd never really bothered to use it for anything. The wall to her right was lined with floor-to-ceiling bookcases, completely filled. Other books that wouldn't fit in the shelves were piled on the floor in the corners. To her left, the wall was covered with photographs—framed memories, color and black-and-white images of moments from Jim Dooley, Sr.'s life. She pulled the high-backed leather chair out from the desk, and sat down, wiping tears from her cheeks with the back of her hand.

Pop-Pop loved spending time in here, she remembered. *He felt comfortable here.* Her mind drifted back to one of the first times she'd visited him, staying in the guest bedroom next door to the study. In the middle of the night—03:00, or thereabouts, she recalled—she'd gotten up to get a glass of water. In the dark hallway, she'd seen the yellow spill of electric light from under the study door. Curious, she'd silently pushed open the well-oiled door. Her grandfather, wrapped in a well-worn robe, had been comfortably ensconced in this very chair, so engrossed in the book he was reading that he hadn't even noticed the door open. Even now, years later, Sam could remember the smile of utter satisfaction on the man's face.

With an effort, she shook off the memories. *I'm here for a reason,* she reminded herself.

The desk was the most logical place to start, she figured.

One by one, she opened the three drawers. Standard office supplies in the first: pencils, pens, a stapler, three pads of yellow Post-it notes. A couple of green pseudo-leather folders in the second. She took them out, pulled the flaps away from their Velcro closures, and opened them on her lap. Insurance policies, she saw at once: life insurance, home owners' policies, and another that she assumed covered *Yellow Bird.* Feeling uncomfortable—*I don't want to* think *about life insurance yet, let alone look at the policies*—she closed the folders and returned them to the drawer. The bottom drawer contained a spiral-bound notebook, unlabeled. *Bingo,* she told herself as she extracted it and opened to the first page.

She saw at once that this was just the logbook for *Yellow Bird*; details on operation hours, maintenance, fuel costs, and the rest. She flipped quickly through the log. Nothing even remotely like memoirs. Frowning, she returned the logbook to the drawer and pushed the leather chair back from the desk. Where else could the memoirs be? She swiveled the chair around slowly, scanning the room. No filing cabinets or other obvious storage places, she saw. *The bookshelves, then.* She stood and crossed to the floor-to-ceiling bookcases. *Might as well do this methodically,* she told herself. *Start at one end, and work along the shelves.*

She was smiling—a little sadly, perhaps—before she'd finished scanning even the first shelf. *I'd forgotten about his tastes in reading,* she mused. *Already I've forgotten.* Jim Dooley had always been a voracious reader. Unlike other hard-core readers she'd known, however, Jim Dooley had read and absorbed just about *everything,* from potboiler fiction to biographies to military histories to treatises on philosophy. And he'd liked to *own* his books, rather than borrowing them from the library; he found something attractive about the knowledge that they were *his.*

Just look *at all this stuff.* She scanned the shelf again. A single hard-bound volume of *Lord of the Rings,* next to *Gray's Anatomy,* next to Attenborough's *Life on Earth,* next to *The Complete Works of William Shakespeare,* next to Irving Wallace's *The Seven Minutes.* She remembered him telling her once that he had so many books that the only logical way to arrange them on the shelves was by size, rather than by title, topic or author, to avoid wasting space.

Sam sighed. This was going to take a while, if she went over every book on every shelf. What other choice did she have, though? She bent to look at the next lowest shelf, resting her hip against the dark oak frame.

As she leaned against it, the bookcase frame seemed to shift slightly, and she heard a faint but sharp metallic *click*. Instinctively, she jumped back a step, covering her head with her arms. *What a stupid way to die: knock over a bookshelf and get brained by the classics of literature.*

Nothing fell; nothing collapsed. Puzzled, she walked back to examine the bookshelf.

Something was different, she noticed at once. The edge of the three-foot-wide section of bookshelf against which she'd put her weight extended about two inches beyond the edge of the adjacent section. *It wasn't like that before, I* know *it wasn't,* she thought to herself. She hesitated, then reached out and pressed against the protruding portion of the frame. The wood frame shifted a little, then resisted her pressure. *As if it's on a spring,* she realized. She applied more force, until the protruding section was flush with the adjacent frame. As the two sections aligned, there was another sharp *click* and the pressure under her hand vanished. She took a step back, knowing already what she'd see. The bookcase was one large unit again; even knowing what to look for, she couldn't see how that one section was different from the others. *That section hides . . . what? A secret compartment of some kind? The kind of place you'd keep private documents—like personal memoirs?*

She pushed on the same spot again, knowing what to expect this time. She eyed the section of bookcase that moved, and found her guess confirmed; it covered an area about three feet wide by seven feet high. About the size of a door.

The part of the wooden frame that extended beyond the neighboring shelves offered an adequate handhold. Gingerly, she pulled the frame toward herself. There was resistance at first, and she wondered if there was some other kind of catch or lock she had to release. But then the force of her effort overcame the inertia of the wooden case with its load of books, and the section swung slowly, silently outward, just like a door. She paused when the gap between the moving section and the rest of the wall was a couple of feet wide. There was darkness beyond the door. She couldn't see how far the space extended, but somehow it *felt* quite large—at least the size of a walk-in closet. *A whole concealed room. . . .*

The half-light coming through the closed blinds was enough for her to navigate around Pop-Pop's study, but didn't reach into this new area. Where was the light switch? There had to be one. Maybe just inside the door.

For a long moment she hesitated. There was something . . . not quite frightening, but a little *unsettling* . . . about reaching into a dark, mysterious chamber looking for the light switch. Then she laughed weakly, embarrassed by her own reaction. *Too many horror movies,* she chided herself. *"No, Sam, don't go down into that dark basement all alone. . . ."* She slid her hand along the wall into the darkness, feeling for the switch.

The moment her hand crossed the threshold, a light flicked on, banishing the darkness within. She stifled a yelp of surprise. *Get a grip,* she told herself disgustedly. *So Pop-Pop set up the light on a motion detector. That's no reason to wet yourself.*

She took a deep, steadying breath, stepped through the concealed doorway, and stared into the room beyond.

6

So this is Pop-Pop's inner sanctum. His sanctum sanctorum.

For a moment, Samantha felt disconnected, cut loose from the real world. *I'm losing it,* she thought dully. *It's like I'm in a . . . a* movie *or something. Real people don't have secret rooms.*

But then, why not? Why *couldn't* they, if they felt the need and they were designing and building their own house? The more she thought about it, the more the idea appealed to her. I *wouldn't mind having something like that,* she had to admit, *and Pop-Pop would find the idea irresistible—a kind of joke he was playing on the rest of the world.* An "inner sanctum" also explained a few things that had always puzzled her. For a man with a fifty-year career as a professional aviator, Jim Dooley, Sr., seemed to have kept very few mementos and knicknacks. Sure, he had his books and his photographs, both those on the study wall opposite the bookshelves and those elsewhere in the house, but that was about it. He didn't have any of the airplane models, the logo-emblazoned coffee mugs, or the other "trophies" that pilots seemed to collect as a matter of course. *Hell, even* Mags *has her ashtray as a memento of one of her first planes.* Instead of assuming that Pop-Pop was so different from all other pilots she'd ever met, wasn't it more reasonable to guess that he'd just found a more private place to store his precious gewgaws?

The windowless "inner study" was bigger than she'd expected: seven or eight feet wide, she estimated, and maybe twelve feet long. And it was cluttered, practically beyond comprehension. Photographs—framed and unframed, black-and-white and color—covered two of the walls. A third bristled with small shelves and racks covered with a bewildering array of *stuff:* models, plaques and citations, even a couple of medals in a glass-fronted display box. Sam suddenly realized her mouth was gaping open, and shut it with an audible click. She felt a warm rush of bittersweet nostalgia. *His life's here,* she thought, *Pop-Pop's whole life. Everything that was important to him.*

Slowly she approached one of the photograph-covered walls, tenderly reached out to touch the nearest photograph. A grainy color group shot, it showed Jim Dooley in his mid-forties, surrounded by half a dozen other men, all wearing military-style jumpsuits. A small child, maybe four years old, sat on the shoulders of one of the men. Sam leaned closer, trying to make out the unit patch on the chest of Pop-Pop's jumpsuit, but the resolution of the photo just wasn't good enough. She started to move away, but one of the faces in the back row caught her eye. Again she leaned in, squinting. She shook her head. It certainly *might* be Simon Warner, but she couldn't be sure.

The next photograph was much older—black-and-white, with the flat contrast that Sam always associated with pictures from the World War II era. There was Pop-Pop again, now a vigorous young man in his mid-twenties, climbing out of the cockpit of a P–51 Mustang. Kill markers painted on the fuselage under the cockpit showed he'd downed two enemy planes and had a "probable" kill on another.

Sam didn't recognize either of the men in the next photograph. Again, it was a grainy black-and-white shot, this time of two men in old-fashioned suits standing in front of something that reminded Sam of an early bathyscaph.

Samantha stopped dead-still in front of the next framed photograph. There was Jim Dooley, Sr., again, a tall, gangly youth in his late teens, maybe as old as twenty. Standing beside him was a slender, graceful-looking woman in her thirties wearing an enigmatic half-smile, her hair slightly tousled and eyes that seemed as deep as oceans. Both were dressed for flying: high, laced boots, broadcloth pants, and well-worn leather flight jackets. Sam stared in amazement. She recognized the woman; she'd seen that face smiling that same smile from the pages of a dozen biographies and aviation histories. *Amelia Earhart, it can't be anyone else. Pop-Pop* knew *Amelia Earhart—flew with her, it looks like.* She couldn't believe he'd never bothered to mention it to her!

Unless it was some kind of promotion, she thought suddenly. *Pay a dollar and have your picture taken with Lady Lindy.* That's how it could have worked.

She really didn't believe that explanation, though. Carefully, she removed the framed photograph from the wall and turned it over. Slipped into the frame was a business card, aged and yellowed. G.P. PUTNAM'S SONS, PUBLISHERS, the card read, giving a phone number in New York. But it was the handwritten scrawl across the card that drew Sam's attention. *To Jimmy,* it read. *No limits but the sky! Your friend, AE.*

Slightly dazed, she returned the framed photograph to its place on the wall. *What was it Sid Warner said the other day? "Still waters run deep"* . . .

She skimmed over the photographs more rapidly now. Jim Dooley at various stages in his life, standing before different types of planes. Group shots, both casual and formally posed, of men and women who were strangers to her. Amateur snapshots of friends and colleagues.

She stopped abruptly as another photograph caught her eye. Jim Dooley, now in his late thirties, she guessed, grinning broadly as he shook hands with a stoop-shouldered man with unruly gray hair, a mustache like a scrub brush, and the sad eyes of someone who had looked firsthand on the darkest secrets of the human soul. *Albert Einstein.*

Sam shook her head slowly. *This just isn't possible,* she told herself. *Einstein. Earhart. How did he meet them. How did he know them? Just what the hell was Pop-Pop involved in?*

And yet another picture caught her attention. Farther along the row from the Einstein photograph, it was larger than the rest, in brilliant, vibrant colors. It was a landscape, apparently viewed from the air. A beach of black sand, textured with sinuous lines of brilliant blue-green, lined the shore of a great ocean. An indeterminate distance offshore, massive, jagged pillars of rock rose from the waves, standing in line like monolithic sentinels. Sam had seen similar formations off the Oregon and California coasts, but there was something about these pillars that made them seem immensely larger. *Yes,* she thought as she studied the picture, *I can see the waves breaking against the foot of the pillars. If those waves are to scale, then. . . .* Again she shook her head. *No, that can't be right,* she told herself firmly. *There's nowhere in the world where you'll find rock pillars a mile high.*

It was a painting, she decided. An incredibly detailed, photorealistic painting, but a painting nonetheless. *That must be what it is.* When she'd dabbled in science fiction literature a few years ago, she'd seen some absolutely amazing paintings that could almost have been depicting familiar subjects, except for some fantastical element: two suns in the sky, for example, or a knight in armor riding a dinosaur. *Amazing workmanship. Also amazingly disturbing. . . .* Quickly, she turned away from the strange landscape.

What was that?

She jumped as though she'd been jolted by an electric shock.

A sound from downstairs. A metallic click—*Like the front door being unlocked. The rent-a-cop. . . .* She looked around wildly, guiltily.

A second later she had herself back under control. *No cause to panic, for God's sake,* she chided herself. *Maybe he just needs to use the john.*

She heard another quiet click as the front door closed. *He's being very quiet, now that I think about it. As if whoever he is doesn't want to attract attention.*

Sam suddenly felt as though she were on very uncertain ground. *If you're being strictly legal, I suppose I'm breaking the law being here,* she reminded herself. And the proximity of the puzzling pictures and unlikely mementos only added to her sense of discomfort. *It's like coming back to a place you think you know, and then finding that a lot of what you thought you knew is wrong.*

Noiselessly, she stepped out of the hidden room into Pop-Pop's study. She held her breath, listening. Silence.

So it's Mr. Rent-a-Cop, she reassured herself. *He'll use the john; then he'll be outside again patrolling the garden, or whatever the hell he thinks he's doing.*

Then another sound gave the lie to her facile reassurances, a faint creaking of wood. *The stairs,* she realized with a shock. *Someone's coming up the stairs.*

What the hell's going on?

Again, guilt tightened her chest. *No,* she told herself firmly. *I'm not in the wrong here. Or, at least, I'm not the* only *one in the wrong. Whoever's on the stairs is trespassing as much as I am.*

Another creak, and a scuffing sound of something brushing against the wall of the upstairs landing. A chill passed over Sam's skin as adrenaline pumped into her bloodstream. Her senses felt suddenly enhanced, as though someone had "turned up the gain" of her nervous system. She felt poised, energized—*Like I'm on the jujitsu mat, waiting for a bout to begin,* she thought. It felt as though her feet didn't touch the floor as she glided toward the open door of the study. Just inside the doorway, she froze again, straining her senses to their expanded limits.

Silence. Absolute silence. She closed her eyes for an instant, concentrating on all her other senses. In the past, when she'd been really keyed up and cranked out, she'd sometimes believed she could *feel* the presence of other people around her by "listening to" a combination of subliminal cues from her senses; that's how she chose to interpret it, at least. Now, she felt nothing. No reading.

She took another deep, steadying breath, letting it out

slowly, silently. She edged into the doorway, stole a quick glance around the corner.

The intruder was less than a yard away, right at the top of the stairs. A tall man, big and broad, wearing nondescript dark clothing. Short, black hair, the kind of face you'd never pay attention to in a crowd. A glint of metal in his right hand—a ring of keys. Sam saw his gray eyes widen with surprise.

But that was the only indication that he'd been caught off-guard. He reacted instantly, lashing out with a fast left jab at her face.

Her own response was as fast and instinctive, as her jujitsu training kicked in. She fell back a half step, simultaneously deflecting his blow with her left forearm. Before he could recover, she grabbed his right hand with her own, digging her thumb into its back, and her four fingers into the palm. An instant later, she was gripping with her left hand as well, applying pressure in the move called the Eagle Grip. Pivoting on the ball of her right foot, she stepped in on him, bending his elbow painfully backward as she crossed her left leg behind his. With a grunt of effort, she finished the maneuver, slamming her left elbow into his chin with all her strength. The big man yelled in pain and alarm as he went over backward.

Sam tried to maintain her Eagle Grip on his hand, but even before he'd hit the ground he was lashing out with his leg, a quick snap-kick at her exposed left knee. She danced back out of range, losing her hold on him as she did so. *Damn it!* she thought as she recovered her balance. *He's had some kind of training too.*

She moved in again, poised for a kick, but before she could close, her opponent was back on his feet as if he were on springs. Sam saw him shift his weight, and her finely honed instincts hurled her backward.

Just in time. Blindingly fast, his right foot licked out in a high sweep-kick aimed at her throat, powerful enough to rupture her larynx. Jesus Christ! She braced herself for his follow-through attack.

There wasn't one. Instead, the big man turned on his heels and sprinted back down the stairs. Sam was in pursuit an instant later, but he'd already built up a good lead. He flung open the front door before she'd even reached the first landing and plunged out into the driveway. An engine roared, and Sam knew what she'd see as she sprinted out onto the front step.

A nondescript Chevy van, bright green with primer-gray patches, was in the driveway, engine running, passenger-side door open. Sam's opponent hurled himself bodily in through the open door, just as the driver hit the gas. Spraying gravel, the van accelerated away, fishtailing wildly up the drive toward the road.

Where the hell's Blondie? Why's there never a rent-a-cop around when you need one? The yellow Ford Bronco was still parked in front, but there was no sign of the security guard. *Damn it!* Sam kept moving, sprinting up the drive after the retreating van. Obviously not expecting immediate pursuit, the van driver had slowed as he turned onto the road heading toward Gold Beach and the coast, and Sam was only a couple of dozen yards behind when she reached the gate. Legs pumping, she drove into the turn. The van's engine roared again, and it accelerated away; the driver had apparently seen her in his mirror. But that was okay. Grendel was less than a hundred yards away.

Twenty seconds later she was vaulting into the driver's seat, jamming the key in the ignition and firing up the Mustang's big engine. The green-and-gray van was out of sight, but not for long. Sam knew there weren't any turnoffs from this road until you reached the coast highway itself.

The engine caught. Sam stamped on the gas and popped the clutch. Grendel leaped forward like a trained hunting beast released from its chain. Tires shrieked, and the pungent smell of burning rubber filled her nostrils. The powerful car started to fishtail, but she kept it in hand, right on the hairy edge of control with an experienced touch on the wheel and the throttle. The tachometer needle slid into the yellow band as she bang-shifted into second, then a few moments later into third. Wind lashed at her hair. Her cheeks felt tight, and she realized she was grinning with a kind of fierce joy. *You're mine,* she told the van driver mentally. It was just a matter of time. There was no way a junker of a van could outrun a juiced Mustang five-liter. For each yard of road that passed under her wheels, she knew the gap between the vehicles was closing.

Then she realized it didn't really seem to be closing at

all. As Samantha hurtled out of the trees and sped toward the U.S. mail boat dock, there was still no sign of the van. *Ha!* There it was, a flash of lime-green, already climbing the hill toward Highway 101. She floored the gas, letting the engine wind out.

Movement! Her peripheral vision caught a hint of motion—a station wagon pulling out of a side street to her right. She leaned on the horn, snapping the wheel to the left then instantly centering it. The Mustang slewed out into the oncoming-traffic lane, skidding sickeningly on a patch of gravel. An instant later, Sam had it back under control. The station wagon's own horn dopplered into the distance behind her.

God, but that van's fast! In the second or two she had been distracted, it was almost to the top of the hill where the river road met Highway 101. Sam slapped the gearshift into fourth, and stamped on the gas again. The speedo needle climbed from "bloody fast" to "patently ridiculous" as the engine howled. Grendel hit the foot of the hill leading up to the coast highway, bottoming out on its springs with a sickening *crunch.* Sam braced her left knee hard against the driver's door in an effort to steady herself.

The van didn't seem to slow in the slightest as it hit the intersection at the top of the hill and turned right—north. With a tortured shriek of tires, it hurtled into a wild four-wheel drift, narrowly missing the stop sign and a concrete divider and leaving quadruple black streaks across the pavement. For a moment Sam thought the driver had really blown it, and half expected to see the heavy vehicle slam through the guardrail before plunging over the precipice beyond the highway and into the ocean. But the van's handling was obviously much better than she'd expected. The van slewed madly across the road as the driver fought it back under control. Then the engine roared and the tires screamed as it accelerated once more.

Grendel was almost to the top of the hill. The stop sign and concrete lane dividers of the intersection seemed to fill her vision. *Holy shit, holy shit. . . .* The speedo needle was up around 65, and Sam was running out of maneuvering room. Desperately, she downshifted directly from fourth to second and feathered the clutch. The tachometer needle leapt into the red, and the engine screamed like a mechanical soul in torment. Her right foot stabbed the brake pedal once, lightly. Then she cut the wheel all the way over to the right.

That was where she almost lost it. She hadn't taken the time to put on her seat belt before giving chase, and without the support of the shoulder strap the sharp turn almost threw her out of the seat. She braced her left shoulder and knee against the driver's door, her left foot jammed against the floorboards, forcing herself back into the leather upholstery.

I'm not going to make it. She was going too fast; the road surface was too gritty for the wide Pirellis to maintain maximum traction. She had the steering wheel cranked all the way to the stop, but still she was hurtling toward the guardrail on the other side of the highway. In a last-ditch attempt to regain control, she pumped the throttle once, then took her foot completely off the gas pedal.

"Trailing-throttle oversteer"—that's what one of the guys who'd taught her performance driving had called it. That's what she was after. The engine's compression slowed the drive wheels *just enough* and the rear Pirellis broke loose of the road, while the front tires maintained their traction. The rear end of the car snapped around in a skid, threatening to put the car into an out-of-control spin. But Sam steered into the skid, knuckles ivory-white on the wheel. She hit the gas again, pouring power to the rear wheels. The tires bit again, and Grendel lunged forward. As quick as thought, Sam reversed the wheel, then again, and once more, to fight the powerful car's tendency to fishtail. The engine screamed as she floored the pedal and bang-shifted up into third, then again into fourth. Her skin felt cold—an early aftereffect of the adrenaline still coursing through her system—and the muscles of her jaw ached from grinding her teeth together. *But I made it, goddamn it,* she told herself firmly. *I* made *it!* Now where was the van?

Improbably, the van had managed to open the gap between the vehicles. It was at least a hundred yards ahead of her and seemed to be pulling away. Sam watched in amazement as the van hurtled into the turn at Otter Point, taking the bend in the road like it was on rails, with almost no body-sway at all. *Custom mill, custom suspension,* she realized. *What the hell's going on?* She kept her own gas pedal to the floor, watched the tach needle climb toward the red line. Bracing herself again, she threw Grendel through the Otter Point turn, still accelerating.

The speedo was reading a hair short of 100 mph as she rocketed out of the turn. Ahead, the van was maintaining its lead, but at least it didn't seem capable of extending. Sam tried to remember all the details of this stretch of Highway 101. Past Otter Point, it was a pretty straight pull up toward Nesika Beach, she recalled, then farther north toward Ophir. She allowed herself a tight smile. On a nice, open straightaway, Grendel would eat the van for breakfast.

There was almost no traffic on the coast road—*Thank God for that,* Sam thought fervently. A pair of huge, tricked-out Honda Gold Wings cruising south, plus a pack of northbound cyclists who'd pulled over onto the shoulder to watch the chase, and that was it. The Mustang was up to 120 mph, and the roar of the wind was louder than the engine. Turbulence slapped at the back of Sam's head, blowing her long hair almost straight forward. She'd never driven the car this fast with the top down. *What's the drag and the turbulence going to do to the handling if I have to make an emergency maneuver?* she wondered, a little sickly.

The speedometer needle crept up to 130, then 135. Grendel was starting to develop a disturbing speed-wobble, a rhythmic vibration that shook the entire body on its stiff suspension. The wheel in Sam's hands quivered like a live thing. Quickly, she backed off on the gas, let the speed creep back down under 130. *That's fast enough,* she decided. Finally she was starting to close the gap—slowly, but unmistakably. *And what am I going to do when I catch the van?* She banished that thought instantly. *One thing at a time.*

Every thirty seconds, another mile flashed by under Grendel's wheels. She was less than fifty yards back of the van by now. *Nesika Beach is coming up,* she realized. *The van's going to have to slow down to go through town, isn't it?*

She was past the beige-painted police car before her brain even registered it. The car was parked on the shoulder, its engine idling as Grendel streaked by. In her rearview mirror, Sam saw the flashing lights come on, the cop car's rear wheels spraying gravel as it accelerated onto the pavement. *Oh great, now things are really delta sierra. What the hell am I supposed to do now?*

Even as she asked herself the question, her instincts answered it. She backed off on the gas and rode the brake lightly as she shifted down to third then second, bleeding off the powerful car's head of speed. The green-and-gray van didn't slow at all, and vanished around a wooded curve. *Damn it!*

When she had her speed down to something reasonable, she pulled half off the road, Grendel's two right wheels crunching on the gravel shoulder. She watched the police car coming up behind her. She half expected it to cut out and around her, pursuing the van—wasn't it obvious that the van's driver was the one who was really responsible?—but instead it pulled off the road behind her. With a fierce curse, she stopped the car, cramped on the hand brake, and killed the engine. She watched in her wing mirror as the cop car came to a stop a foot from her rear bumper.

Through the sun's glare reflecting off the cop car's windshield, she could see the two occupants only as dark shapes. Neither seemed in any hurry to get out of the car. Over the metallic ticking from Grendel's cooling engine, she heard a faint electronic crackle. *They're talking on the radio,* she realized. *Calling for a roadblock to stop the van?*

Finally both front doors of the cop car opened, and the officers emerged. The passenger remained behind the cover of the open door; Sam could imagine his hand resting lightly on the butt of his pistol, ready for trouble. The driver, a handsome black man, walked slowly forward, expression stony, his eyes invisible behind mirrored sunglasses. Sam kept both her hands clearly visible, gripping the steering wheel. The cop stopped alongside her car, slightly behind Sam's left shoulder—*So I can't slam the door open into him,* she realized. *He's not taking any chances.* She looked up at him, keeping her own face expressionless.

"Morning, ma'am. Do you have any idea how fast—?"

"About one-thirty," Sam cut him off shortly. "Look, Officer . . ."—she glanced at the name tag on his uniform shirt—" . . . Officer Belmont, I'm chasing a burglar, somebody who broke into my grandfather's house and then tried to kick the crap out of me."

Belmont turned slowly to gaze north up the highway. "I don't see anyone."

It took all of Sam's strength to keep her composure. "Of course you don't see anyone," she said slowly and clearly. "*He* was going one-thirty too. You cover a lot of ground that way. He's probably through Nesika Beach by now."

"*Who's* probably through Nesika Beach?"

"The burglar," Sam grated through clenched teeth. "The man who beat me up. The green van I was chasing."

The officer was silent for a moment. Then he said flatly, "I didn't see any green van."

"What?" Samantha stared at him uncomprehendingly. "*Jesus,* man, it was fifty yards ahead of me, going like a bat out of hell. You *must* have seen it."

"Sorry." Belmont shifted from foot to foot. *He's uncomfortable,* Sam thought. *Why?*

"You didn't see the van."

"Sorry," the officer repeated.

"Then what the *hell* were you doing on the radio?" she demanded hotly.

Belmont's jaw worked silently. Then he said, "Running your tag with the DMV." His voice was flat, emotionless. "No outstanding warrants."

Tag. What the hell was the van's tag number? For an instant, Sam closed her eyes, trying to build up a picture of it in her mind. Once she was in pursuit, she'd never got close enough to the van to see its rear plate. But when it was still in Pop-Pop's driveway, she knew she'd caught a glimpse of it. Now if only she could dredge up that image . . . *got it.*

She opened her eyes and glared up at Officer Belmont. "If you want to run a tag, why don't you try XBF–254? Oregon plates. A green Chevy van, five or six years old."

Belmont just stared at her. Sam tried to look into his eyes, to gauge what he was thinking, but all she could see were distorted images of herself in his shades. Finally, he said, "I didn't see a green van."

I don't believe *this!* Sam fought back the sudden anger that churned and twisted in her gut. "So you're not going to run the tag number, is that what you're telling me?" To her own ears, her voice sounded cold and brittle.

The cop gave a minuscule shrug. "*What* tag number?"

"I see." Sam nodded slowly. *Even though I don't see at*

all. "Then what *are* you going to do, Officer Belmont?" she asked sweetly. "Give me a ticket?"

Belmont looked really uncomfortable. "The radar wasn't up," he muttered.

"*Radar?* Gee, I think the sonic boom would have been a dead giveaway." *Something really weird is going on here.* "So *what,* then?"

The cop adjusted his glasses, and regained control of his expression. "I'm letting you go with a warning," he said gruffly. "Keep your speed down, okay?" And with that, he turned on his heel and strode back to his car—looking like he was in a hurry, Sam thought. In the wing mirror, she watched as the two figures conferred for a few moments. Then Belmont turned off the light bar and pulled out onto the highway. As the car passed the Mustang, both cops kept their eyes directed straight ahead, not even so much as acknowledging Sam's existence.

7

Samantha wheeled out onto the highway and drove slowly back toward Gold Beach. She felt chilled, even though the sun was beating down, and her hands had a tendency to tremble if she didn't keep a tight grip on the wheel. Her stomach felt hollow, her head packed with cotton wool. *Adrenaline hangover,* she knew: the aftereffects of the high-speed chase.

Something just happened, she told herself, her thoughts flowing as sluggishly as molasses in winter. *Something important. But* what? *What the hell can it mean?*

Officer Belmont's story made no sense. It was ludicrous—totally and utterly unbelievable—to think that he hadn't seen the van blaze by. Yet he'd denied it. *Why?*

Sam remembered the crackle of the police car's radio. *Because somebody* told *him to? Who? And, again,* why?

And just as unbelievable, now that she considered it, was the fact that he'd let her off with a warning. *All because the radar was down? I think not.* She'd been doing 130 miles per hour on a two-lane highway, for chrissake—and she'd *admitted* it. No police officer worthy of the name needed any damned radar to charge her with speeding, dangerous driving, undue care and attention, and probably a few other violations she'd never even heard of. But Officer Belmont just let her go. *For the third and final time,* why?

Who the hell were *those guys in the van?*

It took her almost ten minutes to retrace the course that had taken about two on the way out. As she turned onto the river road, she saw the black skid marks Grendel's Pirellis had left on the pavement, cutting clear across both traffic lanes and coming within an arm's length of the guardrails on the far side. She shuddered. *Geez, that was too close. . . .*

The blond-haired rent-a-cop was standing in the driveway as Sam turned into Pop-Pop's gate. *Where the hell were* you *when it mattered, Blondie?* she wanted to yell at him. Instead, she kept her face impassive as he signaled for her to stop.

There was something different about the way he handled himself, Samantha decided as he strode up to the driver's-side door. Not more confidence; he still looked like a kid trying to do a man's job. *That's it,* she thought suddenly. *He's trying harder*—much *harder. Almost as though someone's watching over his shoulder.* She looked down the curving drive toward the house. Through the trees she could see glimpses of yellow—that had to be the rent-a-cop's Bronco—but there were other vehicles there now, too. Beige ones, she thought. *Like the local police cruisers.*

Blondie hooked his thumbs in his belt and drew himself up to his full height. "Ma'am," he said brusquely. "Can I help you with something?"

Sam hesitated. Her first instinct was to go talk to the police, to report the intruder, but then she thought about it. *Not smart, Dooley,* she told herself firmly. First, she'd have to explain what she was doing in the house in the first place, when an official security officer had told her it was off-limits. And second. . . .

Second, can I trust *the police?* That was a disturbing thought. The police had always been the good guys when she was growing up—respected, dependable, even admired. Now, though, there was something going on—*And at least* some *of the cops are at least peripherally involved,* she thought, remembering Officer Belmont.

She kept her worries to herself as she smiled up at the rent-a-cop. "Just turning around," she said pleasantly.

"That's just bloody ridiculous!" Maggie Braslins leaned back in her armchair, frowning. "What the hell have you got yourself into now, kiddo?"

Samantha smiled, but there was little humor in it. "That's the question, isn't it?"

"And you didn't get the memoirs you were after?"

Sam shook her head. "Never so much as saw them."

Maggie pulled a pack of cigarettes from her pocket and shook one out. As an afterthought, she offered the pack to Sam. The younger woman grinned as she pulled out her own pack. Maggie shook her head in mock despair. "Demon weed's got you again, I see." She lit her own cigarette, then tossed the Zippo over to Sam.

They smoked in companionable silence for a few moments. Sam blew a smoke ring toward the ceiling. *I'm getting better at that,* she mused. *It doesn't look* quite *so much like a bagel.*

With a snort, Maggie leaned forward again. "And there's no way the cops *could* have missed the van?" she proposed quietly. "Maybe they had their snouts buried in a box of doughnuts."

Sam chuckled as she shook her head. "Even so. Hell, Mags, a van doing one-thirty pushes a pretty good shock wave, don't you think? That cop car must have shaken like it was in an earthquake."

"I suppose." Maggie was silent for a moment. Then, "And they wouldn't run the tag number for you?" she said.

"Didn't even write it down."

Maggie snorted her derision. "Then they're either totally incompetent, or they're on the take. Or both."

"What if they *didn't* see the van?"

"That don't butter no parsnips." Maggie stabbed the air with her cigarette. "Cops run the tag on *anything.* Hell, they pull up behind a car at a stoplight, and it's even odds they'll run the tag—standard operating procedure, SOP, just in case there's a warrant out. Even if your friend Belmont didn't see the van, SOP would be to run the tag anyway. If it comes up a green van the way you claimed, he's got some reason to believe you. If it comes up something different, he's got a case of obstructing justice, if he wants to push it."

She paused. "I've got a friend up in Salem," she said at last. "Maybe I'll get him to run the plate unofficially. Couldn't hurt, I guess."

"Couldn't hurt," Sam echoed. *Something* very *strange is going on here.*

Samantha leaned against the front of the small legal office—*Kerr & Simons, Ltd.* the sign read. It was right on the "main drag" of Gold Beach—which was Highway 101, of course—right across from the town's single tiny movie theater. Even before mid-morning, the sun-heated sky-blue stucco was hot against her back through her white cotton shirt.

She smoked thoughtfully as she watched the light Wednesday-morning traffic pass by her. Sunlight glinted off chrome and glass in bright spectrals that shimmered in the heat. Suddenly she gave a wry chuckle: half-subconsciously, she realized, she was keeping a watch for a green-and-gray Chevy van. *Not much hope of that,* she told herself, a little grimly.

Maggie's friend up in the state capital had run the license plate Sam had spotted. Mags had given her the results before Sam left the house for the lawyer's office this morning. The older woman had seemed a little hesitant about discussing it—*As well she might,* Sam recognized—as though she didn't know what kind of news she was bringing to her friend.

"We didn't get a match in the DMV computers," Maggie had told her.

Sam had nodded slowly. "I suppose that makes sense," she'd said. "Stolen van, stolen license plates. . . ."

"No," Maggie had cut her off firmly. "That's not what I mean. I mean no match *at all.* According to the Oregon Department of Motor Vehicles, the plate XBF–254 doesn't exist. It's never been issued." She'd paused. "Are you sure it was an Oregon plate you saw?"

Samantha had hesitated, struggling to rebuild the mental image of the van as it accelerated out of Pop-Pop's driveway. White background, blue "sky" along the top, purple "mountains" toward the bottom, a single green tree—*A Douglas fir, probably; that's the state tree, isn't it?*—in the center of the plate. "I'm sure," she'd confirmed.

Maggie had shrugged. "Then you saw something that officially doesn't exist," she'd said flatly. "Make of that what you will."

Sam sighed. *What I will?* she asked herself. *I haven't got a clue* what *to make of it.*

She took another deep drag of her cigarette, then stared moodily at the burning tip. *Didn't take me long to get completely hooked again, did it?* she thought sourly. She checked her watch: a couple of minutes short of ten. She tossed the half-smoked cigarette to the pavement, ground it out with her heel. Then she turned and went inside, slipping her Ray-Ban aviators into her shirt pocket.

The receptionist, a rather brittle-looking blonde, gave her a plastic smile and gestured to the open office door behind her. Sam brusquely nodded her thanks and strode through the door.

Morton Kerr, Jr., Pop-Pop's lawyer, was sitting behind an oversized desk, its nearly empty surface polished mirror-bright. He was comfortably ensconced in a high-backed leather chair, sharp elbows on the armrests, long fingers laced in front of his chest. His thin face was expressionless, but his gray eyes—*Sharp eyes,* Sam thought, *like an eagle's*—flicked about the room as if unwilling to miss even the slightest detail. Sam settled herself in one of the chairs arranged before the lawyer's desk. There were only three chairs, she noted, and one of those was off to the side, as though not fully involved in the proceedings. That meant only one other person was going to hear the reading of the will, she presumed. Who? Sid Warner, perhaps?

A phone rang, a muted electronic burr. Without a change of expression, Kerr opened the top drawer of his desk and extracted a telephone handset. "Yes?" he said quietly. Sam saw his eyes hood for a moment as he listened; then he nodded, as if to himself. "I see. That will be . . . acceptable. Please join us now, Arlene." He hung up the phone and closed the drawer again.

His predator's eyes fixed on Samantha. "I'm afraid the other . . . um, participant will be unable to attend," he said smoothly. "Dr. Macintyre has been unavoidably detained, but has instructed me to continue without him."

Sam blinked in mild surprise. Dr. Macintyre? Could that be the Ernest Macintyre she'd met on her first visit to Pop-Pop's bedside? *Considering what Pop-Pop said about Macintyre's upbringing, that would make sense, wouldn't it?*

She didn't have time to think about it any further. The bottle-blonde from the reception area came into the office, shutting the door behind her. She perched herself on the single chair that was apart from the others, flipped open an old-style dictation notebook and poised her pencil.

Kerr opened another drawer and extracted a thin stack of papers, which he arranged on the desk before him. He perused them for a few moments, then looked up and fixed Sam with his sharp gaze. "The purpose of this meeting is to read the last will and testament of Mr. James R. Dooley, Sr.," he said, enunciating his words as clearly as if he were on stage. "Afterward, I would be glad to answer any questions you may have—to the limits of my knowledge and abilities, of course." His faint smile communicated clearly how unlikely he considered the possibility that anyone could ask a question beyond his ability to answer. "If I may proceed?"

"Please." Sam shifted in the hard chair, trying to find the position that was least uncomfortable.

The self-conscious-sounding legal phraseology washed over her as Morton Kerr read slowly and precisely. Once she got used to the cadence and style of the language, she found she didn't have to listen carefully to every word of every phrase. Instead, she found herself extracting a kind of précis—a paraphrase of the legal verbiage that condensed its meaning down to a few key statements. (*Why don't lawyers write like that in the first place?* she found herself wondering. *Of course, if they did, we might come to suspect that we don't really need the exalted legal priesthood after all.*)

Basically, nearly everything was hers—that's the way she interpreted it, at least. A trust fund of some kind that Pop-Pop had set up two decades ago would go to one Dr. Ernest Macintyre of Ontario, California. (Sam idly wondered about the size of the trust account, but knew better than to ask the lawyer. *Lawyers won't breach confidentiality far enough to let their left hand know what their right is doing,* she reminded herself, smothering a smile.) Also going to Dr. Macintyre was Pop-Pop's red Jensen Interceptor III.

As he read that statement, Kerr shot Sam a speculative look from under his dark brows, almost as if he expected her to voice a complaint. She just smiled. *Pop-Pop knew what I thought of his car,* she remembered fondly. *It's significant to me because he liked it so much, and that's the only reason. Maybe one of these days, British sports car manufacturers will figure out how to design electrical systems that* work. Her grin turned mischievous. *I hope Macintyre doesn't mind dealing with a* positive-*ground system, and enjoys trying to figure out just what the hell a purple-and-white-striped wire is supposed to be. . . .*

A whole section of the will was devoted to Jim Dooley's mementos, a list so detailed it might as well have itemized them all. Apart from a couple of family photographs that were earmarked for Samantha, the rest—models, decorations, physical souvenirs, photographs and "other images"—were bequeathed to an outfit called the Museum of Flight, located in the small town of Rogers, California. Sam raised an eyebrow at that, but held her tongue even when Kerr gave her another of his speculative glances. She would have liked to receive her grandfather's mementos—particularly the ones from the "inner study," and specifically the photograph of Pop-Pop with Amelia Earhart—but she was not so disappointed that she felt the need to take issue with Jim's will. He must have known that Sam would feel some kind of sentimental attachment to his knickknacks; still, he specifically bequeathed them to the museum. Obviously, the Rogers Museum of Flight must have some major significance for him, even though Sam had never even heard of the place.

The lawyer paused for a few seconds, as if to give Sam a chance to recall her straying attention. Then he began to read the list of bequests that Pop-Pop had left her.

First on the list was the house just outside Gold Beach, plus all those contents that hadn't been dealt with earlier in his will. The will stated that Sam had a choice of how to handle the property. If she wanted to take over the house as hers, all well and good; ditto if she wanted to put it on the market and sell it herself. The legal document specifically laid out a third option, however: she could leave the actual process of the sale to the executors—in other words, to the firm of Kerr & Simons, Ltd. (That was the way these things usually worked, she figured, but it was typical of Pop-Pop to go out of his way to let her know she didn't have to take on a potentially onerous burden if she didn't feel up to it. Sam smiled sadly. *I think I'll take the "escape route" he gave me,* she mused. *It'd tear me apart to go through the process of listing and selling Pop-Pop's house.*)

Jim Dooley's heavily customized Glasair plane—his beloved *Yellow Bird*—went to Sam, of course, as did the (unspecified) proceeds of two separate trust funds, and the balance of the old man's life insurance policies after the payment of funeral expenses, estate taxes, and the like. *I suppose that makes me quite a wealthy young woman,* Sam realized with a faint feeling of shock. *Still, I'd much rather be poor if I could only have Pop-Pop back again.*

And that was it. Kerr finished reading the will and set it aside, sitting back in his chair once more. Samantha blinked in surprise. "What about Pop-Pop's memoirs?" she blurted.

The lawyer gazed at her over his interlaced fingers. (*The perfect poker face,* Sam thought irrelevantly.) He remained silent for a moment, as though scripting out his response—*Or waiting for me to withdraw what he considers a stupid question,* Sam thought. Finally, he pursed his lips and commented, "Personally, I should classify memoirs under the category of 'mementos,' hm?"

Which means they'd go to the Rogers Museum of Flight. Unacceptable. Sam made an effort to keep her voice reasonable and calm. "Your client specifically stated that those memoirs should go to me," she pointed out, "as his single surviving relative."

Kerr was unmoved. "If that were the case," he pointed out, "one would presume he would have included that provision in his will."

A bolt of pain shot through the muscles of Sam's jaws as she ground her teeth together. She knew her response was a vast overreaction born of the emotion of the moment, but . . . suddenly she *despised* Morton Kerr, Jr.—his studied, overprecise mannerisms, his persnickety way of talking, even the way his eyes seemed to glint with a dry amusement he couldn't, or *wouldn't,* share with someone not initiated into the Great Mysteries of the law. She imagined lunging over and grabbing his hair, smashing his face down onto the mirrored finish of the desktop . . . and the image was a pleasant one. It took much of her willpower to keep her expression and voice under control.

"One *might* presume that," she countered, her enunciation almost as cold and precise as his, "unless one assumed that his personal wishes, stated directly and personally, took precedence over a mere legal document. Hm?"

If he noticed that she was mimicking him, he gave no sign. Instead, he just cocked his head slightly to one side—*Like a bird of prey deciding whether to slaughter another field mouse,* she thought suddenly—and made a soft, skeptical noise in his throat. "Possible," he allowed finally, "even though unwise." He opened another drawer and pulled out a second thin sheaf of papers. Quickly, using the tip of his finger as a guide, he scanned the contents of the top sheet. Then he set the papers, face down, on the desk before him. His sharp gaze settled on her face once more. "As it turns out," he went on calmly, "that's not the case."

"What are those?" Her gesture indicated the papers.

"Among other things, an itemized list of the items that are destined for the Museum of Flight."

"The mementos."

He nodded millimetrically.

"Let me have a look." She reached out for the papers, but he swept them smoothly from the desk, returning them to their drawer and shutting it silently.

"I can have Arlene provide you with a *copy* of the list, of course," he said, his voice even more aloof than normal. "You can take my word, however, that there is nothing on it like a journal, or a set of memoirs."

"Who made the list?"

His dark brows arched slightly at that. "Associates of this firm. They are very efficient, I assure you."

Efficient enough to walk out with Pop-Pop's memoirs before they were added to the list? She shook her head. No, that didn't make too much sense, did it? She hadn't found Jim Dooley's memoirs; granted, her search had been interrupted, but why would Pop-Pop have gone to a lot of trouble to hide them? Unless she wanted to start down the twisted path of paranoia and assume that the executors and the police—and everyone else, for that matter—were in cahoots with . . . *someone* to . . . *do something* to her . . . it made a lot more sense to assume Kerr was right. The memoirs weren't in the will because Pop-Pop had expected that she'd take them away before the executors came in. And they didn't appear on Kerr's list of mementos because they weren't in the house when the list was made. *Let's face it,* she reminded herself, *lots of people had access to the house—people who might know about Pop-Pop's memoirs.*

But why would those hypothetical people have reason to take them?

Suddenly she thought of another item that was conspicuous by its absence in the will. "Mr. Dooley had some land," she began.

He nodded immediately. "Yes, the Eagle Mountain property."

"Exactly." She paused. "I had reason to believe that. . . ." She hesitated again, trying to choose the best words.

Kerr saved her the trouble. "That the property would be coming to you?" he finished for her. A cool smile flickered across his thin lips, there for a moment, then gone. "Unlikely, I'm afraid, Ms. Dooley, since the records show Mr. Dooley sold the property seven years ago."

"But he didn't," Sam blurted out. "He would have told me." The expression on the lawyer's face told her just what he thought of that line of reasoning. She reined in her emotions and started again. "I'm sure he *can't* have sold the property. A couple of days before he died, he told me. . . ."

Her voice trailed off. *Just what did he tell me?* she asked herself suddenly. *That he still owned the property?* She tried to remember, to recall exactly what had been said. *Pop-Pop was talking about how he wanted to handle his ashes. I asked if he wanted me to take them to Eagle Mountain. He made a joke, something about having better things to do with eternity than getting up my nose and in my hair. . . .*

No outright statement that he still owned the property and that it would be coming to her, but certainly a pretty strong implication.

The lawyer had been waiting for her to finish her sentence. Now he shrugged. "Perhaps," he said coolly, "you would be better off to place your trust in legal documentation rather than in the memory of a possibly senile, dying man."

Anger flared in Sam's gut, and again she flashed on the picture of slamming the lawyer's face against his spit-polished desk. *Not smart, Dooley.* She took a deep breath, held it for a moment, then let it sigh from her lungs, taking with it at least a fraction of her anger and tension. "When did he sell it?" she asked. She thought her voice sounded brittle as mica-crystal, but at least she avoided giving the impression of a direct attack. "Did you handle the paperwork?"

He shook his head, answering her second question first. "I only joined this firm full-time four years ago," he said. "According to the records, my father handled the Eagle Mountain sale."

"Can I discuss it with him?"

Kerr didn't answer immediately, and his expression, if that were possible, grew even chillier. "That would be rather difficult," he said at last.

Oh, it's like that, is it? Without warning, a nasty little thought struck her. Sam schooled her face into an expression of sadness. "I'm sorry," she said contritely. "I didn't know. It's hard, losing a father. How long ago did he ... did you lose him?"

"Just slightly more than a year ago."

Sam nodded. *That was a paranoid idea anyway,* she chided herself—but still, she felt faintly relieved that something like six years separated the purported sale of the Eagle Mountain property and the death of Morton Kerr, Sr.

The lawyer paused, then continued a little defensively, "I *have* reviewed the contracts, however, as a matter of course. If you have any thoughts of impropriety, I can assure you. . . ."

"The thought never crossed my mind," she lied smoothly. Then, "Can I get copies of the sale paperwork, please?" she asked.

Kerr hesitated, then shrugged minutely. "Arlene can provide you with copies," he allowed. Abruptly, he squared the blotter with the edge of the desk. "Do you have any further questions?"

Sam gave him a smile that quirked her lips but came

nowhere near her eyes. "If I do, I'll be in touch," she assured him coolly.

There was a white, midsize moving truck in the driveway of Pop-Pop's house when she arrived ten minutes later. "Jones Cartage," the red-and-blue logo on the side read. As she pulled to a stop beside the truck, a man in blue overalls emerged from the open door of the house, carrying a large cardboard box. Tears misted Sam's eyes as she recognized some of the items protruding from the open top of the box. Framed photographs, both color and black-and-white, a mounted diploma or citation of some kind. *Pop-Pop's mementos.*

The blond-haired rent-a-cop—accompanied by an older man in a similar uniform; *Blondie's supervisor,* Sam realized at once—were striding toward Grendel from the right of the house. Before they could reach her, she powered down her window and called to the overall-clad mover. "Hey!" When he glanced her way, she beckoned to him.

He didn't come toward the car, but at least he stopped, temporarily supporting some of the box's weight with his hip. "Yeah?" he asked, suspicion coloring his voice.

"Jones Cartage?" He nodded. "Who's hired you to move that stuff out?"

The workman hesitated. "Maybe you'd better talk to my supervisor," he said slowly.

Sam glanced to her right. Blondie and his boss were almost on her. "Some museum?" she called to the workman.

His face cleared. "Yeah," he assented, apparently happier to confirm Sam's statement than to volunteer the information in the first place. "Some flight museum. In California."

"Rogers?"

"That's it." He nodded agreeably.

"Thanks, I appreciate it." Blondie's boss was almost to the car, opening his mouth to speak—probably to tell her to wait. Sam slapped Grendel into reverse and gave the big car some gas. Gravel spattered against the car's underside as she reversed back up the driveway, and the two rent-a-cops flinched away.

Damn it, she thought. *So much for doing things the easy way. I'll have to give this some consideration.*

8

Samantha drove slowly along the narrow streets of Venice, California. Her eyes were gritty and dry from a dozen hours of driving, and the streetlights had a tendency to blur, to smear if she let her attention wander even slightly. Fortunately, the streets were deserted—*Even Venice shuts down eventually,* she reminded herself. The muted rumble of Grendel's engine echoed off the buildings as she turned onto 25th Avenue, then into the alley. She pulled up behind the shabby apartment building, killed the engine, and secured the steering wheel with The Club locking bar she kept under the seat. Stifling a yawn, she hefted her carry bag out of the convertible's backseat and unlocked the building's back door.

Apartment D was on the second floor at the back. Her legs felt like lead, and a sharp ache twinged in the small of her back as she trudged up the stairs. She unlocked her apartment's front door, swung it open, stepped inside, and pushed the door shut. Dropping her bag unceremoniously in the hall, she groped for the light switch. Then she crossed the hardwood floor and slumped down in the large, black-fabric papasan chair that dominated a corner of the living room. She kicked off her shoes and stretched her legs out luxuriously. Without turning, she reached back to the stereo system on the shelf behind her, powered up the amplifier, and hit PLAY on the CD unit. She closed her eyes as the light jazz of Spyrogyra filled the room.

I'm cooked, she told herself. *Burned, trashed, exhausted, fried—physically, mentally* and *emotionally*. It had been another grueling drive. This time she'd gotten caught in the tail end of rush hour on Interstate 5 outside Sacramento. If she'd been thinking, she could have bypassed the city, taken the connector down to Davis, maybe, then followed the blue highways to rejoin I–5 somewhere around Thornton. But no, she'd been letting her mind drift—*Car and brain both on cruise control,* she thought wryly—and hadn't realized there was a problem until she had no option but to sit it out. It had been brutally hot, sitting there on a highway that looked more like a parking lot. If she closed her eyes, she could still see the line of traffic that had stretched out ahead of her, shimmering off into the heat-hazed distance like a warped mirage.

She rubbed tiredly at her face, snatching her fingers away instantly as their touch brought a sharp pain to her nose. *Crap,* she thought in disgust, *I fried my nose.* She'd heaped on the SPF–25 even more liberally this time, but it still hadn't been enough. *When am I going to learn? The better your sunglasses are—the more ultraviolet they reflect—the more protection you need on your nose.* It had been Pop-Pop, of course, who'd pointed that out to her. "Where do you *think* the reflected UV goes, Samantha Rose? It's like putting your nose in a solar oven."

Sam laughed softly, reaching back again to turn up the volume, but not too high; the old building didn't have the best sound insulation, and even her Bohemian-wannabee neighbors were probably trying to sleep. She smiled as the band launched into "Rasul," the light, lyrical melody line of Jay Beckenstein's saxophone seeming to drain away her stress. She took a deep breath, expanding her lungs to their limit, held it—held it—then let it sigh out again. *Much better.* She still wouldn't be able to sleep for a while, but at least the painful tension across the tops of her shoulders was easing.

Eyes still closed, she pulled a pack of cigarettes from her pocket, shook one out and lit it with a disposable Bic she'd bought at a convenience store in Red Bluff. She drew the smoke into her lungs, then blew it in a thin stream at the ceiling.

Quite the week, she thought. *Lose a grandfather, regain an old vice. . . .*

She'd reviewed the events of the last few days a couple of times during the drive back to Southern California—the burglar, the car chase, Officer Belmont's selective blindness to the nonexistent green van, the absence of the journal, and the indecently quick transfer of Pop-Pop's mementos to the Museum of Flight. *There's something going on here,* she told herself for what felt like the hundredth time, *something I'm missing.* The question was, of course, *What?* She believed there must be a pattern to the strange events, each event small, almost insignificant when seen as an isolated anomoly, but if linked correctly they should make sense. *Unless I'm so trashed my mind's playing tricks on me,* she amended.

She took another drag from her cigarette, then butted it out in the soil of the potted ficus beside the chair. She made a mental note: *If I'm going to be doing this regularly, I'd better get myself some real ashtrays.* Stifling another yawn, she pried herself out of the comfortable depths of the papasan chair and shambled off to bed.

Morning came just too damn soon. Sam had shut the drapes against the morning light, but that didn't do much to block out the sounds of the beach and the Ocean Front Walk, only half a block away: dogs barking, people talking, and music of all kinds, from folk to rap, coming from countless portable stereos. Her normal routine was to stroll on down to the Sidewalk Café for a coffee and a croissant, but she just didn't feel up for it this morning. Even at 07:30, she'd be surrounded by too many people—some of whom would want to be sociable, and she decided she couldn't face that at the moment. *I'll have to be polite to people all day,* she reminded herself. *Why start early?* She made a single mug of coffee, too hot and too strong, just what she needed to jump-start her body, and drank it down quickly. Thirty minutes after waking up, she had Grendel back on the road and was cruising north toward the Santa Monica Municipal Airport.

WestAir Helicopter Sightseeing ran its operation out of a small fenced-in area that Sam thought of as "The Compound," on the outskirts of the airport proper. Its owners ran the office operation out of a trailer that had seen better days—up on blocks, wheels removed, the only access a set of rickety wooden steps, paint bleached and cracked by the California sun. In contrast, the small hangar where the helicopters were stored was scrupulously clean and well maintained. Sam occasionally found it amusing, in a disturbing sort of way, that the hardware was treated better than the "wetware"—the people who worked for WestAir—but in some twisted way, it made sense. The helicopters represented revenue and profit; the office staff, from the owner on down to Becky the receptionist, were overhead.

Sam drove through the open gate and parked Grendel in his accustomed spot beside the hangar. As she climbed from the car she watched a figure approaching, a short, squat man wearing oil-stained coveralls, patched here and there with swatches of cloth only slightly less threadbare than the rest of his garb. Walking across the apron—even this early in the morning already hot enough to create a shimmering heat haze—he looked almost as broad across the shoulders as he was tall. His face seemed carved out of rock by a ham-handed sculptor, an assemblage of intersecting planes and fracture lines not yet smoothed into a semblance of human shape. His hair was cropped in such a short buzz cut that she could never be really sure of its natural color. His skin was pale. In all the time she'd known the man, she'd never seen him tan; but she'd never seen him burn, either, even though he spent much of his time out in the sun.

"Hey, Joe!" she called to him.

The man she'd nicknamed "Joe the Mountain" waved. His rocky face split in a broad smile, and his small eyes almost disappeared in a network of deep wrinkles. "Hey, Sam," he called back, his voice surprisingly soft for someone who looked as if he could take a bulldozer two falls out of three. "Good to have you back." He took her extended hand in one of his, his grip gentle to the point of delicacy. "Gertrude's missed you."

"Gertrude" was what Sam had dubbed the company's first-line vehicle, a spit-polished Bell Jet Ranger. "How is the old girl?" Sam asked. "And how's my replacement been shaping up?"

Joe's face twisted into a scowl that would have been frightening if she hadn't known the heavily muscled man. "Don't call him that, Sam. You know you're irreplaceable."

"Problems?"

The mechanic sighed heavily. "Oh, not really, I s'pose," he groused. "He's good enough, but he doesn't have your touch. Doesn't know how to treat a lady." His thick lips quirked in a half-smile. "Still thinks he's dodging small-arms fire over the Mekong, if you ask me, the way he jinks

Gertrude around. Little Japanese lady had a bilge evac a couple days back. Took me two hours to clean it all out."

Sam chuckled. "Bilge evac" was the company's code phrase for violent airsickness, a term less likely to scare away potential customers if they overheard someone making a report. "Sad movies, Joe," she agreed. "Still, that's why they pay you the big bucks."

He gave a single sharp bark of laughter. "Ain't that the truth?" He paused, and his eyes twinkled. "Anyhow, good to have you back in God's country. How'd things go up north?"

It was Sam's turn to pause. Normally, she'd have finessed Joe's question with an offhand comment, some witty comeback to deflect any personal revelation. But today. . . .

She shrugged, a little uncomfortably. "My grandfather died, Joe," she said quietly. "I had to . . . do what was necessary."

He frowned, and squeezed her hand again. "That's tough, Sam, real tough. It's always hard losing kin. Everything squared away, or are the legal vultures jerking you around?"

"Some," she admitted. "Some." She forced her troubled thoughts as far back in her mind as they could go and patted the mechanic on the shoulder. "Come on," she told him, "let's see what's on the frag list for today." Together, they headed over toward the office-trailer.

It was a long day. It would have been grueling if Sam hadn't so relished the joy of getting back behind the controls of Gertrude. Four flights: three short, one-hour jaunts up and down the coast, then a longer, three-and-a-half-hour "special" out to Avalon on Santa Catalina Island. By the time she was through for the day, she felt as though the earpieces of her Ray-Ban aviators were digging right through her skull into her braincase.

The sun was a distended crimson fireball sinking into the ocean by the time she parked Grendel behind her apartment building. Often after a long day, she'd head to the Sidewalk Cafe on the Ocean Front Walk and sip a beer while watching the scenery stroll by. Not tonight, though. Maybe it was a reaction to her time in Gold Beach—the entire population of the small Oregon town seemed, to her eyes, smaller than the number of people on the beach near her home—but she just didn't feel like facing a crowd tonight. Four groups of tourists aboard Gertrude had used up her entire stock of sociability, it seemed.

Besides, she reminded herself, *I've got some things to think through.*

She shut and locked the door of her apartment, and slumped down into the comfort of her papasan chair. For a moment she debated turning on some music, then decided against it. She pulled out a cigarette and lit up, closing her eyes, relishing the feel of the smoke in her lungs.

Throughout the day, she'd been running the weird events of the past week through in her mind. (*One of the advantages of flying a helicopter,* she mused. *The engine noise is so loud only the most determined passengers try to strike up a conversation. Lots of time to think.*) The trick to making any headway on her mystery, she'd found, was keeping track of all the questions, facts and suppositions.

After a few moments, she pushed herself out of the cocooning depths of the chair and crossed to her small desk, set up in one corner of the room. She rummaged around in the drawers, finally retrieving a stack of index cards and a pen. Returning to the papasan, she sucked on the end of the pen as she tried to order her thoughts. Then she started writing, assigning to a single card each of the strange events, the anomalies, the questions, and basically any stray thoughts she had about the events surrounding Pop-Pop's last days. Halfway through the process, she considered whether she should be using different-colored cards to distinguish between facts—like the burglar—and questions or suspicions—like what happened to Pop-Pop's memoirs. She shook her head in frustration. *Why bother?* she asked herself grimly. *It's not as if I have that many facts. . . .*

When she was through, she returned to the corner by the desk. A corkboard took up part of the wall, the result of a years-old, half-hearted attempt to get the "administrivia" of her life, bills and the like, in better order. She'd never fully followed through with her grandiose plans for efficiency. On occasion, she'd posted a phone bill or a parking ticket on the board as a reminder to herself to pay it on time, but she'd found herself just as likely to forget to follow up if the bill was in plain sight or buried in a desk drawer. (*Some of us are just born to need secretaries,* she thought with a smile.)

Now she cleared off the contents of the corkboard—a reminder to renew her car insurance, now long out of date, and a couple of pictures she'd clipped from travel magazines—and pinned up the index cards she'd made. She made no attempt to organize them, just put them up on the board where she could see them all simultaneously. Then she took a step back and considered her handiwork.

Okay, she told herself, *let's see what we've got here.* She moved forward again and started shifting the three-by-five cards around into new arrangements. *The burglar and the cop's refusal to admit that he'd spotted the getaway van—there* has *to be a connection there. Now, what about the missing journal?*

No, she decided after a moment, she could see no *direct* connection there. She'd spooked the burglar before he had a chance to find and make off with the memoirs. *Unless the journal wasn't upstairs at all,* she amended, and he'd already scooped it up before coming upstairs.

Or unless that wasn't his first *visit* to the house. But, in that case, just what the hell was he doing, coming back to the scene of the crime? What else might he have wanted? *Pop-Pop's mementos, maybe? Or just some of them?* Unbidden, her memory dredged up an image of the strange, photorealistic painting she'd seen of that otherworldly landscape. *Now why did I think of that just now?* she asked herself. *Does it have some significance I'm missing?*

She added the painting to a new notecard, but stuck it off to the side. *I just don't know enough about it at the moment,* she decided.

Was there some kind of connection between the strange happenings and the seemingly endless string of people who'd come to see Pop-Pop during those last few days? Earlier, she'd considered that any one of them might have made off with the memoirs. But why? Motive was the biggest question there.

Ah, to hell with it. She sighed. It was all very well to try to figure things out on her own, but she was just spinning her wheels here. She needed to talk things over with someone else—someone who knew Jim Dooley, Sr., as well as she did, if not better. She pulled out her wallet and extracted the piece of paper Simon Warner had given her in the undertaker's waiting room. The ink had smudged slightly, but the phone number was still readable. *Area code 303—that's Denver, isn't it?* She settled herself back in the papasan chair, snagged the phone from the end table and dialed.

For a few seconds she listened to the faint ghost-voices that echoed on the line; then the distant phone began to ring. She heard a sharp click. Then came that most hated of all messages: "The number you have dialed is not in service. Please check the number, and dial again. This is a message from the 3–0 exchange."

With a quiet curse she hung up and carefully redialed the number. She listened to the electronic burr of the ring tone, then, "The number you have dialed. . . ."

"Damn it!" She scrutinized the slip of paper. Smudge or no smudge, Warner's writing was precise and clear: no potential errors, like a *one* that could be a *seven,* or a *four* that might be a *nine.* Painstakingly she dialed again, rechecking each number as she pressed the key. "The number you have dialed is not in service. Please check. . . ."

Maybe Warner had moved. She stared at the wall for a moment, then dialed another number.

"Directory assistance. What city, please?"

"Denver, I guess."

"Go ahead."

"I'd like the new listing for Warner," Sam said. "Simon Warner."

"I'm sorry," the operator replied after a moment. "I have no new listing for that name."

Sam frowned at the scrap of paper. "Give me the current listing, then."

"I'm sorry. I have no listing at all for Simon Warner."

"Try 'Sid', then."

"I'm sorry. I have no listing for Sid Warner."

"Then how about just the initial?"

"I have twelve listings for 'S. Warner'. Do you have an address?"

"No." Sam ground her teeth. "Okay, thanks." She hung up.

Damn it! she thought, slumping back into the chair. *Something's not right here.* No listing for Sid Warner, and the number he gave her not in service. Conceivably, he could have an unlisted number and have written it down wrong—*Or maybe he hasn't paid his phone bill,* she thought wryly. But taken with everything else that had been going on lately, didn't that seem just a *little* too coincidental? Discard that possibility, and the only option was. . . .

He gave me a bogus number, just to dust me off.

Crap!

After a moment, she reached out and grabbed the phone again. She dialed an Oregon number.

Maggie Braslins picked up on the second ring.

"Hey, Mags."

"Sam?" Sam smiled as she heard Maggie's throaty chuckle. "Can't get enough of me, huh? How's the return to what we laughingly call 'real life'?"

"No worse than I expected." Sam paused. "Look, Mags, I need some help with something."

"Sure," her friend responded without hesitation. "Name it."

"Tell me what you know about Sid Warner."

"The guy at Jim's funeral?" Maggie thought for a moment. "I know the name. Part of the old flight-test fraternity, isn't he?" She paused again. "But you probably know that already, don't you?"

"I'm looking for something a little more detailed," Sam admitted.

"Hmm." Samantha could picture her friend's grin. "A little background research, huh? What kind of stuff are you after, specifically?"

Sam shrugged, even though she knew Maggie couldn't see her. "Where he's living these days, for starters. What he's up to. I don't know, anything that might be interesting."

"I see." Mags paused again. "You're asking me if I can dig up the dirt on Simon Warner, is that what you're asking me?"

"That's about it, Mags."

"I see," Maggie said again. "Can you maybe tell me why? Tell me what this is all about?" Her voice changed slightly. "Are you thinking this Warner's got something to do with that deal with the cops?"

"I don't know, Mags," Sam conceded. "Maybe, but . . . I just don't know."

"Hmm," Maggie mused doubtfully. But then, "Okay, Sam," she said, "for you, I'll do it. Anything else?"

It was Sam's turn to pause. "Yes," she said after a moment. "There are some other people I'd like the background scoop on, too."

"The same kind of poop? Present whereabouts, activities, anything that makes my eyes pop?"

"You got it, Mags," Samantha confirmed. "Got a pen handy?" Quickly, Sam ran down her mental list of people who'd visited Jim Dooley during his last week.

When she was finished, Mags didn't speak at once. "Some of those names ring bells," she said finally, "but probably from the same places you've heard of them. I don't know any of them personally." She chuckled again. "But hell, I guess I've always wanted to play private investigator. Do you want me to put the names out over the 99s grapevine?"

"That's what I had in mind," Sam agreed. "But I'd appreciate it if. . . ."

"If I could keep it kinda sub rosa," Maggie finished for her. "No worries. Nobody'll know it's you who's asking."

"How do you think you'll start?"

Maggie considered. "I'll probably start with Amy Langland," she said thoughtfully. "Amy knows everybody and his cousin."

"Where's Amy living now?" Sam cut in. "Still in Milwaukee?"

"Uh-uh, she moved out your way awhile back. Somewhere in Glendale, I think." Maggie paused. "Want me to give you a call when I've got something? Or do you have a fax machine? That might be the most efficient way of doing it."

"Since when have you been efficient, Mags?" Sam countered. She considered for a moment, then, "Why don't you fax it to WestAir?" she suggested. She pulled her business card from her wallet and read off the fax number. "You sure this isn't too much trouble?"

"If it is, I'll let you know," Maggie reassured her. "You can count on that."

After she'd hung up the phone, Sam pulled out the sheaf

of photocopies Arlene, Kerr's legal secretary, had made for her. For the dozenth time, she went over the inventory of mementos and personal effects that had been willed to the Museum of Flight in Rogers. Not that she thought she'd missed something obvious, like Pop-Pop's journal, but on the off-chance that some item might prompt a new idea. After a few minutes, she tossed the inventory aside in frustration and started flipping through the records of sale for Pop-Pop's Eagle Mountain property.

As far as she could tell, everything looked to be in order. The land had been purchased, according to the official records, in early 1980 by some outfit called New Horizons Industries. (She snorted. *Typical California New-Agey kind of name, that,* she thought. *Probably grows tofu or makes flotation tanks, or some crap like that.*) True, Sam didn't have the background or expertise to check through the legalese—the "parties of the first and second part," "henceforths" and "heretofores" making a grotesque parody of the English language—for irregularities, but at first glance it seemed to hang together. The payment provisions, "for one dollar in hand, plus other valuable considerations," caught her eye at first, but then she remembered how an old boyfriend had bought a car in a similar arrangement to avoid paying tax. For a few minutes she considered taking the contract to a lawyer and paying to have him review it. But then she decided against it. *Morton Kerr, Jr., has already looked it over,* she reminded herself, *and he didn't find anything wrong with it. He seemed competent enough . . . snotty, but competent.*

She tossed the contract after the inventory list, in the general direction of her desk, and stared again at the corkboard. *Am I totally overreacting?* she asked herself a little grimly. *Maybe Morton Kerr was right—maybe I* should *trust legal documentation more than I do the memory of a possibly senile, dying man . . . even if he* is *my grandfather. And maybe Officer Belmont really* didn't *see the van. And maybe the burglar was just a thief who reads obituaries and hits houses where people have died. And maybe. . . .* She laughed bitterly. When she looked at it that way, it was ridiculous. Any of those events alone could easily be explained away. But taken together, an innocent explanation would require a ludicrous string of "coincidences." *Remember Ockham's*

Razor, she told herself, *the principle of economy: the simplest hypothesis that covers all the facts is usually the best.*

And the simplest hypothesis here is that something *is going on. Call it a conspiracy of silence, or whatever: there's* something *more than paranoia operating here.*

She reached for another cigarette, found she'd smoked her last. With another curse, she tossed the empty pack at the corkboard.

9

It was difficult—bloody difficult, at times—but Samantha managed to put her speculations on the back burner over the next couple of days. There wasn't anything meaningful she could do until Maggie got back to her with whatever information the 99s grapevine managed to develop on the list of people who'd visited Pop-Pop. In the interim, hard though it was, she carried on with her normal life: flying, mainly, and just existing until it was time to fly again.

When she was in the air behind Gertrude's controls, it was easy enough to lose herself in the intricacies and sensations of flight. On the ground, though, it was much harder to forget about the strange events. When her thoughts threatened to overwhelm her, she got into the habit of firing up Grendel and winding the big car out on the freeways of the Los Angeles basin. Over five or six days, she discovered parts of the sprawling city she'd never known existed, even after living there for almost a decade. Her favorite drive, though, remained Griffith Park north of Los Feliz Boulevard, where she could throw the Mustang around the narrow roads that climbed the dry hills and flanked the scrub-choked arroyos.

On the first of August, two days after her return to work, she found a message from Morton Kerr waiting for her on her telephone answering machine. Apparently, Pop-Pop's house was already attracting interest, and several people had made offers on the property. The sums the lawyer mentioned so casually were staggering—more money than Sam had ever thought of receiving from any single source—and his message implied his confidence that she'd eventually end up selling for even more. *Maybe I should become a lady of leisure,* she mused, *or maybe I should take the money and start my own flying school.* With a snort, she filed those thoughts under the mental heading of future business. She'd never been comfortable letting go of anything until she was damn good and ready—it was one of the traits, she thought, that made her such a good pilot—and she certainly wasn't ready to ignore the weirdness that had gathered around Pop-Pop's death. *Once I've got* that *out of the way,* she promised herself, *then I'll think about the future.*

Despite her intentions, by the evening of August 4 she'd almost managed to forget her suspicions and anxieties. Her life had settled back into its natural rhythm, and it would have been relatively easy to convince herself that nothing had changed—that the events in Gold Beach had never happened. It came as a surprise, then, when Sam saw that Joe the Mountain was waiting for her as she put Gertrude down in the center of the lighted helipad after a sunset flight. As the rotors slowed overhead, she helped the passengers—another Japanese family, three generations in all—out of the copter, reminding them with gestures to keep their heads low. Once she'd seen them clear of the rotating blades with heads still attached to torsos, and accepted their thanks and a generous gratuity, she headed toward the burly mechanic.

"Look at this," she told Joe, holding out the fifty-dollar bill the head of the household had stuffed into her hand. "You think we can get the Japanese to give the other tourists lessons in how to tip?"

Joe barked with laughter. "Guess you're buying the beer, then," he pointed out. "It's Miller time."

"When *isn't* it Miller time for you, Joe?" She punched him lightly on the shoulder; it was like punching the helicopter. "I figured you'd already be gone for the night."

He shook his large head. "Thought you might want this before you left." He reached into a thigh pocket of his overalls and pulled out a carefully folded sheaf of fax paper. "Came in over the box just before Becky headed out for the day," he explained. "Figured you might not want to wait until tomorrow morning before you saw it."

Sam took the sheets from his thick-fingered hand and unfolded them. She scanned the first page quickly, then refolded it and put it safely in her own pocket. "Thanks, Joe, you figured right. Mind if I buy you that beer another night?"

The mechanic hung his head in mock sadness. "Story of my life," he moaned. "Guess I'll just slink off home and tip a few cold ones with my close friends Sam Donaldson and David Letterman." He patted her shoulder. "Catch you in the morning, Sam."

It took all of Sam's self-control to drive home, park Grendel, shut and lock the door, and settle herself comfortably before she unfolded the fax paper again and read it. It was from Maggie, scrawled by hand on the letterhead of the Ophir Flight School, where she worked.

Sam, the cover page read, *sorry it took me as long as it did, but the 99s grapevine isn't as efficient as it used to be in the Good Old Days. Something to do with the women being too concerned with Real Life, that's my opinion at least. As if there's anything more important than sisterhood and all that bilge.*

I've got the word out on all the names you gave me, but like you asked I put a "rush" on Simon Warner. This is what I've got—hope it's what you're after. (Hey, kiddo, you're sure moving in rarefied and intriguing circles these days. Do you happen to know if Simon's got a steady bedmate at the moment? Thought I might apply.) Later.

Sam chuckled to herself and flipped to the second page of the fax. Again handwritten in Maggie's generous scrawl, it was laid out more or less like a résumé, listing the key dates and events in the life of one Simon Warner, Esquire. Much of the early stuff Sam already knew, albeit in nowhere near as much detail. A long stint with the air force as a flight test engineer, based out of Edwards from 1963 to 1967, pushing the envelope in a staggering range of experimental aircraft. Apparently, he'd found his niche in the X–15 rocket-plane program—turned down an opportunity to get involved with the NASA Mercury space-flight program because he had no desire to be "Spam in a can" (Sam had to smile at that)—and racked up half a dozen major records in that hybrid plane-spaceship before leaving the military and going into industry.

Flight Test Engineer with McDonnell Douglas. FTE with Fairchild. FTE with Grumman. FTE with General Dynamics.... Sam shook her head in amazement. *Geez,* she thought, *this guy's probably had some contact with every major series of fighter planes developed in the last thirty years.* She skimmed through the rest of the list. Nothing significant....

Wait a minute; what was this?

The key line in the handwritten column of jobs seemed to jump out at her: 1971 to 1978, Flight Test Engineer for Generro Aerospace.

Sam sat back in the papasan, staring at the fax. Generro Aerospace. *The company Dad flew for when he was killed.*

Did Warner know Dad?

Over the almost two decades since Jim Dooley, Jr.'s, death, Sam had tried on several occasions to track down people who'd known him, who'd flown with him. To little avail, as it turned out. By the time she was old enough to pick up the trail and follow up on names she remembered from her childhood, it was almost completely cold. In some cases, she just didn't have enough information: "Pat and Maureen from Pax River" wasn't enough to find out anything meaningful. In others, the people had died, left the military for the more sketchily documented civilian world, or had become lost in the labyrinthine bureaucracy of the armed forces. What were the chances that she'd stumble upon, totally by chance, the closest connection yet? *Coincidences happen,* she told herself ... *but don't bet on them.*

She skimmed the details of Sid Warner once more, trying to extract a gestalt of the man's career, and his life in general. After a minute or two, she set the papers aside and tried to synthesize a coherent picture. *He's the test pilot's test pilot,* she had to admit. *Out on the pointy end throughout his career, never "left behind"—that great fear of the careerist—except in the case of the space program, and it seems that was his own choice.* She shook her head. *And maybe he made the right decision there if he wanted to remain a real* pilot, *and not a combination laboratory animal and public-relations figurehead.* No record of any wife or family—unusual, but not unheard of. And, again, that could well have been a career choice; the plum flight-test assignments back then, the ones that could really give a cat-shot to your career, were often deemed to be what amounted to suicide missions, and maybe he figured having no entanglements would give him an edge on those gigs.

Warner held memberships in the most prestigious and important associations and clubs, though some were honorary. That included the Society of Experimental Test Pilots (the SETP, the highest pantheon in the flight-test fraternity) and—Sam was wryly amused to note—the unofficial "Caterpillar Club," whose membership was limited to pilots who'd had to bail out of an aircraft to save their lives. She wondered through which association he'd met Pop-Pop.

There were no anomalies in his career, nothing that really stood out. Granted, it was interesting that he apparently hadn't held a full-time job, flying or otherwise, since he left Generro Aerospace nine years earlier, but that didn't necessarily mean much. According to Maggie's dossier, Simon Warner was born in 1926, which made him fifty-two when he left Generro. That wasn't an unreasonable age for someone to retire, particularly someone with a track record like Warner's—and presumably the pensions to go with it. Apparently, that gave him the freedom to do whatever the hell he liked, which seemed to include brief stints of consulting and public-relations work for a bunch of engineering outfits: a week or two here and there. Maggie's dossier listed the major ones—Sam had heard of a few of them—but hinted that there were more she hadn't bothered writing down.

She sighed, debating whether or not to light up a smoke. *Interesting background,* she decided. Very *interesting background. Particularly since he could well have known both Dad* and *Pop-Pop.*

She gave in to her body's craving for nicotine and lit another cigarette. She blew a thin stream of smoke at the ceiling and closed her eyes.

Okay, she told herself. *I've got background information on Simon Warner. Background, but nothing current.* Was it worth pushing, trying to find out what he was up to these days and where she could get in contact with him? After all, there was nothing to even vaguely suggest that he was connected to the weirdness surrounding Jim Dooley's journal.

Yeah, it is *worth it,* she told herself after a moment. Something deep in her gut, some kind of instinct, nagged at her, telling her Warner was somehow a key figure in all of this. Logically, she couldn't understand how or why; there was no clue here that made sense to her rational mind. But over the years, she'd learned to pay attention to that *ir*rational part of her.

So what I really need is information on where Warner is today. *I guess I didn't stress that clearly enough to Mags.* She glanced over at the clock on the stereo. *Not too late to call and ask her to scrounge up his phone number or address.* She reached for the phone.

It rang the instant before she touched it, the electronic buzz jolting her with surprise. She picked it up. "Mags?"

There was a pause at the other end, then a voice that Sam recognized at once. "Could I speak to Samantha Dooley, please?"

Sam could feel the breadth of her smile. "It's me, Amy. How're you doing?"

"As well as can be expected," Amy Langland replied dryly. Her voice had the same edge to it that Sam remembered from their first meeting—the edge that convinced people who didn't bother looking beneath the surface that she was a frosty old bitch. Voice and Corn Belt rasp always made Sam think of an aging tomboy who smoked and drank and cussed right alongside the men—which described Amy Langland to a T. "I hear you're going through some problems at the moment."

Sam blinked in surprise, then she said, "Did Maggie Braslins tell you that?"

Langland hesitated an instant before she answered slowly, "Well, yes, she did." A longer pause, then, "Have I said something wrong?" she asked, her voice as soft as it ever got.

"No. No, it's okay." Sam frowned. *Mags, I thought you said you were going to keep this sub rosa.*

"She didn't tell me much about what was going on," Langland continued. She snorted. "Maybe because she realized she'd just contracted a case of foot-in-mouth disease, I reckon.

"If you want to tell me the details, maybe I can help,"

the older woman continued. "And if you don't, well, that's okay with me, too. I won't mind."

Sam hesitated for a moment. Then her smile broadened. "I can do with the help, Amy," she admitted. "I'm trying to get a line on one Simon Warner."

"Hm. That's what you've got Maggie looking for?"

"Not only Warner," Samantha amended, "even though he's the important one at the moment." And, as she'd done with Braslins, she listed off the other names in which she was interested. When she'd finished, there was no answer from the other end of the line. "Amy?"

"I'm still here," Langland announced a little testily. "I'm just thinking—something you younger gals don't take enough time for, if you ask me." She paused, then hummed musingly to herself, an out-of-tune snatch of an old Count Basie melody. "Quite the illustrious group you've got yourself there, girl."

"You know the names?"

"Most of them," Langland allowed. "Some of them I haven't seen in years. I'll admit, but there's only one or two who are complete strangers. What do you want to know about them?"

She paused, ordering her thoughts. Finally, "*Everything,* basically," she admitted. "Or," she corrected quickly, "anything particularly interesting about them."

"Do you think maybe you can give me something more to go on, child?" Langland asked dryly. " 'Interesting' covers a lot of ground, to my mind. Makes it easier for me to narrow it down if I know you want to shoot 'em, sue 'em or screw 'em."

Samantha laughed out loud. "You've got a point." She paused again. "Okay," she said at length, "let's just say 'anything suspicious,' anything that catches your interest. Anything that doesn't fit. I'm sorry, Amy," she added, "I'm not trying to make it difficult for you. I really don't *know* what I'm looking for.

"Except for Warner," she went on. "I just want to know where he's at these days, and how I can get in touch with him."

"Hmph." Langland snorted again. "And I suppose you can't tell me why you're looking in the first place? No, no," she went on quickly, overriding any answer Sam might have begun, "don't tell me, just an old woman's prurient curiosity.

"I'll need some time on this," she continued thoughtfully. "My memory isn't what it used to be."

"Thanks, Amy, I really mean it."

"Hmph, whatever." Langland brushed off Sam's thanks as if they made her faintly uncomfortable. "You've got Margaret Braslins looking into these same people, have you?"

"That's right," Sam confirmed. "Mags said she'd put it out on the 99s grapevine."

"She did, did she? Hmph, no need to go bothering the other sisters over this. But I guess what's done is done." Langland inflected the last phrase almost like a question. But before Sam could answer—or could even decide if an answer was necessary—she went on, "No matter. I'll call you in a few days, Samantha, when I've wrung the right memories out of this old head of mine."

"Thanks, Amy," Sam said again.

"Yes, well, save that until you see whether I come up with anything." And with a click, the line went dead.

To Sam's surprise, it was Maggie and the 99s grapevine that came through with additional information first. Over the next couple of days, notes from Maggie came in over the WestAir office fax—additional background details, in dribs and drabs. Sam's first instinct was to take each note as it arrived and go through it, but after a little thought she decided it might make more sense to wait until she had a reasonable "body of data" before working her way through it. That way, at least, she'd have a better chance of noticing any unusual connections, correspondences or anomalies.

When she finally sat down with the sheaves of fax paper, she quickly realized she needn't have bothered to wait. Even if she hadn't been alerted by the report on Sid Warner, she wouldn't have missed the one thing that an inordinate number of the people had in common.

They'd all been associated with Generro Aerospace at one time or another.

Samantha climbed out of the papasan and butted out her cigarette half-smoked. She spread the sheets of fax paper out on the floor and went over them again. There was no mistake. Of the dozen names she'd given to Maggie, eight of them had some association with Generro (nine, including

Sid Warner). Granted, the nature of the association varied—only a couple had been pilots; the others had been consultants, managers or tech-reps—and none of their periods of employment seemed to overlap by much. Still, she considered it significant.

She set the sheets aside, picked up the phone book and flipped through the *L*s. Sure enough, there was a listing for a "Langland, Amy J." on the whimsically named Aloha Street—in Los Feliz, not Glendale, but close enough. (Sam shook her head. *It's a small world.* On her high-speed cruises through Griffith Park, she'd probably driven within a mile of Langland's home without even knowing it.) She noted down the number on a scratch pad, then picked up the phone and dialed.

Langland answered almost immediately. "Samantha," she said, once Dooley had identified herself, "I'm sorry I haven't gotten back to you sooner. Some things came up, and I haven't had the time I thought I'd get."

"That's okay, Amy," Sam reassured the aging pilot. "Whenever you get around to it. I do have a couple of specific questions, though."

"Oh? Did the grapevine come through for you, then?"

"More or less," Sam allowed.

"Shoot, then."

"Simon Warner, first of all. Did you get a phone number or address on him?"

"Uh-uh," Langland responded at once. "Got skunked there. I've got some old poop on him, but he moved on without leaving a forwarding address. Pilots tend to do that, y'know."

"That old address: was that in Denver?"

"Huh?" Sam could imagine Langland blinking in surprise. "No. Burbank. That's *quite* a few years back. I tried to pick up tally on him, but no joy.

"Second?"

"Amy, what can you tell me about Generro Aerospace?"

Langland paused. "Generro," she said at last. "Generro. . . ."

"Based in Moreno Valley," Sam added helpfully.

"I know where it is," Langland almost snapped. "I'm just trying to remember." She paused again. "Your father used to fly for Generro."

"Did I tell you about that in Kansas City?"

"You told me about it *somewhere,*" Langland corrected. "Generro—the Thunderflash, right?"

"That's the outfit."

"They were hot for a while, I seem to recall," the old woman went on, almost to herself, so quietly that Sam had to strain to hear. "They had some good engineers, good designers. If they'd had the breaks, they might have been real big. *Real* big. Just bad luck that they weren't, really. But that's the way it was back then. Ideas weren't enough—you had to have the luck for lightning to strike."

"What was it about the company that made it so attractive?"

"Attractive?" Langland snorted. "*Nothing,* really. Just another aerospace startup, that's how I remember it."

"Then how come so many of the people I talked to you about worked there at one time?"

"Huh?" Langland sounded surprised. "What?"

"Those twelve names I gave you the other day," Sam elaborated. "Nine of them had links with Generro. *Nine.* I was just wondering why, what attracted them."

"That's just the way it was back then," Langland said flatly. "It was a smaller industry than it is now, a small, tight little community. Hell, girl, all *twelve* of them were connected with McDonnell Douglas from time to time, weren't they?"

"True, but there's a big difference between Generro Aerospace and McDonnell Douglas. Billions of dollars' difference."

"I suppose." Langland was silent for a moment, then, "Can you tell me why you're interested in these folks?" she asked.

Sam debated for a moment, then shook her head, even though she knew Langland couldn't see her. "It's just curiosity, Amy," she said finally. "It's probably nothing really important."

"Hmph." The older woman wasn't convinced. "You don't put word out so wide on the grapevine for 'just curiosity.' " She paused again. "But if you want to keep your own council, that's your right, of course. This is still a free country, more or less."

"Do you know anybody who's still connected with Generro?"

"More curiosity?" Langland asked tartly. "No, not that I can recall right off the top of my head. They changed their whole operation five, six years ago, y'know. Big management shake-up, heads rolling in the corridors, blood knee-deep in the corporate suites, that's how I hear it."

"Why?"

"The goddamn recession, of course," Langland shot back. "Probably a bunch of pigeon-livered cowards among the major shareholders panicked. Happens all the time, I hear.

"Pretty near gutted Generro, I understand," she went on. "All flight operations closed down." She snorted. "Bean-counting bullcrap, more than likely. Flight operations cost a pile of money, but it's that kind of costly R&D that keeps a company healthy."

"Generro isn't healthy these days?"

"I'd better not say any more, or some uppity stock-broker's going to charge me with handing out investment advice without a license." Sam had to chuckle at the grim tone of the old woman's voice. "Anyhow," Langland finished, "far as I know, there's none of the old guard left there, nobody who worked there in the seventies or earlier." She hesitated. "Is that any help, child?"

Sam wasn't sure. Langland's description certainly made Generro sound like a dead end.

But she had that strange feeling in her gut. "You never know, Amy," she said. "You never know."

10

The headquarters and primary research facility for Generro Aerospace Technologies Incorporated was located in Moreno Valley, some 65 miles east of downtown Los Angeles, not far from March Air Base. *That must have been convenient when they were actually developing aircraft,* Sam had thought as she'd spotted a brace of fighters—fast, lethal-looking darts ripping across the sky—silhouetted for a moment against the thin cloud-deck before vanishing from sight.

Sam had found it easy to arrange for a meeting with a Generro representative. All it had taken was a phone call and a request. None of the plausible excuses on which she'd lavished such effort were even needed. The receptionist had simply taken down her name and phone number, and told her that a Mr. Jacques Leclerc would be able to see her at 11:00 on Thursday, August 6. Thursday and Friday were her days off from WestAir anyway, so there was no trouble on that score. *Of course, Jacques Leclerc's going to be some kind of PR flack,* she'd recognized, *but at least he's a start.*

At about 10:40, Sam drew up to the main security gate of the Generro facility. *The Generro* compound, *more like,* she corrected mentally. With its high reinforced fencing, the top angled out and laced with barbed wire, and the heavy automated gate, the approach reminded her more of a penitentiary or a high-security military facility than a civilian research establishment. The gate itself was set well back from the main road, at the end of a well-paved private roadway lined with cultivated plants. Only a small sign marked the turnoff, and an even smaller panel identified the entrance as belonging to Generro Aerospace. *Interesting,* she thought. *It's like the military in that way: if you don't know where you're going, you shouldn't be going there.*

She stopped Grendel a yard short of the gate, and watched a security guard—carrying a holstered pistol, she noticed, a 9mm automatic with a grip that looked as though it had been used—emerge from the gatehouse and approach the car.

He flashed her a perfunctory smile—polite enough, but certainly not friendly. "Good morning, ma'am. Can I help you?"

She responded with a bright grin. *It's not his fault he's supposed to be coldly efficient,* she reminded herself. "I hope so," she said lightly. "I've got an appointment with a Jacques Leclerc. My name's Samantha Dooley."

"Okay. Hold on." The security guard glanced back over his shoulder toward the gatehouse, and for the first time Sam noticed there was another figure behind the faintly green-tinted windows. (*Bulletproof glass?* she wondered suddenly.) The second guard had apparently heard what she'd said—that meant some kind of exterior microphone, probably; security was more intense than she'd expected—and was leaning forward as if examining a clipboard or a computer screen. After a few moments he nodded.

The guard beside Grendel smiled again, this time a little more genuinely. "Welcome to Generro Aerospace, Ms. Dooley. You're a little early, but Mr. Leclerc *is* expecting you." He reached into his pocket and extracted what looked to Sam like a badge of some kind, about the size of a playing card. He handed it to her. "Please wear this at all times when you're in the facility. It identifies you as a guest. When you leave, please remember to turn it in to me or one of my associates. Okay?"

"Okay." Sam turned the card over in her hand. It was plastic, rather like an oversized, unusually thick credit card. She saw no raised numbers and no magnetic stripe, however; in fact, the only marking at all on the light gray material was the word VISITOR printed in broad, black letters. *Why's it so thick?* she wondered silently. *Probably a 'smart card,' maybe with a locator circuit in it. Interesting.*

Attached to one side of the card was a small metal alligator clip. She used this clip to attach the pass to the collar of her white cotton shirt. Smoothing it down, she smiled back up at the guard. "I guess that makes me official."

His answering smile was fully real this time. "Guess it does, at that." He pointed through the gate, down the blacktopped road that led to the nearest of several low buildings she could see ahead of her. "Stay on the main road, Ms. Dooley," the guard instructed. "At the T-intersection, turn right. You'll find the visitors' lot right in front of the reception building. Mr. Leclerc will be meeting you there. Okay?"

"Right at the T," Sam echoed. "And if I turned left . . . ?"

He chuckled. "That's the part of my job I always hate, notifying the next of kin.

"Have a nice day, Ms. Dooley." As he stepped away from the car, the gate slid back silently on its metal track.

Sam pulled forward slowly, keeping her speed down to the ten miles per hour posted on the sign beside the road. As she passed through the gate, she noticed for the first time a closed-circuit video camera mounted atop one of the metal gateposts, pivoting to follow her. She glanced away quickly—*Nothing makes security wonks more uncomfortable than people paying too much attention to their toys*—but examined the image of the camera held in her mind's eye. A big lens—probably a high-power zoom, she figured. No doubt the boys in the gatehouse would know in an instant if she *did* decide to turn left instead of right.

The two-lane road led straight from the gate toward the complex of buildings. The distance was about a quarter of a mile, she guessed. On either side of the road, beyond the cultivated and irrigated border plants, the land was flat and dusty scrub. No building, no fences, nothing—*A buffer zone,* she realized, *separating the fence from what matters. These guys don't fool around with their security.* Presumably it was a carryover from the company's glory days, when it was involved in heavy-duty military contracts. *But why haven't they relaxed things since?* she asked herself suddenly. *Surely security costs money they could devote to more important projects. . . .*

She could see the cluster of buildings a lot better now: sprawling, single-story blocks of concrete, many of them sprouting an impressive array of microwave and telsat antennas from their roofs. Not many of them had windows, and those few windows that did exist contained heavily tinted glass: predominately to keep the building interiors cool, no doubt, but also doing a great job of blocking any glimpse Sam might have of what was within. Some of the buildings had flowering shrubs planted around them in narrow flower beds, obviously a half-hearted attempt to soften the institutional harshness, but most were flanked with parking lots, only sparsely occupied by cars. *This place looks so familiar.* She examined that impression for a moment before she understood: Generro Aerospace reminded her of a cross between a modern industrial park and a government installation like the Manned Spaceflight Center in Houston, which she'd visited as a teenager.

She reached the T-intersection and turned right as instructed, past a large sign reading ALL VISITORS PROCEED TO RECEPTION BUILDING. It didn't come as too much of a surprise that the left fork offered no sign whatsoever. *Just like I thought: if you don't know where you're going, you shouldn't be going there.*

The reception building was smaller than the others and boasted more than its fair share of dark-tinted windows. Sam parked Grendel in one of the spaces marked VISITOR, and strode up the three shallow steps to the frosted-glass front doors.

Beyond the doors was a stereotypical high-tech company's reception area: an inordinate amount of chrome and glass, much of the light coming from tiny, sun-bright halogen track lights. *Quite striking,* Sam thought, *like it's come right out of a design magazine. But totally soulless.*

She gave her name to the receptionist, who was sitting behind a desk that resembled a cross between a NASA mission control console and a reinforced bunker. Identified by her nameplate as Mrs. Parks, the receptionist—a telephone headset partially concealed in her frizzy red hair, so it looked as though the slender microphone boom sprouted directly from her skull—glanced from Sam's visitor badge to a small computer monitor inset into the desk. "Welcome to Generro Aerospace, Ms. Dooley," she said, sounding not exactly bored, but far from completely sincere. She gestured toward a sofa of black leather and stainless steel. "If you'd like to have a seat, Mr. Leclerc will be with you momentarily."

Sam had hardly settled herself on the cold, angular couch when a man emerged from the door beyond the reception desk and approached her, hand extended. "Ms. Dooley? I'm Jacques Leclerc."

Samantha was back on her feet in an instant, examining her host as she took the proffered hand. He cut an imposing figure, she had to admit. From the apparently Gallic name, she'd expected a small-boned, European-looking man with an aquiline nose. In fact, however, Leclerc more resembled Mohammed Ali, still vigorous and in his physical prime: tall and broad-shouldered, handsome as a black Adonis, carrying himself with the grace of an athlete. His gray, summer-weight suit was impeccably tailored, but somehow seemed totally natural on him, not affected or over-formal. The only faintly Gallic touch about him—besides his name, of course—was the faintest trace of a European accent to his midnight-and-velvet voice.

"Mr. Leclerc," she said formally, matching his grip pressure for pressure. "Thanks for taking the time to see me."

"No problem, no problem." He smiled, showing improbably white teeth. "Welcome to Generro Aerospace." He gestured toward the door. "If you'd like to follow me . . . ?"

Leclerc led her to his office at the front of the building, overlooking the parking lot through dark-tinted windows. As he opened the unmarked office door, Sam noticed a small panel on the wall beside the door frame. A green light blinked as Leclerc passed through, blinked again as she approached. Leclerc gestured to a comfortable-looking conversation grouping away from the office's large desk, and settled himself down in one chair once Sam was seated in another. Only then did Sam notice that Leclerc wore a "smart-card" identification similar to hers, except that his had his photograph on it. Apparently, the panel beside the door had registered the proximity of their passes, both of which authorized entry into the office and—presumably—recording their location and movements in some central computer database.

Leclerc noticed her gaze and immediately grasped its meaning, because he smiled and touched his ID card a little self-consciously. "A little bit of . . . *technological overkill,* yes?" He chuckled ironically. "I think so, too, but"—he gave a very Gallic shrug—"sometimes when one works closely with, er, certain patrons, one has to allay their institutional anxieties."

Sam hadn't expected to come to the point quite so quickly, but she took the opening. "So what is Generro Aerospace doing these days?" she asked. "I thought you'd closed down all your flight operations some time ago."

"That's true, we did. Before my time, of course." He shrugged again. "The cost of developing entire new aircraft was growing so great, while the . . . the institutional hurdles one must deal with . . . were growing ever larger as well. The board of directors decided it was necessary to narrow the scope of the company's operations."

Sam nodded in understanding. "So you develop subsystems, then, rather than whole planes."

Leclerc beamed, as if with pride at a brilliant student. "Precisely. As you say, subsystems. Technologies in their pure form, which we then license to others for integration."

"What kinds of technology?" She saw the slight change

in Leclerc's smile, and went on, "I know, I know. You can tell me, but then you'd have to kill me. Right?"

He showed her his empty palms in a gesture of helplessness. "Government restrictions and regulations. One must understand."

"I understand." She paused. "Can you give me any hints? Not aerodynamics, I take it."

"Correct."

"Mainly avionics and remote sensing, then?"

Leclerc's smile broadened. *He's enjoying this,* Sam recognized with a mixture of amusement and irritation. "I can say," he responded judiciously, "that there are elements of avionics and remote sensing in our work, yes."

"And your 'patron,' as you call it: the air force? The army?"

Again that gesture of helplessness. "I'm sorry, Ms. Dooley."

"Doesn't matter," she said lightly, disarmingly. "Just curiosity."

"I understand," he said magnanimously. "Quite natural to be interested in the company for which one's father once worked." Sam knew her expression must have shown her surprise, because he chuckled softly. "Don't you think we would be a little remiss if we didn't do at least some superficial checking on people who want to visit us?"

"You mean I might be a spy?"

Another shrug, which was answer enough.

Sam drew a breath, and launched into the spiel she'd prepared beforehand, the "cover story" she'd concocted to conceal the real reasons for her interest. "Actually, Mr. Leclerc, it's to do with my father that I'm here today. If you've checked my background, you'll know he died when I was five. Combine that with the fact that my home life wasn't the most stable"—he nodded in understanding—"and you'll understand I didn't have the chance to get to know him at all.

"I know it's taken me a while to think of it, but I've gotten to wondering about the people he flew with when he was at Generro, back in 1967. I got to thinking that *they*'d know him better than just about anybody, and they'd be able to tell me about him." She shrugged. "Not the same as getting to know him myself, of course, but better than nothing."

He nodded slowly, his expression one of understanding and empathy. "Certainly, Ms. Dooley, a fine idea. Who specifically did you have in mind?"

Sam feigned embarrassment. "Well, you see, that's the problem, Mr. Leclerc. If my dad ever mentioned any colleagues at Generro, I was too young to remember their names. I was hoping you could help me out."

Leclerc pursed his lips in thought. "You understand, Ms. Dooley," he responded slowly, "that there was a . . . *cycling* of personnel since the time in question. None of our current personnel had any connection with the company back then." He flashed a strobe-bright smile. "Myself, I only joined the company four years ago."

"I understand," Sam pressed. "But you must have records from that time. You knew about my father. . . ."

"Of course," Leclerc went on smoothly. "Yes, such records exist, but there is a corporate policy of confidentiality. Not management's idea, as it turns out; often it proves quite troublesome for the personnel department. Yet the employees themselves requested it."

"I know about records confidentiality," Sam allowed, "but in this case, when I'm practically Generro 'family'. . . ."

"I'm desolated, Ms. Dooley," Leclerc said, and his expression matched his words, "but it would be more than my job is worth to tell you. If you had a name, perhaps. . . ." He shrugged.

Silently, Samantha ground her teeth. Stonewalling was stonewalling, polite or not, for good reasons or not. "There's one, I remember," she said slowly. "Something Warner: Sam? Sal?"

Leclerc's face brightened. "Simon," he corrected her. "Simon Warner. Yes, he served as a flight test engineer from 1971 to 1978, I believe it was." He looked relieved that he was on safe ground again, Sam thought. He pulled a leather-bound day planner from an inside jacket pocket and flicked it open. "If you can give me your phone number, and the message you wish relayed to Mr. Warner. . . ." He extracted a Mont Blanc pen and poised it expectantly.

"Can't you just give me the contact information?" Sam asked. "Phone number, at work and at home . . . ?"

"Again, I'm desolated," he said, "but no, I cannot. Confidentiality again. And there's no message?"

Sam sighed and shook her head. "Nothing that would make sense to Mr. Warner without any background," she lied smoothly.

Leclerc put away the pen and planner. "I'm truly sorry, Ms. Dooley," and again he sounded as though he meant it, as though his failure to help a damsel in distress would keep him awake nights. "I wish I could be of assistance. Is there anything else with which I can help you?"

"I suppose not," Sam replied after a moment's thought.

Leclerc was on his feet immediately. "A tour, then?" he asked, voice and expression hopeful.

Samantha smiled, as she stood too. "But what could you show me, Mr. Leclerc?" she asked, a touch of irony in her voice. "The cafeteria? The parking lots? Probably even the photocopier's classified, isn't that true?"

"As you say." Leclerc nodded sadly. Then he brightened slightly. "Perhaps you would like to visit us again, Ms. Dooley, if you have any further questions?"

Sam shrugged. "You never know, Mr. Leclerc," she said demurely. "You never do know."

On the way back to the main gate, Sam drove even slower than she had on the way in. In the parabolic passenger-side wing mirror, she scrutinized the building complex receding behind her, looking for any features that stood out, anything that offered a hint as to their activity.

There wasn't much. The buildings were unmarked and generally undifferentiated. Granted, some had more antennas sprouting from their roofs than others, but Sam didn't know enough about telecommunications technology to make any real sense out of them. *For all I know, they're investing in the hottest satellite television system this side of CNN,* she thought wryly. A couple of the buildings in the distance, beyond the reception building, looked similar in design to hangars, but she was pretty sure they'd been converted to other uses. *If Generro was still running flight operations, Leclerc wouldn't lie about it,* Sam recognized. *It's kind of hard to hide a fighter-plane prototype practicing touch-and-goes.*

Wait: there *was* one unusual feature. First of all, there was a relatively small building—blocky, heavy, constructed totally out of concrete—isolated from the rest of the structures by almost a hundred yards. High-tension lines, graceful arcs gleaming in the sun, connected that building to the angular, Erector-set complexity of an electrical substation. From there, other lines arced off to some of the larger buildings. *They're using a lot of power,* Sam realized with a faint shock, *a hell of a lot of power. What for?* At first glance, it looked as though the squarish concrete structure was the source of the power, channeling it to the substation, and then to the other buildings. *But that doesn't make sense.* The substation had to be the distribution node. Which meant the concrete structure—whatever it was—had the greatest power requirements of all. What could need that kind of power?

Lasers? High-powered lasers? she wondered. *A lot of money's still being poured into SDI research, Star Wars. Maybe some of it's finding its way to Generro.* She shook her head. She could speculate all she liked. What she needed was hard information, not guesswork.

As instructed, she handed in her visitor's pass at the front gate. The guard needn't have made such a point of it when she'd arrived, it turned out: they wouldn't have opened the gate to let her leave until they had the pass in their hands. She turned right onto the highway leading back toward central Los Angeles. In her rearview mirror, she saw a large white truck approaching from the other direction, signaling for a turn into Generro's private road. Then a turn in the road hid truck, gate and complex from view.

The phone rang, jolting Sam out of that warm, floating sensation that precedes true sleep. "Crap." She rolled over in bed, glancing at the clock. Almost 01:00. *Figures, doesn't it?* she groused mentally. *The one night I go to bed early. . . .*

She picked up the phone. "Yeah?" Her voice sounded like ten miles of gravel road.

"Good evening. Did I interrupt your beauty sleep?"

The Corn Belt rasp was unmistakable. Sam brushed her hair from her eyes, sat up in bed and flicked on the reading light. "Hi, Amy."

"I was doing some thinking," the aging 99 said. "I guess I brushed you off some about Generro Aerospace, and I got to feeling guilty about it."

"Generro?" Sam struggled to clear the mental cobwebs from her thoughts. "I was just there today."

"You were? Hmph. Maybe I didn't need to go to any trouble after all. That'll teach me to be responsible."

"No, Amy, it's okay," Sam reassured her friend. "It's not like I learned much. What did you remember?"

"Not me, other people," Langland corrected her. "I did some asking around. I'd gotten myself curious about what Generro was doing when they weren't flying Thunderflashes into the desert."

"What did you find out?"

"Not much, all in all. And that told me a lot."

"Huh?" Sam brushed another errant lock of hair back from her face. "Sorry, Amy, I guess I'm not quite awake yet."

"It's like seeing a shadow," Langland explained, a touch impatiently. "A shadow's nothing, right? But something has to *cast* that shadow. That's what I found when I asked around about Generro. Shadows."

Sam blinked as the first light of understanding dawned. "Top secret projects, you mean?"

"More than top secret," Langland corrected. "You've heard of 'black' projects? Top secret projects are concealed. Black projects simply don't exist. The Strategic Defense Initiative: that's top secret. The replacement for the SR-71 Blackbird spy plane, the Aurora, that's black."

"And that's what Generro's involved in?"

"That kind of thing," Langland confirmed, "that's my conclusion. For what it's worth."

"So what could that have to do with Pop-Pop?" The words were out of Sam's mouth before she realized she'd never told Amy Langland why she'd been interested in Generro. "I mean . . . ," she began hurriedly.

Langland snorted, cutting her off. "Your grandfather, I know. Child, I'm not a total *idjit*." She chuckled dryly. "You're asking if Jim would get involved in a 'black' project? Mister 'The Taxpayers Have a Right to Know Where Their Tax Dollars Are Going'? *You* tell *me*."

Sam had to laugh out loud. Through her sleep-roughened throat, the sound came out something like a rusty gate. "No. No, I guess you're right."

"Of course I'm right." Langland sounded downright affronted. "It also explains why an outfit like Generro that looks like small potatoes might manage to attract some high-profile talent, huh? Hell, girl, I'd have *killed* to get involved with Aurora."

"You're probably right, Amy." Sam sighed. "Look, thanks. Okay?"

"Don't mention it." Langland's voice was gruff, as if she were embarrassed by Sam's thanks. "Just trying to help a sister. Get back to sleep, hear?" And she hung up.

Sam returned the handset to its cradle with another sigh. *Dead end.*

11

Sam was dreaming. She *knew* she was dreaming; she knew she was lying in bed in her apartment in Venice. But the knowledge didn't change anything. She couldn't alter the events of the dream; she couldn't shake herself free from it and return to the waking world.

She was back in the Generro Aerospace facility—she knew that too, somehow, even though she saw no familiar landmarks—walking through endless office hallways with Jacques Leclerc by her side. Leclerc was talking as they strolled, apparently with no particular destination in mind. She could hear his voice clearly, could hear the individual words he was saying, but somehow her brain was unable to put them together in any meaningful way. It was as if she'd lost the gift of language.

It was the same with the nameplates on the doors that they passed, and directional signs mounted on the walls. She could recognize individual letters, and knew that they formed words that she *should* know, but they were as meaningless to her as if they'd been written in Cyrillic.

In her peripheral vision, she saw a flash of movement: one of the countless office doors opening. She glanced back just in time to see a figure dart back into the office, closing the door behind it. Someone familiar: Sid Warner? It had to be, she was sure of it.

The voice beside her changed its timbre. Momentarily, it was no longer Leclerc's faintly European accent, but a softer, less assured voice. For an instant, it reminded her of the young engineer she'd met that first day at Pop-Pop's house: Ernest Macintyre. She snapped her head around, but it was still the tall, dark figure of Jacques Leclerc who walked beside her. Even before she'd turned, his voice was back to normal.

The back of her neck prickled uncomfortably—*Someone staring at my grave,* that's how her mother had termed the feeling. Instinctively, she turned around and looked back.

Behind them, the corridor they'd walked stretched off to an impossible distance, miles or more, narrowing to a geometrical vanishing point. Someone was following them. With a strange and unshakable certainty, she knew the person had always been there, though she hadn't been consciously aware of it to this point. Though too far away to make out any details, she thought she recognized the person trailing behind them. *The way he walks, the way he moves . . . Pop-Pop.*

It was her grandfather following silently behind her. For a moment she considered running toward him, but then—in one of those transitions that can happen only in dreams—Pop-Pop, Leclerc and the endless hallway were all gone. She sat in Grendel, driving slowly through the main gate of the Generro facility, out onto the highway. Just like in real life, there was a large white truck approaching from the other direction—from the east. But this time the timing was different, and the truck rumbled right past Grendel as it turned into the Generro compound. Her facility for language hadn't returned. She couldn't read the logo emblazoned on the side of the white truck. But, somehow, the red-and-blue symbol looked very familiar.

Sam's eyes snapped open, then squinted to shut out the bright wash of morning sunlight across the white ceiling. With a muttered curse, she pulled the sheet over her face, rolled over and tried to burrow into the pillow.

Man, she thought, *weird dream. Nocturnal psychodrama, or what? A psychiatrist would have a field day with the symbols.* Like so many dreams, she knew, this one incorporated elements from real life, things she'd been thinking about or worrying about, but mutated and warped into archetypal forms.

Endless corridors? Obviously, that represented the mystery she was trying to solve. (And, now she came to think about it, so did the fact that she couldn't understand what Leclerc was saying, or what the signs on the walls meant.) Leclerc himself, and the fact they'd been at Generro Aerospace? No puzzle there: that was just a replay of actual events from the past day. The momentary appearance of Sid Warner? That was simply her suspicion that he was somehow central to the whole mystery, or at least involved in some way. Pop-Pop? Well, clearly he was the driving force behind the whole thing, the events surrounding his death the underlying reason for her actions.

Of course, there *were* a couple of things that she couldn't interpret so clearly. Why had Leclerc's voice momentarily changed to that of Macintyre? And why did she feel it was important that the truck looked somehow familiar?

The truck! She sat bolt upright in bed. Struggling to sort through her churning thoughts, she tried to form a mental picture of the truck she'd seen. The real one, not the dream image.

Slowly the details came back. It was a standard cargo van, the kind you'd see anywhere, hauling bread or vegetables or office supplies. Or furniture. Even though the angle hadn't been ideal, she *had* caught a glimpse of the truck's side, she realized now: she just hadn't paid it any attention. Now she concentrated on the details she remembered. *Yes, there* was *something on the side of the truck,* she realized. *A name or a logo, painted in bright red and blue.*

Like the logo on the moving truck that had carried away Pop-Pop's mementos. Yes, in her mind's eye the logos looked identical. *It* was *a Jones Cartage truck that was turning in at Generro Aerospace!*

Then reality washed over her like a cold wave. *Get a grip, Dooley,* she told herself disgustedly. *So* what *if it was the same company? That doesn't imply any kind of connection. Surely Jones Cartage has lots of clients. Assuming a connection is as stupid as*—she searched for an analogy—*as assuming that two people in different states are in league with each other because they both rented a car from Hertz.* She flopped back onto the pillow.

Still, a new thought bubbled up without warning, *there* is *an angle I've been neglecting. . . .*

The Rogers Museum of Flight. If Generro itself was the dead end that Amy Langland thought it was, maybe there was some kind of clue that she could pick up in Rogers. Partially reassured that she had at least one possible course to follow, she rolled over and tried to return to sleep.

Rogers was a tiny town just off Route 58, sixty-odd miles north-northeast of downtown Los Angeles. Between the towns of Boron and Four Corners, it was right on the boundary of Edwards Air Force Base. As she cruised eastward toward the Cady Mountains, Samantha heard the distinctive ripping howl of high-speed aircraft echoing through the desert air. As always, the sound made her smile: *The sound of power, the sound of freedom.*

Three miles east of Boron, she turned south off the highway. Rogers was a typical, small, central-California town—*the kind of place where kids grow up dreaming of leaving,* she thought a little wryly. *A good place to be from.* The town comprised a single main street, with a few cars angle-parked in front of the drugstore and a few more in front of a dusty-windowed Pay-'n'-Pak. A small motel—the unimaginatively named Desert Inn, which looked as if it had seen better days—stood forlornly near the entrance to town. Sam drove slowly along the main drag. Only a couple of people were braving the heat on the sidewalks, which was bordering on the uncomfortable even now, around seven in the evening. Several of them watched without curiosity as the white Mustang crept by.

The Museum of Flight was in the center of town, across the street from a Mr. Frosty with its windows boarded up. The building probably used to be a bank, Sam figured as she parked her car out front and rummaged in her pocket for a quarter to feed the meter. It had that blocky, institutional look. The concrete facade had been repainted in the last couple of years, but the date inscribed into the lintel indicated the building had been built soon after the Depression.

She looked askance at the smallish structure. *What am I doing wasting my time here?* she asked herself, shaking her head. She pulled at the fabric of her shirt, stuck to the perspiration on her back and across her shoulders. *Get me back on the highway.*

A hand-lettered sign on the door indicated that the museum was open until seven-thirty in the evening. That gave her only half an hour. Not enough time to go through a *real* museum, but probably more than enough for this one. She pushed the glass door open and stepped in.

The air inside was cool, almost cold, and she felt the perspiration chill on her back. In contrast to the bright sunlight on the street, the interior of the building seemed gloomy. She stopped in the doorway, blinking until her eyes adapted.

Despite its somewhat grandiose name, Sam's first glimpse of the Museum of Flight was underwhelming. It comprised a single large room—"gallery" might be the correct word, she thought—no more than sixty feet long and forty wide. Most of the illumination came from fluorescent lights mounted along the walls, a couple of feet below the ceiling. The walls themselves were bright enough, but the center of the room was heavy with shadows.

She'd been right, she saw immediately as she looked around: this had almost certainly been a bank. The floor was terrazzo, a simple geometric tessellation of black and white shapes. The ceiling was high, maybe twice the height of a man, with a central cupola at least half again as high. Four skylights in the cupola, almost opaque with a coating of grime, let in feeble beams of sunlight, clearly defined in the dusty air. Sam felt a sick bitterness in her stomach. *Pop-Pop bequeathed his mementos—his* memories*—to this place?*

Something moved in the relative gloom ahead of her. She squinted, and for the first time she noticed a desk. A figure was rising from behind it, moving eagerly toward her. She looked the man over as he approached. *The curator?* He was short and dumpy-looking, the top of his balding head level with Sam's eyes. He wore a steel-gray suit with narrow lapels, its cut looking dated, like a photograph from the 1950s. Round glasses caught the light, momentarily hiding his eyes. For an instant, Sam had the strange feeling that the man was somehow not real, just a facade, like a figure in a wax museum. Then the feeling was gone. The curator smiled up at her. "Welcome, welcome," he said heartily, rubbing his hands together with what looked like glee. "Welcome to the Museum of Flight."

"Uh . . . hi." Sam hesitated a little uncomfortably, then, unable to think of what else to do, stuck out her hand. "Hi, Mr. . . ."

The man's eyebrows twitched uncertainly for a moment, as though at a loss as to how he should respond. Then his smile broadened and he grasped her hand. His grip was firm, unexpectedly so. Surprised, Sam looked at the man's hand. The fingers were slender, almost delicate, but the wrist was thick and ridged with tendons that looked like steel rudder-cables under the skin. She blinked in surprise. "Fighter jock's wrist"—that's what she'd always termed the hypertrophy of muscles and tendons characteristic of long-time fighter pilots, developed over years of controlling a stick. *Was this wonk a fighter jock?*

"I'm Timothy Howe," the smiling man said, releasing her hand and stepping back. "Welcome to the Museum of Flight," he repeated. "What can I do for you this fine evening?" He shifted on the balls of his feet, practically bouncing with eagerness.

Sam suppressed a smile. "My name's Sa . . ."—on impulse, she changed her mind in mid-word—"Sandra Dillon," she went on. She paused; if Howe had noticed her slight bobble with the name, he didn't show it. Reassured, she continued. "I was passing through, and I thought"—she shrugged casually—"I'd just stop in for a few minutes."

He nodded. "Of course, of course. Is there anything in particular I can show you?"

"I don't know, Mr. Howe." She looked around in feigned curiosity. "Is there anything in particular that's interesting?"

Howe chuckled, a faint, dry sound. "I'd say 'a lot,' but then of course I'm biased." He paused. "I take it you have some interest in the history of aviation, otherwise you wouldn't be here."

Sam shrugged, again casually, as if the question was almost irrelevant. "Some, I suppose," she said lightly. "I've always liked planes. *Fast* planes."

"Fast planes?" Howe rubbed his hands together again. "Did you know, Ms. Dillion, that Edwards Air Force Base—that's right near here, you probably drove past it—

has traditionally been the home of some of the fastest planes in the world? It's right here, for example, that Chuck Yeager first broke the sound barrier in 1947, in the Bell X–1. . . ." Gently grasping her arm, and still talking, he led her toward a set of photographs on one of the walls.

The wonk does *know his stuff,* Samantha had to admit after an exhaustive tour of the museum. He'd seemed personally and intimately familiar with the provenance, history and background of just about every exhibit in the place. There were only a couple of pictures or models that didn't elicit some brief anecdote or piece of trivia from Timothy Howe. Sam had heard most of them before—though she had to make the sounds of surprise and appreciation that the curator would expect from a non-aviator—but she came to appreciate the man's dry, sometimes ironic delivery. On a couple of occasions, he put enough of a twist on a familiar story that she chuckled aloud in genuine amusement.

Throughout the tour—which didn't take that long; the museum was just one room, after all—she kept a weather eye out for anything that had come from Pop-Pop's house. By the time Howe finally wound down, she'd recognized some photographs that could only have come from Jim Dooley's collection, but not many. Glass display cases contained a couple of plane models that could have been his as well, but there was nothing categorically distinctive about them.

The thing that Sam found most puzzling was that the only items identifiable from Pop-Pop's collection had come from his outer study or from the walls elsewhere in his house. Nowhere did she see any of the unique photos or other items from his concealed inner study. *Why not?* she wondered. *You'd think some of those would be the most interesting, from a museum curator's perspective. Amelia Earhart, Albert Einstein—real historical figures.*

"This is wonderful," she gushed, when Howe had finished his tour. "There's so much *history* here, I can practically *feel* it." (*Don't lay it on* too *thick, Dooley,* she cautioned herself dryly.) "Where do you get all this wonderful stuff?" she asked as casually as she could manage.

"From all sorts of places, really," the curator answered. "From various archives. From the air force and from

NASA directly. And sometimes private owners or collectors donate material to us."

"Donate?"

"Surely," Howe confirmed. "Some of these photographs I just showed you, for example: they were given to the museum by an old friend of aviation." He gestured toward some of Pop-Pop's photographs.

"Just the photographs?"

Howe shot her a sharp, curious glance, his eyeglasses flashing like tiny heliographs. For an instant, Sam feared she'd gone too far. But then the curator's smile returned as he shook his head. "No, as a matter of fact," he said smoothly, "there were some other items as well." He shrugged his narrow shoulders. "But we have to be very selective, you understand. We have limited space. We can only display the exhibits that we judge will have the most interest to visitors. The rest we keep in our permanent collection." He waved a slender hand toward the rear wall of the display gallery.

"You mean you have more stuff?" Sam injected a healthy dose of enthusiasm into her voice. "Can I see the rest, too?"

Howe shook his head again, his lips twisting into an apologetic frown. "I'm sorry, Ms. Dillon, really I am, but the permanent collection isn't on display. It's stored in boxes and crates in the back, I'm afraid." He sighed. "We're hoping to move to larger facilities at some point, and then maybe we'll be able to display all our treasures. But for the moment. . . ." He shrugged again.

"Can I just take a quick look? I'd love to see the back room of a museum, with all those boxes and crates." The dumb-enthusiastic act was wearing a little thin, but Sam forced herself to see it through. *I'll gargle with whiskey later to get the saccharine taste out of my mouth,* she promised herself. "It's probably like that scene at the end of *Raiders of the Lost Ark,* isn't it?" She started walking toward the rear wall of the gallery. "Can we look?"

"I'm sorry, Ms. Dillon, really, but I can't." Howe smiled, almost paternally.

Sam looked crestfallen. "You think I'm going to steal something?"

"Of course not, of course not. It's for your safety, really,

Ms. Dillon. There are things to trip over back there, or hit your head against, or cut yourself on. Our insurance company would be all over me if I let you go back there. You understand?"

She shrugged. "I suppose. It's just too bad, though." She glanced at her watch. It was almost 20:00 hours. She'd already kept the curator after hours, but she was determined to find out what the museum had done with the rest of Pop-Pop's collection. The final piece of a plan to satisfy her curiosity suddenly fell into place in her head. "I'm sorry I kept you late, Mr. Howe. I enjoyed the tour." Sam hesitated shyly, then flashed the curator her best childlike smile. "Can I keep you just a little bit longer, while I go to the little girls' room?"

The tritium paint on the hands of Samantha's watch showed up clearly in the deep shadow of the blocky building. It was coming up on midnight, four hours since she'd watched Timothy Howe lock up the Museum of Flight behind him as he left for the night. Giving the curator one last, cheerful wave, she'd climbed into Grendel and driven away down the main drag, off toward the highway.

A couple of miles later, she'd pulled over to the side of the road and killed the engine, first powering up the convertible top to keep warm as the desert radiated its heat into the clear night sky. She'd reclined the driver's seat and tried to nap, setting her watch alarm.

The alarm had woken her at 23:00. Climbing out of the car to stretch her legs, she'd taken a few moments to stare in unabashed wonder at the stars—crisp, clear, almost harsh, like razor-sharp shards of diamond against the pitch-black velvet of the desert night. Then she'd climbed back into Grendel and driven slowly back toward the town of Rogers.

She'd parked on the outskirts of town, pulling the car off the road into the desert scrub. The white convertible would glare like a beacon in the headlights of any passing car, she knew, but she didn't have the time—or, when it came right down to it, the ambition—to conceal the vehicle. Keeping to the soft gravel shoulder, she'd walked into town.

As she'd expected, the place had been as deserted as a ghost town. Even some of the streetlights had been dark and dead. (Sam had chuckled softly to herself. *Has there ever been a small town where they* don't *roll up the side-walks at sundown?*) She'd hurried down the main street, reaching the museum building in a couple of minutes, and melted into the inky shadows beside it. Now here she was, crouching on the hard ground, her back against the gritty concrete wall.

The small window of the women's washroom was still open, its wooden casement held from closing by the wad of damp paper towels she'd shoved into its track four hours earlier. For the first time since she'd decided to sneak back after the museum closed, Sam thought about what she was doing. She'd done a lot of different things in her life, taken a lot of chances, but none of them had been quite so obviously illegal and *premeditated—and,* she decided, *I really don't want to examine that thought too closely just now. I'll think later about the kind of person I'm becoming.* She grabbed the sill, pulled herself up and squirmed through the window into the dark museum.

She crouched on the tile floor of the small bathroom, feeling the pitch darkness like a physical shroud, heavy around her. She stretched her senses to their limits—listening, *feeling,* for any hints of movement or presence in the building. *Nothing.* After almost a minute, she let herself relax the slightest bit. The building might not be totally deserted—there might be a patrolling security guard, for example—but it certainly *felt* like she was the only person here. She reached into her pocket and took out the penlight she'd retrieved from Grendel's glove box before parking the car. She smiled. *Semper paratis,* she thought wryly. *Be prepared, the old Boy Scout motto. Of course, when I created my "car emergency kit," I didn't expect I'd be using it for breaking and entering.* She turned on the small light—the metallic *snick* of the switch startlingly loud in her ears—and twisted the collar to reduce the beam to the size of a quarter. She wished the light had a rheostat to turn down the intensity of the bulb—her eyes were well night-adapted, after all—but this model didn't have that feature.

Silently, she crossed to the door and pushed it open a crack, then listened. Still no sound. She put her eye to the crack, and saw nothing but darkness: no faint, shifting light that might indicate a guard with a flashlight. Reassured, she pushed the door open and stepped out into the corridor.

So well-adapted was Sam's eyesight that, when she reached the museum's main gallery, she didn't need her penlight. A red Exit sign burned over the front door, casting enough light for her to find her way through the display cases. On impulse, she looked up. The grime-frosted skylights of the cupola seemed to glow faintly, as if with their own internal light. Starlight, she knew; but still, the effect seemed almost magical. Despite herself, she smiled.

Weaving silently between the display cases, she made her way to the back of the gallery. During Howe's tour, she'd spotted the door that must lead to the storage areas where the museum's "permanent collection" was kept. Now, she examined that door with her penlight.

There was nothing particularly secure about the door, nothing to distinguish it from a door you'd find in any house. There didn't even seem to be a lock, just a regular doorknob. She reached out to turn it, then hesitated. *Maybe there's an alarm.* Quickly, she played the beam of her penlight around the frame of the door, looking for wiring or traces of installed contacts. Nothing caught her eye—*But maybe that just means it's well concealed.*

She shook her head with a snort of disgust. *Pretty paranoid, Dooley,* she chided herself. *This is the Museum of Flight in* Rogers, *not Fort Knox.* She grasped the doorknob and turned it.

No siren or bell split the night; no lights flashed in her eyes. She pushed the door open a hand-span, grateful that the hinges were well oiled and silent, and waited. Again, there was nothing but darkness and silence beyond the door. The drumbeat of her own pulse was the loudest sound in the building, maybe the entire town. Forcing herself to take a deep, calming breath, she pushed the door wide open and stepped through.

As she flashed the penlight around her, she chuckled softly, remembering her comment to Timothy Howe. She'd compared the museum back room to the warehouse scene in *Raiders of the Lost Ark. Yeah, right! It is to laugh.* Instead of a cavernous depot larger than an aircraft hangar, she found herself in a cluttered, dusty area not much larger than her own apartment. The wooden crates and cardboard boxes stacked haphazardly around her made it hard to be sure, but she estimated the room to be about half the size of the main gallery. The floor underfoot was concrete, gritty with dust. The ceiling was unfinished; girders and construction elements cast harsh geometric shadows in her penlight beam when she pointed it upward.

Sam paused. Deep down, she supposed, she'd been expecting that the "permanent collection" would be arranged in an orderly fashion, more or less like the collection that was actually on display. Not so, she saw immediately. If there was any organization or order at all to the uneven stacks of boxes, it wasn't visible to the casual observer. *I've seen friends' basements that are better organized than this.* Her heart sank. It was going to be much harder than she'd expected to find any sign of Pop-Pop's mementos. She moved between the piled boxes, silent as a ghost.

Unfortunate metaphor. She stopped, the short hairs along her spine shifting and prickling. A feeling that had been flickering around the periphery of her consciousness suddenly coalesced and grew strong. A chill seemed to run over her skin.

A museum at night: what a lonely, creepy *place.* She was surrounded by memories, she realized, other people's memories. In many cases, the only things that remained to bear witness to their lives. Photographs, cherished possessions. . . . *It's like a mausoleum,* she thought suddenly. *I'm surrounded by the dead.*

And in some ways, she realized, it was *worse* than a mausoleum. *A graveyard holds physical remains. But a physical body isn't who a person* is. *A person is hopes and dreams, thoughts and memories . . . and that's what surrounds me.*

If I were a ghost, I'd haunt a museum rather than a mausoleum any day. . . .

With an effort, she reined in her thoughts. *Flights of fancy, Dooley,* she told herself sternly. *Save your metaphysical woolgathering for a better time and place.* She breathed deeply, the scent of the air sharp with dust. She forced herself to look around, to see the storage area as it really was. *Nothing but boxes,* she told herself firmly, *no more significant than a large rummage sale.* The sense of past lives, of presence, of the persistence of memory—all faded away in an instant. She moved on.

She reached the back wall of the storage area a few moments later and saw, not the bare concrete blocks she'd expected, but the kind of light modular wall common in modern offices. A single, closed door penetrated the wall. Sam hesitated, estimating distances in her mind. If she hadn't lost track, this wall was fifteen or twenty feet short of the rear of the building. That meant this door shouldn't lead out onto the back alley, but to another room. *Another storage area? The curator's office?* She reached out and tried the doorknob, felt no surprise to find it was locked. *Okay,* she told herself, *now we get creative.* She crouched down and examined the locking mechanism in the beam of her penlight.

It was the simplest of locks, she saw at once, nothing high-tech or high-security. It wasn't even a dead bolt, just a standard tongue lock with the keyhole mounted in the center of the doorknob. Once more, she checked around the frame of the door for any indication of an alarm, but this time her scan was perfunctory. *When there's nothing worth stealing, why bother with security?*

From her hip pocket, she pulled out another component of her car emergency kit, a large, elaborate Swiss army–style knife. After a moment's inspection, she unfolded a broad, flat blade made of flexible spring steel, rather like an artist's palette knife. Carefully, she inserted the thin strip of metal between the door and the frame just below the lock, working it in deeply. Then she slid it upward, applying a little inward leverage. The blade engaged on the tongue of the lock. For a few moments she worked the blade delicately, trying to imagine that the steel possessed continuations of the nerves in her fingertips. *Just a little more. . . .* With her other hand, holding the penlight in her teeth, she grasped the doorknob and pulled gently. The lock disengaged with the faintest of clicks, and the door opened. Quickly, she closed her knife and returned it to her pocket. She pushed the door wide and stepped into the darkness.

12

As she flashed the penlight around the room, she felt a momentary sense of déjà vu. *I've been here before. . . .*

Then she realized what had prompted that feeling. *Pop-Pop's inner sanctum,* she thought, that's *what it reminds me of.*

The room in which she'd found herself was shorter than she'd expected—not much more than ten feet from the doorway in which she stood to the far wall—but it was the full width of the building. As she swung her penlight around the room, the beam fell on glass display cases, on models of planes and other devices hanging from the ceiling, on framed photographs mounted on the walls. She took a step forward, then stopped, puzzled. *Another museum? But Howe said. . . .*

The thought trailed off. *No,* she told herself, *the room only* looked *like a museum.* In its superficial details, it was very much like the main gallery. But this gallery *felt* very different.

She stepped forward again, felt pile carpeting give under her feet, instead of bare concrete or terrazzo, and shined her penlight over the pictures on the nearest wall. They were portraits, she saw, posed and professionally composed. Most were photographs, but the collection included a couple of oil paintings. She reached out and touched the frame of the nearest portrait, a painting of a slender-faced woman with a 1960s-style bouffant hairdo. The frame was rich and heavy, finely crafted from a wood with a beautiful, strong grain to it. There was no nameplate or plaque identifying this woman—or any of the other subjects, for that matter—as if anyone who entered this room would automatically recognize her. *But I don't.*

Another detail caught Sam's eye. Across the upper right corner of the frame was a strip of purple velvet, rather like a prize ribbon. She stepped back, and scanned her light down the row of portraits. About two-thirds of them had purple velvet ribbons on a corner.

What does this remind me of? She closed her eyes for a moment as she searched her memories. There was *something,* she knew, something from the past. It lurked just beyond the periphery of conscious thought. With a snort of frustration, she opened her eyes again and moved slowly along the row of portraits.

She stopped with a jerk. Her skin felt suddenly cold. *My God, I* do *recognize some of these people. . . .*

The painting she was standing in front of showed a handsome man in his early thirties, given a rather piratical appearance by the black patch over his left eye. *That's Wiley Post,* she realized, mentally naming a famous American aviator who'd been the first man to fly solo around the world, back in 1933. And a couple of frames down, the thin-faced man with the intense eyes and the brush mustache—*That's another one who'd look at home with a cutlass between his teeth,* she decided—had to be Howard Hughes, a famed aviator in his own right. Both of those portraits were marked with the purple ribbon. Again she moved on, farther down the line.

And again she stopped as if her feet had been frozen to the floor.

Pop-Pop . . . Pop-Pop, it's you.

A young, vibrant James R. Dooley, Sr., grinned insouciently at her from a life-sized oil painting. Through tear-blurred eyes, she saw the purple ribbon adorning the corner of Pop-Pop's portrait. It seemed fresh and new, its color more saturated than those that marked other pictures.

That's it. The thought struck her with an almost physical blow. *I'm in a shrine. A shrine to heroes of aviation. A purple ribbon means they're dead.* A new idea flashed through her mind. *I wonder if. . . .*

She moved rapidly along the wall, scanning each portrait. More than half of them were familiar, now she knew what she was looking at. Charles Lindbergh, Richard Byrd, Fred Noonan. . . . She pulled up short before a portrait of a tall, rangy man in his early thirties, his thick hair already starting to silver. Bright gray eyes seemed to sparkle amidst the network of shallow wrinkles that the years would carve so much deeper. "So good to see you again, Simon Warner,"

Samantha whispered. She ran a finger delicately around the wooden frame, pausing for a moment at the bare upper right corner.

A shrine. She stared into the portrait's unseeing eyes. This *is where you were planning to bring Pop-Pop's ashes, wasn't it?* she asked the picture silently. *"A place to honor the names of people who've pushed the envelope . . . among his colleagues and comrades," that's what you said, wasn't it? Where else could you have meant but here?* She looked back at the portrait of Post. *Wiley, are your ashes here too?*

But where was "here"? *What* was it? A shrine, granted—but whose? Who had established it, and why? *Timothy Howe?* She shook her head. Not him alone. *If I look long enough, will I find a picture of you when you were in* your *prime, Timothy . . . ?*

She scanned her penlight around the walls once more, quickly estimating the number of portraits. *Forty, give or take.*

What do you have to do to get your picture mounted here? What club do you have to join? What criteria do you have to meet? She snorted. *Every time I get close to an answer, all I get are more goddamned questions.*

Frustrated, she spun away from the portrait-lined wall, turning her flashlight on the display cases arrayed throughout the middle of the room. She examined the contents of the first couple of cases. One held a small leather-bound journal, open somewhere near the middle. In the illumination of her penlight, Sam could hardly make out the spider-scratches of crabbed handwriting. Age had yellowed the paper, and faded the ink to a shadowy sepia tone. Stains—water, perhaps—obliterated whole sections of the page. The binding itself looked brittle, charred and discolored in places as if it had been exposed to great heat.

Sam leaned closer, until her nose almost touched the glass case. "*. . . even cut in front of a couple of men with more seniority in the VGL than I have,*" she puzzled out with some difficulty. *"How doesn't really matter. Within minutes, I was wedging myself into the cramped, canvas seat of the cockpit. As two technicians closed the heavy canopy over me, through the quartz glass I could see. . . ."* A stain obliterated several lines. She skimmed down the page, and continued reading where she found intact text.

". . . inside the cockpit myself, the shift was infinitely more intense—almost like a plane dropping when it loses lift, except that this 'drop' was in a direction I never knew existed. For an instant, there was nothingness . . ." And then another stain made it impossible to read further.

A diary of some kind, Sam realized. She glanced down at the small brass plaque that identified the exhibit. PERSONAL JOURNAL OF FREDERICK J. NOONAN (1900–37), JANUARY 1936 TO MAY 1937. VGL CAT. # 335–006.

Samantha blinked. Fred Noonan? That was the name of Amelia Earhart's navigator on the final flight that led to her disappearance. *It couldn't be the same Fred Noonan, could it?* She looked at the display again. According to the plaque, *this* Frederick J. Noonan had died in 1937, the same year as Earhart's last flight. *In fact,* she remembered suddenly, *didn't she fly in late May of that year?*

She shook her head. *Interesting.* She looked at the plaque again. *What's this "VGL"?* she asked herself. Sam had a vague notion that she should recognize the abbreviation as belongiong to *some kind of group or association, but she had no idea what it stood for: V-something G-something Library?* She looked around her again. *Could* this *be the VGL?*

Well, I'm not going to find any answers gaping like a gaffed fish. She forced herself to move on.

The next case contained a model—not the replica plane she expected, but something that looked like a cross between a large steam boiler and a hyperbaric chamber. A submarine-style hatch, with a heavy locking wheel, dominated one end, while a small reinforced porthole marked one side. *And just what the hell is* this *supposed to be? Some kind of archaic bathyscaph, maybe?* She checked the brass identification plaque.

EARLY PROTOTYPE, SYSTEM ONE UFT TRANSPORTER COCKPIT, 1935. VGL CAT. # 032–298.

There it was again, the abbreviation "VGL". And another one, too, this time: "UFT." Sam hesitated. *"UFT": that sounds familiar.* Memory returned with a rush, but left her shaking her head ruefully. *The "UFT" I'm thinking of is "Unified Field Theory,"* she realized. *And that doesn't make any sense in this context.* Adding it to her mental list of mysteries, she moved on.

And yet again she stopped in her tracks. The feeling

of déjà vu was back, but coupled with it was the kind of phantasmagoric dissociation that came from nightmares. The case before her looked, in many ways, like the displays of "moon rocks" that had toured the continent in the early 1970s after the Apollo 11 lunar landing. There were the same small pieces of crystalline rock against plain black backgrounds, with the picture mounted at the back of the case showing where the rocks had come from.

But these weren't the gray-white of lunar rock samples. The three matchbook-sized stones glinted with a brilliant blue-green hue—*Almost cyan,* Sam thought—that she'd never seen before in any mineral or precious stone. And the picture that identified their origin ... *it was the "science-fiction painting" she'd seen in Pop-Pop's inner sanctum.* The mighty ocean, the monolithic rock spires soaring a thousand yards out of the water, the black-sand beach textured with lines of blue-green ... all were the same as she remembered. As she stared, open-mouthed, she realized that the brilliant cyan of the rock samples exactly matched the hue of the lines texturing the beach.

What in the name of all that's holy is going on *here ... ?*

This had to be some kind of overblown hoax, some complex practical joke ... didn't it? But a joke on whom? *Me? Get real, Dooley.* Somebody had gone to entirely too much trouble for this to be a joke. A movie set, then? She shook her head. No, that didn't hang together either. *This is serious.* Somebody *takes it seriously, at least.*

Holy crap, what was that? She heard something, the soft cadence of approaching footfalls. And she instantly realized she'd *been* hearing them for some time, for at least a couple of seconds. She cursed silently. *Damn it, Dooley, this is no time to fall asleep at the stick!* She held her breath for a moment, trying to judge distance and direction.

The pace of the footsteps was slow, casual. In her mind's eye, she saw a fat, sloppy security guard strolling lethargically through the museum gallery. Judging by the volume of the sound, she figured the guard was some distance away—he'd probably just come into the storage area from the main gallery, she guessed—but the sound was getting closer. She moved quickly to the door of the shrine, or private museum, or "VGL," or whatever it was and glanced out.

Yes, she could see a shifting light, silhouetting the untidy piles of boxes and crates. A flashlight, obviously. She watched the shadows' movements for a few seconds, confirming distance and direction. Unless she was misjudging really badly, the guard was making his slow way around the periphery of the storage area in a clockwise direction. That meant he'd be approaching this door from Sam's right. In the moment before she turned off her own flashlight, she stood for a moment in the doorway, looking back into the room as she reached to close the door.

And, for the fourth time that night, she froze as though her muscles were suddenly paralyzed. Her mouth worked silently.

It took all of her willpower to break that paralysis, to point the beam of her penlight directly at the object that had caught her attention and shocked her so deeply. Yes, she hadn't been mistaken. *Oh, my God. . . .*

The guard's footsteps were drawing nearer. In a second or two, he'd see her light. Sam bit her lip, hard, the sudden pain driving away the lassitude of her mental shock. *Later,* she told herself sharply, *I'll think about it later.* She held the penlight to her belly, muffling the sharp *snick* of the switch with her flesh. Pulling the door silently shut behind her, she ghosted her way through the storage area, heading for the door. Even as she hurried through the silent museum and clambered out into the night through the washroom window, her mind was filled with the image of what she'd seen. As she sprinted silently back to where she'd left Grendel, she couldn't shake from her memory the knowing smile on the framed portrait of Amy Langland.

Samantha powered down her window as soon as she was back on the highway, trusting the rush of crisp night air to blow away some of her mental cobwebs. Already, doubt was starting to eat away at the certainty she'd felt just minutes earlier. *Maybe I was wrong. Maybe it was someone who only* looked *like Amy Langland. . . .*

But then she shut that train of thought down, *hard.* "Get a grip," she told herself sharply, the sound of her own voice almost as refreshing as the chill air. "I know what I saw. That was Amy."

It made sense in a way. She still didn't know what the

hell was going on, in terms of the big picture. The big questions—What is the VGL? for example—were still unanswered. But in terms of internal consistency, it made a kind of strange and twisted sense to see Amy's picture there.

Let's take it by the numbers, Sam told herself, striving to keep herself calm and her thoughts under tight control. *Assume that Pop-Pop and Sid Warner are both members of this VGL, whatever it is. Pop-Pop wanted me to read his journal, because it would explain everything. Warner probably wanted the journal—like he wanted Pop-Pop's ashes—to go in the VGL's museum or shrine.* It also made more sense that Pop-Pop would bequeath his precious photographs to the shrine, rather than to the meaningless shell that was the Rogers Museum of Flight. *Suddenly, so much makes sense.*

What about Amy Langland's connection, then? The links were a lot more tenuous, but . . . *Assume that Amelia Earhart was part of this VGL,* Sam mused. *That explains the photo of her in Pop-Pop's inner sanctum. And it fits in with the apparent fact that Fred Noonan was also a VGL member. Since Earhart was one of the founders of the 99s, might that not imply that the 99s themselves—or* some *of them, at least—were, and maybe still are, a kind of "women's auxiliary" for the VGL?* Obviously, not all the 99s had a VGL connection. No one had ever approached Samantha about it, and she was confident that Maggie wasn't involved.

But assuming that Langland *was* connected with the VGL explained some interesting anomalies too. *There was always something that bothered me about Amy's first phone call,* Sam remembered, *I just didn't think very hard about it.* Maybe Maggie *hadn't* told Amy that Sam was researching the people who'd visited her grandfather. Maybe Langland had heard from other sources—*from her VGL colleagues, perhaps*—that Sam was digging into matters best left unexamined. *That would certainly explain Amy's hesitation—her* confusion*—when I asked if Mags had told her. She didn't know that Mags was working the grapevine, because Mags had never even talked to her about it.*

Sam ground her teeth. So that meant that Langland's whole purpose in contacting Sam was to put her safely off the track, off the trail of the VGL. *God*damn *it. I've been* *played for a* fool*!* Her knuckles whitened on Grendel's wheel, and her gaze flicked to the blue-green LEDs of the Mustang's clock. *I think it's time to pay Amy Langland a visit,* she thought coldly. *Real soon.*

The clock on Grendel's dash read 07:45. From where she was in Griffith Park, Sam had watched the pink flood of dawn wash over the city-world that was the Los Angeles basin. Her eyes were gritty, her muscles sore from spending so many hours in the car.

She'd arrived at this lookout near the observatory at three in the morning. For hours she'd sat, staring out over the sea of lights, thinking. Her mind had seemed to be running overspeed, as though a governor had been released on an engine. Physically tired, she'd known there wasn't a hope that she'd be able to sleep if she drove the additional forty-five minutes to Venice. Her energy had been up, her body buzzing as if she'd downed three pots of coffee on an empty stomach. She'd looked down on the district of Los Feliz spread out below her, wondering which light might represent Amy Langland's house. When the sun rose high enough that the air began to warm, she'd powered down Grendel's rag top and relished the sweet-spicy scent of the arid terrain. Insects had buzzed and creaked, greeting the start of a new day.

Langland was an early riser; Sam remembered that from their conversation the first time they met, in Kansas City half a decade before. She turned the key, and Grendel rumbled to life. Slowly, she drove down the winding roads that flanked the arroyos of Griffith Park, out onto Los Feliz Boulevard. She'd already looked up Aloha Street in the *James Guide* she kept under her driver's seat—an absolute necessity for even lifelong Angelenos—and had the directions memorized. Within ten minutes, she was cruising slowly up a steep hill, checking house numbers.

She found Langland's house near the top of the hill. From the road, all she could see was a white wall—some kind of artificial adobe, it looked like—with a brown double gate presumably leading to a garage. Beside it was a smaller "postern gate" with an intercom unit mounted beside it. There was nothing visible of the house itself. Sam figured it had to be one of those characteristic California structures, built down the slope of a steep hill, with the entrance giving access to the top floor. She parked Grendel close against the high curb, killed the engine and climbed out.

She paused in front of the intercom, going over in her mind one last time the way she was going to approach her conversation with Amy. She took a moment to pat the hard, rectangular bulge in her shirt pocket—a purchase from one of the 24-hour "everything markets" that dotted Los Angeles—to reassure herself it was both safe and concealed. Squaring her shoulders, she pressed the buzzer.

Langland's voice answered almost immediately. "Yes?"

"It's me, Amy," Sam said, striving to keep her voice light and casual. "Samantha Dooley. Do you have a few minutes to talk?"

The older woman paused; Sam could almost hear her thinking. Then, "Of course, Samantha," Langland said. "Please, come in." Sam unlatched the door and stepped through.

Langland was waiting for her in the open front door of the house. The older woman was wearing a terry-cloth housecoat that had seen better days, and her hair was flat on one side. Even so, she managed to seem somehow imperious. As Sam approached, Langland stepped aside and ushered her in.

The top floor of Langland's house was small—basically just the entryway, and a single open door leading to what looked like a study or library. Through the door, Sam could see a window that looked out over the hilly Los Feliz area. Wordlessly, Langland gestured toward the flight of stairs heading down.

Sam led the way downstairs, Langland close behind her. The next floor was considerably larger. The staircase opened into a spacious, comfortable living room. Doors opened off the large room, and the rich aroma of coffee wafted from one of them.

Langland waved Sam over toward a couch upholstered in cream-colored brocade. "I've just had my breakfast," she said. "Want some coffee?" Sam nodded, and the older woman vanished into the kitchen.

Sam settled herself on the couch and looked the place over. The house was apparently quite old, but Langland had renovated it nicely. The plaster walls and ceiling were freshly painted, and only the fact that some of the corners had settled out of true hinted that the building wasn't new. The hardwood floor was marked from years of use, but the blemishes only seemed to add character.

Langland reappeared, handing Sam a mug of coffee. "Hope you take it black. I'm fresh out of sugar and milk."

"Black's fine," Sam assured her, as the slender-boned woman seated herself in an armchair.

Langland's eyes were sharp—*Like those of a bird of prey,* Sam thought suddenly—as she scrutinized the younger woman. Finally, she said, "Well? What is it you need to talk about?"

Sam braced herself. "I want to talk to you about the VGL," she said flatly, her gaze steady on Langland's face.

The aging pilot's expression didn't change. Yet Sam felt sure that *something* had happened behind those dark, bright eyes. "What do you want to know?" she asked. "It's public knowledge that the Virtual Geographic League funds exploration and various kinds of research, kind of like the National Geographic Society. What more can I tell you, and why are you asking me?"

Sam thought fast. *Okay, I guess just because I don't know about an organization doesn't mean it doesn't exist. The easiest way Amy can stonewall my bluff is to feed me some palatable lie about what the VGL is. Even if what she's telling me is true, I know it's not the whole story. It took all her force of will not to smile. Let's see how far we can push this.*

"You know what I'm talking about, Amy. Sam let a hint of steel creep into her voice. "I *know,* I've *seen*. I know you're all members, all of you. Pop-Pop. Simon Warner. Lindbergh, Post, Noonan, Hughes. And *you*, Amy. The VGL might be a public organization, but it's got a secret agenda. I *know,* Amy," she grated again. "I know about the UFT cockpit. . . ."

Sam paused as Langland flinched. "Did Leclerc . . . ?" The woman stared at Sam, then closed her mouth with an audible snap and shrugged. "He's always talking about his pet theories to people who don't understand his enthusiasms."

Sam struggled to keep her own reaction from showing on her face. *Leclerc? Then Generro* is *involved. . . .* She forced a knowing smile onto her face. "No," she said quietly,

"Leclerc didn't tell me anything." She chuckled. "Don't underestimate the contacts I've developed, Amy. That would be a mistake."

"I still don't know what you're talking about," Langland blustered. "As far as I know, the Virtual Geographic League is just what it says it is."

Samantha laughed out loud. "It's too late for that, Amy," she snapped. "Don't humiliate yourself, and don't insult my intelligence." She let scorn tinge her voice. "At least let's see if the sisterhood of the 99s can stretch *that* far, shall we?"

"I . . ." Langland began, then trailed off. "I . . ."

"I respect the honor that the VGL gave Pop-Pop," Sam said, taking a sudden tangent in an attempt to unsettle Langland even further.

Langland blinked, obviously caught off-guard, and answered, "The League takes care of its own."

This is working. I've got to keep hitting her from different directions, Sam told herself. *Don't let her catch her breath, get her mental balance. But how long can I keep it up, without showing how little I really know . . . ?*

"You know," she began again, "I think it was the rocks that amazed me the most—the crystals from that black beach."

"You've seen the museum?" Langland asked faintly.

Sam nodded. "Mr. Howe was most enlightening." She held her breath.

Langland gasped, and Sam knew her gamble had paid off. "Howe *showed* you?"

"As I said, most enlightening." *Time for another gamble.* "I suppose Timothy worked for Generro at some time, too."

Langland shook her head. Seemingly distracted by the turmoil of her own thoughts, she mumbled, "No, he ran New Horizons in the 1970s."

It took all Sam's iron control to keep the shock from showing on her face. *New Horizons? That's the company that bought Pop-Pop's land . . . if that wasn't all a scam as well. My God, they're all connected.*

What in the name of God have I stumbled across?

The older woman seemed to be in shock. "I can't believe he showed you the samples from Elsewhen," she muttered, "the pictures of the virtual worlds . . ."

What in the name of all that's holy is "Elsewhen"? The word had a strange mental "color" to it—*Maybe because of Amy's tone when she spoke it,* Sam thought. *It's important—maybe even the key to the secret of the League.* "Timothy showed me a lot," Sam mused, marking time while she tried to puzzle out another approach. "How about you, Amy?" she asked suddenly. "How long have *you* been a member of the League? Since the 1940s?"

Langland's face was pale. She looked physically trashed, emotionally exhausted. She nodded her head. "Nineteen forty-seven," she said.

"I've often wondered if you had the chance to meet the VGL's founders."

"No." Langland shook her head. She seemed punch-drunk. "No, of course not. Burton and Bell were dead long before I joined."

Burton and Bell . . . Sam racked her brain. The only Burton and Bell she could think of on the spur of the moment were Sir Richard Francis Burton and Alexander Graham Bell. *She can't mean them, can she?* She recalled the photograph in Pop-Pop's study, and to cover her confusion temporized, "And Einstein?"

"Of course. He's the one who proposed me for membership . . . God knows why."

This is unbelievable. Sam's thoughts began to flounder. *I'm way out of my depth here. A conspiracy—what else could you call it?—that's been in existence since the 1940s, if not earlier, that involves people like Albert Einstein. A . . . a* cabal . . . *that selects members secretly, and keeps its true purpose hidden from the rest of the world. My God, I'm in a spy thriller. . . .*

Before Sam could ask another question, Langland fixed her with a sharp, eagle-eyed stare. "You amaze me, child," she said, her voice back under some semblance of control. "How the *hell* did you learn all this so damn fast? Your performance has been . . . staggering."

Sam shrugged. "I'm a Dooley," she said, thinking of Pop-Pop. "It runs in the family, I guess."

"Yes, yes." Langland nodded her head, her eyes narrowing in thought. "You're right. You share your father's determination and his courage." Her voice softened, as she remembered. "Such a great loss, that one. He was one of our most promising recruits."

Sam gasped. It was as if a brilliant light had exploded in her brain, stunning her. Her thoughts were sluggish, confused. *Oh my God. She misunderstood, she thought I was talking about dad.*

He *was part of the VGL too!*

What does that mean about his death? Was the VGL involved with developing the Thunderflash?

Or was that even how he died at all?

Langland was staring at her, eyes like slits. "You didn't know," the older woman said softly, wonderingly. "You didn't know, did you?"

"No, I didn't," Sam admitted. She kept her voice firm—or tried to, at least—striving not to lose the advantage she'd already gained.

Langland was still looking at her intently, as though the older woman was trying to stare right through her. "You *don't* know!" Her sudden statement was almost a crow of realization. "You don't know, do you? You're just guessing."

Sam's bluff had collapsed and she knew it. But it had served its purpose. "I *didn't* know," she agreed, "but I do now. You've told me."

"What I told you hardly qualifies as earth-shattering news," Langland scoffed. "Every society keeps some secrets, and these are pretty mild compared to some."

"I know that the public shell of the Virtual Geographic League supports a secret society," Sam pressed, "and I know the secret part has infiltrated Generro Aerospace and New Horizons Industries." She decided to gamble again. "And Jones Cartage," she added.

Langland laughed out loud, a harsh bark of ironic amusement. " 'Infiltrated,' is it? Child, the VGL *is* Generro and New Horizons and Jones Cartage."

"I'm sure there are some people who'll be very interested to hear that."

The old pilot laughed again. "The only people who will believe you don't even count," she snapped. "You'll come across sounding like a paranoid idiot, and if you drag my name into it, I'll deny I ever even talked to you."

Sam's lips quirked in a hard smile. "You'll find it harder

than you think." She reached into her shirt pocket, pulled out the miniature tape recorder she'd hidden there. With her thumb she hit the STOP button, then REWIND. The recorder's motor squealed. Now she hit PLAY. Langland's voice was tinny, slightly distorted, but nonetheless recognizable.

". . . is it? Child, the VGL is *Generro and New Horizons and Jones Cartage."*

Sam clicked the recorder off and slipped it back into her pocket.

Langland glared at her for a moment, then her expression softened. She tapped the fingers of one hand against the other palm—silent applause. "You've got guts, child, I'll give you that. Guts and brains." She paused. "But who're you going to play that for, huh? Did you think about that?

"The police?" Langland snorted. "No crime's been committed. The newspapers? The only papers that'll publish a wild conspiracy story like that will put it on the same page as the latest Elvis sighting."

Sam felt cold, as though a chill wind had blown down the back of her neck. She tried to keep her sudden doubts out of her voice. "The government is what *I* had in mind," she said flatly.

Langland laughed again. "Child, do you really think we could keep what were doing secret from the government?

"The government's *in* on it. We're *partners."*

13

This can't be true. Sam shook her head to clear it.

She felt as though she were in some kind of dream. She knew she'd gotten up from Amy Langland's couch, left the old aviatrix's house and driven off in Grendel. Now she was rolling south on Vermont—driving aimlessly, almost blindly. Looking back on her memories of the past minutes, it seemed almost as though she'd been a spectator, not a participant. It was as if she'd *watched* herself leave the house—leave the house of someone she'd thought of as a friend. *I don't know Amy.* The thought was chilling. *I don't really know her. And I didn't know Pop-Pop, or Dad, either.* She felt cut adrift, as though the foundations of her life had been wrenched away from her. Involuntarily, she remembered the last thing Amy Langland had told her as she'd left. "I'd forget everything you think you know, if I were you, child," the aging woman had said, her voice cool and distant. "The League *has* been known to kill people who endanger its purpose."

What the hell have I stumbled onto? she asked herself. *A cabal, a conspiracy, big enough to take over entire companies . . . with the complicity of the government! A secret important enough to cost people their lives . . .*

But what was this conspiracy trying to do? What was its purpose, its goal? And by what means was it trying to achieve that goal?

Those are the questions Pop-Pop wanted to answer for me with his memoirs, she realized. *That's what he was hinting at that night—all his talk about understanding, and still thinking kindly of him, all his veiled hints about secrets. He wanted me to know, once he was gone, that he was part of this Virtual Geographic League, whatever the hell it is.*

The secret agenda of the VGL alone explained many of the mysteries she'd been trying to puzzle out. *Obviously, if the VGL is supposed to be such a hush-hush outfit, Pop-Pop was "breaking the code" by giving me the memoirs.*

That's why he wanted me to take them before the executors came in—before the VGL could get its shadowy hands on them and keep them away from me.

But the VGL *had* acquired the memoirs, she reminded herself bitterly, just as they'd arranged so she'd never get Pop-Pop's mementos, or the property at Eagle Mountain. *After all,* she told herself, *how tough would it be to suborn a piddly little legal firm if this VGL is big enough to control a major company like Generro Aerospace?*

Generro . . . That unleashed a flood of new thoughts. *My father—he was part of it, too.* What did Langland say about him? *"Such a great loss, that one. He was one of our most promising recruits."*

Such a great loss? No shit. You don't have to tell me *about loss.*

So what exactly had Jim Dooley, Jr., been doing with Generro Aerospace? And how had he died, really? *Had* he augured in behind the stick of a prototype Thunderflash jet fighter, or was that just a cover story? *What the hell happened to my dad?*

Sam's thoughts, her memories, churned wildly. She pulled over to the side of the road, cutting off a taxi in the process, and sunk her face into her hands as the taxi's horn blared at her. Words, phrases whirled through her mind. *Virtual worlds. Burton and Bell.* Elsewhen. *Albert Einstein. UFT transporter cockpit. . . .* What did it all *mean*? *What was the VGL really?*

She forced herself to breathe deeply, to shake off the emotional reaction that threatened to overwhelm her. She rubbed at her eyes, brushed her long hair back from her face. *Get a grip, Dooley.* She reached into the glove box, extracted her Ray-Bans and slipped them on.

As the sunglasses cut the glare of the morning sun, they also seemed to focus her thoughts, to resolve the blurring of words and concepts. *Get a grip,* she told herself again. *You can do this. You can figure it out.*

She felt a growing conviction in the back of her mind that she had what she needed to make sense of everything. *It's like a jigsaw puzzle,* she thought. *I've got all the pieces, but I don't know how they're supposed to fit together. Not yet.*

* * *

Three hours later, she slumped back in her papasan chair and stared at the index cards on her bulletin board.

From a pay phone on the way home, she'd called West-Air to say she was sick. Her boss hadn't sounded too thrilled; she felt sure he'd be unable to get a replacement for her on such short notice and would have to cancel some flights, but he respected her enough not to question her need for the time off. Then she'd driven back to Venice and started work on the "jigsaw puzzle" that was the VGL, writing down on index cards all the new facts, speculations, questions and other comments she could remember.

Once she'd started, it was amazing how much came back to her. *It's as if just* trying *to organize what I know has opened the floodgates,* she thought wryly. But it wasn't the memories themselves that were so fascinating; it was the *connections* she thought she saw developing between those memories.

Take that cryptic model in the private museum-shrine, the "UFT Transporter Cockpit." At the time, she'd dismissed her interpretation of the abbreviation UFT; after all, she'd thought, what connection could that strange device have with the unified field theory? Now, though . . . now that she knew that Albert Einstein had been a member of the VGL, the connection didn't seem outrageous at all.

Once she'd accepted that as a possibility, it put a whole new interpretation on that strange phrase Langland had used, "virtual worlds," and on the name of the Virtual Geographic League itself. *The unified field theory deals with quantum mechanics, the Heisenberg uncertainty principle, Schroedinger's cat, and all that crap, doesn't it? Could* that *be what Amy meant by "virtual worlds"?*

What was Elsewhen, then? Langland had seemed to imply that the two terms were synonymous, or at least related. *Okay, that's a question I can't answer yet.*

She found herself thinking back to the fragments of text she'd read from Fred Noonan's personal journal. What did the entry refer to?

Obviously to a test flight of some kind, she told herself. *He's in the cockpit of an experimental plane, and the flight technicians are closing the canopy.*

No, she thought, *that doesn't necessarily fit. He mentioned quartz glass*—she struggled to recall the exact words—

"through the quartz glass I could see. . . ." What kind of plane had quartz glass in its canopy back in 1937? Quartz glass was only used when there was a danger of radiation, wasn't it? *And that makes* no *sense whatsoever. This was* 1937, *for chrissake, pre-Manhattan Project, pre-Trinity, pre-Hiroshima. . . .* When did nuclear fission take place for the first time? In 1939, wasn't it? So why quartz glass?

Maybe it wasn't *a plane.* The thought surfaced from nowhere. *What did the rest of the journal entry say? Something about a sensation* almost like *a plane dropping without lift.* Noonan was comparing some experience—*"The shift," he'd called it,* she recalled suddenly—to the behavior of a plane. Would he have used the same phrase if he'd been *talking about* a plane? *What's the point of describing an experience in terms of itself? It's like that old joke about an entry in a dictionary for mathematicians: "Recursion: see Recursion". . . .*

And what was the rest of the journal entry about? That was even harder to fathom. *Something about a "drop in a direction I didn't know existed," or something like that.*

The phone rang, jolting her out of her reverie. "Hello?"

"Hey, kiddo."

Samantha sat up in the papasan. "Mags. Geez, girl, have I got some things to tell you."

"Me first," her friend cut in with a throaty laugh. "I've been busting my butt getting the backgrounds you wanted, and I'm going to get it out if I have to strangle you first."

Sam chuckled. "Go for it."

"Sid Warner," Maggie said. "Did that get your attention?"

"You've got it."

"I still don't have an address or phone number, but I *did* manage to get a line on where he's working these days."

"He's still contracting?" Sam guessed.

"You got it," Maggie confirmed. "Down in your neck of the woods, too. An outfit in Moreno Valley, called New Horizons Industries."

"Oh, crap. . . ." Sam breathed.

"You know the name?"

Under other circumstances, the astonishment in Maggie's voice would have been funny. At the moment, though, Sam wasn't in much of a mood to laugh. "I know it," she agreed dryly.

"Huh," Mags grunted. "Then this isn't going to be the eye-popper I thought it was. You probably know it already."

"Tell me anyway."

"This New Horizons isn't an independent company," Maggie explained, "even though it goes to great lengths to *pretend* it is."

Samantha closed her eyes. *I think I know where this is going.* "And it's owned by . . . ?"

"And it's owned by a name I *know* you know," Mags told her. "Generro Aerospace."

Samantha stared at the ceiling. *It all comes down to Generro Aerospace, doesn't it?* Langland had said, right out, that Generro *was* the VGL, or the VGL *was* Generro. The company was the nexus of so many connections. Simon Warner and Jacques Leclerc—both VGL members. The death of Jim Dooley, Jr. Her instincts had been right all along, she realized grimly. *How long ago did I tell myself that I'd find answers at Generro?*

It was time to pay Generro Aerospace another visit.

But how? The question had consumed her for a dozen painful hours before she hit on the answer. Now, sitting in Grendel on the shoulder of Highway 60 just west of Rubidoux, she had to chuckle. *I was trying to be too subtle, that was my problem,* she told herself. *Sometimes it pays to be direct.*

It was a recurrence of the dream—the endless corridors at Generro, and then the Jones Cartage truck—that set her on the right track. Using Maggie Braslins as a resource, she'd done some research on Jones Cartage, Inc. Since Langland had told her that the trucking company was also part of the Virtual Geographic League, she took as a base assumption that Generro Aerospace would use Jones Cartage for any transportation needs they might have. *Why not keep the money "in the family," as it were?*

Sam didn't know—and didn't really want to know—how Maggie had dug up the information. All that mattered was that Maggie had come through, telling her that Jones Cartage was responsible for delivering food and other supplies to the Generro facility every couple of days.

From there, Sam had done some digging into Jones Cartage's schedule and procedures. It hadn't taken her very long to learn that the Generro delivery was part of a detailed route the truck followed. Each day a delivery was scheduled, the truck would stop at the same destinations, in the same sequence, and at approximately the same time every day. For example, on the morning of a delivery, on its way toward the Generro facility from the direction of Los Angeles, the truck would always fuel up at a card-lock facility on Highway 60 between Rubidoux and Riverside. . . .

Of course, it wasn't as easy as I make it sound, Samantha had to admit. The more she'd thought about what Langland had told her about the extent and associated power of the VGL, and especially the threat she had delivered, the more frightened she'd become. *I can't believe they'd kill the daughter of a member to keep her quiet,* she'd told herself. *But I can think of lots of options they can choose short of death, and I don't like any of them either. Anyway,* she'd reasoned, *it never pays to take chances.*

Accordingly, she'd just hit the road, leaving her apartment without packing any bags, taking nothing with her but the cache of "emergency funds" she kept hidden in the freezer. *If the VGL comes visiting, I don't want them to suspect I don't plan on coming home for a while.* She'd called up WestAir and asked for another leave of absence to deal with a "personal crisis." (She wasn't convinced that her boss had believed her this time, and seriously doubted that her job would be waiting for her when this was over—*If it's* ever *over*—but she didn't feel she had much of a choice.) Then she'd checked into a cheap, roadside motel out in the Riverside area, registering under a false name and paying in advance with cash. She'd conducted all her conversations with Maggie on pay phones, and she'd never so much as given her friend a hint about where she was staying. *Not that I don't trust Mags, but it doesn't hurt to play it safe—and I don't want her getting hurt because of me.*

And now her efforts and planning were all paying off. In her wing mirror, she saw the white truck looming up behind her on the highway. Tossing her cigarette to the road, she turned the ignition key; the Mustang's big V-8 caught at once. Grendel rocked as the truck hurtled by, a massive cliff of white looming over the convertible, marked with the red-and-blue petroglyph that was the Jones Cartage logo. Letting in the clutch, she pulled off the shoulder onto the highway and took up pursuit, hanging back by a couple of hundred yards. At this time of day, around 10:00 hours, the traffic was light, and there was no risk of losing her quarry. After all, she knew exactly where it was going.

As she came within a mile of the card-lock facility, she dropped her speed and let the gap open between her and the truck. By the time she pulled onto the apron of the facility, the Jones truck was stopped at one of the pump islands, and the driver was filling the tank.

On her frequent driving trips, Sam had seen many card-lock diesel facilities, but she'd never given them any thought. It was only to prepare for today that she'd so much as looked at one twice.

The system was efficient, and in its own way almost elegant, she had to admit. Trucks, particularly long-haul tractor-trailer rigs, went through a prodigious amount of fuel and had to refill their tanks at all hours of the day and night. Rather than paying attendants to be on duty around the clock at a truck stop, oil companies had instituted the card-lock system (and were even beginning to extend it into the realm of private automobiles, Sam had noticed recently). Card-lock stations had no staff, no attendants, Truckers pulled in and used their fuel cards—similar to a credit card—to unlock the pumps. The driver would fill up, and the automated system would record how much fuel he'd pumped and charge it to his account, or the account of the trucking company for which he drove. Some card-lock facilities only offered fuel dispensers: a couple of pump islands and the associated card-lock gear. Others were more elaborate, with washrooms, changing rooms, even showers.

The card-lock on Highway 60 outside Rubidoux was one of the latter kind. A small concrete building, well away from the pumps themselves, offered the local amenities. Vending machines filled with pop, coffee, snack food and other supplies took up one entire outside wall.

Sam parked Grendel on the margin of the asphalt apron just off the highway, unfolding and examining a map in a pretty fair imitation of a lost tourist, all the while watching the truck driver from the corner of her eye. She needn't have bothered with her playacting; the man never so much as glanced in her direction.

The driver finished fueling and returned the dispenser hose to its mount on the pump. He started to walk around the truck, probably making a routine check of the tires and lights and other potential problem areas. The instant he disappeared from her view, Sam grabbed The Club locking bar from under her seat, opened the door, and walked quickly across the parking lot toward the truck.

This was where her careful planning ended. She knew what she *hoped* the driver would do, and she'd prepared for that specific action. But she had no way of knowing for sure what he'd do. If he did something unexpected, she'd have to improvise, or maybe give the whole thing up as a bad job and try it again another time. As she reached the truck, she crouched low, looking beneath its undercarriage. She could see the driver's legs, striding toward the back of the vehicle. Her chest was tight, her pulse pounding in her ears. *If he comes around and starts to get back into the cab,* then *what do I do?* She tried the balance and the heft of The Club in her hand.

No, she saw with relief, he wasn't coming around to the driver's side of the truck. Finished with his visual inspection, he was heading toward the concrete building that contained the washrooms. Ducking into the cover of the truck's rear, Sam watched him disappear into the men's room, pushing the door shut behind him.

Now she ran, sprinting to the door the man had just closed. This was just what she'd been hoping for—*A pit stop to break up a long drive,* she thought with a kind of manic glee—and the contingency for which she'd planned. She slipped the U-shaped end of The Club over the shaft of the doorknob. Then, pressing the other end of the bar flush against the wall, she slid the mobile J-shaped bracket of the locking device until it hooked around a drainpipe mounted next to the door frame. With fingers that trembled so much they almost dropped the key, she locked it in place. The red handle end of The Club was jammed against the wall. There was no way the driver could pull the door open while The Club was still locked onto the outside.

The driver must have heard the click of The Club's lock

engaging. Something thumped hard against the inside of the door. "Hey, what the hell—!" the driver bellowed.

But Sam wasn't waiting to hear the rest of what he had to say. She sprinted back to the truck's cab, pulled open the driver's door, and jumped in, reaching for the ignition.

"Who the hell are *you*?"

Sam physically jumped with alarm, clearing the driver's seat and nearly smacking her head on the roof.

There was someone else in the truck's cab. The relief driver—*trainee*?—was slumped low in the passenger's seat, only now pushing back the Dodgers baseball cap he'd pulled low to cover his eyes as he napped. *It never occurred to me there might be* two. . . .

The second driver was coming awake fast. Sam's initial impression was that he was short and scrawny, with a face like a malnourished weasel. But as he grabbed the dashboard to pull himself upright, she saw steel-cable tendons stand out in his tanned forearms. He glared at her with narrowed eyes, and Sam could suddenly smell the bitter tang of imminent violence. "What the hell you think you're doin'?" the weasel demanded.

Reacting instinctively, Sam shoved the driver's door open and tried to leap out. Before she could shift her weight, though, the weasel's left hand flicked out like a striking snake and grabbed her right wrist. Sam yelped as his fingers sunk deep into her flesh. "Not so fast there, girlie," the man snapped.

Sam's instincts kicked in again, but this time the instinct came from a different source. The trained reactions of the jujitsu mat took over, the muscles acting before the mind was even aware what was coming. Twisting in the driver's seat, Sam grasped the weasel's thumb with her left hand, bending it back with all her strength. The man gasped in pain, releasing his grip on Sam's right wrist. In an instant, she'd shifted her hold on his hand, now applying pressure to it with both of hers, in the Eagle grip. She shifted her weight toward him, hooking her right elbow over the crook of his arm. Her opponent screamed as she applied pressure, an agonizing lever movement that twisted both his elbow and wrist.

A smart man would have surrendered before his arm broke under the pressure. The weasel wasn't smart. Even as he yowled his agony, he lunged at Sam, throwing a wild right at her face. She threw herself back, away from him, "slipping" the punch while increasing the pressure on his wrist and elbow.

On the jujitsu mat, she'd have easily converted the move into a hip throw, and that's what her trained reactions tried to do. She'd shifted her weight, fully committing herself to the maneuver, before her brain sounded a warning. Too late. She cried with alarm as she realized what was happening. *I'm not on the mat, I'm in the cab of a* truck. . . .

She felt herself overbalancing, falling out of the truck's open door. Even as she saw the asphalt rushing toward her, her body finished the practiced move. The laws of mechanics, leverage and momentum worked just as well in mid-air as they did anywhere else. In fact, the energy of her falling body added to the lever effect. She fell clear, but as she did, she dragged the weasel with her, his cramped arm a lever around the fulcrum that was Sam's center of mass. With a shocked yell, the weasel was dragged from his seat, baseball cap flying from his head, out the door of the cab. He pivoted in midair around the fulcrum Sam had created of his arm.

Sam hit hard, but the weasel was underneath her when they struck. His back slammed flat against the asphalt, Sam's knees driving into his chest and stomach an instant later. The air *whooped* from his body, spraying spittle up into Sam's face. Her momentum rolled her aside, off him, the gritty asphalt abrading the skin from her right arm and her cheek. Even though her mind was stunned by the impact—it's a long way from the cab of a truck to the ground—her reflexes were still in high gear, and she was instantly on her feet again, panting with exertion and adrenaline rush.

The weasel drew his knees up to his chest, fighting to drag air into his lungs in great, asthmatic wheezes. His lips were faintly blue, his cheeks red. His eyes were screwed shut in torment. He rolled to one side and began to vomit. Sam backed away before the smell could reach her.

She stood there on the apron, shifting from foot to foot in indecision. *I should help him, I should do something. . . .*

But then the more rational part of her mind took over. *He'll be okay,* she told herself. *He's just badly winded.* She winced, remembering the pain when an overeager jujitsu practice partner had accidentally tagged her with a knee to the solar plexus. *You don't die from a gut-shot like I gave him. You just* wish *you could.*

Taking one last look at the incapacitated second driver, she climbed back into the truck cab and fired up the engine. She shook her head in amazement. *Quite the morning, Dooley. Unlawful confinement, followed by a little assault and battery—and that's on top of the breaking and entering job at the museum, and not counting what she was planning to do at Generro. How many years in jail does all that represent?* Not for the first time since her grandfather's death, Samantha wondered how she came by her apparent gift for inventive law-breaking, and flinched at the thought of trying to explain her actions to Pop-Pop. But if this VGL thing shaped up the way she figured it would—well, Pop-Pop might just have understood.

Well, what was done was done, she told herself firmly, forcing herself to forget her moral qualms for the moment. *And since I created this opportunity, I ought to take advantage of it.*

The transmission ground as she put the big vehicle into gear and pulled away.

14

The Generro gate guard stared suspiciously at Samantha. "You're not the regular driver," he said.

Sam shrugged. She sat well back in the big truck's driver's seat, not even bothering to look in the guard's direction, as though completely unconcerned. She wore the Dodgers baseball cap the weasel had involuntarily left behind in the truck, her long hair crammed up underneath it, the peak pulled low over her brow. A cigarette dangled from the corner of her mouth. A thin tendril of smoke had found its way up under her Ray-Bans and was making her left eye water, but she didn't move the cigarette. She shrugged again. "Joe's sick," she said flatly. (Joe Lindroos was the name she'd found on the truck's paperwork when she went through the glove box.) "Something he ate . . . or drank."

The guard—it wasn't the same one who'd let Sam into the Generro site a few days earlier, she was glad to see—chuckled to himself. "It's the twenty-six ounce flu, you ask me." But then his amusement faded. "We weren't notified of any change."

With an effort, Sam smothered her sigh of relief. It didn't seem as though Joe—the driver she'd locked in the washroom—or the weasel had reported the theft of their truck to the powers that be at Generro. *And why should they?* she asked herself. *If your car gets stolen, you report it to the police. You don't bother to inform the person you were planning to visit when the theft occurred, do you?*

"Take it up with the dispatcher," she said with another shrug. "No skin off my butt if I don't make this delivery."

The guard looked uncomfortable. "Let's see your swindle sheets," he said after a moment.

Swindle sheets? Sam had an almost uncontrollable urge to laugh out loud. The only time she'd ever heard that term was in the lyrics of some stupid novelty song—"Convoy," or something like that—which was popular back in the 1970s when CB radios were the latest fad. *People actually* say *that?* Concealing her amusement—*Relax, damn it, Dooley: it wasn't* that *funny*—she handed down to the guard the manifests she'd found on a clipboard under the driver's seat.

He flipped through them quickly.

"Are my papers in order, sir?" Sam said dryly.

The guard's jaw set. He thrust the paperwork back at Sam. "Head on through," he grunted. "You know where to go."

"Actually, I don't," Sam said. "As you pointed out yourself, I'm not the regular driver."

"T-intersection, turn left," the man almost growled. "You'll see the loading bay." He signaled brusquely to the other guard inside the gatehouse. With a metallic click, the gate started to roll back.

Sam flipped him an ironic salute, touching the peak of her baseball cap with a finger. Then she put the truck in gear—carefully!—and rolled forward through the gate.

Softly, she began to whistle the chorus from the song "Convoy."

The wheel was heavy as she turned left at the T-intersection. As the truck took the corner, she glanced in the right side mirror. The parabolic surface distorted the reception building she'd visited a few days earlier, making it curve like an example of avant-garde architecture. The left arm of the intersection ran straight toward one of the larger buildings, a sprawling structure that looked like a converted airplane hangar. Farther to the left, separated from the rest of the buildings, she saw the small concrete blockhouse that she'd noticed on her first visit. The high-tension lines that connected it to the electrical substation gleamed in the bright sun, like laser beams that had been impossibly bent into graceful hyperbolic arcs.

A smaller road led off to the right; a sign read LOADING BAY, with an arrow below the words. She wrestled the big truck around to the right. Ahead of her, a shallow ramp led downward, butting right up against the side of the converted hangar. She saw an empty concrete loading dock, with two large up-and-over cargo doors. Obviously, things were arranged so that when a delivery truck backed down the ramp, the concrete dock would be just at the height of the truck's bed. To the left of the ramp was a wide asphalt apron—like a parking lot, except for a large sign that warned DON'T EVEN THINK ABOUT PARKING HERE. *Space for the delivery driver to turn his truck around, so he can reverse it down the ramp,* she realized.

Sam slowed the truck to a stop, air brakes wheezing, and thought for a moment. Should she try and back the truck into position at the loading bay? *Not smart, Dooley. Driving into the corner of the building when you misjudge the turn—what better way to blow your cover?* She chuckled softly, the tension in her chest emerging as amusement with a slight hysterical edge to it. *I'm just lucky I haven't run into anything so far.* She pulled the truck over into the turnaround area and eyeballed her surroundings. There was nobody in sight—nobody walking on the concrete paths that connected the different buildings, nobody on the loading dock itself. The sprawling hangar had no windows that she could see. *Okay, time to move,* she told herself. She killed the engine and put on the parking brake, opened the door and dropped to the asphalt. She tossed down her cigarette and ground it out with her heel. Then she walked purposefully toward the converted hangar.

Around the corner of the building, to the left of the loading bay, was a single door. As she strode toward it, new doubts assaulted her confidence. She remembered the guest pass she'd been given on her first visit and the "smart card" that Leclerc had worn, that had registered with the security system beside his office door. *If there's security like that on* this *door, this is going to be the shortest infiltration mission on record.* She glanced back over her shoulder at the truck. *What the hell am I supposed to do then? Ram the truck through the gate to get out?* With an effort, she pushed the fears from the forefront of her mind. *Too late for second thoughts now, Dooley; you're committed.* She smiled, but the expression felt like a grimace. *Remember the osprey—full investment. . . .*

The door was closed, but she didn't see a security panel mounted on the wall beside it. Bracing herself for disaster, she grasped the doorknob and twisted.

The knob turned; the door opened with a metallic click that sounded as loud as a gunshot in her ears. She pushed the door open and stepped inside.

In contrast to the brilliance of the California sun, the corridor in which she found herself seemed gloomy. At least it was empty, though; no one confronted her and demanded to know her business. Quickly, she moved down the corridor, glancing at the doors on either side of her.

WOMEN'S CHANGE ROOM, read the plate on the third door to her left. Without stopping to think, she pushed the door open and stepped through.

She found herself in a low-ceilinged room, two of the concrete walls lined with banks of metal lockers. Two long wooden benches flanked the lockers. From an open door in the far wall, she heard the sound of a shower running. The room was empty.

Quickly, she looked around the room, hoping against hope. . . . Yes, one of the full-length lockers was ajar, a cheap combination lock hanging open on its door. She hurried over to it, and swung the door open. In the small storage space at the top of the locker, she saw a pair of running shoes and a small purse. Hanging from a hook below was a set of olive-drab overalls, the name PETRIE embroidered above the right breast-pocket. Involuntarily, she glanced at the door that led to the showers. The water was still running, but she expected the sound to stop at any moment. *Hurry, hurry!* she told herself. She reached in and pulled out the overalls. Instantly she could see they were too small for her. *Just as well,* she realized a moment later. When she finished her shower, Petrie would sure as hell notice that her overalls were distinctly missing.

On impulse, she searched through the pockets of the overalls. *Maybe, maybe. . . .*

Yes! Through the fabric of one of the breast pockets, she could feel something stiff, a little larger than a playing card. With a gasp of relief, she pulled out the ID smart card. Like Leclerc's, there was a photograph mounted on the light gray plastic, but no other markings. *God looks after idiots after all,* she thought wryly. For a moment, she looked at the photograph of Petrie, saw a petite, small-boned woman with the short-cropped red hair. Then she returned the overalls to the hook, closed the locker door to the same position again, and bolted from the room.

Only once she was out in the corridor again did she take a moment to attach the smart card ID to her collar with its small alligator clip. She experimented with attaching it a couple of ways, until it hung so that the photograph wasn't immediately visible. *If anybody takes the time to actually* look *at the ID, I'm dead,* she recognized. *But at least the security system shouldn't worry about why Petrie's wandering around the facility.*

At the far end of the corridor, she saw a double door painted red. Walking confidently, as though she knew where she was going, she strode toward the doors, stopping a few feet in front of them. AUTHORIZED PERSONNEL ONLY, a large black-on-white warning read, and beneath it a smaller plate said: UFT TRANSPORT. *"Unified Field Theory Transport"? Maybe.*

Mounted on the wall beside the double doors was a small metal panel, marked by two small LEDs, one red, one green. It was a twin of the panel mounted outside Leclerc's office in the administration building. Sam hesitated, touching Petrie's ID card tentatively. Then she stepped up to the door.

The green LED lit, and Sam heard a soft metallic *snick* from the door as an automatic lock disengaged. It was only when she let out a loud sigh that she realized she'd been holding her breath. She pushed open the left-hand door and stepped through.

For one, bewildering instant, she felt as though she'd stepped into a movie sound stage, the set of a high-budget science fiction feature. *Maybe* that's *what Generro's into,* she thought distractedly, *making movies.* She contradicted herself a second later. *This isn't a movie set; this is* real.

The building was a converted aircraft hangar, as she'd suspected; the design was unmistakable. The roof was high overhead, crisscrossed with girders and support stanchions, easily sixty feet above the floor. Unrecognizable equipment towered around her, casting strange, angular shadows in the light provided by banks of bright fluorescent tubes suspended from the roof girders. Sam stepped away from the door, flattening herself against the wall in the shadow of something that looked like a cross between a huge Van de Graaff generator and a massive stack of batteries. Out of the view of anyone who walked through the doors, she looked around.

15

What the hell is going on here? The room in which Sam found herself was huge, cavernous. Immense pieces of equipment towered over the area, their sheer size making it difficult to accurately judge the room's square footage. Even so, she figured the area to be at least one hundred feet wide and perhaps twice that long. Some of the mysterious equipment was free-standing, like a bank of six ringed ceramic towers off to her right, huge cylinders thirty feet high and almost five feet in diameter. (Something about those cylinders stirred an old memory, from a high school physics course. *They look something like Tesla coils,* she thought, *but what would you do with six Tesla coils that big?*) Other units were surrounded by scaffolding, and some were connected by latticework catwalks. On the far side of the open area, she saw an overalls-clad figure crouching on a platform, performing some kind of maintenance on a device that resembled an enormous high-voltage transformer.

The whole area seemed to vibrate with a pervasive hum, so low-pitched as to be almost subliminal. Sam touched one ear. Yes, she *felt* the hum through the bones of her skull more than she *heard* it. *Power,* she thought. Lots *of power.* She sniffed the air, and recognized the ocean tang of ozone. She remembered the electrical substation outside. Obviously, this was where all that electrical energy was going. *But why? What for?*

Over the subliminal hum, Sam could hear voices. She'd been hearing them for a while, she realized; she just hadn't paid any attention. She held her breath, trying to make out what they were saying, but the electrical hum acted like white noise, muffling the actual words and obliterating the meaning. Still, she could tell that there were clearly three voices carrying on a conversation: two male, one female. One of the male voices sounded familiar. Her overstimulated brain couldn't quite place the memory, but there was something about it—the tone, maybe the intonation and cadence of words—that convinced her she'd heard the voice before.

She scanned the room again. The only person she could see was the "technician" working on the raised gantry. She took two deep breaths to ease the almost excruciating tension in her chest. Then she moved, flitting like a ghost from shadow to shadow, around the towering blocks of equipment. Warning signs reading HIGH VOLTAGE, reinforced with graphical icons of a human figure struck by lightning, only strengthened her determination not to touch anything. Using the voices to navigate by, Sam crept toward the middle of the room.

The center area was more brightly lit. Reinforcing the illumination of the fluorescent tubes, a series of smaller lights—burning with the hard, flat radiance of quartz-halogen bulbs—seemed to highlight a partially clear area that was surrounded by unidentifiable gear reaching nearly to the girders overhead. She dropped into a crouch, inching forward in a cramped duck-walk, staying to the deepest shadows. Finally she found a vantage point that gave her full view of the brightly lit region yet screened her from casual discovery by a ten-foot-tall green metal enclosure that emitted a faint whine reminiscent of a recharging capacitor. Again, she struggled to make sense of what she was seeing.

Arranged in a large, hollow U-shape were three consoles of computer equipment. Text—unreadable from this distance—scrolled on monitor screens, while a complex array of annunciator lights flashed at a frenetic tempo. Across the top of one console was a large bank of closed-circuit video monitors. The angle she was at prevented Sam from seeing what they showed. From the backs of the consoles, Medusa-heads of wires, gathered into loose harnesses, snaked out over the floor. Something about what she was seeing made her certain that the entire setup was somehow temporary—*Like a prototype of a NASA mission control room.*

Three figures clustered in front of a particularly dense panel of computers. A large monitor displayed complex waveforms in bright green phosphor. There were *two* waveforms, Sam realized suddenly, overlapping but not synchronized. Both were, at their heart, simple sine waves, but modulated in a complex manner as if by additional signals. One of the figures—a small Oriental man apparently in his late twenties, wearing a white lab coat—was punching commands into a keyboard below the monitor. The green phosphor light glinted off the lenses of his round glasses. Behind the Oriental man stood a woman, also wearing a white lab coat. She was taller than the man but still shorter than Sam herself, thin-faced and light-boned, her mouse-brown hair pulled back into a severe bun.

It was the third figure that held Sam's attention, though. No lab coat on this one; instead, he wore a pair of gray slacks and a white shirt, sleeves rolled up, perspiration stains under his arms. Tall, medium build—his brown hair looked slightly disheveled. Behind his wire-rimmed glasses she saw the flash of cornflower-blue eyes.

Ernest Macintyre. Fancy meeting you *here.*

The young engineer who she'd met by Pop-Pop's sickbed was craning forward, staring fixedly at the screen. He reached out to tap the monitor with a slender forefinger. "We're still getting channel crosstalk." His voice was as soft as she remembered, but now it held an undertone of authority. *This is where he belongs,* Sam thought. *He's in his element here—dealing with computers, rather than with people.* "Can you isolate the feed from the quaternary coupler, and bring up the harmonic on the secondary?"

The young Oriental man glanced questioningly at Macintyre, then shrugged his thin shoulders. "You're the boss, Mac." He typed a long instruction string into the keyboard.

Samantha jerked as the whine from the enclosure beside her jumped in pitch. She worked her jaw from side to side, trying to lessen the sharp pain that stabbed into her ears. On the screen, the wave forms shifted, overlapping further, starting to coalesce. Then they shifted apart again. Even though she hadn't a clue what she was watching, Sam couldn't help but share the tension that was etched in every line of the three people's bodies. *It's like watching surgeons at work,* she thought.

Macintyre made a *tsk* sound. "Resonance effects," he muttered.

"I thought we had that licked," the woman said.

Macintyre tapped the screen again. "Bring up the tertiary five percent." The waveforms shifted again. "Another five." Millimeter by millimeter, the waves crept closer to each other. "And five more. . . ." The waveforms merged, one perfectly superimposed over the other. A single, sinuous line of intense green burned on the screen. "*Congruence,*" Macintyre announced. "Lock it in." As the Oriental man tapped another command string into the computer, Macintyre turned to the woman with a gentle smile. "I think we're ready for the team, Andrea."

Andrea nodded sharply and walked quickly away. Macintyre looked at the single wave form again, and clapped the Oriental keyboard artist on the shoulder. "I think it's going to be a good day, John," Macintyre said mildly.

Sam shifted her position, easing the tension in her knees. *Something important just happened. But* what?

And what's this about a team?

She needed a better view, she realized. There had to be more to . . . to whatever it was that was happening than these computers. *As far as I know, you don't need three-story-tall Tesla coils to run computers.* Trying to keep one eye on Macintyre and John at the console, she started to move counterclockwise between the stacks of equipment.

She stopped again after she'd moved a couple dozen feet. From this angle, she had a better view of the bank of closed-circuit TV screens. Of the two horizontal rows of eight screens, only the top row was operating, each showing what seemed to be an identical image. She squinted for a better look. Yes, each screen displayed something that resembled the interior of a plane cockpit, except that the canopy enclosing it was opaque. She could see a joystick on the right, a simple throttle on the left. Banks of buttons, annunciator lights and LED data displays surrounded the pilot's seat. *I thought Generro had given up on flight operations. . . .*

Frustrated by her inability to understand what she saw, Sam shook her head and continued to move past the stacks of equipment. The young Oriental man was still at the keyboard, she could see, but Macintyre had moved to another console and was pushing buttons on what looked like a bank of videotape recorders. Over the ever-present electronic buzz, she could hear him humming tunelessly to himself. She moved on.

Rounding the corner of a huge, humming bank of . . . *of* some *electrical device* . . . she stopped once more. *What the hell . . . ?* Now she saw what was beyond the U-shaped arrangement of consoles.

Eight . . . *cockpits,* she guessed, *what else could they be?* Each unit was rectangular, maybe eight or ten feet long, four feet wide, and five feet high. They were arranged in two rows, side by side, separated by a four-foot aisle. All eight were open; sliding canopies had been pushed backward on rails, exposing the interiors. Multicolored lights gleamed inside the cockpits—the annunciators and data displays she'd seen on the closed-circuit TV screens, Sam assumed. The metal exteriors were dark, institutional gray, spotted here and there with cryptic symbols, text labels unreadable from this distance, and warning banners, like the airframe of a fighter plane. Complex wiring harnesses connected the cockpits to the equipment around them, and eventually to the computer consoles where Macintyre still stood. *No,* she decided a moment later, *the cables* aren't *connected to the cockpits, not directly.* Instead, they seemed to be linked to the rails or frames—gantries, maybe—on which the cockpits rested. Though she couldn't see for sure, she suspected that nothing connected directly to the cockpits themselves. *Now, why would that be?*

She shifted position again for a better look, and spotted something that really piqued her curiosity. Near the front of each cockpit was a blaze of color: a bright, almost garish illustration of some kind. *Like nose art on World War II bombers,* she thought. The cockpit nearest her showed an Annie Oakley–style cowgirl, blowing the smoke from the barrel of her six-shooter. The words "Calamity Jane" framed the figure in looping script. The next cockpit down the line bore the name "Privateer," the word superimposed over the image of a swashbuckling pirate lunging with a bell-hilt rapier. And next to that was a cockpit identified as "Call of the Wild," the emblem comprising the silhouette of a wolf howling at the night sky. She couldn't see the nose art on the remaining five cockpits, but she assumed it was there.

She nodded slowly as understanding dawned. Cockpits that aren't part of planes, connected, if only indirectly, to complex computer systems. . . . They had to be simulators of some kind. Much less sophisticated than the ones she'd used at Edwards—these didn't have any kind of motion control, no hydraulic systems to simulate movement—but simulators just the same.

As quickly as it had come, her certainty began to fade. *What kind of simulators need all this electrical power? And what's the significance of those waveforms on the monitor?* This whole thing just continued to refuse to make sense.

She heard voices behind her and ducked farther into the shadows. The woman, Andrea, had returned, followed by six pilots.

Well, they look *like pilots,* Sam amended. They wore khaki overalls that looked like flight suits, but it was the way they carried themselves that clinched it for her. Each one of them—five men, one woman—moved with the graceful self-assurance, just one short step away from arrogance, that she associated with Ben Katt and the other jet-jockeys at Edwards. All of them were young, around Sam's age, with hair cropped in almost-military styles. Their eyes were steady, and they seemed to radiate energy and excitement.

One of the pilots, a muscular man with sandy-blond hair and steel-gray eyes, walked up to Macintyre. *The flight leader,* Sam recognized. "Hey, Mac," he said. "I hear we're a go?"

Macintyre nodded. He was taller than the pilot, but something about his posture made it seem as if he were looking up at the other man. "We had some unexpected resonance effects, Will, but we managed to balance the harmonics and. . . ."

The pilot shrugged and gave Macintyre a lopsided smile. "Can the techno-babble, Mac," he cut in, his tone robbing the words of any offense. "All I care about is, are we going?"

Macintyre took a look at the monitor. The waveforms were still perfectly superimposed, a single line of green. "You're going," he said simply.

Will turned to his fellows. "Gentlemen, ladies," he announced, "we're going to Solaris. U–N–V one-thirty-seven awaits. Translocation in . . . ?" He looked questionably at Macintyre.

"Five minutes," the young engineer replied.

". . . In five minutes," Will echoed, louder. He pointed toward the line of cockpits. "Mount up," he ordered.

Sam watched as the six pilots climbed into their cockpits and slid the canopies shut around them. As the canopies *thunked* into place, Andrea went along the line, ensuring that they were seated and latched properly. The two cockpits nearest Sam—"Calamity Jane" and "Privateer"—remained open and empty.

She turned to the bank of closed-circuit TV monitors. As she'd expected, two displays on the top row were unchanged, showing empty cockpits. On the other six, she saw Will and his team getting ready for whatever simulation Macintyre had in store for them. (*What was it Will called it—"Solaris"? And "U–N–V one thirty-seven"?*) The eight monitors on the lower row seemed to be powered up—occasional "snow" flickered across them—but still showed nothing meaningful.

Andrea had taken a seat at the console beside John. She ran her hands over the array of buttons and keys, apparently powering up new systems. Macintyre stood near her, occasionally glancing over her shoulder but not interfering. *He's training her,* Sam suddenly understood. *He's staying close enough to bail her out if she gets into trouble, but otherwise she's on her own.*

As if to confirm her speculation, Macintyre rested his hand on Andrea's shoulder for a moment, then said quietly, "I'd like you to handle the translocation yourself."

She glanced up at him, and Sam could see the doubt on her face. But Macintyre smiled reassuringly down at her. "You know what you're doing, Andrea," he told her calmly. "I'd like you to send them through in . . ." —he glanced at a digital clock mounted on the console— ". . . two minutes and 25 seconds. Okay?"

Andrea hesitated, then nodded once. Sam watched her take a deep breath, then turn back to the control console. She punched a few more buttons and watched the data readouts change. Then she reached for a gooseneck microphone that extended from the panel in front of her and brought it nearer her mouth. "Team Alpha, check in, please." Her voice sounded firmer than it had before, as though she'd already been changed by her new responsibility.

"Alpha One, check." The lead pilot's voice came through an overhead speaker. On the leftmost TV monitor, Sam saw Will smile. "Ready whenever you are, Andrea."

"Alpha Two, check."

"Alpha Three, check."

In sequence, the six pilots checked in. Andrea nodded with satisfaction. She pressed another button and a new sequence of annunciators lit up on her board. "Telemetry good," she announced. "UFT cockpits on line." (In her hiding place, Sam blinked. Those *are the 'UFT cockpits'? Then I guess 'UFT' doesn't stand for 'Unified Field Theory.'*)

"How are the waveforms?" Andrea asked. "Any drift?"

"None," the Oriental technician responded. "We're locked down tight over here."

Andrea nodded. Sam could feel the tension. "We're at Stage Two," Andrea announced. "Primary inductance system steady at two billion volts." (*What?* Sam thought, her mind reeling.) "Confirm coordinates."

Again, it was John who answered. "Entered and locked in. We're set for the hills outside Roland Fields."

"Did you copy that, Alpha One?"

"Copy, Control." Will chuckled, sounding like a pirate who's just spotted a ship ripe for plundering. "This is going to be fun."

Macintyre spoke up suddenly. "I want you to take it easy, Will," he cautioned. "These are only preliminary tests. You know how it is with new technology. . . ."

Will laughed out loud. "Don't worry, Dad," he chided, "I'll bring the DeSoto back in one piece."

Macintyre shook his head, but didn't answer.

Andrea pressed another series of buttons. "Confirm retrieval criteria."

"Retrieval criteria standard, Control," Will responded.

"Automatic sequence start," Andrea announced as she depressed a final key. "Inductance fields read stable. Gantry system powering up."

Samantha shifted uncomfortably. She could feel something happening. The hairs on the back of her neck moved with a life of their own. Her teeth seemed to be buzzing, and her vision blurred slightly. Those physical sensations didn't disturb her, though, as much as something else that she felt—if "felt" was exactly the right word—not through her normal five senses but . . . *otherwise.* It was as if the cavernous chamber were echoing with a new sound, beyond the range of human hearing but of a frequency that somehow set up a sympathetic vibration in her very soul. *Something is going to happen. Something important.*

"Gantry at full power," Andrea announced crisply. "Steady at two billion volts, one gigahertz." Sam noticed that Andrea, Macintyre and John were shielding their eyes with their hands. *Now, why . . . ?*

"Translocation in five . . . in four . . . three . . . two . . . one. . . ."

Sam gasped with pain as a silent concussion of light stabbed her eyes. She fell back deeper into the shadows. Through the pain, she felt a strange thrilling in the core of her being, as if the harmonic frequency that had set up that strange sympathetic vibration in her soul had just jumped to a higher octave.

"Translocation successful." Andrea's voice carried a distinct tone of satisfaction. "Welcome to Solaris Seven, ladies and gentlemen."

Fighting down an unreasoning impulse to just turn away, to *flee,* Sam forced herself to move forward again. Through streaming eyes, she looked toward the row of cockpits.

Only the closest two remained; the other six gantries were empty.

16

Sam stared disbelievingly at the empty gantries that had, a second before, supported six clunky "cockpits." *It's got to be some kind of trick. It's got to be. . . .*

Her mind no longer trusted the evidence of her senses. *What I just saw is against all the laws of physics. So I* can't *have seen it.* Her thoughts were hurried, harried, edged with panic. *It's a trick, parlor magic. Hell, I've seen David Copperfield make the* Statue of Liberty *disappear on TV. 'Course, he knew he had an audience. Are these guys just practicing some elaborate vanishing act?*

But while her intellect rebelled, another part of her—something closer to the core of her being—knew she'd just witnessed something significant and overwhelming, something not quite impossible. Her intellect could bluster and posture all it liked, but the cockpits had truly vanished. They'd gone . . . *somewhere.*

"Virtual worlds." "Elsewhen." Amy Langland had spoken those words to her. *Have the cockpits traveled to some "virtual world"? Are they now in* Elsewhen?

She leaned against the large metal enclosure beside her, reassured by its solidity, by the touch of the cold metal against her flesh. *At least* something's *still dependable,* she thought. *Steel is still hard, the floor still supports my weight, I can still breathe the air . . .*

As she observed her mental gymnastics, she felt the sense of dislocation, of rebellion—*All right, why not use the word? Of* fear—diminish. *The world still is as it is,* she reminded herself firmly. *Just because I've seen something I can't explain doesn't mean my whole world view has to lose its underpinnings.* She took a deep breath, stretching her lungs to their maximum capacity, then let the air out slowly in a soft hiss. The tension in her throat and chest, the incipient panic crowding her mind, eased dramatically. She turned back to the array of cockpits, and for the first time she could look at the empty gantries without a rush of numbing fear.

Fact: the cockpits had been there, but now they were gone. Fact: the six people who'd climbed into them had been preparing for some kind of mission. Fact: the "translocation"—that was the word, wasn't it?—had been controlled, and thus had been initiated, by Andrea, through the use of the complex computer consoles. Fact: this wasn't the first time that this had been done. Conclusion. . . .

Sam shook her head. *I don't have an effing clue.* What she needed was more data.

"Control, this is Alpha One." Will's voice sounded from a speaker, startling Sam so that she almost yelped aloud. "Translocation successful. How's the telemetry?"

Samantha turned to look at Andrea and the control consoles. Six monitors on the upper bank still showed head shots of Will and his teammates. The lower monitors were still blank.

Andrea was scrutinizing her data readouts. "We're receiving telemetry five-by," she confirmed. "How's your reception?"

"Five-by-five and treetop-high," Will responded with a broad grin. "Are you receiving our beacons?"

Andrea glanced questioningly at John, who smiled. "We got a hot lock on your gadgets, Team Alpha," he responded happily.

"Everything looks good here," Andrea said. "Proceed with mission, Alpha One."

Will's smile broadened further. "That's a big roger, Control."

Macintyre leaned in close, bending the microphone's gooseneck to bring it near to his lips. "Will," he said. His voice was quiet, but there was no mistaking the seriousness of his tone. "Take it easy, please. I mean it. I don't want to have to explain to anyone why we lost some people. Okay?"

On the monitor, Alpha One's smile faded slightly. "Copy that, Mac," he said sincerely. "We'll take it slow and easy." A soft click sounded from the speaker. On-screen, Will's lips moved silently. Apparently, he'd switched to another frequency to communicate directly with his team.

Macintyre gestured to the lower bank of monitors, which still flickered with occasional snow. "Where's visual?" he asked.

Andrea was making adjustments to her console, watching the results on her data displays. "We've got some harmonic distortion," she mumbled, "just trying to filter it out. . . ." The leftmost six monitors in the lower bank flashed pure white for a moment, then turned into windows looking onto churning chaos. "Boosting the primary gain . . . *now.*" The six screens cleared.

Sam stared at the screens, frowning in puzzlement. *A blasted wasteland*—that was her first impression. The six lower screens all showed views of bleak plains, similar to the rutted hardpan of the "fly-over states" like Nevada and eastern Utah. The video displays were in color, but since the scenery, such as it was, seemed to be made up entirely of shades of gray and faint brown, a monochrome image would have done it justice. Overhead was a low, solid cloud-deck. It didn't seem to be raining at the moment, but the ground looked drenched, if not muddy. In the distance, Sam thought she could make out the beginning of foothills. (*That's right,* she remembered, *the tech said something about "the hills outside Roland Fields."*) Only after a few seconds did Sam notice that the six images were slightly different in terms of parallax and angle of view. Obviously the screens showed images from six distinct cameras—presumably one associated with each cockpit.

So now *what happens?* Sam imagined the six cockpits, mysteriously relocated to this bleak, harsh environment, sitting motionless on the hard ground. *What do they do—sprout wheels and drive around . . . ?*

"Okay, Team Alpha." Sam glanced toward the screen displaying Will's image, watched as he moved his fingers and gripped his cockpit's stick and throttle. (*Stick and throttle? What the hell good are they going to do?*) "Radial dispersal. Head out half a klick, then report in. Let's go." On the screen, Sam watched him push his throttle forward.

The point of view of the screen at the left end of the lower rank immediately shifted. Sam stared as the terrain began to rush past. It was hard to judge distances without anything to confirm scale and size, but she figured that Will's vehicle—whatever it was—had to be cruising over the rutted hardpan at thirty miles an hour or more. At the same time, she realized that the vantage point wasn't right on the ground, as she'd believed, but fifty or sixty feet above the landscape.

Okay. He's apparently flying some kind of plane or helicopter. But how? The cockpits had precisely zero means of propulsion, she knew that—they weren't some kind of high-tech, science-fictional "air car": there simply wasn't enough space in them for the necessary equipment. And she'd already agreed with herself that this was no simulation. With a sigh, she put the question aside, mentally adding it to the bulging file marked "for later."

She checked the other displays and saw much the same thing, except that the angles of view were different. The six members of Team Alpha seemed to be heading for the hills, splitting up. (*Well, duh,* she told herself wryly. *What did you* think *"radial dispersion" meant?*)

Finally, the six moving points of view came to a stop. Sam checked the second hand of her watch. *If the team moved out half a kilometer, that means*—she did a quick calculation in her head—*those things, whatever they are, are traveling at something like eighty kilometers per hour. That's fifty miles per hour, give or take.*) She focused on one of the displays that was still moving, and watched carefully as it slowed and came to a dead stop. As far as she could tell, its altitude didn't change as it decelerated and stopped. *That means a helicopter of some kind,* she told herself.

A woman's voice sounded from the speaker. "Alpha Four, checking in."

"Alpha Two, ready to go."

"Alpha Three, ready."

When the rest of the team had sounded off, Will's voice announced, "Okay, Team Alpha, listen up. Remember what Mac said, take it easy, this is just a shakedown mission. Okay, let's kick some butt."

The images on all six lower screens pivoted rapidly—presumably as the members of Team Alpha wheeled their vehicles. The separate views were too confusing for Sam to make sense of the overall picture, so she focused on only one display: Will's.

The team leader seemed to be heading for the nearest of the foothills, the rough and rugged terrain flying by beneath him. Sam estimated his speed at close to sixty miles per hour—ninety kilometers per hour. For the first time, she noticed that the vehicle's motion, judging by the display screen at least, wasn't smooth. Instead, there was a kind of vibration to it, a regular jar or impact occurring about twice a second. *Low-altitude turbulence?* she wondered, then discarded that hypothesis—no turbulence could be that regular and uniform. *It must be some kind of harmonic effect,* she decided, *maybe some artifact of the engine the vehicle's using.* She grinned, satisfied she'd figured out the puzzle.

"Hey, Alpha Three!" Will crowed over the loudspeaker. "Let's party!" On the team leader's display, the horizon tilted as though he were banking his vehicle into a tight turn. Sam's eyes flicked to the upper line of monitors. Will was grinning like a bandit, punching controls on the wraparound panels. "Shall we dance?" he called out. Sam looked down at the lower display, waiting for something meaningful to appear. There it was, a flash of movement at the periphery of the screen. . . .

And then, with a burst of static and electronic snow, the closed-circuit monitors went dead. The overhead speakers crackled and hissed in the white noise of lost radio contact.

Andrea and the tech were on their feet instantly, yelling instructions at each other, punching buttons, fingers flying across keyboards. Many of the digital data displays on the computer consoles were blank or filled with garbled gibberish. Macintyre grabbed the microphone. "Team Alpha, come in," he snapped. "Team Alpha, do you read me?" He turned to Andrea. "Do we still have telemetry?"

"We've got the low-band carrier, the secondary modulation and that's it. What the hell happened?" Sam could hear an edge of real panic in Andrea's voice.

"Oh, shit. . . ." That from John. He pointed to the large waveform monitor. The complex modulated sine wave was starting to blur, starting to separate into its two components. "We're drifting."

"*Ride* it." It was the closest Sam had heard Macintyre

come to raising his voice. As the technician hunched over his keyboard, Macintyre turned to Andrea. "What about the beacons?"

The woman typed a command string onto her keyboard, and stared at the results as they appeared on a display. In the bright quartz-halogen light, Sam could see a sheen of sweat on her forehead. "Decaying," she said. "Amplitude's down 35 percent and dropping, data-link integrity's failing. . . ."

"Can you bring them back?"

Andrea turned and looked straight into Macintyre's eyes. "I don't know," she said softly.

"Try it," the young engineer ordered. *"Now!"*

The woman nodded and turned her attention back to the console. Her fingers flew across the controls. "Alpha Team, come in." Now that she had a task to focus on, the panic was gone, and her voice sounded almost detached. "Emergency return translocation. Repeat, emergency return translocation. We're bringing you back." She turned to the other technician. "Ready? On my mark.

"Translocation back—three . . . two . . . one . . . *Reverse polarity*!"

Three sets of eyes—four, including Sam's—fixed on the empty gantries. For a long second nothing happened. Then that same brilliant flash of light punished Sam's eyes. When she'd blinked away the tears, the six cockpits were back, as if they'd never been gone. Except that the dark gray metal seemed to be misted with white, Sam noticed. *Condensation?*

The canopy of Will's cockpit unlatched and slid back with a slam loud enough to make Sam jump. The muscular pilot swung himself out of the cockpit and stood motionless for a few moments, then moved down the line and helped the rest of his team disembark. They were all back, all six of them, and as far as Sam could see they were unharmed. (Physically *unharmed, at least,* she amended. Emotionally, they all looked like they'd just qualified for the Caterpillar Club.) Sam retreated farther into the shadows as the members of Team Alpha moved toward the center of the room.

Macintyre was waiting for them near the control center. "What happened, Will?"

"Unexpected company." The stocky pilot smiled. He

tried to make it rakish and devil-may-care, but to Sam it looked like a twisted rictus of a child whistling his way through a night-cloaked graveyard on a dare. "Remember how I said the locals would eventually spot us and get interested?"

"We can repeat that argument later," Macintyre replied. The relief was evident in his voice. "Tell me what happened."

Will shrugged, and brushed a lock of hair back from his forehead—then frowned at his fingers as if surprised to see sweat on them. "It was a good translation—clean and smooth," he said. "No problems, no glitches. We're just setting ourselves up for the mission when we pick up the bogies."

"Bogies?" Macintyre repeated.

"Eight of them," the pilot confirmed, "maybe ten. Deeper in the foothills so we were losing some sensor acuity, but they were there all right. Maybe a klick away, and hauling serious ass toward us. And that's when the jamming hit us.

"My radar screen's an omelet, my targeting system starts locking on to rocks and birds and shit, and all I get over my comm link is static."

"Local *and* base communications were down?"

"Both, Mac," Will confirmed. "Down *hard.*" He tried another smile, and this time it came out a lot better. "Damn good thing you hauled us back when you did; otherwise things would have got *real* interesting in a hurry."

Macintyre didn't look one bit happy. "You were jammed?" he repeated quietly.

"I know what jamming looks like, Mac. Trust me on this one, okay?"

"This hasn't happened before." Macintyre shook his head. "Are you sure the jamming was meant for you?"

Will rolled his eyes. "It's kinda hard to tell, you know?" he said ironically. "All the comms gear that might be able to tell me something about the jamming is too busy getting jammed, if you know what I mean."

Macintyre went on as though the pilot hadn't spoken. "And the bogies—were they after you, or did they just happen to be in the vicinity?"

The pilot shrugged eloquently. "I remember one of the

first things I learned in flight school, Mac," he said. "You always make decisions based on capabilities, not on intentions. Eight or ten bogies, *with* jamming support, had the capability to slag my people down. Did they have the intention? I'm sure as hell not going to stick around and find out."

Macintyre nodded. He patted the lead pilot on the shoulder. "You're right, Will. I'm just glad we were able to pull you back."

Will laughed. "No more glad than I am." He glanced over at the other members of Team Alpha, standing in a tight-knit group, talking softly among themselves. "Do you need my people anymore right now?"

"I think we can wait awhile for the debriefing," Macintyre allowed with a faint smile.

"Okay, people." Will turned to his comrades. "Hit the showers; then it's Miller time." He cocked an eyebrow at Macintyre. "Control crew's buying, right, Mac?"

Sam sat on the concrete floor with her back against the equipment enclosure. The pressure of the metal against her back had become a familiar, if uncomfortable constant, and a faint vibration seemed to conduct through her flesh into her ears. She was deep in the shadows now, out of sight of both the console arrays and the cockpits of their gantries. Alarms were ringing at the edges of her consciousness; every moment she stayed here greatly increased the risk of discovery. The odds were good that someone already had connected the abandoned truck with Petrie's missing ID badge, but still she ignored the alarms. *I need time to think,* she told herself for the dozenth time. *I've got to figure it all out, figure out what it has to do with Pop-Pop. Figure out what it has to do with* me.

She could hear Andrea moving around near the control consoles. Will and the other members of Team Alpha had left the area ten minutes ago, presumably to shower and change. As soon as they were alone, Macintyre, Andrea and John had held a low-voiced, tense discussion about what might have gone wrong on the mission. From where she was crouching, Sam hadn't been able to hear more than every third or fourth word, and those she did hear were technobabble like "resonance heterodyning" and "pulse-modulation patterns." Working together, Macintyre and Andrea had resynchronized the two waveforms on the main display. From what little she could make out of their conversation, apparently the jamming that had caused the "drift" was gone and the system was stable again.

After a few more minutes of testing, Macintyre and John walked away, leaving Andrea to run some diagnostics on the command and control systems. It was at that point that Sam had pulled back from her vantage spot to a position where she was less likely to be noticed.

Okay. Let's make sense of it all, Sam told herself firmly. Cockpits containing six "pilots" vanished—*Or* appeared *to vanish,* she corrected automatically—and then returned. Where did they go? "To somewhere called Solaris Seven" was the superficial answer, but that just posed more questions.

Will had talked as if he and his team had been put into some kind of combat situation, where they'd been bushwhacked by a group of "bogies"—hostile craft belonging to an opposition force. She sighed, shaking her head. It could easily be the same kind of simulated mission that fighter jocks went through at Edwards. *How about this?* she asked herself. *Two simulator setups, distinct but networked together. Will and his crew went on their own mission without knowing that another group—call them Team Beta—was in their* own *simulator setup at the same time. Team Alpha is surprised to find that Team Beta is waiting for them in the simulated "battlefield" . . . and is even more surprised that the hostile force is using jamming to screw them up.*

Sam nodded slowly. This was making some sense. *So let's push it one step further,* she decided. *Team Alpha and Team Beta are involved in some kind of long-term war game. Both teams are assigned missions to complete, but they've also got some freedom to play "aggressor" and foul up each other's plans. Almost like real combat operations.* She shifted positions, trying to work some of the tension out of her knees.

That's one hell of a training regimen, she thought, impressed. Even Edwards Air Force Base didn't have anything that sophisticated—not that *she* knew about, at least. *Can Generro Aerospace be working on some new kind of training program for interceptor and strike pilots?*

Okay, now that she had a preliminary hypothesis that

covered at least *some* of the strange events she'd witnessed, it was time to start trying to poke holes in it.

First problem: when Team Alpha got jammed, Macintyre and the others had reacted as if the team was in real danger. Why, if it was just a simulation?

Maybe because victory in the ongoing war game was on the line, she mused. *This new tactic by the aggressor force would have cost them points in the final standings.*

And sometimes when you're in a simulation, you get drawn in all the way—you forget that it's not real. She smiled as she remembered her own reaction the last time she'd "flown" in the Edwards simulator. She'd felt a rush of real anger when her "wingman"—actually a computer simulation—had been splashed by a MiG–29 Fulcrum.

Second problem: what the hell kind of vehicle, and combat, were they trying to simulate here? Chopper combat didn't make any sense; the tactics Will and the others seemed to be using would have been elaborate methods of suicide in a helo battle. So why simulate something that's patently unrealistic?

Maybe because this is just a capabilities test, she thought, *a kind of "shakedown cruise" for new technology. When Macintyre and his cronies have worked the bugs out of the technology,* then *they'll work up a good simulation of something that* matters.

Third problem: she sighed. Well, this was the big one, wasn't it?

Where did the cockpits go? When that brilliant light flashed, *what happened to them?* She could play all the mental games she liked to justify her hypothesis that she'd seen a simulation, but that didn't answer the central question. *What happened to the cockpits?*

Finally, she gave a bleak laugh. *How long can I keep putting off the inevitable?* she asked herself scathingly. *How long can I keep playing mental games? I* know *what I've got to do if I want the real answers to any of these questions.* With a grunt, she forced herself to her feet and ghosted her way between the humming stacks of high technology, planning her next set of lies.

She strode up to the U-shaped command station from the same direction in which she'd seen Macintyre and the others leave. Andrea didn't notice her approach, so she cleared her throat sharply. The thin-faced woman spun with a gasp.

"Sorry to startle you," Sam said. It took all her willpower to keep her voice even, her smile innocent and friendly.

The woman blinked. "It's all right, uh. . . ."

Sam stuck out a hand. "Samantha Dooley."

Andrea hesitated for a moment, but social conditioning quickly took control. She grasped Sam's hand in a firm, dry grip and shook it. "Andrea Wallinger. I, uh, I haven't. . . ."

"I know," Sam cut her off with an apologetic grin. "I haven't made the time to meet everyone, like I should have."

Andrea blinked again. "You're new?" A faint tinge of suspicion in her voice set off alarm bells in Sam's mind.

"In a manner of speaking," Sam went on smoothly. Mentally she crossed her fingers as she tried a gamble. "I've just been seconded from New Horizons."

The other woman relaxed visibly. "Oh, of course." She paused. "Dooley?" she repeated hesitantly. "Have I heard of you?"

"Not me, probably," Sam admitted with a laugh. "Maybe someday, though." She paused, as though a new thought had struck her. "You're probably thinking of my father," she suggested, "or my grandfather." Andrew frowned. "Jim Dooley, Junior and Senior?"

Andrea's expression cleared. "Oh, yes, certainly. You're part of *that* family?" She shook her head with a smile. "Quite a legacy."

"Quite a pair of shoes to fill," Sam corrected with a smile.

The other woman laughed. When she smiled, her face was actually very pretty, Sam noticed. It was only Andrea's serious expression that made her look plain. "I'm sure you'll fill them in time, Samantha," she said.

"Well, actually, I've got a chance to start right now." Sam braced herself. *Time for the big lie.* "Mr. Macintyre ran into me in the hall and sent me in here. He told me he wants me to go through the U–N–V one-thirty-seven."

"Oh?" Andrea frowned again. "When?"

"Now." Sam held her breath.

"*Now?*" Andrea sounded scandalized. "You can't be serious."

Sam blinked in feigned surprise. "Why not?" she asked. She gestured to the main display, where a single synchronized waveform burned brilliant green. "He said you've got Solaris Seven all locked in."

"Well, yes, but . . ."—Andrea's hands fluttered like wounded birds—". . . but we've been having some serious problems. . . ."

Again Sam cut her off, this time letting a hint of impatience into her words. "I know about that. Will told me all about it. And that's why Mac wants to send me back right now. Reconnaissance, to check out how the situation's developing." She gestured toward the waveforms again. "You have congruence," she pointed out. "You can translocate me now, and I can report back to Mac before he gets impatient. Okay?"

Andrea didn't look at all convinced. "Maybe I should talk to Mac directly." She reached for a telephone that Sam hadn't noticed before, mounted on the console.

Sam struggled to hide her sudden crescendo of tension. She shrugged carelessly. "If you have to disturb him, I guess," she said lightly. "He's in a meeting with Mr. Leclerc at the moment, but if you really need to ask him for permission. . . ." She let the thought trail off.

The technician shifted her weight uncomfortably. Sam could see the indecision in her eyes, could almost hear her thoughts: *Do I take responsibility myself, or do I run to Mac for permission?*

I've almost got her, Sam told herself. *All she needs is one more little shove . . . but I can't push too hard.*

Sam glanced at her watch, and shrugged. "It probably doesn't matter anyway," she said. "We've almost missed the window of opportunity." She shrugged. "Next time, maybe." She started to turn away.

"Uh . . . Samantha . . . ?"

Yes! Sam thought. As casually as she could manage, she turned back. "Uh-huh?"

"If it's really important. . . ."

Sam shrugged. "Mac seems to think so."

Andrea's expression cleared as she made her decision.

She even flashed Sam a brief smile. "How long *is* your window?"

Sam looked at her watch again. It was 12:11. She shrugged once more. "He wanted me to translocate by 12:15 . . . if we can make it."

Andrea glanced at a time display on the nearest console. "We can make it," she confirmed. "Take Privateer. I'll power up the gantry."

"Thanks, Andrea. I owe you one." Fighting to keep her expression calm and sober, she hurried over to the row of cockpits.

Privateer was the second cockpit from the right, one of the two that hadn't been involved in the first mission. To its right was Calamity Jane; to its left, Call of the Wild, still frosted with a faint layer of condensation. Sam swung into Privateer, settling herself into the seat.

The cockpit wasn't nearly as confining as it looked from the outside, and from the monitors. The hip, shoulder and leg room was better than in most of the flight simulators she'd tried at Edwards, and the cockpit was *much* more spacious than the Indy-style racing car she'd once had a chance to drive. Even the headroom was ample. Reaching up and back, she grabbed the opaque canopy and slid it along its rails until it locked into place. Inside her metal cocoon, she could no longer hear the hum and burr of high-energy electronics that filled the cavernous space outside. The only sound she could hear now was the faint soughing of air conditioning.

Quickly, she tried to orient herself to the cockpit. Two rudder pedals lay under her feet. She wrapped her hand around the joystick mounted on the right-side console. Her forefinger naturally fell on a pistol-style trigger, while on the top of the stick were one blue and one green thumb button. At her left hand was the throttle—a simple T-stick, like the automatic shift in an old car, with a thumb button on the right end. (*So this* can't *be a helicopter simulation,* she decided. *The controls just aren't right.*)

Directly in front of her, between two vertical consoles studded with buttons in red, green and blue, and red LED data displays—now blank—was a large TV-style monitor screen. There was no image on it, but faint dots drifting around the screen's periphery told her it was powered up.

Below the main screen was something that resembled a radar screen, or perhaps the threat display in an F–16 Falcon. Two intersecting lines divided the screen into quadrants, while a shape similar to a slice of pie—with its apex positioned at the center of the screen—glowed a different color. (*A radar arc of some kind?* Sam wondered. *Some type of limited-arc weapon targeting?*) On the same panel, to the left of the radar screen, she saw a compass rose and what seemed to be a speed scale, ranging from zero to 170. (*Miles per hour? Kilometers per hour? Or—like on the Falcon—knots divided by ten?*) To the right were two additional display windows—both currently blank—marked DISPLAY KEY and DAMAGE. The rest of the consoles. . . .

She shook her head. *More buttons, basically*—illuminated push buttons and small-format alphanumeric keypads. Few were identified, and those that were had cryptic labels like AC-10 and PPC. While the overall complexity fell well short of that of a modern fighter jet cockpit, it was a cinch she wasn't going to comprehend everything on first glance. *Just stick with what you know, Dooley,* she cautioned herself. *Stick, throttle and rudder pedals are a good start.*

"Samantha?" Andrea's voice crackled from a small speaker mounted somewhere behind Sam's head. "Everything okay?"

Sam looked up above the main display screen, saw the faint glint of glass that marked the location of the closed-circuit camera. She smiled up at it as she adjusted a small gooseneck microphone. She glanced down, trying to find the "transmit" button. *There, that should be it: the small red button near the throttle.* She pressed it and heard an electronic click from the speaker. "Dooley One, check," she announced crisply.

"Telemetry good. UFT cockpit on line."

"How are the waveforms, Andrea?"

"Locked in," the technician confirmed. "Stage Two, primaries at two billion volts."

Sam closed her eyes, trying to concentrate on her sensations. If what Andrea said was true, two *billion* volts—two *gigavolts*—of electrical potential was flowing through the metal gantry supporting the cockpit. (*What kind of charge does an electric chair use?* she wondered suddenly. *Only two* thousand *volts, isn't it . . . ?*) She could feel a faint tingling in her skin, particularly at the nape of her neck, but she had no way of knowing if that was a consequence of the electrical current or just a symptom of stress.

"What coordinates do you want, Dooley One?" Andrea's voice asked.

Sam hesitated. "U–N–V one-thirty-seven," she replied at last.

"Yes, I know," Andrea said patiently, "but what *coordinates*?"

Uh-oh. Sam racked her brain. What had Will or Macintyre or whoever said about coordinates? "Same as the last mission, please," she said, forcing her voice to be firm. *What was it?* "The hills outside Roland Fields. Drop me on the same spot as you did Will, if you can."

"Well, I can get you close," Andrea said slowly. "Will plus-or-minus ten centimeters be good enough?"

She's joking, Sam realized with a rush of relief. *Maybe the big lie is going to work.*

"Confirm retrieval criteria, Dooley One."

"Standard."

"Automatic sequence start," Andrea's voice announced. "Inductance fields stable. Gantry power coming up."

For a moment it felt as though a million tiny bugs were crawling across Sam's skin. With an effort, she fought back the impulse to brush at her legs, her face. *It's just a magnetic field,* she told herself, *a* strong *magnetic field. The flux makes the tiny hairs on your skin repel each other.*

"Steady at one gigahertz," the crackling voice stated. "Translocation in three . . . in two . . . in one. . . ."

And, sickeningly, the bottom dropped out of Samantha's world.

17

She was struck blind.

For one, horrible moment Samantha could see nothing. Not darkness; darkness was an attribute of *something.* This was very different—an absolute absence of all visual sensation whatsoever. She thought she whimpered, but she couldn't be sure.

What made the blindness worse was the sensation of falling. Vertiginous, terrifying on the most basic level. *The cockpit's plummeting like a broken elevator,* her mind yammered, but another part of her realized that wasn't quite true. She was falling, yes, but . . . *What did Fred Noonan write in his diary? ". . . This 'drop' was in a direction I never knew existed. . . ."* That was precisely how it felt.

The nothingness lasted less than a second, but the disorientation that accompanied it persisted considerably longer. As suddenly as it had struck, the sense of falling vanished, and Sam saw the confines of the cockpit—now reassuring, almost familiar—close around her.

"Dooley One." Andrea's voice sounded strange—not just distortion, but almost a kind of phase-shift effect. "Are you all right?"

Sam glanced down at her hands, noticed they were shaking. She tightened her grip on the stick and throttle and the shaking stopped. "I'm okay, Control," she said, unable to keep the quaver out of her voice. "Er . . . A bit of a glitch on translocation, that's all."

"Glitch? What kind of glitch?"

"Momentary instability, that's all," Sam blustered.

"Nothing showed up on my readouts," Andrea countered. There was a hint of something—*suspicion*?—in the woman's voice.

"Well, nothing to worry about anyway," Sam told her. "Everything's stable now."

Andrea made a noncommittal sound. "Hmm."

I've got to watch myself, Sam thought firmly. *She can terminate this whole thing in an instant if she figures out I'm an impostor. Which probably doesn't give me much time.*

She looked at her cockpit's main display screen. The image it showed was faint, washed out. After a brief search, she found and adjusted the contrast and brightness controls for the screen. The image came into clear view.

It was the same terrain she'd seen on the slave displays in the control center: the blasted wasteland of rutted hardpan, sloping up in the distance toward distant hills. A watery light shone down through the low cloud cover. As before, she seemed to be steady at an altitude of 50 or 60 feet above the ground. She closed her eyes for a moment, trying to *feel* the vehicle—or whatever it was—around her. A faint vibration transmitted itself through the seat and floor, up her spinal column, into her jaw and ears, the almost subliminal hum of an idling engine. There was none of the high-amplitude, low-frequency vibration she associated with a helicopter.

"Dooley One, what's your mission?" Andrea asked suddenly. This time the suspicion in her voice was unmistakable.

Sam's eyes snapped open. "Simple recon, Control," she replied as calmly as she could. "I was just sightseeing." *I'd better do something.* She centered the joystick, tested the play of the rudder pedals, and gingerly pushed the throttle forward.

She gasped aloud as the vehicle lurched forward. Not the steady acceleration of a fixed-wing plane or the nose-dipping surge of a helo, this motion was . . . *something else.* It was discontinuous, jerky, jolting.

My God, this is real! For the first time, as the vehicle lurched forward, true and total conviction penetrated and took hold of her emotions. *This isn't a simulation. This* can't be *a simulation. I'm . . .* somewhere else, *I've been "translocated."* All of her hypotheses fell apart in an instant, revealed for what they really were: facile justifications and evasions, denials of reality. She heard a sound that was a cross between a bitter laugh and a whimper—and realized it came from her own throat. Viscerally she *knew,* at last. She'd been physically translocated to another place (another *time*?).

"Dooley One, come in."

Sam's pilot's instincts kicked in, suppressing the fear that threatened to incapacitate her. It was almost as if a screen suddenly slammed shut, separating her intellect from her emotions. Her gut still churned, her heart still raced, her throat still spasmed . . . but she could control it. Her thoughts were cold, emotionless—crystalline and precise. *Man,* she thought, *I am going to have one* gonzo *of an emotional reaction when I let myself go. . . .*

She smiled coolly up into the closed-circuit video camera. "Dooley One here, Control." Her voice was crisp, professional. "Receiving you five-by. I've got a green board here, everything's fine."

Andrea hesitated. When she finally replied, Sam could hear that the other woman's suspicion had eased. "Roger that, Dooley One. Keep me updated."

"That's a roj." Sam looked down at the speed display as she pushed the throttle forward another fraction of an inch. A yellow bar crept up the graduated scale, steadying at the "50" tick. *Time to see what this baby can do,* she told herself. Slowly she edged the throttle forward until the speed bar touched 70.

The motion of her vehicle changed drastically, she noted. Her ride still lurched along in its discontinuous motion, now reinforced by a rhythmic pounding vibration strong enough to jar her teeth together unless she kept her jaws clenched. The cycle of the pounding was close to one per second, she estimated—*Almost like the footsteps of someone walking briskly,* she thought. Tentatively, she nudged the throttle farther along its track until the speedo read 80. As she half-expected, the cadence of the pounding, jarring impacts increased. *What am I supposed to make of that?* she wondered. The vibration obviously wasn't a harmonic effect, as she'd suspected earlier—it was too powerful and precise for that.

She stretched the fingers of her right hand, and took a better grip on the joystick. *Let's see how this thing corners.* Gently, she pushed the stick to the left.

Instantly, the view on the main display screen moved, shifting to the right. She centered the stick; the sideways movement stopped. *Okay, I just made a turn. . . .*

But no, she realized suddenly, she *hadn't* turned the craft. Something was wrong with the view on the screen, and it took her a couple of moments to figure out what it was. The parallax and perspective were wrong; the sense of motion didn't match. Her vehicle was still following the same trajectory; it was just her angle of view that had altered. *It's like a person walking forward, turning their head to the left,* she understood. *Or like a tank pivoting its turret to the left without changing its actual course.* (Could she be driving some type of *tank*?) She looked down at what she took to be the radar or threat display. Yes, she saw, the pie-shaped sector—the targeting arc?—was offset by about 20 degrees from the top of the screen. Using that as a guide, she moved the stick to the right, stopping again when her field of view was aligned with her direction of motion.

So the stick pivots my . . . my what? *My turret?* That meant the pedals had to control direction. She pushed gently on the left rudder pedal, watched with satisfaction as the view of the screen shifted. Yes, she saw, this time the perspective matched properly; she *was* turning the vehicle. (She imagined a huge tank, kicking up plumes of dust as it churned its way across the hardpan.)

Only one thing left to try. . . . Gingerly, she pulled back on the joystick. *If this* is *a tank, nothing should happen, should it?*

Even through her tightly imposed mental control she felt a flash of alarm as the cockpit tilted backward—*Like a plane going into a climb.* On the forward display, the distant horizon moved toward the bottom of the screen. Her altitude above the hardpan hadn't changed, however, she noticed immediately. For the first time, she saw a cursor—*No,* she corrected, *a crosshair*—in the center of her screen. Before, it had been positioned on the horizon, which presumably was why she hadn't spotted it. Now, though, it showed up clearly against the gray of the sky. She centered the stick again, feeling the cockpit tilt forward once more until it was horizontal. *Oh, man. . . . I have no idea what I'm doing.*

"Dooley One." Andrea's crackling voice jolted her. "Telemetry's reading multiple bogies, bearing 94 degrees relative. Can you confirm?"

Bogies? Sam looked down at her threat display.

Yes, there they were—two strange, angular shapes near the top of the lower right-hand quadrant of the screen, about halfway between the center and the outer edge. *What's the distance scale on this display?* Sam wondered suddenly. She scanned the panel, but couldn't spot anything that looked like a scale. *I guess that's another one of those things you're supposed to* know. If this were a Falcon, a blip at that spot on the threat display would be 15 nautical miles out. *But this isn't a Falcon,* she reminded herself firmly.

"Dooley One?"

"Roger that, Control," she said calmly. "I'm showing two bogies."

"What range, Dooley One?"

You had *to ask that, didn't you . . . ?* "I'm closing to investigate," Sam stated, ignoring Andrea's question.

"Your mission's recon, isn't it?" the technician asked sharply. "You're supposed to avoid close contact."

"I'm closing to investigate," Sam repeated, voice firm. She applied pressure on the right rudder pedal, wheeling her vehicle around in a wide turn to the right. *Turning radius sucks,* she told herself. She edged the throttle back, dropping her speed to about 50. As she'd expected, the turn radius tightened up.

On the display screen, the two angular bogies were moving around toward the top of the screen as Sam's angle changed. They weren't quite in the V-shaped acquisition arc, but they would be in a couple of moments. *Then we'll see what we shall see. . . .*

"Dooley One." There was a real edge of command to Andrea's voice this time. "You are forbidden to make contract. Break off immediately and prepare for translocation back."

"Negative, Control. This is what Macintyre told me to do."

A new voice—male, this time—sounded from the speaker, and Sam cringed. She felt her cheeks burning with a child's embarrassment at getting caught out in a lie. "Ms. Dooley, this is Ernest Macintyre. Break off and shut down before you get yourself killed. We're bringing you back."

Anger flared in Sam's chest, overcoming the embarrassment and fear. *Like hell you are, Mac! I haven't learned enough yet.* She looked around the cockpit desperately. There had to be some controls somewhere for the telemetry that linked her cockpit to the control system at Generro Aerospace.

"Translocation back . . . in five . . . in four . . ." Andrea's voice sounded in her ears like a countdown to disaster. ". . . in three . . ." Sam began to panic.

There they were—a small panel of toggle switches mounted on the panel below the throttle. Unlike most other controls in the cockpit, these actually had labels attached: TELEMETRY, BEACON and COMMS. Desperately, she flipped the first two toggles to OFF.

". . . In two . . ." Andrea's countdown stopped, and the woman gasped. "She's turned off her beacon, Mac."

"Dooley, you don't know what you're doing," Macintyre snapped. (*You got that right, Mac,* she answered mentally, with a wry smile.) "This isn't a game. We've lost people before . . . and that's been *with* an active beacon."

"Like my father, you mean?"

She'd said that more to give herself time to think than anything, but Macintyre's response shocked her into momentary immobility. "That's right, Dooley. And if you don't want to join him, turn your beacon back on." Sam heard something scrape against the microphone—presumably Macintyre's hand, covering it. His next comment was so muffled she could barely make out the words. "Andrea, manual override. Get me that beacon back on line."

"It'll take time."

"We don't *have* time. Just do it." The muffling hand was removed from the microphone, and Macintyre's voice was clear again. "Dooley. Samantha—*Sam* . . . Please. Turn away from the contacts and extend. When you're out of range, power up your beacon again and we'll try to get you back in one piece. Okay?"

With a snort, Sam snapped the third toggle switch to the OFF position. The intercom speaker went silent. "That conversation was getting boring anyway," she muttered.

Dad . . . ? He died on a mission like this . . . ?

Get a grip, Dooley, she told herself firmly, forcing those thoughts from her consciousness. *You can think about all that later . . . if there* is *a later.*

While she'd been dealing with Andrea and Macintyre, Sam's instincts had put her vehicle back onto a straight course. Now, however, she pulled the throttle back even farther and initiated a tight right-hand turn. The distant hills, nearly invisible through the mist, swung across the forward screen, as did the two bogies on the threat display below. The first of the blips entered the acquisition arc on the display . . .

And she felt her mouth drop open as the bogie appeared on her forward screen.

Despite what she knew, Sam still had been expecting to

see some kind of helicopter hugging the contours of the ground in a nape-of-earth flight path. Instead . . .

Instead, through the faint mist, she saw a figure—a humanoid, bipedal figure. For an instant, her sense of scale went wild, like a tumbled gyro in an inertial navigation system. She shook her head to clear it. *If that's a person, then. . . .*

But it *wasn't* a person—she saw that a moment later, and once again her sense of scale shifted wildly. The figure ahead *was* bipedal and roughly humanoid, but it wasn't human. Its lines were angular, blocky—mechanical. Planes of metal glinted in the dim light seeping through the cloud cover. What she'd initially taken to be arms were weapons mounts of some kind, with huge, gaping muzzles in place of hands. The feet were clawed monstrosities, on metal-jointed "legs" the thickness of a telephone booth. The head, looming 50 feet or more above the ground, was . . . well, she couldn't make out *what* it was—a sensor platform of some kind, perhaps? For all the world, it looked like a robot—a huge, brutal-looking robot from some cheap, cheesy science fiction movie.

Except that every robot she'd ever seen on the late-late sci-fi movie was clumsy and slow, slogging along at a crawl. *This thing's seriously hauling ass.* Its legs were pumping like a long-distance runner's, driving the gargantuan mechanism forward at a speed that was almost literally unbelievable. A huge rooster-tail of dust trailed behind it.

The robot—that's how she labeled it in her mind, at least—wasn't heading straight for her. Instead, it was on an almost parallel course.

Not for long, though. In response to some cue that she'd missed, it changed direction, lumbering around in a wide-radius turn. As it shifted direction, its movements brought home to Sam just how massive the thing really was. *It's got to weigh 50 tons if it's an ounce,* she realized, *and it's* running. . . .

Before it could complete the turn, four beams of ruby light lanced into Sam's screen display, bracketing the running robot. *Holy crap! Lasers*—powerful *lasers* . . . The beams flicked out of existence, then flashed on again. This time one of the beams caught the robot in the torso. Sam flinched as fragments of thick metal—*Armor*?—exploded away from the impact point, raining to the ground like shrapnel.

The target robot's torso pivoted, twisting to face back the way it had come. Sam was completing her turn, her angle of view on the main screen—That*'s what the pie-shaped segment on the radar display represents,* she realized—coming around to include the second bogie. It was another robot, on a similar scale to the first, but of a slightly different design. This figure was less humanoid than the first, with large open-fronted cubes mounted on its hulking shoulders. In the dim light, Sam thought she could make out arrays of red-tipped cones mounted within the open cubes. *Missile racks . . . ?*

The first robot's torso stopped pivoting, and Sam saw its arms move, bringing their own weapons to bear. Ruby light—so brilliant that the beams looked like solid bars—flashed through the dust, flicking and blinking like camera strobes, there then gone. From the robot's massive right arm, a beam of azure blue—*The color of Cherenkov radiation,* Sam thought—lashed out with the sound of a thunderclap.

Jesus Christ, they're trying to kill *each other!*

Sam slammed her throttle all the way back in its slot, her stomach lurching as her vehicle—*Another one of those giant robots . . . ?*—decelerated hard and came to a stop. She closed her eyes, trying to ignore the mechanical carnage that filled her forward screen. She felt a sudden, desperate need to escape, to *withdraw*—to close herself off from what was happening around her, to return to a place where everything followed the normal, familiar laws of physics . . . even if that place was just in her own mind. The sounds and the sensations surrounding her seemed to retreat. As if from a huge distance, she felt her muscles shift as she brought her legs up, hugging her knees to her chest, sinking her face down to shelter against her thighs . . .

No!

No! Dooley, you . . . cannot . . . withdraw! With all the considerable strength of her will, she fought the overwhelming desire—the *need*—to sink into a fetal position and ignore the outside world. *You've got to hang tough, Dooley, goddamn it! There is no easy way out of this.*

Remember the osprey, Dooley. Full investment.

Slowly, agonizingly slowly, she straightened her back, pushed her legs back into the well under the console, placed her feet on the rudder pedals. She squared her shoulders, pushed some wayward hair back from her eyes. *Stay with it, Dooley.* She took a deep breath, held it as long as she could, then let it out silently. Another . . . then another. The feeling of distance, of detachment, was fading—*Thank God for small favors,* she thought wryly. She clenched her fists tightly, reassured by the sensations in her forearms. Yes, her body was back under control of her mind. Fighting back the urge to shudder, she returned her attention to the forward screen.

The situation had developed—or maybe "deteriorated" was a better word—while she'd been fighting her traitor body. Another two of the giant robots had entered the fray from somewhere offscreen, and all four of the fighting machines were locked in the equivalent of a close dogfight, a "furball." The air was filled with dust, kicked up by pounding metal feet, cutting visibility down to considerably less than a mile. Lances of ruby light flashed and flicked through the haze, boiling armor away from whatever they struck, or more rarely blowing unrecognizable mechanisms away in secondary explosions. Bolts of azure blue were much less frequent than the laser beams, but seemed to do considerably more damage when they struck. Sam flinched in sympathetic pain as she saw a blue bolt blow the arm clean off a target robot.

My God. . . . These things can absorb a horrendous amount of punishment, she realized. *And dish it out, too.*

Damn, what could one of those things do to a tank platoon? She remembered the row of cockpits at Generro Aerospace. *Let alone* eight*!*

On the screen, one of the monster robots had pivoted to face directly toward Sam. A barrage of laser fire strobed out, blowing gaping furrows in the hardpan a dozen yards in front of her vehicle. As if the barrage had been a silent cue, the other three robots held their fire, then began lumbering turns in her direction.

Holy shit*!* Dooley, *it's time to get your butt out of here. . . .* As she slammed the throttle full forward and stamped on the left rudder pedal, another fusillade of laser fire flashed around her. A harsh metal *crang* sound echoed through her cockpit, and the seat-back slammed her in the kidneys. *Shit, I've been* hit . . . *!* For the first time, the portion of the lower display screen labeled DAMAGE came to life. On it was a schematic of a squat, angular but roughly humanoid robot. (*That's what* I'm *driving . . . ?*) Most of the vectors making up the schematic were green. The lower right quarter of the torso glowed yellow, however, and the upper portion of the right leg gleamed orange.

The speedo bar was climbing up the scale, and Sam's vehicle—*My giant robot*—was swinging around to the left in a wide turn. The other four robots shifted to the right of the forward screen, quickly disappearing completely from view. They were still visible on the threat display, though, she saw, and seemed to be taking up the pursuit. The cockpit jolted hard again, then yet again, and heavy concussions punished her ears. Yellow, orange and red flickered over the damage schematic. *I'm getting pasted here.*

There was something psychologically terrifying about turning her back on people shooting at her, she found. Even as her speed climbed toward 90 and she saw the distance between her and her pursuers extending on the threat display, she couldn't shake the paranoia and fear—the overwhelming *need* to see what was happening behind her. As she completed her turn and continued to accelerate, she pushed the stick hard to the right. The view on the forward screen and the visual arc on the threat display pivoted rapidly. After watching the other robots, she knew what was happening now: the torso of her robot was pivoting at the "waist," turning to look back, while it was still sprinting forward at high speed. Her four pursuers quickly swung into view, and she centered the joystick. The pivoting motion stopped.

The view on the screen was disconcerting. The ground seemed to rush *away* beneath her. It was like driving a car forward at highway speed while twisted around to look out the rear window. She did her best to ignore the disconcerting motion cues, while focusing her attention on her pursuers.

They were eight or nine hundred yards behind her, she guessed. Three were falling back even farther, but one—the unit with the missile racks looming over its shoulders—seemed to be matching her speed. *Uh, oh. . . .*

The cockpit jarred and jolted again—not from a weapons hit this time; Sam hadn't seen anything fire at her. She jammed the joystick over to the right again. As the torso started to twist, she realized with a cold shock what was happening. She was already into the rough, broken ground that preceded the foothills. And that meant she was sprinting, in a 50-ton robot five dozen feet tall, into terrain striated by chasms and streambeds and dotted with boulders. She shuddered as she imagined her robot stubbing its metallic toe against a rock—*At 90 kilometers per hour,* she reminded herself—and going flying. She had no choice, she realized; she hauled back on the throttle, and watched the display as the speed plummeted.

Her four pursuers weren't slackening their speed, she saw immediately; they were eating up the distance with their long strides. *Beam me up, Scotty,* she thought fervently. *There's no place like home, there's no place like home. . . .* Reaching down, she flipped the three toggle switches—TELEMETRY, BEACON and COMMS—back to ON. A babble of panicked voices burst from the speaker, almost deafening her.

". . . Powered down, I can't override . . ."

". . . a rescue team?"

"We don't have the gantries configured for multiple time-offset insertion. Give me an hour, maybe . . ."

"Damn, damn, damn, damn . . ."

Sam recognized two of the voices: Macintyre and Andrea Wallinger. The others were unfamiliar. "Hey," she called out, "I'm ready to come home anytime you're up for it."

The babble shut off as if someone had flicked a switch. Then she heard Macintyre's voice. "Dooley, your comms are back on line."

No shit, Sherlock, she wanted to say. But she kept her mouth shut.

"What's your status?"

"Delta sierra, Control," Sam announced, managing to keep her voice at least halfway calm, "and getting worse." Quickly, she filled Macintyre in on the pursuit and the damage displayed on her monitor. "If you want to pull me out of here now, I'll come quietly," she concluded. "I'll take my medicine."

Macintyre didn't answer right away, and Sam's blood ran

suddenly cold. "I'm afraid it's not that simple, Samantha," he said quietly. "How far out are the bogies?"

"Maybe half a mile and closing fast. *Why* isn't it that simple, Macintyre? I've powered up my beacon again."

"It may be powered up, but it takes time to synch with your signal." He made a *tsk* noise. "Do you have any idea how complex the physics involved are?"

"I honestly don't *care* at the moment, Macintyre," she snapped. Panic was rising, and it was getting more and more difficult to fight it back. "We'll talk tech all you like after you get me the hell *out* of here!"

"Hang tight, Dooley. This is Will Zdebiak." She recognized the voice of the pilot who'd led the mission she'd watched. "Mac's working on it. He says he'll have a lock in . . ."—his voice faded as he turned aside for a moment—"sixty, Mac?" He turned back to the microphone. "Sixty seconds. Give me your status again."

Sam scanned the forward screen and all her displays. Some of the yellow areas on the damage schematic had turned orange or even red. *What does* that *mean? Am I on fire . . . ?* She clenched her fists around stick and throttle until the tendons in her forearms ached. Then she released her grip, forcing her muscles to relax, feeling the tension flooding out of her body. When she spoke, the calm tone of her voice came as a surprise even to her. "Okay, Control. I'm on the edge of the foothills, getting into rough terrain."

"Don't go any further, Dooley," Will cut her off. "The 'Mech data-models we're using are great for flat ground, but the balance algorithms go to hell in a handcart once you're into broken terrain. Do you read me?"

"Face plant, you mean."

"You got it. And trying a headstand in a 50-ton BattleMech don't work too good, if you get my drift."

Part of Sam's mind—that part not consumed with the worries of immediate survival—filed some of Will's words away in her memory for later consideration. *'Mech,* she thought. *BattleMech. So* that's *what these things are.* "And I take it the bandits don't have the same restriction?" she said dryly.

"You got that right," the pilot confirmed. "Are they still closing?"

"Two are hanging back," she told him, checking her forward screen and radar display. "The other two are still closing, but they've backed way off on their speed."

"Good." She heard the predatory satisfaction in the pilot's voice. "They don't know what to make of you yet. Have you returned fire yet?"

"With *what*?" she asked simply.

Will chuckled. "Oh, the usual," he said lightly. "Autocannons. Lasers. Missiles. Particle projection cannons. You might not know it, but you're riding in a pretty decent armory, Dooley."

"Good enough to slag down four 'Mechs?"

"Not *that* good."

I didn't think so, she thought dryly.

"I want you to give them something to think about," Will went on firmly. "Call it suppression fire. Give us a little more time to lock in on your beacon and yank you out of there. Okay?"

"Hey, I'm open to suggestions here."

The pilot chuckled again. Sam imagined his steel-gray eyes flashing with amusement. "I'll talk you through it," he said reassuringly. "You've probably figured out that your joystick controls your targeting crosshairs." Sam grunted acknowledgment. "Have you reconfigured your weapons?"

"How?" she demanded.

"Good point," he allowed. "Okay, that means you've got everything—and I *do* mean everything—assigned to the trigger on your joystick. All you've got to do is put your crosshairs on a target—like the nearest 'Mech—keep it there, and just keep pulling that trigger. You're going to spike your heat into the stratosphere, but since we should have you out of there real soon now, you won't have to worry. Got it?"

Sam shrugged. "I'll give it a try," she said. "And give Macintyre a firm kick in the behind for me, okay?"

"Forty-five seconds, Samantha." That was Macintyre's voice. From his tone she knew the young engineer was trying to reassure her, but it wasn't working. *He said* sixty *seconds last time. . . and that was more than a minute ago. This is like a two-minute drill in football.*

Only one of the hostile BattleMechs was continuing to advance, and even that had slowed drastically. Will was right, Sam realized: the pursuers didn't know what to make of her, and didn't want to rush headlong into an untenable position, or maybe an ambush. Even at cruising speed, however, the lead 'Mech would be on top of her in thirty seconds. She wiped the palm of her right hand—slick with sweat—against her thigh, then gripped the joystick again.

She forced herself to ignore the sensations in her inner ear as she pivoted her 'Mech's torso. The joystick had a surprisingly delicate touch, and it took her a second or two to position the crosshairs on top of the hulking shape of the advancing BattleMech. As she settled the crosshairs on her target, a range designation flashed on the screen. *Three hundred fifty meters. That's plenty close enough, bucko.* Bracing herself, she pulled the trigger.

The noise was incredible, echoing harshly within the cockpit. It combined the scream of high-rate-of-fire machine guns, the thudding of a weapon with a much lower rate of fire but launching larger projectiles, the distinctive *pah* of discharging capacitors, and a discharge that sounded like a lightning bolt striking the canopy. Sam's ears rang with the aural distillation of modern combat.

On-screen, the enemy 'Mech disappeared. Lasers flayed away metallic skin and armor. Machine gun rounds sparked and flashed off the angled facets of the BattleMech's head. An azure-blue bolt detonated the ground directly beneath the target's feet, throwing thousands of pounds of dust and debris into the air. A second later, fireballs bloomed all across the 'Mech's torso as a volley of missiles struck home. Secondary explosions flared. Smoke boiled up in a black-and-red puffball that completely engulfed the BattleMech.

"Holy *Christ* . . ." Sam gasped. She couldn't even grasp the magnitude of the firepower she'd just brought to bear. She forgot about pulling the trigger again as she stared at the screen, waiting for the smoke to disperse so she could see the wreckage of her target.

She almost shrieked in shock as the target 'Mech lurched toward her out of the smoke cloud. It was obviously damaged, blackened and charred across the entire head and torso with a couple of gaping craters showing some of its internal structure. Its right arm hung at a strange angle, as though its elbow had been shattered. But it was still on its feet, and still moving toward her. Mauled as it was, it looked even more intimidating than it had before her attack.

"Mac," she called, the edge of hysteria in her voice clear even to her ears. "I'm ready to leave, Mac."

"Thirty more seconds, Samantha."

The two open-faced cubes mounted on the shoulders of the target 'Mech belched white smoke. A dozen small, stubby missiles—white, with bright red nose cones—hurtled clear, six from each rack. She saw them wobble in the air for a moment, then straighten out as they acquired their target.

"I don't have *three* seconds, Mac. Incoming missiles." She watched the projectiles arc toward her, leaving surprisingly delicate white smoke-trails. And she braced for impact.

18

The impact as the missiles hit was horrendous, cataclysmic—as if the entire arch of the sky had collapsed on top of Samantha. The cockpit rang like a gong with the impact, a single overwhelming concussion as if all the missiles had detonated simultaneously in a perfect time-on-target salvo. Sam's head was slammed against the canopy, and a brilliant light exploded in her brain, followed by darkness.

She regained consciousness a couple of seconds later. It was pain that returned first, a brutal hammering in her right temple and a sharper, searing agony in her left knee. For one horrible instant, she didn't know where she was, what had happened. Then memory flooded back, making sense of what she could see around her.

The cockpit was lying on its left side; obviously the 'Mech had fallen, or been blown off its feet by the missile impacts. If there was a harness or seat belt, Sam hadn't seen it, so when the giant robot had hit the ground—*Christ, think of the impact! Fifty tons falling sixty feet . . .*—she'd been slammed hard against the side of the cockpit. *I'm lucky I didn't break my neck or crack my skull,* she realized with a chill. The T-stick of the throttle was digging painfully into her ribs. She cursed, and moved off the protrusion.

It was dark in the cockpit, the only illumination coming from the few buttons and data displays still functioning. The forward view-screen and the radar/threat display were both dead. A couple of annunciator panels glowed sullen red.

What about the radio? she wondered. Suddenly, that question filled her mind. She reached over and clicked the radio transmit key a couple of times. The speaker was totally silent—no hiss of static, no electronic pop as she keyed the microphone. That didn't mean she wasn't transmitting, she reminded herself hopefully, just that she couldn't receive.

She keyed the mike again. "Control, this is Dooley One." She tried to keep her voice emotionless, professional. It wasn't working, she recognized with chagrin. "I'm still in one piece, but I can't say the same for my ride. Most systems seem to be down or damaged, and I think the only way this thing's going to move again is if somebody tows it. Can you get me out of here? Over."

She released the transmit key. The speaker remained dead.

A chill wind seemed to blow across the back of Sam's neck. She keyed the mike once more. "Control, this is Sam Dooley. I'm alive, and I'm requesting immediate retrieval. Do you read me? Over."

Silence. *What if they think I'm dead?* she asked herself suddenly. *What if they've lost contact? They know missiles were inbound; I told them that myself. If I get knocked out of contact immediately afterward, what are they going to think?*

And are they going to bother translocating back what they expect to be a dead body?

Unwilling to give up hope, she keyed the mike once again. "Mac, this is Sam Dooley." She heard the hint of hysteria in her own voice and scorned herself for it. "If you can hear me, pull me out of here. Repeat—my BattleMech's down, but I'm in one piece and feeling awful lonely, if you get my drift. If there's any way of letting me know you've got this message, Mac, do it, okay?" She released the transmit button and tried to find a more comfortable position.

The ventilation system was dead, the near-subliminal soughing of the fan silent. For the first time, Sam realized how hot it was in the cockpit. She was bathed in sweat, her hair matted, her clothes sticking to her skin. Some of that was a reaction to fear and stress, she knew, but most of it was due to the fact the cockpit felt like a dry sauna. *What was it Will said over the radio?* she asked herself. *Something about "spiking my heat into the stratosphere,"* she recalled after a moment. *Is that the problem here?*

Or is the 'Mech on fire . . . ?

That thought jolted her like an electric shock. *Christ!* She'd seen secondary explosions when weapons had struck the other 'Mechs. Some of them might have been delayed warhead detonations from armor-piercing rounds, but at least a few of them must have been from ammo cooking off. *This thing's got to be chock-full of machine-gun rounds,* she realized. *I'm sitting on top of a powder key and the fuse is burning . . .*

She shook her head. *Oh,* great. *Like I* need *to make this choice right now . . .* What was she supposed to do—stay put and hope Macintyre would translocate her home before she died in an ammo explosion? Or bail out and stay alive for the moment, but abandon the one link with the world she'd left behind? *The lady or the tiger . . . ?*

A dull, thudding concussion from somewhere below her made up her mind. Somewhere in the bowels of the fallen 'Mech, *something* had detonated. She pressed the transmit key for the last time. "Mac, it's Dooley again. I'm bailing out, Mac. I don't have any choice. But I'll stay in the vicinity, okay? If you can arrange some kind of extraction, I'd be very grateful." She fought back the urge to laugh—there was something so ludicrous about her attempts to sound like the cool professional when she was terrified of being blown up or marooned. "Come get me, Mac, okay? I'll be waiting. Dooley over and out."

Another secondary explosion jolted the cockpit, and half of the data displays that were still functioning went dead. Fighting back the wave of panic that threatened to engulf her, she felt around blindly for the canopy release. After what felt like minutes, she found the locking handle, and pulled.

Nothing. The handle didn't even shift. *Oh, God . . .*

Could the impact—either the original missile hits, or the subsequent fall—have buckled the cockpit's structure, jamming the canopy? *If so, I'm dead,* she realized. Desperately, she threw her weight against the locking handle—difficult, considering the cramped quarters and the unnatural angle of the cockpit. At first the handle stayed frozen. Then, with a metallic creak, it gave way, slamming to the OPEN position. The sliding canopy shifted minusculely on its rails.

Sam could have cheered aloud as she saw the hair-thin line of light. She grabbed the handgrips, and pushed.

The canopy rails were buckled; she realized that at once. Back at the Generro site, the canopy had moved smoothly and silently. Now it ground and creaked and groaned, and she needed all her strength to shift it. But shift it did. The crack broadened—a finger's width, a palm's breadth. The canopy jammed momentarily, and fear squeezed Sam's heart like a cold fist. She took a deep breath, and put her back into the effort.

She could almost hear her tendons crack with the effort, but the canopy wouldn't move any farther. The opening was almost a foot wide now. Through it, she could see the hard terrain of the foothills, the solid gray cloud-deck. *It* can't *be jammed,* she thought wildly. *I'm almost out of this death trap.* Again, she threw her weight against the canopy handgrips, strained with all her strength until her vision swam with exertion. Panting, she fell back.

A sense of futility overwhelmed her. *What a stupid way to die!* she raged mentally. *Trapped in a goddamn* robot *in some other world. . . .* She blinked back the tears that blurred her vision.

Once again, she closed her eyes, forced herself to breathe slowly, deeply. *Get a* grip, *Dooley. If anything's going to kill you, it's going to be panic.* The fringes of hysteria began to retreat, like an outgoing tide on a black, icy sea.

Struggling to stay calm, to analyze her situation objectively, she opened her eyes and examined the canopy and what she could see of the rails on which it was mounted. There *was* some buckling, she saw, but the situation was nowhere near as bad as it could have been. The canopy was just stuck on a largish wrinkle. If she could apply enough force, she *should* be able to slide the canopy past the obstruction. What she needed was leverage, a good solid base from which to apply force.

Looking at it that way, the answer was simple. Because the cockpit was lying on its side, she was crouched uncomfortably on the left-hand console, her shoulders turned so she could grab the canopy handholds. That meant that when she tried to open the canopy, she could only use the muscles of her arms, and the muscles that turned her at the waist, her obliques. What she needed to do was bring the strong muscles of her legs into play. She looked around again, and suddenly smiled.

I'm too socialized, she realized wryly. *Even when I'm trying to save my own life, I remember my mother telling me not to put my feet on the table. . . .*

She shifted her body in the cramped cockpit, placing her feet against the main display console in front of the pilot's seat. Knees bent, she rolled onto her side and grabbed the canopy handgrips. Taking a deep breath, she hauled on the canopy, using all the strength of her legs and back. Under the soles of her light hiking boots, keypads, buttons and data displays crunched and shattered.

For a split second the canopy held, then with a tearing *scream* came loose, slamming back on its rails. Sam was caught by surprise, losing her balance and her grip. With a yelp, she fell out the open canopy, giving her already punished head another clip on the cockpit combing on the way out.

She hit the hard ground on her shoulder and hip, sending bolts of pain shooting through her body. Martial arts instincts kicked in and she rolled, dissipating some of the energy of the fall. She fetched up against a boulder the size of a Volkswagen, delivering herself another sharp rap on the head. Tears stung her eyes and blurred her vision as she forced herself to a crouch.

Pain erupted in her left knee, making her gasp as she put weight on it. The joint felt swollen, pumped full of fluid. It throbbed and pulsed when it was at rest, much of the pain coming from the pressure of fluid within the joint capsule itself. When she flexed it or put weight on it, though, the dull, blunted pain became knife-sharp, as though a sadistic doctor were probing her injury with a red-hot scalpel. *What* a great *time to blow a knee, Dooley,* she told herself in disgust. *Anything* else *you can think of to make this tougher . . . ?* At least the joint would hold her weight, she decided after a couple of painful experiments. She wasn't going to enjoy a moment of it, but she *could* walk if she had to.

Will *I have to?* That was the key question, wasn't it? For the first time, she really looked around her . . . and stopped short in astonishment.

Her BattleMech was ten feet away, lying on its side. For a moment she gawked in absolute awe, temporarily forgetting about her pain and her predicament.

She'd known the fighting robots were big, but knowing and seeing—particularly from this close—were two different things. It was massive, the BattleMech, the size of a small building—bigger than an F–111 fighter-bomber, and probably heavier.

She shivered. Even smashed to the ground, mauled and shredded by missile fire, it was intimidating, as though the designer had consciously intended for it to strike fear into its opponents. (*And maybe he did,* she thought.) Its torso was narrow, mounted on "hips" and "legs" that would have made an excellent gantry for a heavy crane. Its "head" was low, sunk between its huge, hulking "shoulders," making Sam think of a huge vulture rendered by an industrial artist with paranoia. In the top of the "head" she could see the open canopy hatch from which she'd fallen. *My God,* she thought, *I was* piloting *that thing!*

The salvo of missiles had ruptured the fallen 'Mech's armor in half a dozen places, she saw. The right "knee" joint was almost totally gone, the two parts of the leg held together by nothing more than a couple of power cables. The right "arm" was buckled, trapped under the mass of the torso, while the left wasn't much more than a scorched, twisted metal stump. A great crater gaped in the center of the BattleMech's "chest," the metal within still glowing cherry-red. Sparks flashed and flared inside the yawning hole, reminding Sam of arc welders. Black smoke gouted from another tear in the fighting machine's structure, and she thought she could see the flicker of flames. *Damn good thing I got out of there,* she told herself.

Of course, ten feet was still a tad close if anything unpleasantly energetic happened. Keeping low, she crept around the boulder, interposing its bulk between her and the downed machine. Feeling at least partially safe, she struggled to get her heart rate and breathing under control.

The 'Mech—my *'Mech,* she corrected mentally—wasn't dying quietly. Electric sparks crackled and spat. Overheated metal groaned and cracked as it cooled. Deep within the guts of the machine she heard a high-pitched burring whine, like an engine running on a faulty bearing.

Now there was another sound, too, a rhythmic thumping that she felt through the ground more than heard. *Oh, my God,* she thought suddenly. *I forgot the other 'Mechs. . . .*

There were four more of them out there, and at the very least the one she'd shot at would be coming to investigate the results of its missile salvo. *What do they do with incapacitated 'Mechs?* she wondered. *And what do they do with captured pilots—particularly "outlanders" like me . . . ?*

The rhythmic concussion—just like the footsteps of an approaching monster in a Godzilla movie—were coming closer, their amplitude increasing by the second. She could imagine the robot that had destroyed "her" 'Mech eating up the distance between them with its huge strides.

She shifted slowly around the car-sized boulder, staying in a crouch to minimize her exposure. Her knee stabbed her with agony, but she muffled her impulse to curse. *Do those things have exterior microphones? And how sensitive are they?*

There it was, the ambulatory missile platform that had damn near killed her. It was maybe two hundred feet away, advancing slowly across the broken ground. Its right arm still hung limply from its smashed elbow, but the huge weapon mounted in its left was trained steadily on the head of the fallen 'Mech. Sam shook her head in disbelief. *Come* on, she thought, *do you* really *think this might be a trick . . . ?* But then she remembered how much punishment she'd seen the other 'Mechs take. It *wasn't* inconceivable that the downed machine might be able to fire off one last, devastating attack at point-blank range.

Behind the missile platform, two more of the gigantic machines were approaching. The three finally stopped in a small group, their torsos slightly turned so they "faced" each other. There was no sound beyond that of the dying

'Mech, but Sam knew the three pilots were discussing what to do next.

Finally the fourth 'Mech lumbered up to break the deadlock. It strode right past the other three, pulling up only forty or fifty feet from Sam's machine. With its elongated left arm, it pointed at the incapacitated BattleMech.

Oh, shit! In a flash of insight, Sam knew what was coming next. She flung herself flat, in the cover of the boulder.

Her ears were filled with the high-pitched shriek of pressurized gas escaping, with the roar and crackle of flame. She screamed into the ground as the air was sucked from her lungs, as she felt her hair crisp and shrivel. *I'm roasting alive. . . .*

The killing heat lasted only a couple of seconds. The furnace roar shut off, and unheated air—brutally cold on her skin in contrast to the dragon's breath of a moment before—rushed in to fill the partial vacuum. Sam gasped, sucking the life-giving air into her lungs.

Cautiously, she raised her head over the top of the boulder.

The wreckage of her 'Mech was well and truly on fire, coated in a flaming liquid something like napalm. The BattleMech that had just fired stood over the wreckage, liquid fire still dripping from the muzzle of its arm-mounted flame thrower. As Sam watched, the 'Mech brought its flamer to bear again.

I can't stand another shot! The heat will kill me. Before the thought was even fully formed, Sam was on her feet and running. As she put her weight on her left leg, her knee flared with agony. The joint held, though. She bit back on her screams as she sprinted across the broken ground toward a ravine-scored boulder field a couple of dozen yards away. Behind her she heard the rushing of flames again, felt the heat pulse on the back of her neck.

"You! Stop right there!" The voice was impossibly, inhumanly loud—like a titan screaming in rage. Reflexively, Sam looked back over her shoulder.

One of the 'Mechs—the one that had almost killed her with the missile salvo—had pivoted its torso to face her.

"Stop or you're meat!" the electronically amplified voice boomed . . . and only now did Sam realize consciously that it was speaking English.

She almost pulled up, almost raised her arms in surrender. But then she remembered the sight of her downed BattleMech flaming with napalm. *Is* that *how they treat enemies? No thanks.* She put her head down and poured on all the speed her damaged knee could manage.

"Bad choice, snake." A ripping burst of machine-gun fire punctuated the wry comment. Sam yelled as she heard the bullets hammering the hard ground behind her, ricochets wailing and howling into the sky. The 'Mech pilot triggered another burst—closer, this time, but still behind Sam. Rock splinters flayed the backs of her legs through her thick trousers. *His next burst's going to be right on the money. . . .*

But an instant later she was in the boulder field, and one of the countless narrow ravines—deep-scored dry streambeds, maybe—opened at her feet. She flung herself headlong into it, hitting the bottom hard. She rolled, forcing herself back to her feet, and scrambled along the bottom of the rocky cleft. Behind her, another burst of fire tore up the ground and spattered off boulders. A quick, panicked glance over her shoulder told her she was hidden from immediate view. But she knew all too well that if the 'Mech pilot really wanted to take her out, he'd be able to do it with a single missile. *Whoever said 'Close only counts in horseshoes' wasn't using high-explosive missiles . . .*

A narrower chasm branched off to the left, and she lurched up it. Another branch, another turn. Two more—the ravines or arroyos or whatever were interlinked like a maze—and she wasn't even sure what direction she'd come from. Her vision was tunneling down from exertion and from the agony pounding in her knee, but she forced herself onward.

Eventually she collapsed, simply unable to push herself any farther. Her vision blurred; her thoughts were muzzy. *If the 'Mech pilot's still on my tail, I won't even give him a moving target,* she thought drunkenly.

But nothing tore into her body; nothing turned her into a flaming pyre. The silence was heavy around her.

Without warning, her stomach cramped. The emotional reaction was finally hitting her, she realized. She gagged again, then spewed the contents of her stomach onto the rocky ground.

When the spasms stopped racking her body, she wiped

her mouth with her sweat-drenched sleeve. *Ugh. Just charming, Dooley,* she thought.

A chill wind had blown up out of nowhere, whistling and howling through the interlinked ravines. Above, the slate-gray clouds threatened rain. Exhausted, she looked around. A couple of yards away was a small overhang—not quite a cave—where the side of the ravine had been partially undercut. Groaning with the effort, she dragged herself to the shelter and wedged herself as deep into it as she could manage. She drew her knees up to her chest, hugging her legs tightly. And—so far from home that miles couldn't even measure it—she sunk into a kind of mental withdrawal that could only distantly be classed as sleep.

19

The small creature was back again. Sitting miserably in her shallow cave, Samantha watched it through dull eyes.

It was about a foot long—eighteen inches including the tail—and looked like some kind of lizard . . . except that it had a thick coat of wiry brown hair. It had appeared from nowhere about half an hour ago, watching Sam with its beady red eyes from across the narrow arroyo. After a few moments, it had scurried away to vanish among the rocks.

Now it was back, and it was closer, no more than ten feet from her shoes. It seemed to quiver with tension or fear. For the first time, Sam noticed a sharp, bitter smell, like musk mixed with ammonia, wafting from the small creature. She'd never seen anything like this furred lizard in all of her travels, or in any of the nature books she'd read.

Of course not, Dooley, she thought wryly. *All those nature books describe species native to Earth—Sol Three—not Solaris Seven.* The wire-haired lizard was just one more reminder—if she really needed one—that she was a long way from home. *A whole different planet, perhaps centuries in the future, or maybe in an entirely different universe.* She shook her head. Those thoughts were just too big for her to really comprehend.

The furry lizard moved closer, edging cautiously toward her right foot. *What do you want?* She directed the thought like a radio message toward the small animal. *Am I sitting in your home, is that it?*

She laughed, a single bark of bitterness. *Well, possession is nine-tenths of the law,* she thought. *I'm here, you're not, and that's all there is to it. Tough luck, brother.* She picked up a pebble and buzzed it at the creature. It skittered back a few feet, turned and hissed venomously. *I know just how you feel,* she scowled, and threw another pebble. The lizard darted into the cover of some head-sized rocks across the arroyo and disappeared.

Reflexively, she checked her watch. *Just shy of 17:30.* She shook her head. Meaningless, of course. All the watch told her was what the time was back in California. Only by the longest of long shots would that have any connection whatsoever with local time. *I don't even know how long Solaris Seven's day is, for chrissake,* she realized. For the dozenth time, she shifted on the rough ground, craning her head for a look around the overhang at the cloud-deck. Still solid, unbroken, still gray as lead. She knew the sun was still up—the level of illumination was like a Venice Beach twilight—but it was impossible to judge just where above the cloud cover the sun was. *It could be noon, or it could be two minutes before sundown, for all I know,* she told herself glumly.

At least the rain had stopped. A couple of minutes after she'd found her shelter, the sky had opened up. For almost an hour rain had beaten down, a brutal barrage of huge, cold drops. Morosely, she'd watched the bottom of her arroyo churned into mud. At one point, a shaft of fear had penetrated her emotional withdrawal—*What about flash floods? If this* is *a dry riverbed . . .*—but she'd put it aside. *After what I've already survived, a flash flood's not even worth thinking about,* she assured herself.

The rain *had* offered at least one blessing. She'd extended her left leg out from under the overhang, letting the cold water soak the fabric of her pants. The cold had taken some of the pain out of her wounded knee—not quite as well as an ice pack, but much better than nothing—and seemed to have controlled the swelling. And later, when she'd realized how dry her throat was, she'd been able to drink all she'd wanted simply by letting the rain fill her cupped hands like a bowl.

Eventually the rain had slackened off to a drizzle, then stopped entirely. The cloud-deck had remained unbroken—no warming beams of sunlight breaking through—but the mud had dried amazingly fast. *Almost as if the ground itself is absorbing the water,* she'd realized. Within half an hour after the rain ended, the standing puddles that had developed in the bottom of the arroyo were gone, and only a slight softness to the ground gave evidence that the rain had ever happened.

With the end of the rain, the wind—sharp, biting—had picked up again. Unlike the ground, Sam's clothes hadn't dried quickly, and in a few minutes she was shivering with bitter cold.

She looked at the sky again. Was it just her imagination, or were the leaden-gray clouds darkening? *Is the sun going down?* she wondered, and the thought chilled her even more than the wind. *There's no way I'm going to survive a night in the open.*

She looked around her for anything that she could use to make a fire. Nothing—no wood, no grasses, no leaves. Now that she thought about it, the furry lizard had been the only living thing—plant or animal—she'd seen in the boulder fields. She sighed. *Anyway, even if some kind soul delivered me a cord of dry wood right now, I wouldn't be able to light a fire.* She didn't have matches; she didn't have flint and steel, or any other fire-making tools. When she'd checked her pockets for her Bic, the lighter had been missing. *Probably lost it when I fell out of the 'Mech,* she thought. She'd managed to hold on to her pack of Lucky Strikes, but it was crushed out of recognizable shape and soaked through.

So no high-tech solutions to the problem of starting a fire. *What the hell am I supposed to do, then? Rub two dry clichés together?*

Damn it, it was coming down to another one of *those* decisions, wasn't it? If she wanted to save her life, she'd have to abandon another connection—absolutely her last, this time—to home, to Generro, to Earth. Just about an hour ago, she'd had to bail out of her downed 'Mech, abandoning the beacon—assuming it was still functional—that might eventually let Macintyre and the others translocate her home. Now, she had to move out of the immediate area if she didn't want to die of exposure, cutting to almost nil the chances that a rescue mission—assuming that Macintyre even sent one—would be able to find her. She smiled bitterly. *I'm getting pretty tired of these hard choices.*

With a sigh, she forced herself to her feet. Her muscles had stiffened up, and her left knee felt as though someone had implanted a small balloon behind the kneecap that interfered with the joint and limited its mobility. She stepped out from under her overhang into the middle of the arroyo.

Which way? There had to be some kind of settlement around here, didn't there? The BattleMechs that had slagged her down had to have come from *somewhere.* Hadn't Andrea agreed to put Sam down in the hills outside Roland Fields? Roland Fields sounded like some kind of town.

But where was it? Which way should she go? And could she even get there from here?

She sighed again. At least she'd keep herself warm—*Warmer,* she amended—by moving. Mentally she flipped a coin. Then she turned right and started heading uphill.

Glancing back over her shoulder, she saw the furry lizard watching her from behind a rock. "It's all yours now, buster," she said wryly, and limped on.

The sky *was* darkening, there was no doubt. To Sam's left, the clouds were shading from dark gray to midnight black, while to her right the cloud-deck nearest the horizon was taking on the faintest of pink tinges. *There's probably one heck of a sunset out there,* she thought, *if only the clouds would part.*

She sighed. Things were just going from bad to worse, weren't they? The temperature had already dropped noticeably. Despite the exertion of hiking over the broken ground, she was chilled to the bone. *If the temperature's dropped this much at sunset, what's it going to be like at midnight?* Real fear twisted in her guts. *Unless I find shelter, I'm dead.*

What a stupid, miserable, *sordid* way to die—hypothermia, in the middle of some godforsaken hills.

At least the changing light made it easier to navigate.

When she'd started out up the narrow, winding arroyo, she'd found it almost impossible to keep track of direction. Soon she'd sensed that the ravine was doubling back on itself, so she'd climbed out and cut across country for a while. A few minutes later, when she'd dropped back into a new arroyo—which looked disturbingly familiar—she'd been terrified that around the next bend she'd find the same shallow cave, the same furry lizard. It hadn't worked out that way—*Thank God . . .*—but even so, the navigational fix of sunset had come as a relief.

Darkness to the left, sunset to the right: that meant she was heading south. She tried to remember the lay of the land as she'd seen it from the cockpit of her BattleMech. *I wish I'd paid more attention to the compass,* she thought grimly. She *guessed* the other 'Mechs—the bogies—had come out of the foothills south of her position. That implied that Roland Fields was probably to the south, didn't it? She grimaced. *I just can't remember the compass reading. I could be 90 degrees off course . . . or more.*

The going was getting steeper and more difficult. Not only was the overall slope increasing, but—now she knew which way she was going—all the narrow arroyos she encountered were roughly perpendicular to her path, rather than parallel. Some were narrow enough that she could jump them without real difficulty; even so, she always erred on the side of caution. Her light hiking boots didn't offer as much ankle support as she would have liked, and she didn't dare put much confidence in her injured knee. Many, though, she had to climb down and then up the other side. And some were wide or steep-sided enough that she had to diverge from her course to bypass them completely.

Looking back over her shoulder, she tried to judge how far she'd gone from her shelter. *Probably no more than two miles, as the crow flies,* she thought grumpily, *or as the BattleMech runs. But probably almost* twice *that if you count vertical distance as well.* Her ankles were sore from walking on the shifting rocks, and the muscles of her calves burned. Her left knee had gone almost totally numb; only the worst shocks or jolts sent jagged bolts of pain through the joint. *Not good,* she realized . . . even though, from one standpoint, the absence of pain was a blessing.

It would be so easy just to sit down in the lee of a rock and rest her muscles. She'd be painfully cold at first, she knew, but that pain would vanish soon enough, and she'd start to feel comfortably warm. Then she'd just go to sleep. . . .

No!

By God, that *wasn't* going to happen. She'd never been able to give up, on *anything*. She hated to lose, and she was innately *unable* to surrender. *If I'm going to die tonight, the Grim Reaper's going to have to beat me two out of three falls and then drag me off in a damn* sack. . . . She straightened her back and squared her shoulders, and forced herself to keep moving.

The light was almost totally gone in the west, and night had come in with a vengeance. The sky above Samantha was unrelieved black. There were no stars. Once, maybe ten minutes ago, her peripheral vision had caught a streak of brilliant gold light to the west, angled upward from the southwestern horizon. It was gone as suddenly as it had appeared, so quickly that Sam couldn't focus on it . . . or even be completely sure it had ever been there. *What the hell was it anyway?* she wondered dully. She *thought* there was some upward motion to the streak, so it couldn't have been a 'Mech's laser fired at the sky. A missile launch, maybe? Or maybe it was some kind of rocket ship—*If Solaris Seven has BattleMechs, mustn't it also have rocket ships?*—taking off from a spaceport. If that was the case, then she was heading in the wrong direction, wasn't she? Surely a spaceport would be like an airport, relatively near a major population center. . . .

She shook her head, struggling to clear her mind of random thoughts. *I'll stick to the course I've chosen,* she told herself firmly. *That's all I can do at this point.*

She was exhausted, she knew—totally and utterly drained of energy. Her body felt like . . . well, it didn't even feel like *her* body anymore. Sometimes she felt as though she were *observing* her body struggling on. She knew that the body she was watching was in pain, was starting to fail, and she sometimes felt sympathy for it. But she didn't feel the pain herself, not really. *I'm losing it,* she told herself muzzily. *I don't have much left.* Her mind, too, was trashed, her thoughts churning uncontrollably, making and breaking nonsensical connections of meaning—*Like the moments just before you go to sleep and start dreaming.* Forcing herself on in the pitch darkness, she knew she'd stumble over something and fall—if not this minute, then the next, or the one after that—and it would be even odds whether she'd be able to force herself back to her feet.

The slope of the ground had decreased, she noticed eventually, almost as if she was approaching the top of a hill. It made the going easier, but still not easy enough. The ground was hard and rough, but at least the baseball-sized rocks that had been threatening to break her ankles for several miles were gone. There was no way, she knew, that she'd have been able to handle that kind of terrain in the dark. . . .

Except that it didn't seem to *be* that dark anymore. For the first time in many minutes, she could actually see some of the details of the ground in front of her—not just vague shapes of black-on-black, but real outlines and objects. It took a few moments for the realization to penetrate her shell-shocked brain. She came to a stop, and looked around through stinging eyes. She was so used to staring at the ground immediately before her feet that it took a couple of seconds before her eyes could focus to a greater distance.

She *was* on top of a hill, she realized—in fact, atop a small range of hills. The badlands were behind her. In front of her, the land sloped down into what looked like a basin or a very wide valley.

And, in the distance, spreading toward the horizon, that basin was filled with a sea of lights. For a few disjointed seconds, she could almost have convinced herself that she was standing in the hills of Griffith Park, looking down over the city of Los Angeles.

Samantha leaned against a large boulder, and just stared. *I've almost made it,* she told herself dully. *I'm almost there.*

Well, that wasn't *quite* true. The city wasn't as large as Los Angeles, and it certainly seemed to have a denser population—judging by the lights, at least. The basin itself was huge (if it actually was a basin, and her eyes and mind weren't playing tricks on her), and the city proper seemed to fill the farther, southern reaches of it. Her best wild guess put the periphery of the city itself a good five or six miles away from where she stood.

She slumped in on herself as that fact penetrated. *Five or six miles,* she repeated mentally. *There isn't a hope in hell I'll make it that far. Damn, to die of exposure* this close *to safety. . . .* She turned away from the sea of lights that seemed to twinkle mockingly in the cold night air.

And saw that a pseudopod of lights extended from the main body of the city toward the hills to her left. In that pseudopod, the lights were nowhere near as concentrated as they were in the heart of the city. There were large areas of blackness, islands of darkness, where no lights at all burned. In other regions, sparse lights seemed to flicker—not twinkle like stars, as a result of currents in the air, but actually *flicker,* as if the light sources themselves weren't constant. And in other parts, the few lights had a distinctly different color to them: the warm yellow-red of fires, rather than the hard, artificial yellow of sodium lights or the harsh blue-white brilliance of carbon arcs.

Sam's heart seemed to leap in her chest, a sudden flame of hope replacing the dirty ice of despair in her gut. She forced herself to walk, then to jog and stumble, toward the nearest of the lights.

She crested a ridge and looked down into a narrow valley directly below. Fires dotted the darkness—small, localized fires. *Like burning embers scattered over a field of black velvet,* she thought, *or like the campfires of a besieging army in a movie set in the Middle Ages. . . .* She shook her head, fighting down the disjointed welter of dreamlike thoughts that threatened to overwhelm her. The pain had returned to her knee, and she groaned as she started down the ridge.

She almost didn't make it. Exhaustion filled her ears with a rushing sound, like distant and continuous surf. Her vision tunneled down until her view of the terrain before her was the size of a fist at arm's length, surrounded by a whirlpool of blood-red. After the fifth time, she lost track of the times she stumbled—sometimes skidding on loose rocks, sometimes falling headlong and rolling down the steep slope until she fetched up against a larger rock and came to a stop. She felt oblivion, unconsciousness, looming behind her like a huge, black wave, threatening to break over her and sweep her away.

She had no idea how long it took—minutes, hours, years—but eventually the ground leveled off under her feet. She stopped, bending forward at the waist, hands on her thighs, as she gasped and fought to draw in the oxygen she needed. Slowly—*so* slowly—the pain in her chest receded, the rushing of blood in her ears diminished, and the red, swirling tunnel through which she saw the world faded away. She was among the fires, she saw—braziers, they looked like, or more likely fires burning in garbage cans or old oil drums. The nearest was thirty feet away. Even from where she stood, she could feel its heat on her body, like a promise of life. She lurched toward it.

A black shape loomed up, seeming to materialize from the darkness. It took her befuddled brain a second to identify it: a bent, malnourished-looking man dressed in a tattered fake-fur coat over ragged clothes. "Ge' back!" the scarecrow figure snarled at her. "Ge' back, or I cut ya, bint." Something flashed in the scarecrow's hand—a knife, mirror-brilliant in the firelight. It slashed toward her.

Sam tensed. Jujitsu-trained reflexes kicked in, determined the best angle of approach, the best way of disarming the ragged figure and taking it down. She moved, stepping inside the arc of his swing. . . .

And her body—exhausted, virtually incapacitated—betrayed her. Her left knee gave out, and she collapsed to the ground in agony.

The scarecrow figure checked its swing. A scavenger's eyes glinted from a grimy face. The scarecrow bared blackened teeth in what might almost have been a smile. "You no' so tough, huh, bint?" the figure croaked. "You no' so tough at all. You ge' back a' my squat, or I cut ya good, huh?" Gesturing warningly with the narrow knife-blade one last time, the figure seemed to compress, to shrink in on itself as the man sank back into a hunched crouch and wrapped his ragged coat around him.

Sam closed her eyes. Her heart was almost palpitating as an aftereffect of the adrenaline that fear had pumped into her bloodstream. Her stomach knotted with nausea. *I'm helpless,* she realized with a sickening shock. *I'm completely helpless.* For the first time in as long as she could remember, she had to accept that she was totally at the mercy of the people around her. She couldn't run, she couldn't fight—not in this condition. Hell, she couldn't even yell for help—*Not that yelling would do that much good anyway, judging by* that *reception,* she thought grimly.

Something touched her shoulder lightly. She yelped with

fright, recoiling from the touch. Again, her left knee gave out, and she sprawled to the rocky ground. She looked up.

The heavy cloud-deck reflected light from the city below, seeming to glow with its own faint light. Silhouetted against that opalescent glow was a looming figure, bending over her. Instinctively, she drew back as the figure reached toward her.

Then she controlled her reaction as she realized the figure wasn't threatening her, but was offering her a hand to help her up. "S'okay," the figure said gruffly. "S'okay, I won' hurtcha. Huh?"

The shape above her seemed to contract, to shrink to its true proportions. It was her fear that had cast the figure as a hulking, looming shape, she realized with some chagrin. It reality it was small, shorter than her by a good eight inches, and scrawny—thinner, even, than the scarecrow who'd threatened her with a knife. As her eyes adapted to the reflected light, she could make out a hollow-cheeked face, a nose hooked like a raptor's beak. Thin tufts of dirty-white hair formed a chaotic halo around the figure's head. A *man,* she realized, *an old man.*

"S'okay," he said again. "C'mon."

With a self-conscious smile, Sam took his extended hand. He staggered as she pulled, almost falling on top of her. His grip was strong, though, and she used his arm for balance as she clambered back to her feet.

"There. Better, huh?" He smiled up at her. Most of his teeth were missing, she saw, and the few he'd retained looked seriously decayed. He chuckled, and the sickening miasma that was his breath—a complex, sweet-sour biological reek combining alcohol, ketones and decay—washed over her. He shrugged rail-thin shoulders and gestured to the scarecrow who'd drawn the knife on her. "Don' let ol' Dog getcha, huh? He just bad, y'know?" He patted her paternally on the arm. "Y'can share my squat, you wanna. Huh?" With a birdlike twitch of his head he indicated a smaller brazier to Sam's right.

Sam hesitated. *I need the warmth. I'll die without it, but. . . .* "Who are you, anyway?" she asked, more to give herself time to think than because she really wanted to know.

"Y'can call me Raven, if y'like." He laughed again, a

bubbling, phlegmy sound. "Ever'body does, those who call me an'thin' at all."

"Raven," she repeated.

The old man nodded. "S'me," he confirmed with a gap-toothed grin.

Sam stared into his eyes. They were open wide, almost bulging out of his head—bloodshot so badly they looked like they'd start bleeding at any moment. The pupils were blown, dilated so wide she could see only the thinnest trace of iris around them. *He's drunk out of his mind,* she realized, *or drugged. And he's mad as a coot.* But the madness she saw in his eyes seemed to be of a gentle stripe: senility rather than hostility. *He's harmless,* she decided, *or at least as close to harmless as I'm likely to find here.*

She forced herself to smile. "Thanks, Raven," she said. "I think I'll take you up on that offer."

Raven nodded, his own smile growing wider, as if she'd just offered him the greatest of compliments. (*And maybe I have,* she mused.) He hobbled toward his brazier. For the first time, Sam saw there were other shapes huddled around the warmth and light. *Raven's family?* she wondered. *His gang? Or his tribe?* She shrugged. She was too tired to think, too tired to worry . . . and *much* too tired to stay on her feet another second. She slumped to the hard ground, hugging her knees to her chest. After the cold of the hills, the radiant heat of the brazier was almost painfully intense. She closed her eyes and, lulled by the crackling of the fire and the mumble of distant conversation, she fell headlong into the black sea of sleep.

When she woke, some unmeasured time later, she found that somebody had draped a ratty fur rug over her sleeping body like a blanket. (She sniffed and wrinkled her nose. Judging by the smell, she didn't want to ever find herself downwind of the animal that had "donated" this fur. . . . *But beggars can't be choosers,* she reminded herself firmly, *and that's definitely what I am here.*)

She rolled into a sitting position, squinting her eyes against the light. The cloud-deck overhead was still unbroken; no blue sky showed through. But the ceiling seemed to be much higher, and the clouds themselves thinner. More light was penetrating to the ground, and the level of brightness was almost the same as a cloudy day in Los Angeles.

Somebody had banked the fire in Raven's brazier, she saw. Wisps of smoke emerged from a couple of air holes punched in the side of the can. A ragged-edged sheet of metal covered the top of the oil can, and a battered pot sitting atop it steamed sullenly. A woman—*I think it's a woman,* she amended—was crouching beside it, staring blankly at the pot. As Sam watched, she reached up and stirred the contents with a "spoon" that looked as though it had started service as an angle bracket.

Suddenly curious—and not a little edgy—Samantha looked around her. She'd found her way into some kind of garbage dump, she saw. *And not just* any *garbage dump,* she amended instantly, *more like a technological burial ground—where old machines go to die.* She was near the periphery of an area about the size of a football field. To the south and east, maybe eighty yards away, loomed a wall thirty or forty feet high made of old, rusted-out cars (or what she *took* to be cars, at least) piled on top of each other. The ground underfoot—which she'd taken in the dark to be grit and gravel—actually seemed to comprise mainly rust: chunks of oxidized metals, most so small they looked like iron filings. Braziers, each surrounded by a cluster of ragged figures, were scattered throughout the area, between looming haystack-like mounds of smashed and rusting metal. Curiously, Sam scrutinized the nearest "metalstack." She could make out some of the components—that looked like a trashed refrigerator over there, and that had to be some kind of hydraulic drill press—but most of the trash was crushed and rusted beyond recognition.

Beyond the wall of dead cars, she could see a stretch of low buildings: two and three stories, most of them, with the occasional taller structure thrown in for variety. They all looked as if they'd seen better days—*No,* she corrected wryly, *be honest: they look as if they should be condemned, and* soon. She could see the movement of people in the streets, but she was too far away to make out any details. *Great,* she thought glumly, *just* great, *Dooley. Less than twenty-four hours in a new world, and you've managed to find the slums. Good eye.* She snorted in disgust.

A couple of members of Raven's "tribe" were watching

her, she noticed suddenly. Two looked like close relations: they had the same scrawny, twisted shape as her benefactor, and could well have stolen their clothes from the garbage of the same tailor. Their faces were gaunt and careworn, devastated by too many years of hardship and too few moments of tranquillity. Sunken eyes watched her steadily, emotionlessly. Suddenly uncomfortable, Sam glanced away.

The third person watching her was as different from the others as night from day. Young, lean and hard, he sat crouched five yards away from Sam. He watched her too, but his dark eyes seemed alive with speculation, and with something that could be grim humor. His skin was pale, his hair night-black. He wore tight-fitting pants of a material that seemed as supple as glove-leather, but had a distinctive snakeskin pattern to it. The pants' legs were bloused over mid-length boots of stiff leather, embellished with silver-colored metal toecaps and chains. Above the waist, he wore nothing but a sleeveless vest of the same material as his pants. His shoulders were broad and strong, she couldn't help noticing, but his long arms didn't seem any more muscular than her own. Discomfited by his steady scrutiny, she looked away.

Raven was still asleep, she saw, bundled up in an ancient cloth coat. His knees were drawn up to his chest, and he lay on his side in the fetal position near the brazier. Sam rolled gingerly to her feet, groaning involuntarily as the stabbing pain returned to her knee. Favoring her left leg, trying to work out the stiffness, she crossed to the old man, laying her hand on his shoulder. He didn't respond to her touch. Gently, she shook him.

"Leave him be."

Sam jumped at the harsh voice behind her. She turned, guiltily.

The young man's expression was hard as stone. *He looked angry. Why?* "I only wanted to thank him," she said defensively. "He saved my life last night."

"Too late for that." The man shrugged.

"Too late?" Sam felt anger flare in her chest, but fought it down. *Now's not the time to get in a fight with the locals, Dooley,* she cautioned herself, "Why's it too late?" she asked, keeping her voice calm and reasonable. "All I want to do is thank him. . . ."

"Frak!" the man spat. He glared at her, naked anger in his eyes now. "He's *gone,* deadload, okay? Raven died in the frakking night. Okay?"

Samantha blinked. "Dead? But . . . ," She looked down at the huddled figure. Instantly, instinctively, she *knew* the younger man was right. The old man who'd called himself Raven was dead. "But what. . . ." Her voice trailed off.

"Doesn't matter, does it?" the other said harshly.

"Maybe it does to me." The young man's hard eyes widened slightly at the soft tone of Sam's voice. "He saved my life," she repeated.

The man didn't move for a long second, frozen like a still scene from a movie. Then she saw the harsh lines of his body soften slightly, some of the tension going out of him. "It was just a matter of time," he said. He was trying to keep his voice unemotional, but beneath the rough tone Sam could *feel* there was real sadness there. Mentally, she decreased her estimate of his age—*Fifteen? No more than that.*

"Why was it just a matter of time?"

He shrugged. "You drink squeeze long enough, one time you're going to get a bad batch. Half his liver was already gone, okay? Even a mild case of toxic shock, and he's gone."

Sam nodded slowly. Some of the words didn't mean anything to her—"squeeze," "toxic shock"—but she understood the gist. "Your father?" she asked gently.

The young man flinched. Then, so quickly that Sam could almost believe she'd imagined his reaction, he was stone again. "Wrong track, deadload," he snapped. (*"Mind your own business, dipshit,"* Sam translated mentally.)

She nodded again. "What . . ." She stopped and tried again. "What happens to him?" She gestured at the body.

"The busters'll pick him up. Sometime."

" 'Busters'?"

He rolled his eyes at her ignorance. "Cops. Police, okay? That's the way it works out here, greenie." He smiled, but there was no humor in it. "Welcome to Roland Fields," he said.

20

Samantha stared at Raven's huddled body. "And you just *leave* him?" she asked. "You let the cops . . . the busters . . . take him away?"

The young man shrugged. "What else?"

"You don't do anything to . . ."—she hesitated, struggling to find the right words—"to show respect?" Unbidden, memories of her last flight in Pop-Pop's *Yellow Bird,* of the private wake she and Maggie had held washed over her. "Some way of saying good-bye to him?"

"*That's* not him. That's just the meat, the dust, okay? *He's* not there anymore."

"Yes, but. . . ."

He laughed roughly. "What do you do with a coat when you don't need it anymore? Throw it a party? Frak, you *are* a deadload." He paused, and his dark eyes took on a new expression. "You're not from around here, are you, deadload? You're not a Fielder. You're an outworlder, aren't you?"

Sam hesitated, then, she nodded once. *That's as good a description as any,* she had to admit.

"Where you from, deadload? And what the frak are you doing *here*?" He leaned forward, interested. "You look like a mechbunny. You some kind of deadload frak-bait mech-bunny out slumming, is that it?"

"It's a long story."

"*Tell* me, deadload," he said, loading his voice with heavy irony. "I *like* stories."

Sam felt suddenly uncomfortable under the intensity of the young man's gaze. Judging by his eyes and his voice, she notched her estimate of his age down to fourteen. About half my age, she thought—but still she felt intimidated. *This is his world, after all,* she rationalized silently. *He knows how things work; I'm the stranger, the "greenie."* She looked around at the devastation surrounding them. *You'd have to grow up fast and* hard *in a place like this.*

Slowly she rose to her feet. "Doesn't matter, does it?" she said quietly, echoing his own words. "I guess I'll be moving on." She glanced at Raven's body, and concentrated on a single thought—*Thanks for saving my life, Raven*—and imagined it winging its way to wherever the old man's soul was now. She started to turn away.

"Where you going?"

Sam turned back. The young man's face was still expressionless, but again, something had changed in his body language. She wished she knew how to interpret it. "I don't know," she said with a slight shrug. Then she smiled faintly. "But you needn't worry. I'm not going to challenge you for your squat." She saw the young man's brow crease in a puzzled frown. "It's yours now that Raven's gone, isn't it?"

He snorted his ridicule of that idea. "I don't squat *here,* greenie," he sneered. "I stopped by last night to visit. Found you sleeping there—dead to the world, grinding metal—and found Raven gone." He shrugged, as if that explained everything.

"So why did you stay?" Samantha asked after a moment.

The young man glanced away. "Nothing better to do with my time," he muttered.

"So you slept here? No," she corrected, "you didn't sleep at all, did you?" The expression on the young man's face confirmed that she'd guessed right. *That's kind of touching.*

"Raven was cracked," the boy said gruffly, unable to meet Sam's gaze. "You offer a greenie a place to crash, the least you got to do is make sure nobody slits her throat for her fancy shoes."

Sam struggled to suppress an understanding smile. *You watched over me all night, didn't you?* she thought. That's *why you didn't go back to wherever you normally live. You won't admit it, though . . . and you won't let me thank you for it, either?*

She nodded slowly. "I see that," she said evenly. "Right is right." She smiled faintly. "I knew Raven's name," she pointed out. "And my name's Samantha, but people call me Sam." She let the sentence hang.

"Renard," he offered after a moment. "Ren."

Sam nodded soberly again. "Okay, Ren."

Renard jumped to his feet, as though he suddenly had

too much energy that he needed to burn off. "Where you going?" he asked again.

That's the question, isn't it?

Some of the emotions churning in her gut must have shown on her face, because Renard frowned. "You got no place to go?" Words and intonation phrased it as a question; his expression turned it into a statement.

Sam hesitated.

And that was apparently answer enough. He snorted in disgust. "Didn't think so. *Frak,* you're a *real* deadload. What in the name of the Five Pillars are you *doing* here, bunny? How'd you *get* here?"

Again Sam shrugged. "Doesn't matter, does it?" she echoed once more.

"Not to me it doesn't, *that*'s for frakking sure."

"No reason it should." Something made her think this hard-edged young man wasn't as cold and heartless as he wanted her to believe—and she could use a friend about now, even just someone to point her in the right direction. Riding a hunch on how to play it out with this Ren, she sighed theatrically and turned away, started to walk off.

"Hey, deadload!"

She suppressed a small, grim smile—*Got you!*—and turned back, her expression dispirited. "Yeah?"

Renard was shifting from foot to foot, his body language clearly communicating the discomfort he couldn't let his face show. "Where you going?" he asked again. "How you going to live, huh?" He gestured sharply toward the shapeless, cloth-swathed shape near the brazier. "Not many Ravens around, not around here."

She shrugged again, and muttered, "I'll figure something out." She turned her back on him again, trying to keep her doubts out of her own body language. *What the hell are you doing playing hard to get, Dooley?* she asked herself harshly. *You've got him hooked.* She snorted softly—disgust at herself, admixed with frustration. *You've always been so damn proud of your independence. You can't even trust this kid in order to save your life? It's not like he could get you into anything you can't get yourself out of.*

"Hey, wait."

Slowly she turned back. There was a strange, complex expression on Ren's narrow face.

"Do you even know where you are?"

"Roland Fields."

Ren hissed impatiently. "Yeah, sure. But *where* in the Fields?"

Sam shook her head. "No," she said honestly, "I don't."

He glared at her, his eyes flashing with exasperation. "And you don't know where you're going, either, do you, deadload? Where you're going to squat tonight? How you're going to eat?"

"I'll make out."

He snorted with amusement, as though she'd said something funny. He pointedly look her up and down. "Yeah, *sure* you will. On your back or on your knees, no other way. You ready to go that route, bunny, huh? Who knows, maybe there's a market in the Fields for outworld meat. Huh?" His voice was harsh, scornful; but something in his eyes contradicted the venom in his words. "Hey, you can probably start your career right around here, if that's what you want."

It took a major effort to keep herself from shivering. She knew the truth in the boy's harsh voice. *God, he's probably right. What other options would I have? I don't know the culture, I don't know the technology, it's just pure luck I even know the* language. Sam forced herself to ignore those thoughts. "I'll make do," she said evenly.

Ren spat on the ground. Samantha watched silently as he paced, almost vibrating with tension as he made up his mind. Finally he shook himself once, like a dog shaking off water. "Well, frak it, I'm going!" he ground out. "Gotta get to work." He turned his back on her, but he didn't walk away—not yet. Without looking at her, he growled churlishly, "If you want to come, come. If you don't, *frak* you!" And he strode away toward the low buildings of Roland Fields.

Even then, Sam hesitated before limping after him.

What the hell is *this place?*

That was Samantha's first reaction to Roland Fields "proper." Her impression from the ridge the night before had been something like Los Angeles—a megalopolis, spread out in a sea of lights. When she'd thought about it—not often, she admitted—she'd imagined something out of a science fiction movie. Roland Fields had to be a "techno-utopia," didn't it? After all, any society that had the technology to build BattleMechs ought to have countless other technological wonders. "Air cars," maybe; great glass-and-titanium skyscrapers half a mile tall; computers, robots, artificial intelligence, and who knew what else?

All right, so the desolation where she'd spent the night and the low buildings she'd seen from the field of "metal-stacks" didn't match the image of gleaming technology. But could you honestly judge the whole of Los Angeles from a wrecker's yard and a block or two of South Central LA? That had to be the kind of place she'd wandered into, she reasoned. Okay, she'd stumbled upon the "slums" of Roland Fields . . . and they were pretty damn depressing. But walk far enough away from the hills she'd descended the night before, and she'd soon get to the *real* city. . . .

Wouldn't she? It didn't take long for doubt to start gnawing away at her certainty. The first few blocks through which she and Ren walked definitely looked familiar. It wouldn't have taken much to convince herself that she was strolling through Watts near the USC campus, or through various parts of South Central. The same low, dilapidated buildings. The same graffiti and gang-style "placa" spray painted onto the walls. The same metal bars over the windows, the same reinforced doors on convenience stores. And the same street denizens, leaning against walls or crouching in doorways, watching the passersby with the eyes of scavengers or predators.

The similarities were deep, structural, significant. The differences she found were more superficial, just errant details more than anything, but for all that she found them disturbing, disorienting.

The smell of the air, for one. Even on the clearest day, the air of the Los Angeles basin had a distinctive smell to it: car exhaust, plus other elements that made up the distinctive exhalation of the city. Angelenos didn't really notice it, of course; their senses and brains adapted, quickly "tuning it out." *This* city, though, had its own, distinct smell: pollution of some kind, though not the NO_X and carbon monoxide she was used to, leavened with the tang of ozone and something else. *The dead, dusty smell of de-*

spair, maybe? And the sharp scent of violence, *just below the surface. . . .*

Then there were the ads, the billboards that covered nearly every available inch of wall space. The ads for familiar categories of products—liquor and junk food, for example—felt subtly *wrong.* It wasn't just the unfamiliar brand names—*Stiletto Gin?*—and the public-service announcements hinting at unfamiliar threats—"Stop BRIADS before it stops *you*!"—though those were disturbing. Even more disorienting was the *look* of the ads, the graphic and typographic designs, the images, the way everything fit together. Sam had never really thought about it before, but now she realized there was a kind of "visual dialectic" in ads—*as in just about everything else*—a kind of shared "visual language" that allowed ad designers to convey a wealth of emotional "data" in a simple series of images. For her, these ads and billboards lacked that familiar visual dialectic; the pictures and graphics used a different visual language, one she didn't understand.

And then there are the ads for weapons. Flashy billboards, next to those selling snack food or soft drinks, sang the praises of one kind of handgun or ammunition over another. "SAGET 9MM—WHEN IT COUNTS!" or "KEYHOLDER UNDER-CALIBER ROUNDS—SAY IT WITH SABOTS!" *This place has got to be an NRA member's wet dream. . . .*

Before they'd left the metalstacks, Sam had caught up with Renard. Now she'd fallen behind again—*Too busy rubbernecking,* she chided herself. Hastily, she picked up the pace, closing the gap between her and the hard-edged kid. She was still a dozen yards back when he turned right, down a narrow sidestreet—*Or maybe alley is a better word,* she corrected mentally. She felt eyes on her; street types were watching her, *evaluating* her. She shivered suddenly, wanting to run to catch up with Renard *right now,* but knowing instinctively that would be very much the wrong thing to do. With an effort, she kept her pace steady—a brisk, businesslike stride, not the panicked scuttle of a victim. She turned the corner . . .

And damn near ran smack into a person emerging from a doorway alcove to her left. She put on the brakes, pulling up a couple of inches short of him.

He was a tall man, six-two, maybe six-three, and broad

across the shoulders and chest. He'd probably been in shape once, but now most of his muscle seemed to have gone to fat. His T-shirt—it bore a low-definition color photo-image of a BattleMech climbing over what looked like a metalstack, with the slogan underneath reading "SCRAPYARD DOG"—was stretched tight over his belly. He leered down into Sam's face, his front teeth glinting the cold gray of steel. His breath washed over her, a choking combination of alcohol, halitosis and decay.

"Hey, bunny," he slurred. "Wanna go with me? Yeah, *sure* you do." He reached out with his left hand to grab Sam—maybe her upper arm, maybe her breast, she wasn't sure.

And she *certainly* wasn't going to wait to find out. She stepped back and moved to grab the meaty hand that was reaching for her, intending to use the same armlock she'd used on the weasel in the Jones Cartage truck cab.

She was fast, but the big man facing her was even faster. His own right hand lashed out, grabbing her wrist in a grip like a manacle. Sam shouted as he lifted the wrist he held to above her shoulder, scrutinizing it blearily with bloodshot eyes. "Spunky," he rumbled. And then he smiled. "I like 'em spunky."

Sam shifted her weight, preparing for a countermove. Before she could follow through, the big man tightened his grip on her, until she felt the small bones in her wrist grind and shift against each other. She bit back on a scream.

"Don't," he growled, his voice suddenly harsh. His piggy little eyes narrowed, and he glared down at her. "Don't do *nothing,* bunny, 'wise I might decide not to be nice to you after all. Yah?"

Samantha lashed out with her right foot, a quick, powerful kick to the man's groin. It never landed. Again he reacted faster than anyone that big—or that drunk—had any right to. He pivoted his hip so her kick hit the big muscle of his thigh. He grunted with the impact; it had to hurt, but it was far from the incapacitating blow she'd intended. Then, with a growl of bestial rage, he tightened his grip on Sam's wrist and jerked her off her feet, shaking her as he squeezed.

She shrieked at the pain, bolts of agony shooting up her forearm into her elbow as the joint hyperextended.

"Bitch," the big man snarled. "Frakhead." He squeezed

even tighter, and Sam felt something give in her wrist. The pain was a red fog clouding her vision, a pounding in her ears.

"Put the lady down, wad."

The voice barely penetrated the pulse-synchrony of pain. Sam didn't recognize it immediately—she'd never heard a voice so cold, so deadly and emotionless. She immediately looked toward the source of the voice, the source of the new threat.

It was Renard. His face was blank, completely expressionless, like that of a corpse. The only sign of life was in his eyes, a cold glint like a knife blade gleaming under a streetlight. In his hand he held a gun—a big, bulky thing with a muzzle like a cave. The pistol was as steady as if his arm, his whole body, were cast out of tungsten steel. "Put the lady down," he ordered again.

Slowly, the big man turned his head to glare at Ren. His eyes narrowed down to angry slits. "Walk away, boy," he rumbled. "Just walk away." Still he held Sam's wrist in a grip like a hydraulic vise.

Ren shook his head, just once. "Put her down." Sam saw his thumb move, heard the sharp metallic *snick* as he flicked the safety catch off the big pistol.

The man's grip loosened slightly, and the pain started to recede. "She's with you?" he asked, his voice an insulting sneer. "*Big* man."

Sam saw the pistol move slightly, as Ren adjusted his aim. Before, it had been pointing at the center of the man's chest. Now, she knew, the point of aim had settled between the big man's piggy eyes. "Big enough," Ren agreed.

Samantha could feel a change in the man's grip. It was still tight enough to hurt, but some of the certainty, the mindless aggression, seemed to have gone out of the man's body. "Big enough to pull that trigger?" he asked.

And Renard smiled, a cruel, cold expression. *I am Death,* it seemed to say. "If I am, you won't live long enough to know it."

"Frak!" The man threw Sam away from him. She staggered, then caught her balance. "*Take* the bait," he snarled. Sam heard the tremor of fear in his voice. "She probably ain't worth the trouble anyhow." And with that, he turned

his back and swaggered off, out of the narrow side street and out of sight.

Ren's pistol tracked him until he rounded the corner. For a couple more seconds, the young man stood there, hard and implacable. Then he let his breath out in a sigh, and the tension went out of his body. He looked down at the pistol in his hand as if he'd never seen it before. He reached behind him, and jammed it into the waistband of his trousers at the back, out of sight under his hip-length vest. "Deadload," he snorted.

Then he smiled at Samantha, a real smile this time, not the grimace of Death incarnate. "You coming?" he asked her.

Sam shook her head in the affirmative, still slightly stunned. *I've never come that close to a murder before.* As Renard began walking, she hurried to catch up with him.

He didn't look her way, didn't respond to her presence at all. He just strode on. Sam tried to read his body language, finally deciphered a faint tremor as the fear that he'd suppressed so successfully during the standoff.

"Thanks," she said quietly. "That's two I owe you."

Ren snorted at that, as though her words meant nothing to him. "Don't like assholes," he explained roughly.

Sam nodded, and walked in silence beside him for a couple of minutes. Finally, her curiosity got the better of her. "Would you have shot him?" she asked quietly.

He stopped and looked at her, face expressionless again.

"*Would* you?" she pressed.

Suddenly he smiled. "Nah," he said casually. "Didn't have no bullets."

She stared at him for a moment, then she laughed aloud. "Renard," she said, "I like your style."

And I was hoping for a science fiction city with soaring glass skyscrapers . . . Sam snorted.

They'd been walking for almost fifteen minutes now—*Call it a mile from the metalstacks,* she thought—and if anything, the surroundings had grown even more depressing. The streets were narrower, nearly blocked in places by piles of garbage—decaying, discarded food, as well as technical detritus. *If I come back here five years from now, will these streets be filled with metalstacks, too?* she wondered.

Scavengers watched them as they walked by—two-legged *and* four-legged scavengers. Down-and-outers watched from shadowed doorways, and little beady eyes glinted from the dark depths of the refuse piles. *Rats,* she thought, until she saw one of the small animals. It was like the creature whose cave she'd usurped in the badlands; a lizard, but covered with a thick pelt of fur, and these were larger, about the size of a malnourished beagle. And it looked nastier, too—leaner, meaner, more feral. Samantha stifled a shiver. *These things fill the ecological niche of rats?* she thought. *If I ever needed evidence that I'm* somewhere else, *somewhere alien, this is it.*

Renard walked on, oblivious to the scavengers watching them. The cloud-deck overhead was unbroken, the dark gray of slate. A light, cold drizzle had started to fall, chilling Samantha to the bone. If Ren even noticed the rain, he gave no sign.

"So you work around here, Ren?" she asked.

The young man grinned, understanding the *real* question behind her words. "Not far now, deadload," he told her wryly.

"Sam," she corrected automatically.

He hesitated; then he nodded. "Sam."

"What do you do?" she asked after another minute. She glanced around at the low, tumble-down buildings. The windows of most of the small stores were boarded up. Many of the walls were stitched with craters the size of baseballs. *Bulletholes,* she realized with a chill.

Ren seemed to have noticed the direction of her gaze, because his lips quirked up in another grim smile. "Do I do the gang thing, you mean? Drive-bys and that shit? Nah, not anymore."

"So . . . ?"

"Got me a real job," he elaborated. "Work for a stable. Saber Stable."

Samantha shook her head. "You've lost me," she admitted. "What's a stable?" She snorted, and cut off his response. "I *know* I'm a deadload, but humor me, okay?"

Ren chuckled. "I know you're a deadload too," he said, but for the first time he didn't use it as an insult. "This is Solaris Seven. You gotta be a *real* deadload not to know what that means."

"Tell me."

The young ex-ganger shrugged his scrawny shoulders. "Solaris Seven—it's the Game World, right? That's why it exists. That's the *only* reason it exists."

"What do you mean, 'Game World'?"

"The *games,*" he stressed. He stopped, settled his fists on his hips and stared at her. "You really don't know? Where the frak are you *from*? And what are you doing here?"

Sam sighed. "Maybe I'll tell you sometime. You were saying . . . ?"

Ren shook his head—in disgust or frustration, she wasn't sure. "The games," he repeated. "The BattleMech games. Combat. One-on-one, in teams, you frakking *name* it.

"There's arenas all over the frakking planet, okay? All kinds of leagues, all kinds of divisions. You've got Mech-Warriors coming from all over to fight."

Sam blinked. "Fight?" she repeated. "Like . . . *fight,* for real? You're talking about gladiatorial combat?"

Ren shrugged again. "Gladiators are something different. I'm talking about fighting in 'Mechs."

"Fighting to the death?"

"Okay, in some arenas and divisions—out in the blood pits, sometimes—they use training weapons and simulators and all that frak." His expression told Samantha clearly what he thought about that. "In the big leagues, up in the Show, it's live weapons, the real scene."

My God. . . . Sam shook her head in disbelief. *What kind of world* is *this?* Images flooded back of the 'Mech-vs-'Mech combat she'd seen—and been *involved* in! The lasers, the missiles, the almost unbelievable firepower and destructiveness. "And people do this for *fun*?"

"For *money,*" the young man corrected her sharply. "A real burner—a real hot MechWarrior—makes a frakking *fortune* . . . if he doesn't get himself killed in the process."

"And people pay to watch people kill each other?"

"Pay *and* bet." Ren pointed to a tattered poster stuck to the wall of a nearby building. "What did you *think* all that was about, huh?"

Sam turned and looked at the poster he indicated. She realized she'd seen dozens of posters like this during the last twenty minutes; she just hadn't paid attention.

It was like an advertisement for a prizefight back in the world she knew, like the announcement of a boxing championship. But instead of pictures of two boxers, the poster showed images of two looming BattleMechs painted in garish colors. PAUL JERRIS V. CASSIE HO, the headline read, and beneath, in smaller letters, SHADOWHAWK V. WOLVERINE—THE FACTORY.

"The Factory, that's the big arena in the Montenegro Sector of Solaris City," Ren explained almost patiently. "Jerris and Ho, they're two up-and-coming jockeys, just starting to build themselves a rep. Jerris pilots a *Shadowhawk*—that's a kind of 'Mech, right?—and Ho's riding a *Wolverine.* Should be a pretty even matchup, considering their records. Lots of money's going to change hands over this one, you can bet your life on that."

Bet your life . . . interesting phrase.

Because that's just what Jerris and Ho are doing, isn't it? Betting their lives. . . .

Bread and circuses. "It's all going to be broadcast on TV, isn't it?" Sam said slowly, thinking out loud.

"Tri-V, yeah," Ren acknowledged, apparently mishearing her. "Everybody watches, if they can't make it to the arenas live."

"And 'stables' are . . . ?"

"What do you think?" Ren snorted again. " 'Mechs cost money—*big* bills—to own, to run, to maintain. And you need techs to wrench on your ride, don't you? *That's* what stables are about."

Again, Sam nodded slowly. It made a strange kind of sense. "So you work for one of these stables?"

"For Saber Stable, yeah." He shrugged, a touch uncomfortably. "It's not big time, not yet. The Sabers, they still fight in the blood pits—the small arenas, the local ones, not part of the Show. Not yet. But they're going to make it . . . *soon.*

"See, the Sabers, they're a two-way stable," he said earnestly. "They got 'Mechs, and they got good pilots, sure. But they also run gladiators."

"You mean real gladiators, don't you?" Sam suppressed a shiver. "Single combat. People fighting to the death while people watch."

Ren's flinty eyes settled on her, and seemed to look deep into her soul. "Yeah, that's what I mean," he said slowly.

"Not always to the death, but . . . sometimes, yeah." He blinked. "You didn't know, huh? You never heard of this before?"

She shook her head. "There's nothing like this where I come from."

"Which is . . . ?"

"A long way from here," Sam said bleakly. *Farther than you know.*

Worry about the future later, Dooley, she told herself firmly. *Right now, you've got to think about the* now . . . *about surviving another day here.*

"So you work for the Sabers," she said, her voice quiet. "Are *you* a gladiator, or"—she hesitated for a moment, trying to remember the words Ren had used—"or a MechWarrior?"

The young man laughed aloud at that, a harsh sound, strangely old for someone who hadn't yet hit sixteen. "Deadload, I sweep the frakking floors!"

She couldn't help herself; she laughed along with him. "Well, Renard," she said, "do you think they might have space for another floor sweeper?"

21

There was no sign to identify the facilities of the Saber Stable, nothing at all to distinguish it from the other broken-down warehouses that dominated this area of Roland Fields.

Samantha had been trying to keep track of the direction they'd traveled, to note the route they'd followed—*Why?* she asked herself wryly. *In case I need to go back to the metalstacks and fight Dog for his squat?*—but the unbroken cloud cover made it difficult. She couldn't pick out north from the position of the sun, and the route that Ren had taken seemed almost deliberately complex. She figured they'd walked maybe a mile and a half—half an hour, with a couple of minutes taken up by the confrontation with her would-be "client"—but Renard could have just been leading her around in circles and she'd never have known. Her knee had throbbed agonizingly for a while, but even before the encounter with the drunk it had gone numb. (She didn't like to think about the possible damage she was inflicting on the injured joint. *Not that I have much choice,* she reminded herself.)

"Here we are," Ren announced, indicating the front of the warehouse with a jerk of his chin.

"Home?" Sam asked ironically.

"Sometimes, yeah."

Instead of taking her up to the rusting metal door, as Sam had expected, the young ex-ganger cut around the side of the warehouse, down a narrow breezeway clogged with garbage. Something hissed viciously at Sam as she followed him past a particularly large pile of refuse—one of the hairy lizard-rats, no doubt—but at least it didn't try to take a chunk out of her leg.

There was more to Saber Stable's facilities than just the warehouse, she noted. A chain-link fence, topped with particularly nasty-looking razorwire, ran along the side of the building and extended beyond the end of the warehouse. There were more buildings making up the "compound," she saw, taller warehouses, the equivalent of six- or seven-story structures, and some others that looked something like army barracks. Overall, she guessed, the compound covered fifteen or so acres.

"This is one of the smaller stables, you say?" she asked.

He nodded. "Compared to the ones in the Show, yeah, it's small." Then he grinned—a little predatorily, Sam thought. "Around here, in the Fields? It's pretty big time."

They continued walking along the length of fence, finally turning a corner around to the back of the compound. From this new angle, Sam could see that one of the taller buildings had a large pair of sliding doors, fifty or sixty feet tall, open to show the darkened interior. She squinted, trying for a look at whatever might be inside.

Suddenly, actinic light flashed and flared in the darkness—*Like an arc welder,* she realized. In the harsh light, she saw an angular metal shape looming in the blackness. A BattleMech of some kind. *My God,* she thought again.

Ren had reached a gate in the fence, a metal door with a smooth, matte-black panel about a foot square mounted beside it. Around the gate, the fence was reinforced, and above it the upper strands of razorwire were angled sharply outward to prevent anyone from climbing over. Without a word, Renard walked up to the door and placed his right palm flat against the black panel. Sam heard a faint electronic hum, then a loud *clack* as the door unlocked. Ren turned the handle and pushed the door open. He held it, a little impatiently, as he waited for her. She stepped through into the Saber Stable compound, and Ren shut the door behind them.

She looked around. Someone was still working on the BattleMech she'd seen—welding armor plating onto one of the gargantuan legs, apparently. Apart from the technician, glimpsed sporadically in the arc-light glare, there was nobody around. She turned to her young guide. "So, now what?"

Judging from the expression on Ren's face, he was asking himself that question. He looked uncomfortable again, on edge as he'd been when she'd first met him. *Second thoughts,* she realized grimly. *He brought me here on impulse; now he doesn't know what to do with me.* She reached out and squeezed his arm, flashing him a reassuring smile. "Thanks, Ren," she said earnestly. "I appreciate what you've done for me, but I can take it from here, okay? You just introduce me to someone around here—*anyone,* it doesn't really matter—then I'm on my own. Deal?"

He hesitated, then he shrugged in a parody of indifference. "Yeah, sure. Deal." She could see from his expression that he was relieved—*Relieved that I'm not going to embarrass him in front of his employer and his peers?* she wondered. That seemed the most likely explanation.

Turning sharply, he strode off again, with a brusque, "This way," over his shoulder. She hurried to keep up with him.

"I don't work in the 'Mech side of things," he explained as he walked, "so I don't know nobody there. Maybe in the gladiator pool . . ." He shrugged again.

"That's fine," she told him.

He was leading her toward one of the smaller buildings, she saw, away from the tall "hangars" like the one where she'd seen the 'Mech. Long and low, it was one of the buildings that made her think of military-style housing. "You live here?" she asked.

He shook his head. "I bunk down over *there,*" he responded, pointing to a smaller barracks near the fence, "with the other workers. This is where the gladiators crash."

Gladiators. Just great, she thought.

Ren was approaching the pitted, peeling door in one end of the barracks when it swung open. Three figures emerged, and stopped.

Older than Ren, they were still young, Sam recognized—twenty, maybe, twenty-one at the outside. There were two men, one woman. All wore simple jumpsuits, utilitarian beige things with a dozen pockets. The tallest of the three was about Sam's height, but their physiques were like Ren's—compact, hard, not overtly muscular but fast and dangerous-looking. The woman's ginger hair was cropped close to her scalp, while the two men wore their hair longer—shoulder-length at the back and sides, but with the bangs chopped short.

"Yo, Jonas," Ren said to the taller of the two men. "Zup?"

The three had been talking when they'd stepped out of the door, but had fallen silent the moment they'd set eyes on Ren and Sam. Now the taller of the men—Jonas—stepped forward, scanning Sam from top to toe with cold, gray eyes. "Bringing your girlfriend around these days, Ren?" he asked scornfully. "Or maybe she's your mother, huh?"

Sam blinked. This wasn't just friendly ribbing; she recognized that at once. There was a sincerely nasty undertone to Jonas's voice, something very unpleasant in his eyes and in the set of his face. *What the hell's going on here?* she asked herself. *It's like he's trying to pick a fight—with Ren or with me, I don't know which. . . .* She glanced at her young guide.

Ren's face had re-formed into the emotionless mask he'd worn among the metalstacks, and when he'd faced down the man who'd assaulted Sam. There was no trace of the empathy, the concern, he'd shown for her. Judging by his eyes, he couldn't have cared less what happened to her.

And that's my cue, isn't it? Sam realized with a chill. *I'm on my own here. Whatever happens, it's entirely up to me.*

"You looking for a playmate, bunny?" Jonas asked, stepping up closer to Sam, his thin lips twisting in a sneer. "Somebody to show you a good time?" He shot a quick, knowing glance at his two companions. "I'm up for it if you are."

And that glance clued Sam in to what was going down. *Pecking order,* she realized suddenly. *These are gladiators, right? That's what Ren said. Fighting's what they do*—all *they do. So how is pecking order—the hierarchy of dominance and submission—going to be established in a group like that?*

Just like this. . . .

From the corner of her eye, Sam saw Ren watching her. His expression was blank, but his body was tense with anticipation—*With* anxiety, she corrected mentally. *He doesn't want me to let him down.*

So now I know how to handle this.

She let her expression twist into a sneer of her own. "Playmate?" she echoed curiously. "Maybe . . . if you can show me someone man enough to know how to go about it."

Jonas's face clouded up, and she wanted desperately to slip into a jujitsu defensive stance. Counter to her instincts, though, she kept her hands at her sides, hip shot provocatively.

The young gladiator glared at her a moment with pure hatred. Then she saw him force a false smile into his face. He chuckled softly, turning toward his buddies as if to turn it into a joke . . .

And, without warning, he came at Sam, snapping a quick right hand at her throat.

Despite her casual posture, Samantha was ready. As the young gladiator threw his punch, she danced back a half-step—almost too late; *he's bloody fast* . . .—and grabbed his right hand with her left. In a continuation of the same movement, before Jonas could respond, Sam stepped in on him, sliding her own right arm over his extended arm, doubling it back under his forearm. Gripping her own left wrist with her right hand, she pivoted quickly to the right, on the ball of her left foot, using her two-point grip to twist

Jonas's arm high in the air, behind his shoulder. To relieve the twisting, wrenching pressure on his shoulder joint, he did the instinctive thing—bent forward at the waist.

Normally, Sam would have finished the move by continuing the pressure, driving her opponent to his knees at her feet. On the jujitsu mat, that would have won her the point.

But this is no game, she knew. In an official bout, her opponent would concede. This was reality. The gladiator still had his left hand free, and she knew he could do a hell of a lot of damage with it. She had to take him down all the way—*decisively,* right now.

Those thoughts flashed through Sam's mind in the briefest fraction of a second as she made her decision. Smoothly, without a break in her motion, she stepped back with her right foot, increased the pressure on Jonas's arm, and brought her knee up, as hard as she could, into the gladiator's face. She cringed at the sound and the feel as her knee smashed his lips and flattened his nose. Instantly, she released his arm and jumped back out of the way as he fell to his knees, stunned by the impact.

For a long second, nobody moved. Jonas's companions had instinctively dropped into combat crouches, but they weren't moving in—not yet. Panting with exertion and the throbbing in her knee, Sam slipped into her own defensive posture.

On the ground in front of her, Jonas shook his head and spat bloody foam. Slowly he looked up at her, his blood-clad face twisted into a rictus of rage. "*Get* the frakker," he grunted. As if his words had freed them from the paralysis that gripped them, the other two gladiators moved forward—cautiously, circling left and right to flank Samantha.

"Stop!"

The voice behind Sam wasn't loud, but it rang out as harsh and sharp as a gunshot. For an instant, everyone froze, a surrealistic tableau. Then Jonas's two companions snapped to attention. Even Jonas himself, still spitting bloody froth onto the ground, reacted. Sam turned.

It was an older man who'd spoken—balding, big and bulky. Her first impression was that he was fat, because he had a bulging gut like the man who'd assaulted her in the alley, but she quickly corrected that mistake. The would-be rapist had let himself go soft. There was nothing soft about *this* man.

He wore the same sort of jumpsuit as the gladiators, but his left chest carried a "unit patch" showing a stylized sword. On his broad belt hung a holstered pistol. Under his right arm, carried like a swagger stick, he held what could have been a short riding crop, except that it was made of metal. *And seems to have some kind of battery pack mounted on the grip,* Sam realized. *Something like a cattle prod . . . ?*

Sam suddenly felt a jolt of recognition: the way he moved, the way he carried himself—*He's like a military drill sergeant,* she realized.

The bald man stopped and looked over the tableau. His mouth was twisted into a scowl of disgust . . . and judging from the way the lines of his face naturally fell, Sam guessed that this was his habitual expression. He glared at the three gladiators and watched without sympathy as Jonas struggled to his feet. "What's going on here?" he demanded of them. *"Well?"*

It was the young woman who spoke. "Nothing, *sensei,*" she snapped. (Sam's eyes widened at the word she'd used. *Sensei* was the Japanese term for "master," a trainer in the martial arts.)

"Nothing," the bald man repeated. "Nothing." He glared at Jonas. "So Mr. Clay here fell down and bloodied his nose all by himself, then?"

None of the three gladiators spoke, or so much as moved.

The drill sergeant shook his head. "Frakking hopeless," he growled. "Get out of here."

"Yes, *sensei,*" the gladiators responded in unison. Then they turned and walked quickly away, disappearing around a corner . . . but not before Jonas Clay gave her one last glare of hatred. (Sam sighed. *This isn't over,* she admitted grimly, *not yet.*)

The bald man watched them go, then turned his hard, dark eyes on Renard. So far he hadn't so much as acknowledged Sam's existence. With another snort, he strode over, bearing down on the young ex-ganger. Sam could see the fear in the young man's eyes, but he held his ground and kept his face expressionless.

"Maybe *you* can tell me what happened, Mr. Gilbert,"

the sergeant said quietly, giving the name a French intonation. (Samantha filed that away for future reference. *Renard Gilbert.*)

Ren didn't flinch. "Nothing, *sensei.* Just a . . . difference of opinion."

Still the sergeant didn't even glance in Sam's direction, but he hooked a large thumb at her. "Did you bring her here?" he demanded.

"Yes, *sensei.* I . . ." Ren's voice trailed off.

"It was my idea," Sam broke in. "I asked him to."

For all the reaction the sergeant showed to her interruption, she might as well have been invisible and mute. "You're on report, Mr. Gilbert," the big man snarled. "Be outside my office when you've finished your duties for the day."

Ren's lips tightened. "Yes, *sensei.*"

"Hey!" Sam said sharply. Angrily, she reached out and grabbed the big man's shoulder, turning him to face her. "I told you it was me."

She gasped as the sergeant swung his swagger stick—or whatever it was—at her head. Reflexively, she blocked his swing with her crossed wrists, grabbed his forearm with both her hands and twisted, pulling him off balance as she hooked his left knee out from under him. He went down hard, hitting the ground; with a grunt. Sam jumped back a step, poised, waiting for him to roll to his feet and come for her again.

He didn't. Instead, he lay there on his side, looking up at her speculatively. Then his leathery face wrinkled into a smile. "Good," he grunted. "Very good." Pointedly, he set the crop down on the ground; then he rolled to his feet. Sam felt her tension ebbing away as he looked her over.

"Good," he said again. "There's a place for you here, if you want it." Then his smile faded, and the steel was back in his face and voice. "But that's the *last* time you'll lay a hand on me, do we understand each other?"

Sam nodded slowly. *Things are happening too fast,* she thought grimly. *But what the hell else am I supposed to do but go along, and see where they take me?* "Yes, *sensei,*" she barked.

Samantha stumbled into the barracks and did a face-plant onto her hard bunk. For a few moments she debated taking off the ankle-high boots she'd been issued, but quickly discarded that idea. *Too much effort,* she decided firmly, *and too embarrassing if I don't have the strength left to undo the Velcro closures.*

This had been the third day of what she mentally labeled "basic training" under the direct supervision of the *sensei.* (Jared Bloch, his name was, Sam had learned, and he never let his very real concern for his "charges" get in the way of the hard-nosed discipline he figured they needed.) The bald man had handed over authority for the rest of the gladiator-trainees to a colleague in order to concentrate on "bringing Sam along" as fast as humanly possible. *Thanks for nothing,* Sam snorted into her pillow. *If it's all the same to you, I'll do without the personal attention.*

Samantha had always considered herself to be in good shape . . . up until now. She'd always been able to keep up with friends and colleagues in any athletic pursuit that came along—jogging, tennis, martial arts, whatever—and had figured that she had the physical wherewithal to handle anything that circumstances threw at her.

It had taken Jared Bloch less than an hour to prove her totally and categorically wrong. The Saber Stable compound included a training "circuit" like Sam had seen in countless "army basic training" movies—a steeplechase course containing just about every kind of obstacle a demented mind could envision. Apparently, every gladiator-trainee began his day with one time around this course before breakfast. By the time Bloch had put Sam through the circuit *three* times, she was ready to die.

And *still* he'd pushed her, forcing her to reach down inside herself and come up with reserves of energy and determination she hadn't known she possessed. She'd dragged into the gladiator-trainees' commissary for lunch after the rest of the trainees had already finished and gone—*On purpose, for obvious reasons,* Sam had decided after the fact—leaving her nothing but rapidly cooling scraps and remnants. Once she'd eaten, Bloch had taken her back out to the circuit, which she promptly dubbed the torture zone, and worked her until the sun had gone down behind the slate-gray clouds. Again the commissary had been empty when he'd finally told her to break for the evening, and she was glad of it. If Jonas Clay had been around and willing to make trouble for her, she'd have been hard pressed to offer so much as a witty comeback, let alone hold her own in a scrap. When she'd eaten, Bloch had shown her to her bunk in the "Transients' Barracks." Currently she was the only "transient" in the compound—whatever transient meant, in this context—which meant she had the small, spartan facility to herself. Bliss beyond imagining! She'd fallen into bed and slept like the dead.

Only to wake up and do the exact same thing the next day, and the day after. *What the hell am I doing here?* she asked herself for the thousandth time. *Compared to* this *torture, working the streets wouldn't be so bad. . . .*

She rolled over and stared unseeingly at the underside of the upper bunk. That wasn't true: she knew that, and she accepted her current tentative membership in Saber Stable as the best of a bad list of alternatives. *But that doesn't mean I have to like it!*

In any case, the level of agony she felt in every muscle was rapidly dropping as her conditioning improved. Bloch might be a hard taskmaster—*A cast-iron son of a bitch is more like it*—but he knew just how far he could push her without breaking her. By the end of the day, she had "low-order" strain-related aches in places she hadn't known she had muscles. Toward the end of her "torture sessions," when she was getting lightheaded and her equilibrium was off, he'd back down on the intensity, or tell her to skip whole series of obstacles on the training circuit. *Sensible,* she knew. *When I'm tired, that's when I'm most at risk of some major injury. And if Bloch's job is to get me in shape for something, having me break a leg or blow a joint would play merry hell with his schedule.*

Now that she thought about it, she realized he'd been moderating the risk of physical damage from the outset. She'd never mentioned her knee injury to him, the pulled ligament she'd suffered when her 'Mech had been toasted, but he'd apparently noticed her favoring her leg. While he'd pushed her to the limits of the injury's endurance, he hadn't pushed her *past* it. By the second day, the stiffness and pain in the joint had diminished, and by the third it was almost gone. *A mixed blessing,* she thought wryly. *If my knee hurt, it would distract me from noticing how much everything* else *hurts, too.*

Bloch continued to arrange her schedule so that she was in the commissary either before or after the other gladiator-trainees, and she was still the only person in the Transients' Barracks. (She wondered if the *sensei* had something to do with that, too.) That didn't mean she never *saw* anyone else besides Bloch, however. On a couple of occasions, when exhaustion hadn't tunneled her vision down *too* far, she'd noticed people watching from the periphery of the training circuit.

Renard had been there at least once, accompanied by a couple of friends who shared his lean hardness and his taste in clothes. (To spare him any potential embarrassment, she hadn't so much as acknowledged his existence.) Jonas Clay was there a couple of times as well, flanked by a couple of his "bootlickers"—that's how she mentally labeled them, at least—watching her with scorn written clearly on their faces. The last time Jonas and his little friends had graced her work with their presence, she'd seen Clay make some comment—obviously highly insulting, though she didn't hear it over the blood pounding in her ears—and then had watched all of them laugh uproariously before swaggering away.

Well, not all, she'd corrected. The ginger-haired woman who'd been with Jonas the first day hadn't laughed. Not as hard as the others, at least, and Sam had a strong feeling that she was laughing only because of peer pressure. She knew she was right when the woman shot Sam a sympathetic look before hurrying after her companions. *There's potential there,* Sam thought now, lying on her bunk. *If not for a friend, then at least for someone who's not an enemy. I should be thankful for anything I can get here.*

She shifted position again, groaning as her muscles complained. *That is, if I live through this,* she added.

She linked her fingers behind her neck, pillowing her head, and she frowned at the bunk overhead. *My God,* she thought, *I'm starting to think long-term here.* She examined that realization. *Long-term? This isn't my world. . . .*

Isn't it? she asked herself sharply. *It may well be, Dooley—face it.* She sighed.

She *had* to worry about long-term survival here. An ugly thought, but an important one. What the hell else was she supposed to do? Leave Saber Stable and Roland Fields and everything else behind her and trek back into the badlands to where her 'Mech had been destroyed?

Why? For what? On the off-chance that Macintyre might *have sent a rescue team after me ... and that I happen to be in the right place at the right time? There's nothing wrong with playing the odds,* she reminded herself grimly, *but they should at least be* reasonable *odds.*

Were these reasonable? No, she had to admit. Assume just for the sake of argument that Macintyre *did* send a rescue team after her. Not a certainty by any means, she knew; he could well have assumed that she'd died when her 'Mech was blasted off the air. When would be a reasonable time to do it? *Immediately,* obviously—as soon after the loss of contact as possible. For all Macintyre and the others knew, even if she'd survived the initial missile impacts, she might have been bleeding to death in her cockpit. Andrea had said something about the gantries not being configured for "multiple time-offset insertion," which implied that it might take a while to stage a recovery mission. An hour? Two? Three? In that case, when the would-be rescuers had "translated" to Solaris Seven, she'd already been driven far away from the downed 'Mech.

Would they have stayed long enough to make a proper search? Not necessarily. Nobody had come out and said it, but from conversations she'd overheard, Sam had concluded that the VGL missions were trying to avoid notice from the locals. That was one of the reasons why Will and Macintyre had been so concerned about the jamming and the ambush into which Will's team apparently had stumbled.) Considering, then, that the VGL wanted to keep a low profile, was it likely that they'd risk exposure to stage a full-scale search for her? No, she decided sadly, not likely at all. She was only one person. And, worse, she wasn't even a member of the Virtual Geographic League; she was a nosy outsider who'd penetrated the League's security, who'd lied and connived to get herself into trouble. She sighed again. *Isn't it much more likely that they'll just say "good riddance to bad rubbish" and forget about me?* Which meant ...

Which means this is *my world,* she told herself. *I'm stuck here—marooned, abandoned. I can't lie to myself; I can't depend on any false hopes, on any deus ex machina.* (She laughed harshly at the appropriateness of that phrase.) *I'm here, and that's it—until and unless I can find some way to get myself back home.* I. *Me. Myself. It's all up to* me.

Her eyes stung, and she rubbed at them impatiently with the back of her hand. She wished she could convince herself that the prickling and the blurring of her vision came solely from being overtired.

22

Oh, God, it can't be morning already . . .

Sam rolled over and pulled the pillow over her head, trying to muffle her ears. It wasn't going to work, she knew. She'd never really understood why armies—at least, judging by a lot of the movies she'd seen—still used buglers to wake the troops even late in the twentieth century. Now she knew. *Because sounds with lots of harmonics to them, like bugle notes, go right through anything you might try cramming into your ears.*

Saber Stable didn't go for a bugler, but the Powers That Be obviously understood the principle all too well. Speakers in the Transients' Barracks, well-concealed so that the inmates couldn't find them and tear them out, sounded a harsh electronic tone that reminded Sam of the "general quarters" alarm in war movies. Impossible to ignore, impossible to sleep through.

With a vicious curse, she rolled out of bed, and yelped as her bare feet hit the cold floor. *(That's something else the Powers That Be have figured out,* she guessed. *Keep the barracks damn cold. That way, the troops won't dog it when they're getting dressed, simply because it's too bloody uncomfortable.)*

And I would kill *for a cigarette. . . .* To her surprise, she was coming to realize that *this* would be one of the hardest transitions she'd have to make. If anyone smoked real nicotine on Solaris Seven, she had yet to see it. *Time to quit again,* she thought wryly, *because what passes here for a real smoke just ain't cutting it for me.*

Less than ten minutes after the "general quarters" alarm, Samantha was showered, dressed and ready to face the day. *As ready as I'm* ever *going to be,* she corrected with a sigh. Bloch was waiting for her outside the barracks as usual, swagger stick (she'd learned it was actually an electric stun baton) under his arm.

"Sensei!" she snapped, drawing herself to attention.

The big man smiled at her. "We're going to pass up our little run today, Ms. Dooley," he told her jovially.

It took all her self-control not to respond visibly. "Our little run" was what he called the brutal three laps of the training circuit with which he usually began Sam's day.

"I think it's time for you to join the others," he said after a moment. His voice was neutral as he continued, "If you think you're up to it."

Sam almost smiled, the trap was so blatant. She didn't answer, just held her ramrod-straight posture and stared straight ahead.

After a moment, Bloch smiled. "You're learning, Ms. Dooley," he growled approvingly. "You're learning. This way." He turned on his heel and strode away, expecting Sam to follow.

She did, catching up with him quickly and falling into step to his left and one stride back. (He'd never told her that this was the way she should follow a superior officer, but she was sure she'd read it in a novel somewhere. Wherever she'd picked it up, Bloch seemed to approve.) As they left the Transients' Barracks behind, Sam cleared her throat.

"Well?" Bloch snapped.

"I wanted to ask about my assignment, *sensei.*"

The big man shot her a quizzical glance over his shoulder. "Gladiator training. That's what we *do* here, Dooley."

"Yes, *sensei,*" she agreed. "But Saber Stable does more than that, doesn't it?" She pointed in the direction of the large hangars she'd seen her first day. "You have 'Mechs."

"Of course."

"I can pilot a 'Mech, *sensei.*"

Bloch stopped so suddenly that Sam almost rear-ended him. He turned the full force of his scowl on her. "What was that?" he rumbled.

Sam held her ground. "I've piloted a 'Mech before, *sensei.*"

"*Bilge.* Where? When?"

"On Solaris. In the badlands outside Roland Fields."

"*Whose* 'Mech?" he demanded.

"I can't tell you that, *sensei.*" *You wouldn't believe me anyway.*

Bloch's eyes narrowed. "What model?"

Sam hesitated. "'Privateer'," she answered, remembering the nose art on the UFT cockpit.

"I don't care what you called it," Bloch sneered. "What *model*?"

"I can't tell you that, *sensei,*" Sam said flatly. *And that's the absolute truth.*

"Bilge!" the instructor snarled again. But there was something calculating, something speculative in his eyes as he looked Sam over, as if he were seeing her for the first time. "This way," he snapped suddenly, and again Sam found herself hurrying to catch up.

He led her toward the 'Mech hangars. As before, the main doors were open, but this time nobody was working on the great, looming shapes inside the darkened building. Bloch stopped at the foot of one of the BattleMechs, and turned to Samantha expectantly. "Go on," he said quietly. "Get aboard and fire her up. Do that, and we'll talk about your assignment."

Sam stared up in dismay at the giant metal figure that towered a good thirty feet over her head. This BattleMech was designed along quite different lines from any of the other units she'd seen. Instead of harsh, angular planes of armor, this one seemed based entirely on curves. Every component seemed to be a segment of a cylinder or a sphere.

Which meant there were no easy hand- or footholds. If she'd been faced with one of the 'Mechs designs she'd already seen, she might have considered scrambling up the outer hull and trying to open the cockpit. Not this one—she'd have had as much luck scaling the outside of a water tank . . . *without* the benefit of ladders. (*Probably just as well,* she told herself. *Getting overconfident, falling and breaking my neck* isn't *a good way of attracting positive attention.*)

She reached out and touched the 'Mech's leg, an articulated metal shaft thicker than her torso. The metal was smooth and chill under her palm. She sighed, and looked at Jared Bloch. "Maybe gladiator training isn't such a bad idea after all," she said dryly.

Bloch chuckled, a sound like a rough-running engine. "So glad you've decided to see things my way, Ms. Dooley," he said sarcastically. "Now, if you're *quite* sure you're ready . . . ?"

Sam's shoulders slumped as she followed Bloch away from the gleaming 'Mech.

The suit of lightweight composite body armor was like a sauna. Samantha felt the sweat plastering her hair to her head under the full-face helmet, and running down her spine to collect under the reinforced kidney pads. Still, she couldn't fight off the frequent attacks of shivering that convulsed her. Not because of the temperature; not because of *anything* physical, as a matter of fact.

I'm watching people training to kill *each other. That* was what brought on the shivering fits, the realization that all too soon the gladiator-trainees she was watching go through their paces would be doing this for real. No armor, and real weapons instead of the padded plastic mockups. No instructors yelling orders and stopping the bout before anyone was accidentally injured. No other students watching from the sidelines, mentally rehearsing techniques for their own training fights. Instead, there'd be paying spectators, absorbent sand underfoot, the bright lights of trivid cameras. And blood, pain and death.

As he'd led her toward the training area, Jared Bloch had given her a brief overview of the gladiator "game" as it was played in Roland Fields. Gladiators were professionals, paid a basic salary and given room and board by their stables. In addition, they received bonuses for victories in the arenas, and were docked pay for making stupid mistakes. When the gladiatorial arenas—the death pits—had first opened in Roland Fields a couple of decades earlier, despite their name they were sites for purely nonlethal combat. Initially, combatants were armored, and their weapons were blunted, incapable of inflicting anything more life-threatening than a bruise, except by the most remote of chances.

While this was initially a hit with the Fielders who came to the bouts, it soon lost its attraction. Apparently, tastes in Roland Fields were just too jaded to care about two opponents, wearing so much padding that a small-caliber bullet wouldn't reach their skin, whaling on each other with fake weapons. Something had to change.

About fifteen years ago, according to Bloch, the gladiatorial "games" were revamped. Pit fighters no longer wore any armor, and the padded weapons were replaced by stun batons of various shapes and sizes. From what Sam could make out from the *sensei*'s description, these worked on the same principle as the taser back on Earth. High-voltage, low-amperage current stunned the muscles wherever the baton hit. A blow to the arm would immobilize that arm; a blow to the leg would make walking impossible; a blow to the torso would cause enough pain to effectively incapacitate the victim. A blow to the head . . .

Well, that was the problem, apparently. A head shot *might* simply knock the victim unconscious, or temporarily incapacitate him with a crippling migraine. But it might kill him, essentially turning off his brain.

The audiences liked that, it seemed; the real risk of death added spice to the sport. Within months, all death pits had switched over to the new stun weapons . . . and had finally begun to live up, or down, to their name.

And now the sport was undergoing another shakeup, Bloch explained. Even stun weapons weren't delivering enough excitement for the increasingly jaded populace. The spectators wanted to see real blood, real death.

So far, only a few of the arenas allowed death matches in their facilities, and fewer than half a dozen stables put their fighters in bouts to the death. Even those stables allowed their gladiators to sign up for these fights rather than assigning them. Stable owners let it be known that no fighter would ever be *forced* to accept a challenge to the death, but then they loaded up those events with such ridiculously high bonuses that many fighters actually volunteered for death matches. After all, the way the bonus structure was set up, a gladiator had to win only five or six death matches to be set for life—rich enough to quit the stable and live comfortably for the rest of his days. Since most gladiators came from the metalstacks or other "garden spots" of equal economic scale, and because quitting a stable would usually mean they'd find themselves right back in the slums again, there was a real attraction to the death-match route.

(Sam sighed. No doubt, most of the gladiators who accepted death-match challenges fully intended to quit after their fifth or sixth victory. But according to Bloch, most of those gladiators found themselves unwilling or unable to quit the circuit. Either the ultimate adrenaline rush of the arena had hooked them, or they'd lived high on the hog, frittering away their money so that they didn't have the savings to retire after all.)

Saber Stable was one of the organizations that refused to let its gladiators accept death-match challenges even if they wanted to, Bloch had explained. The Powers That Be apparently disapproved of the changes in the games, and were planning on holding out as long as they possibly could against the ground swell in favor of deadly force.

They wouldn't be able to hold out for long, Bloch claimed. The spectators—and the trivid broadcasters—were voting with their feet and with their money, and the outcome was a foregone conclusion. Arenas that didn't schedule death matches were losing business rapidly, and would have to change their policies or face financial ruin. The same was true for the stables, of course. The economic writing was on the wall; it wouldn't be too long before the vast majority of gladiator bouts, if not *all*, would be to the death.

No matter how much they may disapprove, the Powers That Be don't seem to have any problem with preparing for the change, Sam thought sourly. The "short sword" she held across her knee didn't have an edge or a point to it. It wasn't even a real sword: it was a "simulated weapon," designed to cause the red composite armor she and the other trainees wore to change color when struck. In that sense, it was less dangerous—and *considerably* less painful—than a stun weapon. Still, it was what it *represented* that so disturbed Sam. This simulated weapon wasn't even close to the size and shape of, and had a completely different balance than, a stun baton. That meant she and the other trainees weren't practicing for stun bouts. *This thing's got the same heft and balance as a real sword,* she told herself grimly. That's *what we're practicing for here—real fights, with real blades in our hands.*

Out on the practice ground, Jonas Clay was locked in combat with another trainee. Both were fast on their feet, and both were very aggressive, but neither seemed particularly comfortable with the simulated short sword he was holding. They were used to longer, heavier weapons, Sam guessed, judging by the way they moved. Their thrusts were always a hand's-span short, giving their opponent enough leeway to move out of the way, and their cuts were too slow and too clearly "telegraphed."

Finally, Clay's opponent scored a hit, a glancing blow across Jonas's upper torso that traced a bright track of green across the electro-reactive armor. Clay swore viciously, while his opponent looked smug over his victory. *Some victory,* Sam said to herself. *You didn't* win, *Clay* lost. She felt a twinge of sadness—of loss, of homesickness—as she remembered her fencing instructor from years ago. *What did he tell me? "In fencing, the first person to make a mistake loses," wasn't that it? Clay, you made a mistake.*

Bloch stepped into the ring and sent the other trainee back to the sidelines. Then he took Clay aside and spoke to him in a low voice for almost a minute. When the *sensei* walked away, Sam watched Jonas take off his wraparound helmet. The young man's face was red—not just from exertion, she saw immediately, but from humiliation. *Bloch must have told him he screwed up,* she thought. *And, knowing Bloch, he wasn't particularly kind about it.*

She thought she was hiding her amusement, but judging by the vicious look Clay gave her as he slouched to the sidelines, she wasn't doing a very good job. *I'm going to have to figure out this guy and his grudge sooner than later,* she thought as she watched Clay join his friends. *As if I didn't have enough to think about.*

"Next," Bloch bellowed, striding out to the middle of the training ring. "Dooley. Priss."

Sam stood up and stepped forward. Her opponent was a couple of seconds slower. It was the girl who'd been with Clay when Samantha arrived at the stable. Sam had since learned her name was Dana Priss. She shot a quick glance at Bloch. *You did this on purpose, didn't you?* she asked silently. *You saw this was the one person who might become a friend, so you're making sure we have to beat the crap out of each other.*

She shook her head sadly. *Well, that's life in Roland Fields, I guess.*

Bloch asked both combatants, "Ready?"

Sam swung the faceplate of her helmet shut. "Ready." She tightened her grip on the short sword as Priss closed her own helmet.

Bloch stepped back, hand raised, then made a sharp, downward cutting motion as he said, "Go."

Sam immediately took up a classic saber *en garde* position—right leg forward, foot pointing at Priss; left leg back, foot perpendicular to the axis of her body; left arm out of the way with her left hand on her hip; right elbow half-bent and relaxed, tip of her "sword" pointing at her opponent's eye. (*Interesting,* a detached, objective part of her brain noted. *Almost six years since I did any fencing, but the moves come back just like that.*) She forced herself to relax, to breathe deeply—to wait for Priss to come for her.

But Priss didn't seem to be in any hurry to attack. Either she was playing the same waiting game as Sam—hanging back, waiting for the other fighter to commit herself so that she could observe strengths and weaknesses—or she was intimidated by the armor, by the simulated weapons, and by what they meant. *Probably some of both,* Sam decided.

Well, let's get this happening if we're going to.

Deliberately, she tightened the muscles in her right arm, letting the tip of her "blade" waver, hoping Priss would interpret it as uncertainty. She shifted cautiously to her right, as though she was starting to circle her opponent. As she moved, she shifted her blade a little off-line, no longer pointing directly toward the other woman.

Just as Sam had expected, Priss took the opening Sam gave her. Lunging in fast, Priss thrust directly toward Sam's exposed torso, right for the heart.

The thrust was short, as Sam had expected it to be. Snapping her own weapon back onto line, she made a textbook saber parry in *quarte.* Before Priss could recover, Sam riposted—a quick snap-cut to the head . . .

A feint. Priss's own blade whipped up to block the head-cut, but Sam had already converted it into a cut to the side. Sam's weapon slammed into Priss's armor near her opponent's ribs, turning the entire side of her torso bright green. Again, Sam's training kicked in. While Priss was still staring in disbelief at the "mortal wound," Sam had stepped back and raised her weapon sharply to *salut*—blade vertical in front of her face, guard touching her lips.

As Sam brought her blade down from *salut,* a meaty hand fell on her shoulder. Bloch's face was expressionless as she turned to him. "You suckered her pretty good," the big man said flatly. "But don't make a habit of that. You give a *good* swordsman an opening like that, and he'll be eating your heart faster than you can think."

"Yes, *sensei,*" she snapped. As she returned to the suddenly silent sidelines, she couldn't suppress her grin—concealed behind her helmet's visor, thank God. For all the criticism in Bloch's words, she'd heard the satisfaction—*pride,* almost—he'd been trying to keep out of his voice.

Sam went against two more opponents that morning, and won both bouts. Despite what Bloch had said, she used almost exactly the same tactic against her first opponent, a woman named Wilkinson. It worked just as well as it had with Priss, and Sam filed that fact away for future reference. *You probably learn well enough from your own mistakes,* she thought silently to Wilkinson, *but you haven't figured out yet how to learn from* other people's *mistakes.*

Her third bout of the day was against Jonas Clay. As the hard-edged young bully swaggered toward her, she glanced over at Bloch—who was supremely unconcerned, gazing off at the horizon. *A potential best friend and a potential worst enemy,* she thought wryly. *Just what kind of twisted psychological game are you playing here,* sensei?

She beat Clay too, but it was a much closer-fought thing. Unlike Wilkinson, he *had* learned from watching others, and he carefully refused to take any of the "openings" Sam offered him. (He also passed up a *real* opening created when her foot slipped on some gravel, which was just the morale boost Sam needed at that moment.) Eventually, he decided to press his attack, coming in fast and hard with a flurry of cuts directed at Sam's head. She parried them all, but he was too fast to give her a clean opening for a riposte. So she just hung tough, weaving a web of simulated steel in front of her that he couldn't get through. Finally, as she'd guessed he would, he succumbed to fatigue coupled with frustration, and let his guard slip just for an instant. She feinted—just with her elbow, this time—drawing his guard up to block a head-cut . . .

Which never came. Sam's blade was still at *en garde,* because her elbow feint hadn't changed the angle of her sword in the slightest, and she came in fast, a simple thrust that drove right into his solar plexus. Even with the reinforced armor, he gasped from the impact. She stepped back—no salute for Clay, she decided on the spur of the moment—and turned away.

Jonas's unexpected blow to the back of her head was enough to blur her vision, even through the padding of the helmet. Her sromach roiled with nausea, and her ears rang with high-pitched, metallic echoes. She staggered forward under the force of the blow, trying to turn and bring her weapon up to block another attack.

There *was* no other attack. Jonas Clay was on the ground groaning, clutching at his right thigh. In addition to the bright green patch on his torso where Sam's thrust had landed, the entire right thigh of Clay's armored suit was brilliant yellow. Jared Bloch stood over him, his stun baton swagger stick poised for another blow should it become necessary.

"Consider yourself on report, Mr. Clay," the *sensei* said, his voice little more than a cold whisper. He turned his back on the fallen trainee, as he would reject something distasteful or totally insignificant. "You fought well, Ms. Dooley," he said to Sam. "But learn from this: a fight is *not* over until your opponent is completely neutralized. Do you understand me?"

She looked at Clay, still writhing in agony from the stun baton. "Yes, *sensei,*" she snapped.

All the other trainees avoided Sam as they walked to the commissary for lunch, leaving her alone to follow along behind the pack. Jonas Clay and his closest bootlickers acknowledged her existence only far enough to glare at her with undisguised hatred. Most of the other trainees seemed happy to stay out of the fight, avoiding both Clay's circle and Samantha. And then there were a couple, Dana Priss among them, who seemed willing to approach Sam—*would* have approached her, if it wasn't for Clay and his close buddies. (*Typical,* Sam thought grimly. *I pick one person to* really *alienate, and it's somebody with real influence among the trainees, somebody who nobody wants to cross. Smooth move, Dooley.*) As they reached the commissary, Priss turned back just long enough to shoot Samantha a quick smile. Then she disappeared into the building. Sam sighed as she walked the last few steps to the door and reached for the handle.

"Samantha Dooley?"

Sam turned. The man who had just walked around the corner of the building was glancing down questioningly at one of the hand-held computers that seemed to function as clipboards here. She hadn't seen him around before; his square, craggy face was unfamiliar. He was wearing the same sort of coveralls as she was, but his seemed to fit a lot better than anyone else's that she'd seen. *Custom tailoring?* she wondered. *Rank hath its privileges, is that it?* "I'm Dooley," she replied.

"Come with me, then," the square-faced man said. "Someone wants to see you."

"Who?" she asked, then belatedly added, "Sir?"

The man nearly smiled. "Mandelbaum, that's who." Sam waited; the name meant nothing to her. "Colonel Mandelbaum," he elaborated, surprise in his voice. "He owns the stable." His smile grew broader. "Trainee Dooley, either you've lucked out or you've frakked up . . . *big* time."

He started to walk away, then turned to say over his shoulder, "Coming?"

23

Her guide led her to a building she'd never approached before, on the far side of the gladiators' training field, as far from the 'Mech bays as it was possible to get inside the Saber Stable compound. It wasn't the newest of the stable's buildings, Samantha guessed—the Transients' Barracks seemed to have that honor—but it was certainly in the best repair. And, unlike most of the other buildings, it actually had *windows.*

It was built on the same ferroconcrete (or whatever) as the others, and it certainly seemed solidly built. But it resembled an office building more than it did a fortress. The lower two floors had only a few windows; narrow, set deep into the surrounding concrete, little more than enlarged arrow slits, but the upper three stories were almost all glass.

They went in through the main door, which was reinforced metal; apparently the difference in architecture didn't extend *that* far, and through a spartan reception area. (Instead of the big-haired, decorative secretary she half-expected to see, the reception desk was staffed by a hard-looking middle-aged man wearing the same style uniform coveralls as Jared Bloch. He nodded a greeting to her escort, but he didn't so much as acknowledge Sam's existence.)

From the reception area they rode a high-speed elevator to the top floor of the building. The elevator foyer opened onto another reception area, this one more opulent, with holographic images of BattleMechs and other fighting craft on the walls. The receptionist—a woman, this time, but no less formidable-looking than the man downstairs—smiled as they approached.

"Major," she said, acknowledging Sam's escort. "Trainee Dooley." She almost smiled, but not quite. "He's expecting you. Go right in." She reached below the top of the desk, presumably to press a concealed button of some kind.

Sam's escort—*Major what?* she wondered—nodded his thanks and strode past the reception desk to stop before a door of dark-grained wood. He knocked perfunctorily, then opened it. He stepped aside, and gestured for Sam to enter.

She hesitated for a moment, suddenly anxious. *What the hell is this all about?* she asked herself for the first time. Then she squared her shoulders, suppressed her sudden fit of nerves and strode past the major into the office beyond. She heard the door click shut behind her.

Once again, she was struck by an incredibly strong sense of déjà vu. I've been here before. . . .

But she knew that wasn't true. When she concentrated on the feeling, she realized what had struck her about her surroundings. Since her arrival on Solaris Seven, everything had been different from the world she'd left behind. The metalstacks, the dilapidated streets of Roland Fields, the strange combination of high- and low-tech throughout the stable compound. Here, though . . .

She could have been in the office of Jacques Leclerc at the Generro Aerospace facility. Everything was just that mundane: a wooden desk, a couple of chairs, bookshelves (holding the first paper books she'd seen since setting foot on Solaris, she realized suddenly). Nothing whatsoever was out of the ordinary . . . for Earth, her Earth. Familiar surroundings were now just as jarring as the sights she'd seen her first day on Solaris Seven.

The only reminder of the world outside was the view from the large picture window that looked out over the training field toward the 'Mech bays. With an effort, she brought herself back to the present and focused all her attention on the man watching her curiously from behind the large desk.

Colonel Mandelbaum—that was what the major had called him. He was middle-aged, in his fifties, perhaps, but still in the vibrant prime of life. His hair, cropped military short, was pure silver and his face was creased and lined, the road map of a life lived to the fullest. But the eyes that stared at her out of that narrow, ascetic face were as bright, as sharp, as those of someone three decades younger.

He wore a uniform jacket quite unlike the loose-fitting coveralls she wore herself. White, piped with red, with a high collar that looked vaguely Chinese in style rising from tan epaulets. For all of fifteen seconds, Mandelbaum considered her thoughtfully, as if measuring her worth with his gaze. Then he nodded to the single chair in front of the desk.

"Please sit down, Ms. Dooley," he suggested. His voice was quiet, but perfectly modulated—*Like a trained actor's,* she thought. *No,* she corrected herself, *like an officer so used to giving orders and receiving instant obedience that he didn't need to raise his voice at all.*

"Thank you, sir," she said, and settled in the chair.

"Mr. Bloch has been very complimentary about your performance on the training circuit," Mandelbaum began. "I believe he actually used the words *initiative, potential* and *persistent* in the same sentence. I don't think he's ever used those words together before, except perhaps to describe himself." He chuckled softly, picking up the cigarette from the ashtray at his elbow, and raised it to his lips.

"Thank you, sir," Sam repeated, then stared at Mandelbaum open-mouthed as the final element of familiarity clicked into place. Her heart felt like it spasmed in her chest as she realized he was smoking *a real cigarette,* at least something with the right mix of tobacco, nicotine and chemicals to make her system believe it was real. She stared in fascination at the cigarette as Mandelbaum returned it to the ashtray and tapped off the build-up of ash.

"Ms. Dooley . . . ?" Mandelbaum followed her transfixed gaze. "May I offer you a cigarette, Ms. Dooley?" he asked, irony heavy in his voice.

Sam swallowed hard, suddenly remembering where she was. "Yes, sir, please," she croaked through a throat gone dry.

Opening a drawer, he brought out a pack—*Marlboros, for God's sake!*—shook out a cigarette and offered it to her. As she took a cigarette, he also passed her a lighter. She took the disposable Bic and concentrated on lighting up, giving herself a moment to get her churning thoughts under some semblance of control. She drew the smoke deep into her lungs, closing her eyes for a moment, feeling the nicotine working its insidious magic. Blowing a cloud of smoke at the ceiling, she set the lighter on the desktop. "Thank you, Colonel," she said, struggling to keep her voice level.

He didn't reply, just watched her again for a few moments—*probably re-evaluating what he sees,* she thought. He retrieved the lighter and returned it to a pocket.

"You're from Earth, too, aren't you?" Sam blurted out, her heart speaking before her brain had much of a chance to fully examine the ramifications of her words.

Mandelbaum regarded her sternly. "We call it Terra in this universe."

"*Tell* me!"

The colonel shrugged, glancing away from her to look out the window toward the distant 'Mech hangers. "It's rather a long story," he replied, but not unkindly.

She accepted the brush-off—*temporarily,* she assured herself—taking another drag on the cigarette while she tried to slow her racing pulse. "Then answer me a question. Where the hell *am* I?"

He shrugged. "I could say, Solaris Seven," he pointed out, "but that isn't the answer you're looking for, is it?" He paused. Then, "Solaris Seven is a planet in the Solaris system," he went on. "It's located on the Marik-Steiner frontier of the Inner Sphere. That puts it 120 light years from Terra—from Earth."

"The future . . . ?"

Mandelbaum shook his head. "*A* future," he corrected quietly. "An alternate future."

Sam shook her head. Once again she felt detached—from her body, from her surroundings, from everything. Just as she had felt when she first understood that the UFT cockpit had become a massive war machine, something that people used to kill each other, it was as if she were observing from afar, remote from her body, remote from Mandelbaum's office. "What year is it?" It took her a moment to recognize the strangled voice as her own.

"It's 3052." Mandelbaum raised a cautioning hand. "In this virtual world, at least. This isn't your universe, Ms. Dooley"—he smiled self-deprecatingly—"or mine either, for that matter. The history of this world diverged from the history of *our* Earth in the late 1980s.

"And history's not the only difference," he elaborated. "I'm not physicist enough to explain it, but there are some significant differences in the natural laws, I believe. For example, some of the technologies used in BattleMechs simply won't work in our world. Believe me, some of the brightest minds in the League have tried, but with no success."

"Macintyre," Sam murmured.

Mandelbaum nodded. "One of the best and brightest," he agreed. "So I hear, at least. He was just a boy the last time I saw him. The last time I saw Earth, for that matter."

Sam shook her head again, trying to comprehend—to comprehend what she was hearing, and what it meant. "You've been here—in this universe—that long? How? Why? I mean, *how*?" Then, before the silver-haired man could reply, she answered her own question. "You're an explorer, aren't you? You came here, to this 'virtual world,' years ago, didn't you? And you didn't go home."

"Correct, Ms. Dooley."

"Why?"

For a moment, the colonel looked away, apparently uncomfortable. "I suppose I could say because there wasn't anything for me there," he answered slowly, not making eye contact. "That's what I've tried to tell myself over the years. But it's not true. I had a family, a career, a life. . . .

"Yet, there was *more* for me here, Ms. Dooley."

"Samantha," she corrected automatically. "Sam."

He accepted the correction with a faint, troubled smile. "Samantha," he agreed. He paused, then continued, "There was more for me here; that's what I thought at the time."

He sighed. "I was a warrior, Samantha. That's what I was at my core. It took me years to realize it, but when I flew jet fighters over Korea in the 1950s, I knew that's where I *belonged.*"

Again he paused. When he went on, his voice was soft, as though he were talking to himself and she were eavesdropping. "I was a historian, too—a military historian, of course. My studies revealed something important, if only important to me.

"Our culture, American society, was one of the first to dispense with a concept I believed to be very important then, and still do." He turned his sharp, dark eyes on her. "Can you guess what it might be?"

She narrowed her eyes in thought. *I think I have a good idea. . . .* But she waited for him to tell her.

Mandelbaum smiled again, a sad smile. "The concept we had abandoned in our society was the idea of the warrior class," he explained earnestly. "A true, distinct class—different from, and apart from, the other classes that make up any society." He shook his head. "Not just soldiers, Samantha, that's not what I mean. Not a civilian militia, not people conscripted and given arms to deal with a temporary crisis.

"*Warriors*—men and women who choose the . . . the . . ."—he paused, then grinned self-consciously—". . . the way of Mars, the way of Ares as the course of their lives. Those who live not to fight—not *only* to fight, at least—but also to understand and make part of themselves the traditions of military science. An educated warrior class, a warrior elite, if you will, who know not only how to fight, but *when* and *why* a society *should* fight . . . and when and why *not.*

"The Romans had it. The Greeks, too. . . ."

"Japan," Sam put in quietly. *"Bushido."*

"The way of the warrior, of course." He nodded his agreement, his approval. "Less complex societies than ours who fought when war itself was less complex understood its importance.

"Yet, somehow, we forgot." He sighed. "We forgot, and we paid the price. I wasn't on Earth to witness the Vietnam War and its aftermath, but I could have predicted the societal costs it incurred."

He leaned forward across the desk, intent. "Think about it, Samantha. We conscripted soldiers and we accepted volunteers, and neither group truly understood the responsibility they undertook. We trained them and we indoctrinated them, and we sent them out into harm's way, onto the most intense, the most bloody battlefield ever. We constrained them with political considerations. We brought them back . . .

"And then we forgot about them." His bright eyes hooded with sadness. "We brought them back to the civilian world and we expected them to return to their old lives as if nothing had happened. As if they hadn't been changed—as if *we* hadn't changed them. It was foolishness."

Sam nodded slowly. It made sense, but . . . "That's not all, is it?" she asked at last.

Mandelbaum's smile twisted, became a grimace of irony. "Of course not," he admitted. "There was more. My other motive—maybe it was my *main* motive, I still don't know—was . . ." He paused. "Well, let me explain it this way.

"I was a pilot, Samantha. A fighter pilot, flying the F–86 Saberjet, the earliest truly successful jet warplane. I understand things are different now, but in the 1950s, in the skies over Korea, we hadn't perfected combined tactics—close formations, wingmen, mutual support. . . . In a very real sense, we were alone up there—alone at the stick of the most potent war machine yet developed. When I was flying MiGCAP—combat air patrol—if I saw a target, I could pursue it on my own initiative. Can you understand the significance, the . . . the *excitement* of that freedom and responsibility? I held my success and my failure completely in my own hands. If I was good—if I succeeded—I lived; I scored kills. If I failed, I died. It was all in these two hands." He looked down, as it to examine the slender fingers he held out over his desk. "Can you understand that?" He looked up again, fixing Sam with his steady gaze. Something seemed to change in those eyes, and he murmured softly. "Maybe you *can* understand, after all."

Samantha watched him change mental gears, the shift almost physical, shaking off his mood, suppressing once more the very real emotion he'd shown. He shrugged, as if the discussion were nothing but idle small talk. "In any case," he continued, "I came to relish my career as a 'wolf of the sky'—that's what we called ourselves, my squadron; foolish in a way, but also accurate."

"And then it ended."

Mandelbaum nodded sharply. "Of course it ended. My squadron was broken up. Some of my old comrades never flew again. Some became commercial airline pilots." His expression communicated clearly what he thought about that option. "One thing led to another. I jointed the Virtual Geographic League. I was one of the first explorers to translate to this universe—to the 'BattleTech' universe, as I dubbed it.

"And I found a world that had a true warrior class—a distinct class, its members respected and *honored.*

"I found a society with a strong foundation, overlaid with a structure that allowed, even *encouraged* people to work outside it. It offered space for wolves, Samantha. More room for a lone wolf than there *ever* could be in the world I'd left behind.

"I never returned." He steepled his fingers before his lips, and he waited.

Waited for what? Sam asked herself. *For me to disagree with him, to argue? But I* don't *disagree. My God, I can understand* exactly *what he's talking about. Would I have made the same decision he did?* She stared into Mandelbaum's dark eyes. His expression changed subtly.

He shrugged again. "I was young," he said flatly. "Now I'm old. Old, and—I hope—wiser."

Sam frowned. "You're saying you made the wrong decision?" she asked.

"Right, wrong"—he shrugged once more—"it hardly matters now, does it?"

"You mean you're thinking of going back?"

He chuckled at that, a dry sound heavy with scorn. "I left your world behind in the 1960s, Samantha," he said. "Almost thirty years. It's not my world anymore. And I'm too old to be a stranger in a strange land again."

She nodded slowly . . . then sat bolt upright in her chair as the next logical thought struck home. *Thirty years . . . ?* "But you know about Vietnam," she blurted; "you know about the aftermath of that war. And these!" She gestured with her half-smoked cigarette.

Mandelbaum smiled faintly. "My last pack," he said lightly. "I haven't smoked for six weeks, and it's pure coincidence that I decided to treat myself today."

"But how . . ." Sam sputtered.

"I *am* in contact with the VGL, yes," he answered her unfinished question. "Occasional contact—*very* occasional, these days."

"*How* occasional?"

"Months between visits," he stated. "Often years."

"How long since the last contact?" Sam pressed.

"Six months." Conflicting emotions churned in Sam's chest. Apparently they showed in her face, because Mandelbaum asked quietly, "Do you wish me to tell them about you when they next make contact, ask them to take you back? Consider it seriously, Ms. Dooley. There might be . . . *repercussions.*"

She nodded. *Bloody* right *there might be repercussions.* "How did you know?" she said suddenly.

There was a hint of genuine amusement in his voice as he replied, "That you're a . . . well, I suppose 'stowaway' is a good enough word. It was rather obvious when your first question after your initial outburst was 'Where am I?' The VGL thoroughly preps its pilots about the target world before translocation. If you were a member and were stranded here, you would have known where to find me—roughly, at least—and would have come to me for help." His lips twisted ironically. "As you may have noticed, Solaris Seven isn't a conducive place for strangers."

No shit! she thought wryly.

He leaned forward again. "So how *do* you come to be here, Samantha?" he asked.

She hesitated for only a moment, then, with a mental

shrug, she told her story. All of it, beginning with Pop-Pop's death to her penetration of Generro Aerospace's security, and her battle with the 'Mechs in the badlands.

Mandelbaum was a good listener, as she'd thought he might be. He listened intently, his gaze steady on her face, her eyes. He interrupted only rarely, but asked incisive questions that cut to the heart of the matter, unerringly picking up on those important things at which Sam only hinted.

When she described her penetration of Generro and the way she'd convinced the technician Andrea to translocate her to Solaris, he chuckled. "That'll give them something to think about," he said, shaking his head. "They're so proud of their security—*some* of them, at least. They're so focused on keeping their secret that they've forgotten one of the core tenets of the League established by its founders back in the nineteenth century."

"Burton and Bell," Sam put in, remembering her conversation with Amy Langland. (*My God, that seems like years ago.*)

Mandelbaum nodded approvingly. "Precisely. Sir Richard Francis Burton, discoverer of Lake Tanganyika, translator of the *Arabian Nights.* And Alexander Graham Bell, inventor of the telephone.

"When they discussed the creation of a league to investigate *Elsewhen*—the virtual worlds, as we now call them—they understood the importance of *recruitment,* of finding those of like mind and spirit—like *soul*—and bringing them into the League." He sighed. "Sometimes I fear that the security that's built up around the League's activities is excluding the very people we need to *attract* to lead us into the next century."

He smiled. "I'm relieved that it didn't keep *you* out, Samantha."

"It almost did," she admitted. "You know, if it hadn't been for the van . . ." She paused. "That's something I still don't understand," she admitted. "What were those people doing at Pop-Pop's house? The League already knew it was getting his memoirs."

Mandelbaum shrugged. "I can't really answer that question, of course. But what makes you so sure the people in the van belonged to the League?"

"But who else . . . ?" She cut herself off in mid-sentence. "The government, maybe?"

The silver-haired man inclined his head. "That would be my guess," he said judiciously. "Again, I can't tell you for sure, but . . .

"The League's relationship with the United States government has always been rather rocky." He smiled ironically. "Something to do with both parties trying their damnedest to keep secrets from the other, I'd imagine.

"In any case, I wouldn't be surprised to learn that the people in the van were from the government, trying to acquire your grandfather's journals before the League secreted them away."

Sam nodded slowly. That made some sense. She sat back in her chair and closed her eyes for a moment, giving herself a moment's respite from the world around her. Finally, she asked quietly, "What now?"

"That's up to you, I'd imagine."

"What about a rescue mission?" She fixed her gaze on Mandelbaum's eyes, watching for any clue he might reveal. "Would they send one? Or would they just write me off?"

Mandelbaum gestured with his empty palms. "How could I know?" he asked calmly. "If he had reason to suspect you were still alive, Macintyre would do what he could to bring you back. But Macintyre isn't in overall charge of the operations. . . ."

"And he might not *have* any reason to think that," Sam finished bleakly. "I understand that. So. . . ."

"So your question remains: what now?" Mandelbaum turned to look out the window. Sam remained silent, watching the man's profile. Finally, he turned back to her. "There's a place for you here, if you want it," he said simply.

"Jared Bloch already made that clear," she said, her tone dry.

"I'm sure he did," Mandelbaum laughed. "Bloch knows a good catch when he sees one. I had something else in mind, though. Do you have any interest in learning to pilot a BattleMech? The real thing, I mean, not the emulation the UFT cockpits can provide."

"So I can fight in the games?"

Mandelbaum must have noted the sarcasm in her voice,

but chose not to respond to it. "Eventually, of course. That *is* what I established Saber Stable for, after all. And that *is* what the economy of Solaris Seven is based on.

"It provides a good living," he went on carefully. "There *are* risks, it's true . . . but there are risks in even getting out of bed in the morning. MechWarrior is an honorable profession—on Solaris, and throughout this universe." He smiled, an almost predatory expression, shockingly out of keeping with his "elder statesman" mien. "And it's one of the best professions for a lone wolf . . . or one who wishes to become one.

"What do you think, Samantha Dooley?"

Sam paused. *If this* is *going to be my home, doesn't it make sense to carve out something for myself?* She felt her lips draw back from her teeth in a matching smile. "Where do I sign, Colonel Mandelbaum?" she asked.

24

Sam slumped down on her bed—a *real* bed, not a bunk, this time, in a tiny private room—and stared at the ceiling. *And I thought gladiator training was tough. . . .*

She was exhausted—so exhausted that she couldn't summon the energy to walk the twenty meters down the hall to the MechWarriors' commissary, despite the fact that her stomach felt like a fist clenched around nothing. In one way, it didn't make any sense. *What did I do today?* she asked herself. *Physically, I mean.* Nothing, *or next to it.* No running around Jared Bloch's torture course. No sparring with Jonas Clay and the others. *Hell,* she thought, *from one perspective, all I did was sit on my butt. How come I'm so tired, then?*

She smiled. *I think I asked my dad that very question once,* she remembered. *We were on vacation and he'd been driving for hours. When we finally stopped, he remarked how tired he was. "How can you be tired?" I asked him. "All you've done all day is* sit down."

She could relate to his fatigue after her experience today.

In terms of running or climbing or jumping or fighting, she'd done next to nothing. But she'd spent more than four hours in one of the stable's sophisticated BattleMech simulator cockpits being put through her paces by simulator techs who were as daunting and demanding in their way as Jared Bloch. Learning how to make the gargantuan war machines—the real thing, this time, as Mandelbaum had said—walk and run, punch and block. Learning the strengths and weaknesses of the staggeringly powerful weapons: pulse lasers, autocannon, short- and long-range missiles, particle projection cannon, and the rest. Learning how to manage heat buildup from the powerful engine and from the weapons she fired.

It was like the first time she'd climbed into an F–16 fighter simulator at Edwards. . . . *No, even worse,* she corrected quickly. When she'd first "flown" a simulator, at least she'd been experienced with the general mechanics of flying. She'd had no trouble herding the simulated plane around the sky, leaving her with a lot of spare mental horsepower to think about things like weapons management and tactics. Now?

Now she had to learn to pilot an entirely new vehicle—*from scratch*—as well as learn how to survive in combat. After her first half-hour session, her clothes had been wringing wet with sweat, her muscles trembling from the tension and mental exertion. And in her subsequent three sessions spaced throughout the afternoon and early evening, the pressure had grown worse. *It makes sense, I suppose,* she thought tiredly. *Other recruits for the stable have probably read all there is to read on BattleMech technology and piloting, watched countless battles in the arenas or on the tri-V. Me?* She chuckled dryly. *The only time I ever saw* real *BattleMechs in action, I was too busy getting my butt kicked to pay attention to trivia.*

She scratched at the dry, itchy patches on her scalp. A tech named Dawn had come to her room this morning with battery-powered clippers and shaved away patches of hair on both sides of her head. She'd gone along with it, even though she hadn't really understood Dawn's explanation of why the patches were necessary.

When she'd showed up for her first simulator session, though, and when the chief technician had given her helmet to her, she'd understood. The acrylic-composite shell was more than just a protective measure. It was a "neurohelmet," a device with inductance-pad electrodes mounted on the inner lining. From what she'd come to understand—none of the techs had answered her questions with more than the bare minimum of brusque words, as though talking to a lowly recruit was beneath them—the inductance-pad electrodes read her brain waves. Particularly those produced by the parts of the brain responsible for "conscious proprioception": her sense of body position and balance. The output from those parts of her brain was fed into the gyroscopic stabilization system of the giant BattleMech, allowing it to keep its balance and stay upright. If she understood properly, her senses and her brain were being used as the huge vehicle's "inner ear."

My God, she thought wryly, *Mandelbaum* understated *the case when he said the VGL simulator was simpler than the real thing. Rudder pedals and a single stick . . . ? Give me a break!*

In the real BattleMech cockpit, she had control over every aspect of her giant fighting machine. *Every* aspect. When she wanted to move forward, she had to control the legs of the humanoid vehicle, and the arms too, since it was often necessary to use them for balance. Sure, a lot of it was automated; she could put certain facets of the controls on autopilot. That was fine for perfectly flat terrain, but as soon as she needed to walk over broken ground, she had to take over control of things like stride length, how far she raised the vehicle's "knees," and countless other factors. *All the factors that I have to pay attention to when I'm walking,* she realized. *That's what it's like—learning to stand, to walk, to turn, to run, all over again . . . except with my balance and physical capabilities totally changed.*

It was complex—hideously complex—but she could see the value of this kind of micromanagement. If you had control over every aspect of the 'Mech's function, you could use that control to your advantage. There was no way she could do it yet—and she was sure she *wouldn't* be able to do it for a good, long time—but she'd heard a good 'Mech pilot could make his ride climb a damned *mountain* using footholds and handholds, as a human climber would.

That kind of thing's way *in the future, Dooley,* she told herself firmly. *At the moment, be proud of the fact that you didn't fall flat on your metallic hind end more than twice in that last session. . . .*

Someone rapped on her door, quietly but sharply. "You decent in there?" a male voice asked.

Sam rolled over, her muscles complaining, and tried to husband the energy to glare at the door. "Is this a social call, or are you here to view the body?" Then she sighed. "C'mon in."

The hiss as the door slid back didn't obscure the warm chuckle at her response.

A young man was standing in the doorway. *No, not so young,* she quickly decided. With his boyish face, bright green eyes and fine blond hair, he could have been a self-confident teenager. But when she looked closer and saw the fine network of crow's-feet wrinkles around his eyes, she realized he was at least a couple of years older than she was. "Can I come in?" he asked. His voice was strong and vibrant.

"I said you could, didn't I?"

He shrugged, and his crooked half-smile didn't waver. "Just checking." He strode in and looked around. Sam was sprawled across the bed—the only piece of furniture in the closet-sized room—so he leaned against the wall, ankles crossed. It hardly looked comfortable, Sam thought, but he didn't seem to mind.

"Are you just going to stand there and look at me?" she asked him.

He shrugged again, but didn't answer. With a sigh, Sam forced herself into a sitting position on the bed and gave her visitor a closer look.

He was medium height, maybe an inch taller than Samantha, but considerably broader across the shoulders. He looked strong enough, but had the ropy muscles of someone who had developed that strength doing strenuous physical labor, rather than in a gym. He was handsome, she had to admit . . . but his expression made it clear that he knew it all too well. She sighed again. *I know you,* she thought silently. *I've never met you before, but I* know *you.* Unbidden, images of Ben Katt and the other fighter jocks she knew flashed through her mind. *It's the same type, the same* archetype, she realized. *Some things stay the same, even between different universes.*

He'd noticed her scrutiny, of course, and his lopsided smile broadened. "Glad to see you're not *quite* dead," he remarked. "We haven't met. I'm Eric Silver, but people call me 'Sterling.' "

Sam shook her head. *Right down to the call sign. . . .*

"Sterling" Silver's smile faded momentarily. "Anything wrong?"

"No. No, nothing." She held out her hand to him. "I'd stand, if I had any muscle tone left. I'm Samantha Dooley. People call me Sam."

He took her hand. For a moment, Sam thought he might be going to kiss it, but then he just shook it with a firm grip. "Pleased to know you, Sam Dooley," he said, as though he really meant it. "Tough day in the can?"

"The simulator?" She nodded earnestly. "Tough isn't the word for it."

Silver smiled agreement. "I hear you did right well for a newbie, though," he went on. "Some of the techs were pretty impressed."

Sam grimaced, remembering how the chief technician had sworn at her in some language that sounded like Cantonese when she'd stumbled and fallen in her simulated 'Mech for the sixth time in an hour. "I don't know about that."

"I do," he corrected calmly. "First time an outworlder's come in here and picked things up so fast."

"Everybody seems to know I'm an outworlder just by looking at me," Sam said wryly. "Is it really that obvious?"

"Well . . . *yes,*" Silver confirmed with a laugh. "Some of the pilots have taken up a pool on what planet you're actually from."

Samantha raised her eyebrows. "Is that why you're here, Sterling Silver?" she laughed. "To get the inside track on your betting pool?" She shook her head firmly. "Sorry, my friend."

"Ah, well." He gestured with his empty hands. "Worth a shot. I guess it only makes sense that you'd be keeping your secrets, considering who recruited you."

Sam leaned forward, frowning. "What do you mean?" she asked.

"Mandelbaum," he said, as if that should explain it all. When her expression showed it hadn't, he went on, "The mystery man himself. Nobody knows where he came from, and the man's not talking." He shrugged. "Okay, everyone knows he carved out quite the career for himself in House Kurita before retiring to Solaris. But where did he come from before that? Where was he born? Where did he get his training?" Silver gestured widely. "Mate, he's got ideas on tactics and strategy I've never heard before. *Nobody*'s heard them before—even the other snakes, the other Kuritas I've talked to. No wonder he worked his way up the ranks so fast. So where did he *get* those ideas, that's what we all want to know."

Sam struggled to suppress her amusement. "You're asking the wrong person, Sterling," she said as ingenuously as she could.

"Yeah, *right,*" he snorted in mock disgust. "I've got some of my pilots guessing that you're the old man's daughter, or *some* kind of kin, at least." He looked hopefully at her. "Any comments on that?"

She smiled sweetly. "Sorry."

"Yeah, that's what I figured." His frown faded to be replaced by a hopeful smile. "Well, look, Sam Dooley, how about giving a pilot a chance to wheedle more of a scoop out of you over dinner? I'll even buy."

Sam couldn't help but laugh at the expectant look on his face. "Why not? Lead on, Sterling Silver."

The decor of the MechWarriors' commissary wasn't much more inspiring than the gladiator-trainees' facility, Sam noticed. The same refectory-style tables, the same bare walls, the same stamped-metal cutlery.

The food was much better, though, she had to admit. Most importantly, here people actually got a *choice.* Instead of a single dish, turned out by the kitchen staff in industrial quantities, the MechWarriors' commissary was set up like a cafeteria. People had their choice of three hot entrees and as many cold dishes, as well as a reasonable selection of side orders like salads and vegetables. As she looked over the selections, Sam developed a strong suspicion that the foodstuffs used in the dishes weren't what they looked like. Did that stuff that looked like potato salad actually contain potatoes, for example? And the pan containing what she'd expect to be chicken salad—well, she'd never seen chicken quite that hue or texture before.

Silver was behind her in the line for food, and he chuckled over Sam's hesitation. "Outworlder, I knew it," he crowed triumphantly. With a snort of exasperation—only partially feigned—Sam scooped a generous dollop of what *might* be spinach lasagna onto her plate.

Only half a dozen people were still in the commissary. Sam hesitated as she carried her plate away from the serving area—despite Silver's comment about "buying her dinner," no one had asked for any kind of payment. (*Just as well,* Sam realized suddenly, *since I don't even know what kind of money people use on Solaris.*) Her hesitation gave Sterling enough time to catch up to her and take her gently by the arm.

"Why don't we join them?" he asked her, inclining his head toward a man and a woman sitting together in the far corner.

"Fair enough," Sam allowed. "I guess it's time I started meeting the troops."

The two diners looked up as they approached, flashing quick smiles at Silver and trying to keep their obvious curiosity out of the glances they shot at Samantha. "Sam," Silver announced, "I want you to meet a couple of the stable's better MechWarriors—Mary-Margaret Richardson and Lucas Trent. Meg, Luke, we've got us a new jockey: Sam Dooley."

Sam looked the two over as she shook their hands and returned their greetings. In terms of body type, both could have come from the same mold—as could Sterling Silver, now she thought about it. They were compact of build, probably very strong but not over-muscled. Their hair was cropped short with the same "electrode tracks" as she had on her own scalp. But it was their eyes, and the way they carried themselves, that she noticed immediately: steady, self-assured, confident just short of the point of arrogance.

"Pull up a stump," Meg suggested, indicating the seat beside her.

Silver settled himself across the table, next to Luke Trent. "You guys got time to jaw awhile?" he asked the other two MechWarriors. "Sam here's probably got a few dozen questions, and maybe she wants more than just my opinion on things."

"Let me deal with some of this first," Sam said, digging into the "lasagna." As she'd suspected, it wasn't pasta at all. The layer that could have been pasta was crispy, almost like thick filo pastry, and the filling combined the flavors and textures of ground beef, eggplant and something sweet-sharp, almost (but not quite) like cloves. It certainly wasn't like anything she'd eaten before, but she thoroughly enjoyed it once she'd got used to the strange combination of tastes. She polished off a couple of mouthfuls before asking, "You've been with the stable for a while?"

Meg answered for both of them. "Three years for me, two for Luke." She smiled, a cheery expression that Sam didn't expect from someone with such a no-nonsense gaze. "Sterling's the old man: four years, isn't it?"

"Coming up," Silver agreed easily.

"And you're all from around here?"

"The Fields?" Meg chuckled. "Not a chance, mate. I'm the only Solaris local here, and I came from Kobe—about as far away from Roland Fields as you can get and still be in the city. Luke and Sterling, they're outworlders—like you," she added.

Sam raised an eyebrow, but didn't comment.

Luke spoke for the first time. "Heard good things about you from the can techs," he said quietly. "So you're going to be training with us, huh?"

Sam drew breath to respond, but Silver answered for her. "I'll probably be running her through a few more simulations," he said casually, "but by the end of the week—yeah, she'll be ready to go live."

Samantha stared at the pilot. This was the first time she'd heard any of this, including the suggestion that Silver had anything to do with her training, but she held her peace. "Thanks for the vote of confidence," she said, keeping the irony in her voice to a faint edge.

The table was silent for a moment, giving Samantha another chance to work on her "lasagna." Then Meg remarked, "I'm sure you've got questions, Sam."

Sam snorted. "I don't even know enough to ask intelligent questions," she grumbled around a mouthful of food.

"Why don't you guys tell me anything particular you think I should know? How's that for a start?"

The three MechWarriors exchanged quick glances, and their smiles faded slightly. "I guess you haven't been off-compound yet, right?" Luke asked.

"You're joking, right?" Sam chuckled. "It feels like this is the first time I've had a chance to *think*, let alone go for a stroll." She paused, and her own smile vanished. "Why?"

It was Sterling who answered. He kept his voice light, but Sam could hear the seriousness in his words. "Sometimes it's not a smart thing to be identified as a member of Saber Stable. Not in the Fields, at least."

"Not in a lot of Solaris City," Meg amended quietly.

"Why?" Sam leaned forward intently. "What's the problem? People don't like MechWarriors? That doesn't make much sense."

The three pilots laughed aloud at that. Sam felt her cheeks burn with embarrassment before she realized the others weren't laughing at *her,* but at what she'd said . . . and there *was* a difference, she knew.

"Mate," Luke answered earnestly, "the city—the whole world—is *crazy* for MechWarriors. Most warriors, they go *anywhere* and they're followed by a flock of mechbunnies—female and male. Hangers-on, groupies, that whole trip."

"Same with us, really," Meg continued, picking up the narrative. "It's just that if you're wearing Saber Stable colors, you can't be sure that one of those mechbunnies won't slip a vibroblade over your kidney the first time you turn your back."

Sam frowned, suddenly remembering her impressions of the stable compound's architecture, the sense that the buildings were reinforced to resist attack. "I'm not sure I understand," she admitted slowly. "The stable's got enemies? Rivals in the games, maybe?"

The three MechWarriors hesitated, exchanging looks. It was Silver who broke the silence. "It's a little more complicated than that," he explained. "Sure, the stable's got rivals. We're on our way up, and that means we're climbing over the backs of other stables, which in turn will do whatever it takes to hang on to their position in the hierarchy. At the level we're talking, though—not up in the full-on Show yet—'whatever it takes' usually doesn't get really nasty.

Sure, there's backstabbing, but in the symbolic sense: dueling rumors to trash the other guy's reputation, political manipulation, that kind of crap."

He chuckled. "We've probably got one or two ghosts for other stables on the payroll. Not among the MechWarriors, probably, but almost certainly among the maintenance and tech teams. Just like Saber Stable's probably got its own ghosts in place inside major rivals.

"Up in the top leagues—up in the Show—you'll sometimes see ghosts sabotaging rivals' 'Mechs, even doing the dirty to individual jockeys. When Saber Stable gets up there, we're going to have to sweat that as well. At the moment?" He shrugged. "Typically, the worst a ghost's going to do is a little low-level industrial espionage. If one of our techs comes up with ways to improve heat sink efficiency, let's say, given a couple of days all our rivals are going to know about it and be trying to reverse-engineer it based on the data their ghosts have fed them."

Silver's smile faded. "We're talking about more than that, though." He fixed Sam with a steady gaze. "You asked if Saber Stable's got enemies," he reminded her. "The answer is, more or less. To be accurate, I guess the issue is that *Colonel Mandelbaum*'s got enemies. And they're not above causing real problems for anybody who's signed on with the stable."

Samantha shook her head. "I don't understand," she conceded. That earned her a disbelieving look from Meg and Luke, but, "I really don't," she stressed. "Look, I can't control what you think, but believe me—I've got no ties to Colonel Mandelbaum. I don't know a *thing* about his background, or about who might be after him. And I'm starting to get the feeling maybe I *should* know. Okay?"

After a moment, Silver nodded. "Okay, mate, your call. From the beginning.

"First off, Colonel Mandelbaum *is* a colonel . . . unlike some of the self-styled military types you find running around Solaris City. He served with the Draconis Combine, and that's where he earned his rank . . ."

"Hold on a minute," Sam interrupted. "I thought you told me he was with 'House Kurita.' "

Again, the three MechWarriors exchanged glances. When Silver continued, there was a strange undertone to his voice. "House Kurita, Draconis Combine—same thing." He didn't voice it, but Sam could see the question to his eyes—*Where the hell do you come from that you don't know* that?

"Go on," she said calmly.

Silver pursed his lips in exasperation, but he did continue. "The way we've heard it—not from Mandelbaum himself, of course," he explained quickly, "from the usual kind of rumors—he earned a killer rep out on the pointy end: out in combat, in harm's way. According to the rumors, he's a real butt-kicker of a MechWarrior, but he's also a pretty fair arrowhead, an aerospace fighter jock."

He looked quizzically at Sam, as if expecting her to ask another question. She held her face expressionless, and said simply, "Go on."

"Once he'd gotten himself noticed," the 'Mech pilot continued, "he moved up *fast* in the officer corps. Various command posts, then a kind of lateral shift into military intelligence. He retired with a rank of full colonel.

"That was maybe four years back," Silver elaborated. "From Luthien, Mandelbaum came here, to Solaris. He'd made himself a pile, apparently—either that or he was independently *very* wealthy—because the first thing he did was set up Saber Stable. Both sides of it, to be precise, the gladiator school *and* the 'Mech stable. I was one of his first recruits."

"And the only one who stuck around," Meg added.

For a moment, Silver looked embarrassed. "Maybe I just didn't get the right offer," he mumbled.

Meg explained to Samantha, "Some of the higher-league stables make it a point to poach promising 'Mech jockeys from Saber Stable. Mandelbaum's got one frak of a good training program, and he's got a rep for turning farmers into wizards. Problem is, once he's got a jockey up to scratch, one of the high-profile and big-budget stables—like White Hand or Starlight—comes along and lures them away. Mandelbaum just can't match the amount of money the big boys can splash around." She shot a meaningful look at her friend. "Now Sterling, here, he's turned down every poaching attempt that's come his way."

"Maybe I like being a big rat in a small hole," he grumbled, "instead of being a small rat in a *big* hole."

Meg's lips quirked in an ironic smile. "Whatever you

have to tell yourself, Sterling, just so you don't have to say scary words like 'loyalty,' huh?"

"You were telling me about Mandelbaum," Sam reminded Silver gently after a moment.

"Yeah, right." He paused, ordering his thoughts. "Okay," he said at last, "this is where it starts to get a little hazy, because Mandelbaum never talks about himself"—he shot Sam a quizzical look—"not to us, at any rate. . . ." He let the thought trail off. When it was apparent that Sam wasn't going to respond, he snorted and continued, "You can't climb the Combine hierarchy—*any* hierarchy, for that matter—without stepping on some toes. Inside *and* outside the Combine, come to think of it. It seems there's a number of people out there"—he gestured vaguely toward Solaris City and, by extension, to the worlds beyond Solaris Seven—"who are still holding grudges against the colonel. And they're willing to take them out on anyone associated with him."

"Who?" Sam asked. "Who's got such a big mad on for Mandelbaum?" She saw the MechWarriors' wry smiles. *Okay,* she admitted mentally, *dumb question, Dooley.* "You've got to have some guesses," she pressed.

It was Luke who took up the thought. "Guesses are all we've got, but . . ." He paused, then, "Okay," he went on, "here's the way we've come to figure it. Colonel Mandelbaum resigned his commission with the Combine and came to Solaris . . . but people just don't *do* that. Colonels in military intelligence don't just resign, and *certainly* not to come here, okay? So what are people going to think?"

Samantha blinked. *It's pretty obvious, isn't it?* she thought. "That he never really resigned," she suggested, "that he's here on some kind of TDY—temporary detached duty."

Silver nodded. "Right in one. Now, just for the sake of argument, say that Mandelbaum *has* hung 'em up, really retired for good and all, okay? Are the other Successor States—Davion, maybe, or Marik—going to believe that?"

Successor States . . . ? Sam thought in puzzlement. But she kept her mouth shut.

"Of course they're not," Silver answered himself, warming to his theme. "They can't *afford* to, just on the off chance that Mandelbaum *is* up to something shady—something that'll cause them problems, either now or in the future. Okay, assuming that the colonel *isn't* some kind of deep-cover ghost, the closer the other Successor States' security assets look, the less they're going to find. But how's a career ghost going to respond to that, huh?"

She knew the answer to that one. "By looking closer."

Silver nodded in satisfaction. "Again, right in one," he commended her. "Career ghosts, they're going to *assume* that something sinister's going on, and if they don't find any evidence of it, they're going to assume that it's just very well hidden . . . which implies to the ghost mind that the person they're investigating is *very* good at covering his tracks. In other words, a shit-hot ghost in his own right. Right?"

Slowly, Sam nodded. She'd never had any personal experience with that kind of "military intelligence" mind-set—*If that's not an oxymoron,* she thought wryly. But Ben Katt and some of the other pilots could tell some pretty disturbing stories about the "spooks" they'd come into contact with. *The spook mind-set is "Guilty until proven innocent." And an* appearance *of innocence just implies your subject is a pro at covering his tracks. . . .* "So agents from these other Successor States are working against Colonel Mandelbaum, is that what you're saying?"

"Not directly," Silver corrected carefully. "They don't want to be linked with anything like that. If Mandelbaum *is* still part of the Combine's intelligence apparatus, if he *is* on TDY, they know that taking any overt action against him will just escalate the shadow games that the Successor States are always playing. Kurita assets will ice a couple of their assets, and tit for tat until everything settles down again. A couple of operations get wrecked, a couple of ghosts get their brains burned out. Bad business all round.

"And if Mandelbaum *isn't* a Kurita ghost, he's still a Kurita citizen," Silver added, "and the Combine's always looking for some excuse to jack with someone else's intelligence network. Unprovoked interference in the life of a Kurita 'civilian' is an ideal excuse, as those things go."

Samantha sighed softly. *And I thought the Cold War was baroque and weird.* "No direct intervention," she echoed. "Indirect, then?"

"Through Mandelbaum's . . . well, call them *natural rivals* here on Solaris," Silver confirmed. "Other stables, mainly.

"Okay." He leaned forward intently. "As an outworlder you probably don't realize it, but Saber Stable is a success story to end all success stories. Four years ago, there was no Saber Stable—nothing. See, Mandelbaum didn't come in and take over a stable that already existed. He built all this"—he gestured around again—"from scratch.

"Four years later—today—Saber Stable is one of the hottest up-and-comers in Roland Fields. Its rep's still growing, even faster than it was a year ago. If the colonel can keep it up, two years from now Saber BattleMechs are going to be in the Show, fighting in the major arenas."

Samantha nodded. She didn't have any background against which to evaluate Silver's comments, but, *I might as well take it at face value,* she decided. "So how's he been able to do that?" she asked.

The blond-haired 'Mech jockey grinned. "And that's the question, isn't it?" he asked rhetorically. "There are only two basic answers. One: he's just frakking *good* at what he does. He started with all the same advantages and disadvantages that face other stable owners, but he's done it *right.* He's managed his resources and his people well. He's set up a good training program, and, with all due modesty," he added with a smirk, "attracted some damn fine people. He's got some innovative ideas about tactics, weapons allocation and 'Mech design . . . but nothing that anyone else couldn't have thought of.

"And two?" He chuckled grimly. "Two: he's got some kind of *edge,* something he brought with him from Kurita. Some new, hot tech." He snorted. "Don't ask me what it could be. I've been here since the stable opened its doors, and there just *isn't* any secret tech that's given Mandelbaum the successes he's earned.

"Okay," Silver concluded. "Of those two options, which are the other stable owners going to believe? That they're getting their butts kicked because Mandelbaum's simply better and smarter than they are? Or that they're losing out because Mandelbaum's got some kind of unfair advantage—no matter how irrational that explanation is?" He fixed his green-eyed gaze on Samantha. "Well?" he asked. "Which?"

She smiled wryly and nodded understanding. "I get your point. It's just human nature."

"Right," Silver agreed. "Okay," he went on, "to get back to the original point, why should any of the other Successor States make any direct moves against Mandelbaum when . . ."

"When they've got all those jealous stable owners to use as pawns," Samantha finished for him, "as 'deniable assets.' Right?"

"You got it! And *that,*" Silver concluded, "is the tale of Saber Stables . . . and why it's a good idea to watch your back anytime you're outside the compound." He chuckled suddenly. "Not that your training schedule's going to give you much free time, Dooley. You're up for some long days, mate, let me tell you *that.*"

25

Sterling wasn't kidding, Sam told herself wryly as she strolled slowly from the simulator facility—the "can crate," as the other 'Mech jockeys dubbed it—toward her quarters. *Long days indeed.* For the first time since she'd arrived in Solaris City, she could actually see the sun, a bloated red spheroid almost touching the horizon. She glanced at her watch—the new digital model that Meg Richardson had loaned her when she'd discovered she couldn't adjust her cherished aviator's watch to Solaris's twenty-six-and-a-half-hour day. According to the plasma-red digits, she'd been in the "can" for more than ten hours, running through incredibly grueling simulated scenarios, fighting against one, two and finally *four* opponents under a range of conditions and environments. Her eyes were so tired they felt sandblasted, and a tension headache squeezed her skull like a steel band of pain around her brow. Muscles in her legs and back complained with each step.

But she'd survived, that was the key thing. In all three simulations—under the close observation of the "can" techs—she'd managed to bring her 85-ton *Sasquatch* BattleMech through the virtual carnage in one piece. *Pretty badly mauled, true,* she amended mentally, *but still in one piece.* Granted, in the last scenario—the four-on-one dog-fight—she'd survived only through pure luck. With her *Sasquatch* badly damaged and her heat level hovering just short of shutdown, her single surviving opponent—a nasty thing called a *Shadow Hawk*—should have had her dead to rights, but missed cleanly with a missile salvo. Before it could take another shot, she'd "racked" her own 'Mech, spiking the heat into shutdown with a last-ditch attack that slagged the *Shadow Hawk* down into scrap. *Those missiles* shouldn't *have missed,* she told herself wryly. *Did one of the simulator techs take pity on me, and diddle a byte or two in the software?*

Well, it didn't really matter, did it? Even if the *Shadow Hawk* had taken her *Sasquatch* down, she'd still acquitted herself pretty damned admirably—if she did say so her-self—taking out all three of the *Hawk*'s "wingmen" (that's how she thought of them, at least) before getting herself splashed. She chuckled suddenly, remembering her first few disastrous sessions in the can, when it had been all she could do to keep her lumbering BattleMech on its metal feet. By now, she'd mastered the mechanics of movement to such a nicety that she was able to pull off a couple of unexpected maneuvers that had caught her simulated opponents well and truly by surprise.

This is better than Edwards ever was. The thought caught her by surprise. She stopped in the middle of the Saber compound and thought about that feeling.

I'm part of something, I'm accepted. She noticed again the unfamiliar weight at her right hip, glanced down to see the pseudo-leather holster on her belt. *I'm a MechWarrior now,* she thought, *and MechWarriors—in Saber Stable, at least—wear sidearms.* Silver had presented the holstered pistol to her that morning before she'd gone into the simulator for her first run. Though the blond 'Mech jockey had joked about it, Sam could tell that he took the symbolism quite seriously. So she'd taken the weapon and put it on her belt as he'd looked on . . . deciding against telling him that she didn't even know how to take the safety off the unfamiliar weapon.

I am *fitting in here, aren't I? Fitting in . . . and enjoying it.* The realization disturbed her, at some deep level.

But why *should it disturb me?* she asked herself. *I'm* here. *Marooned, abandoned, whatever you want to call it. Why* shouldn't *I fit in? And why shouldn't I enjoy it?*

She smiled, then. *In a way, this is what I always wanted, isn't it? It's the freedom that Mandelbaum talked about—the freedom to be a lone wolf, to carve out something for* myself, *to rise to the challenge, to survive. . . .*

The smile faded. *So why do I still feel like I'm missing something?* She looked to the upper floor of the compound's administration building. As she'd expected, the only light on in the entire upper floor was from the window she'd tentatively identified as Colonel Mandelbaum's office. She squinted, trying to make out details. Was that shape Mandelbaum himself, sitting at his desk . . . ?

"Why don't you just go up there and scratch on the door, like the miserable little bitch puppy you are?"

Startled, Sam turned at the sound of the harsh, scornful voice behind her.

It was Jonas Clay, of course, the gladiator-trainee she'd scrapped it out with on her first day with at the stable. He was standing a dozen feet away, fists on his hips, sneering at her with open dislike. *Hatred?* Sam wondered.

"Bad day, *Sammy*?" he asked, lacing the question with all the contempt he could. "Going to run on up to your outworlder sugar-daddy and cry on his shoulder? Oh yeah, I'm sure you and the mystery man have *lots* to talk about, don't you?"

For a moment, Sam just stared at him—bewildered, put off stride. The level of hostility she heard in his voice, his manner—directed not only at her, but at Mandelbaum as well, she realized—was . . . well, *inappropriate.* His attitude seemed to have little to no relationship to reality. *What the hell have I done to you—has* he *done to you—to warrant this kind of reaction?* she asked mentally.

"Skavel got your tongue, Sammy?"

Sam put her own hands on her hips, her right hand unconsciously brushing against the pistol on her belt as she did so.

Clay's eyes narrowed as he looked down at the holstered sidearm. "Oh, oh," he yelped in feigned fright, "oh, is Sammy going to shoot me now?" He laughed harshly. "Stupid cow," he spat. "You'll get yours." And with that he turned away and strode off.

Samantha watched him until he disappeared into the gathering shadows. *Why the hell would Jonas Clay have such an ax to grind with me, and with Mandelbaum?* she wondered. *Or is that just the way he* is, *generically mad at the world?* She'd met other people like that . . . and, she recalled, gone a long way to avoid them once she'd realized what they were like.

"Enjoying the sunset?" Another voice behind her.

She turned—more slowly, this time—and gave Silver a half-smile. "More or less," she said, impulsively deciding against mentioning her encounter with Clay.

"I hear you had a good day." The MechWarrior was grinning like a bandit, she saw.

"More or less," she repeated.

Silver snorted his derision at that. "Tube the false modesty, okay?" he told her. "The can techs told me how the simulations went today. I've never seen them that impressed. Particularly after the last scenario."

Sam shrugged, a little uncomfortably. "I got mauled," she pointed out.

He chuckled. "You don't get it, do you? You frakking *won,* Dooley. You weren't *supposed* to win. That scenario—four on one? It's a no-win situation, okay? That's what it's *supposed* to be, at least," he corrected quickly. "The lesson you were *supposed* to learn there was how to evaluate a superior force, and how to frakking *bug out* and save your ride before you got slagged down.

"And what did you do?" He snorted. "You kicked their frakking *butts,* Dooley." He barked with laughter. "Don't you *ever* play by the rules?"

Unexpectedly, Sam's memory flashed back to her last session in the F–16 simulator at Edwards. She shrugged, trying to look unconcerned. "I like my life challenging," she remarked lightly.

Silver slapped her on the shoulder. "You've got juice, Dooley. I've got to give you that." He paused, and his expression changed. "Got a couple of minutes?" he asked. "I've got something to show you."

Samantha stood under the actinic glare of the hanger

lights—a hangar she hadn't visited before—staring upward. A BattleMech towered above her, its polished hull gleaming—mirror-finish silver, instead of the sometimes-garish color schemes on the other stable 'Mechs. *The mark of a new unit,* she realized, *fresh off the assembly line. I guess that's why it's not in the same hangar complex as the other BattleMechs.* She reached out toward the thick leg—hesitated, before she could bring herself to touch the cold metal.

She turned to Silver, who was watching her with a broad smile. "Mine?"

He nodded. "I told you you'd be going live by the end of the week," he reminded her. He shrugged. "It's the end of the week."

Sam shook her head slowly. This was . . . well, just too big to wrap her mind around. She brushed the smooth armor lightly with her fingertips. "What . . ." Her voice broke. She tried again. "What is it?"

The 'Mech jockey laughed. "It's a SQS–TH–001 *Sasquatch,* of course. VEST's latest and best. Why else would we have been drilling you on *Sasquatches* in the can?"

"And it's mine?" she repeated.

"Yours," Silver confirmed. "The techs have already configured it using the telemetry from your simulator sessions." He chuckled indulgently. Then he tossed her something that glinted in the lights.

She plucked the object out of the air reflexively and examined it in her hand. A metal tag about the size of a dog tag, on a chain. Serial numbers and other data were engraved into one side. In the other, something glittered like an imbedded gem—some kind of optical data chip, she guessed. "What's this?"

"Code-key for your 'Mech. Tomorrow I'll take you out into the badlands and you can put it through its paces. Okay?"

For a few seconds, all Sam could do was shake her head. Then she slipped the code-key's chain over her head, flipping her long hair back out of the way. She laughed aloud. "*Okay?* Sterling, it's a little better than 'okay.' " She knew her eyes were dancing in the harsh overhead lights. She caressed the 'Mech—my *'Mech!*—once more. Then she turned to her trainer and friend. "Suddenly, I'm in the mood to celebrate," she said cheerfully.

Silver's grin grew even broader. "I think I can be up for that," he allowed judiciously.

Sam rolled over, staring at the faint wash of light across the ceiling in momentary befuddlement. *Where the hell* am *I . . . ?* Then she felt the warm presence beside her in the bed. Memory flooded back, and she smiled. *That's right,* she thought comfortably, *the "celebration" went a little further than I'd expected, didn't it?*

Or was this what I had in mind all along . . . ? She sighed contentedly. It didn't matter. For the first time in a *long* time, she felt really *good*—at peace with the world, and with herself.

Sterling Silver's quarters were larger than hers—reasonable, she figured, considering he was the stable's senior 'Mech pilot—but the additional space wasn't anywhere near as attractive to Sam as the fact that his room had a *window.* Granted, the view could have been better—the featureless wall of a 'Mech hangar, mostly—but at least she could see the sky. Lying in bed, she stared up and out. The lights of Solaris City were reflecting off the underside of the unbroken cloud-deck, a strange, ruddy glow.

Not only did Silver have a window, but it actually *opened. What I wouldn't give for some fresh air in* my *quarters,* Sam thought.

Of course, that was something of a mixed blessing. At the moment, the acrylic window was halfway open, letting in entirely too much of the cold night breeze for Sam's tastes. After a few seconds' consideration, she climbed out from under the bed's single cover—carefully, so as not to wake Sterling. Naked, Sam padded across the room and quietly slid the window closed.

As she returned to the bed, her 'Mech code-key swung on its chain between her breasts. She stopped, touching the small piece of metal with a fingertip. *Not such a bad day, all in all,* she thought with a smile. She climbed back under the cover, pressing her body close to the warmth of Silver's skin. The MechWarrior mumbled something in his sleep, blindly reaching out to wrap an arm around Sam's shoulder. Tenderly, she reached up to brush a wayward lock of blond hair away from his face. She lowered her head to the pillow, and closed her eyes.

* * *

It seemed only seconds later that the noise jolted her awake, the dull *crump* of an explosion from oustide the building. An instant later, a closer concussion rattled the acrylic windowpane in its frame. Sam jerked bolt-upright in bed. "What the hell was *that*?"

It took Silver a couple of seconds longer to react to the sounds. But when he *did* respond, it was by rolling out of bed, groping blindly for the clothes piled on the floor. "We're under attack," he grated, pulling on his jumpsuit.

"What?" Sam stared blankly. "But . . ."

Silver snagged Sam's jumpsuit from the floor and tossed it toward her. "Get dressed. *Do* it, Dooley!" Another explosion outside punctuated his words, a brilliant strobe-flash of light, followed an instant later by a pressure-pulse powerful enough to nearly crack the acrylic window.

Reflex took over. Sam jumped from the bed, pulling the cool fabric of the jumpsuit over her bed-warm skin. "Who?" she asked as she dressed.

"Frakked if I know. I don't have time to make a list." As he spoke, he buckled on his weapon belt, pulled the large pistol from the holster and checked the load. "Let's *go*!"

"Don't wait for me. I'll meet you outside."

Silver shot her a pirate's smile. "Head for the 'Mechs," he told her. Then he sprinted from the room.

It took her only a couple of seconds to finish dressing and pull on her boots. For an instant, she debated taking her own weapon belt. Instead, though, she just grabbed the pistol from the holster and crammed it deep into one of the jumpsuits' pockets. Then she, too, bolted from the room.

Out into the hall, down the single flight of stairs toward the building's main door. She was quicker on her feet than Sterling, catching up with the MechWarrior just outside the building.

The compound was in chaos. Lights that should have been burning were dead; harsh, glaring emergency lighting cast deep, sharp-edged shadows. Dark figures sprinted across the compound; she couldn't make out whether they were friends or foes . . . or even if there *were* any foes around. She cringed instinctively as another explosion split the night. A fireball roiled into the sky from the direction of the gladiator training course. Behind her, more of the stable's MechWarriors were boiling out of the barracks building like hornets from a burning hive.

A step ahead of her, Silver grabbed a person running past. *"What the frak's happening?"* the 'Mech jockey screamed.

The figure turned, and Sam recognized it as the *sensei,* Jared Bloch. "Under attack," the big man barked.

"Frak, I *know* that! Who? No, *how*?"

Bloch's snarl was a horrible rictus in the harsh lighting. "Sabotage," he spat. "Power down on five grids, security off-line. We're wide open."

" 'Mechs?" Silver demanded.

"Three mediums inbound," the *sensei* snapped back. "Eyeball reports only."

Silver nodded, slapping the big soldier on the shoulder. "Come on," he yelled back over his shoulder to the other MechWarriors. "Mount up, Sabers." The 'Mech pilots sprinted in the direction of the BattleMech hangars. Sam hesitated, then ran after them.

This doesn't make sense. The thought pounded in her head. Not just the attack—that didn't make sense to her, but apparently did to *some*one—but the *nature* of it. How many operational BattleMechs did Saber Stable have? Seven at least, in the standard hangars toward which everyone was running. And how many attacking 'Mechs? Three? *What was it Bloch said . . . ?*

She skidded to a stop *"No!"* she screamed after the running MechWarriors. "*No!* The 'Mechs are sabotaged too!"

Only Silver seemed to hear, stopping in his tracks to turn back toward her. In the harsh emergency lighting, she saw his frown . . . saw his eyes open wide as her words penetrated. "Stop!" he yelled after the other pilots. "Don't . . ."

He was too late. Luke Trent was in the lead, the first to reach the nearest of the 'Mech hangars. The big sliding doors were shut, as they always were at night. Luke grabbed the handle of the small, human-sized door to the right of the main door. An explosion blew him off his feet, flinging his broken body like a rag doll. The other Mech-

Warriors, a step or two behind him, yelled with alarm and agony as shrapnel tore into them.

"Ah, *frak*!" Silver screamed. He was running again, through the knot of pilots. The explosion that had slaughtered Luke had blown the door off the hinges. Without slowing, Silver sprinted through the doorway. Sam followed him, a step or two back, into the dark interior of the hangar.

Except it *wasn't* dark in the hangar, as it should have been. Flickering, ruddy light cast shifting shadows across the floor and walls. She almost slammed full into Silver, who'd stopped in his tracks again. "No . . ." he gasped.

Sam followed his gaze. Three huge 'Mechs loomed above her. Their armored bodies were pristine, untouched . . . but flames licked and roared from inside their open cockpits. Someone had unlocked the cockpits and tossed in incendiary grenades, or the local equivalent.

Silver seemed frozen in shock. *Of course,* Sam realized suddenly, *of course he's in shock. He's under attack. . . .*

And he's not a MechWarrior anymore! She grabbed her lover's shoulder. "The other 'Mechs will be booby-trapped too," she said.

He turned toward her, his face pale even in the red firelight. "I know it." Then his eyes seemed to focus, and his jaw set. "By the Name of Blake," he growled, "they're not going to bring us down without one frak of a fight." His gaze frightened her with its intensity. "Got your gun?"

She nodded wordlessly. *Not that I know how to use it.*

Dully, she followed Silver back outside. "Get to the armory," he yelled at the MechWarriors under his command. "We're going to have to fight this one as groundpounders."

A flash momentarily blinded Samantha; an instant later, a shock wave slammed her to the ground. Dazed, ears ringing, she forced herself up to a kneeling position.

My God . . . ! The MechWarrior barracks building was just *gone,* blown to rubble by a single explosion. As she knelt there, something flashed into her visual field from her left—a comet trailing fire, to slam into the wreckage of the building and explode again. *Missiles,* she knew. She turned.

Something loomed above one of the compound's low maintenance buildings: a massive, angular head and shoulders, silhouetted against the city-lit clouds. The first of the attackers' BattleMechs, she knew. As she watched in horror, more missiles lashed out from the racks on the 'Mech's shoulders, tearing gaping holes in the walls of the hangar to her right.

From the darkness across the compound, muzzle flashes flared—the strobe-flashes of single shots, the less ephemeral fire flowers of autofire. Rounds sparked off the armor of the approaching BattleMech—harmlessly, she knew.

The enemy 'Mech smashed its way through the maintenance building, destroying it with its sheer mass like a child kicking his way through a sand castle. As it walked, it pointed in the direction of the muzzle flashes with its right arm. Fire lanced from its wrist, a long, ripping burst of high-caliber autofire, raking through the Saber defenders. Muzzle flashes answered from the darkness, but fewer than before.

And now figures were pouring from the darkness, in the shadow of the BattleMech. Ground troops, she realized, like mechanized infantry supporting the heavy armor that was the assaulting 'Mechs. Desperate, chaotic firefights broke out throughout the compound as the Saber defenders tried to deal with this new threat.

My God, I'm just standing here in the open! The thought struck Sam with an almost physical impact. Instinctively, she pulled out her pistol, holding it clumsily before her. Even if she didn't know how to use the advanced weapon, just holding it seemed to bolster her confidence.

What the hell am I supposed to do now? I'm worse than useless.

I have to do something. . . .

Her 'Mech. What about the shiny new *Sasquatch,* fresh off the assembly line? The attackers—whoever they were—had sabotaged the stable's 'Mechs. . . .

The ones they *knew* about, at least. How good was their intelligence, though? *That* was the question. Did they know about the *Sasquatch,* in its secondary hangar on the other side of the compound? Sam hadn't known about it until Silver had "assigned" her to it. But did that mean anything? She was the newcomer, the outworlder, after all.

If I guess wrong, I'm dead like Luke, killed by a booby trap. She cringed as a burst of autofire spattered off the metal wall of the hangar behind her. *But if I don't do anything, I'm dead anyway, aren't I? Blown up or shot—dead's* dead, *isn't it?* More missiles streaked through the night, this time slamming into the concrete administration building.

And she was off, running, before she could talk herself out of it. Across the open space of the compound, past the training area where Jared Bloch had put her through her paces those first couple of days. She heard gunfire around her, screams and yells, the crackling of fire, the roar of explosions. A bullet whip-cracked by her head, near enough that she *felt* the wind of its passage, but she ran on.

There was the secondary hangar, its huge sliding door shut. The building seemed to be intact; no missiles had blown rents in its walls. She put on the brakes, skidding to a stop before the side door. She reached for the doorknob, hesitated—*What did Luke feel?* the thought whispered through the back of her brain. *Did he know he was dying?*—then grabbed it firmly, turned.

Nothing, no explosion, no agonizing pain followed by oblivion. The lock clicked open. Sam let air hiss through her teeth, the breath she didn't know she'd been holding. She flung the door open and dashed into the darkened hangar.

There was the *Sasquatch—her Sasquatch*—an angular shape of deeper black on black. No flames licked from the open cockpit. *Maybe,* she thought, *just maybe.*

She sprinted up the stairway that led to the gantry partially enclosing the 'Mech. Her boots clattered on the metal steps, the echoes shockingly loud in the hangar.

Her eyes were adapting to the darkness; vague shapes were starting to resolve themselves into details. On the gantry handrail to her right, she saw the control panel for the large sliding door. Without breaking stride, she pounded the OPEN button with her fist. The high-pitched whine of an electric motor filled the cavernous space.

The *Sasquatch*'s canopy was open, a gaping hole in the BattleMech's angular head. The gantry's narrow walkway extended between the complex array of antennae and sensors that sprouted from the giant vehicle's metallic skull. With no hesitation, Samantha sprinted along the walkway, jumping the last foot into the waiting cockpit. As she hit the seat, she reached up and slapped the RETRACT button mounted on the underside of the walkway.

Sensors in the cockpit detected her presence, and telltales danced across the complex consoles. By their light, she picked out the slot that would accept the code-key Silver had given her. She unzipped the neck of her jumpsuit, reached down and extracted the small piece of metal from where it hung between her breasts, pulling the chain over her head.

And then she hesitated, as the enormity of what she was doing really penetrated. *My God, this is for real. A real 'Mech, live weapons. Now we'll see if I'm really as good as everyone* tells *me I am.*

She slammed the code-key home, watched more lights blossom across the console. Beneath her feet and the pilot's chair, she felt a high-frequency vibration—something the simulator designers hadn't bothered to replicate, she realized—as the BattleMech's fusion engine came on-line. She picked up the neurohelmet resting atop one of the control panels—it was exactly the same helmet she'd used in the simulator, she noticed—and pulled it on, feeling the cold metal of the inductance electrodes against the shaved spots on her scalp. Instinctively, she went through the security lockout procedure as the simulator techs had taught her, feeling rather than hearing the BattleMech's systems coming on-line around her. Her eyes scanned the data readouts in a practiced pattern: available power at 100 percent, heat sink efficiency nominal, gyro spinning up normally, capacitors charging in the 'Mech's lasers and the massive Gauss rifle that made up its right arm. Green lights across the board.

The huge sliding door before her was almost completely open now. She felt the BattleMech quiver, almost expectantly, as her brain sent preliminary balance data to the gyro that was the war-machine's heart.

What's that . . . ? A dark figure slipped through the open door into the hangar. On reflex, she triggered the *Sasquatch*'s infrared systems, painting a computer-enhanced picture of the scene on the 'Mech's HUD.

Yes, it *was* a figure . . . holding a large rifle at the ready. It was looking up toward her, a harsh smile on its face.

Jonas Clay, she realized. A chill breeze seemed to brush

the back of her neck. *Bloch said the security systems were sabotaged,* she remembered, *which means an inside job. And didn't Clay say something about me "getting mine" . . . ? Is* this *what he meant, this attack?*

Clay had moved to the side, away from the door . . . out of the field of view of the *Sasquatch*'s IR system. Sam squinted at the dark figure through the open side of the cockpit.

Oh, my God, open *side* . . . She hadn't closed the 'Mech's canopy, hadn't buttoned up yet. If Clay *was* behind the attack—if he wanted to finish off the only operational MechWarrior the stable had—a single shot with his rifle would do it. She grasped the 'Mech's controls in a death-grip, ready to pivot the *Sasquatch*'s torso-mounted machine guns and cut him down, knowing all too well that the gladiator-trainee would have all the time he needed to snap up his rifle and take a shot before she could bring her own weapons to bear. She felt her muscles tense—*As if that's going to stop a bullet or a laser beam,* she thought.

But Clay *didn't* bring his rifle to his shoulder. Instead, his fierce grin grew even broader. "*Go,* Sammy!" he yelled up at her. "Kick some frakking *ass*!" And with that, he turned and sprinted back out into the compound, firing from the hip as he ran.

26

A shiver racked Sam's body before she could suppress it. *No time for emotional reactions now,* she told herself firmly. With a fist, she pounded the CANOPY CLOSE button, feeling her ears pop as the cockpit sealed itself around her. One last scan of the data readouts and she was ready. *Okay, Sterling,* she thought, *let's see how good a mentor you've been.* Her hands caressed the controls, and the *Sasquatch* strode forward out of the hangar.

And into the midst of a fierce firefight. Even with the *Sasquatch*'s image-enhancement systems, it took her a long couple of seconds to even *start* to make sense of the chaos.

Small packs of Saber Stable personnel were huddled here and there behind whatever cover they could find, while assaulting fire teams leapfrogged forward, covering each other's advance with suppression fire.

It was one of the tight knots of Saber warriors who spotted the *Sasquatch* first. Through the 'Mechs external pickups, Sam heard their sudden burst of cheering. The attackers spotted the new threat a moment later. Muzzle flashes lit the night, as small-arms fire—laser and projectile—spattered harmlessly off her 'Mech's armor. Sam grinned fiercely. *The game's just changed, boys,* she thought as she tracked the *Sasquatch*'s machine guns and small lasers to bear on the nearest assaulting fire team. She cringed as her fire tore through the attackers, slaughtering half of them in the first fusillade—the carnage all too clear on her HUD—but steeled herself to the bloodshed she was causing. *They brought it on themselves, remember that.*

Her arrival seemed to re-energize the Saber defenders. Within seconds, the tide of battle seemed to have turned, the initiative wrenched away from the attackers. Around her, she saw her stablemates staging counterattacks throughout the compound. *Go to it,* she thought grimly. Her hands flickered across the 'Mech's controls, quickly reconfiguring her Targeting Interlock Circuits, or TICs, isolating her lighter antipersonnel weapons from the "big guns" that she thought of as her 'Mech-killers. As she configured the TICs, she scanned the area for the assaulting BattleMechs.

There was one, silhouetted against the flames of the gladiator-trainees' barracks—the angular, insectlike shape of a *Locust* light 'Mech. The enemy pilot didn't seem to have noticed the new threat yet. Instead of turning her way, he was busy engaging a knot of Saber warriors with the small BattleMech's machine guns and single medium laser. *Let's see if I can get his attention,* Sam thought wryly as she tracked her targeting crosshairs over to the *Locust. Range—75 meters: damn near point-blank.* She squeezed the trigger gently, lighting off all the weapons configured on TIC A.

The *Sasquatch*'s heat scale spiked into the orange as the four medium pulse lasers in the 'Mech's left arm and the huge Gauss rifle in the right cut loose. Sam hooted with glee as the combined firepower slammed the smaller *Locust* off its feet, boiling away armor and staving in the side of the enemy 'Mech's hull. An instant before the downed *Locust* vanished in a fireball, the pilot's cockpit ejected, rocketing two hundred meters into the air. *Splash one. First kill!* Bringing the *Sasquatch*'s speed up, she checked around her for the other two attacking 'Mechs.

There they were . . . but there weren't just two of them—there were *four. Holy shit,* she thought, *reinforcements.* This time, the attackers had spotted her before she'd located them. A salvo of long-range missiles was already in flight, streaking across the intervening space. She hardly had time to brace for impact before they slammed home, almost engulfing the *Sasquatch* in dirty-red fireballs. Warning tones screamed before she silenced them, and red lights flickered across damage displays. Whole sections of armor had been flayed from the *Sasquatch*'s torso, she knew, and already lasers from the attacking 'Mechs were probing into the weakened areas to slash away at her vehicle's internal structure.

Time to move. Sam kicked the *Sasquatch* into a shambling run, ducking into the cover of the as-yet-untouched secondary hangar. As she did, she scanned the data displays on her console. The computer had already identified three of the enemy 'Mechs firmly and one tentatively. She was facing two *Griffins,* a *Rifleman* and either a *Thunderbolt* or a *Warhammer*—her computer imaging system hadn't got a good enough look at the fourth 'Mech to be sure. Either way, she knew, it spelled trouble—*A* T-bolt *or a* Hammer *by itself is a good match for my* Sasquatch, she realized grimly, *and the* Griffins *and* Rifleman *just make things nastier.*

This is one of those times Sterling was talking about, isn't it? When you're supposed to evaluate a superior force and bug out, save your ride?

But I can't *bug out, not this time. It's full investment again, just like the osprey.*

Tightening her jaw, she kicked the *Sasquatch* up to its full running speed, almost 64 kilometers per hour, sprinting along the back wall of the secondary hangar. She slowed as she reached the far end, creeping forward slowly until she could poke the 'Mech's head—and its right arm—around the corner of the building.

She chuckled grimly. *I* figured *you might do that. . . .* One of the *Griffin* pilots had seen the *Sasquatch* turn tail and run—that's how he'd interpreted it, at least—and had hurried ahead of his wingmen to pursue and hopefully drop the Saber 'Mech from behind. *Make him pay,* Sam told herself as she brought the *Sasquatch*'s Gauss rifle to bear and took careful aim.

Some subliminal clue seemed to warn the *Griffin* jockey before she could take the shot. The enemy 'Mech's rounded head turned toward her, and a salvo of missiles ripple-fired from its shoulder-mounted rack. The pilot didn't have a lock on her, though, and the missile spread went wide, shredding the forward wall of the secondary hangar. *Make him pay,* Sam thought again. She brushed the trigger. The recoil was enough to rattle her teeth, despite the *Sasquatch*'s sophisticated compensators.

The Gauss rifle's massive nickel-iron slug took the *Griffin* full in the "face." The round didn't explode, *but then, it doesn't have to, does it?* With the staggering muzzle velocity that the electromagnetic cannon could generate, sheer kinetic energy did all the damage that was necessary. Sam saw the structure of the *Griffin*'s cockpit implode from the impact, in the instant before a secondary explosion tore the entire head to shrapnel. For a long moment the decapitated *Griffin* stood there, swaying. Then it crashed to the ground, flames licking from its "neck." *Splash two!* Sam cheered mentally.

No more than 60 meters away, another 'Mech hove into view—the *Rifleman.* She tried to pull the *Sasquatch* back into the shelter of the hangar. A second too late. Shafts of ruby light flickered out from both the *Rifleman*'s arms, blowing away a couple of hundred pounds of armor from the *Sasquatch*'s right shoulder. More red lights flashed across Sam's damage displays.

Damn it, what now? Common sense told her she should withdraw—and *right now.* If she stayed put, the three enemy 'Mechs would be able to flank her, and then just chew her apart. If she cut and ran—or, more sensibly, withdrew to another defensive position—the *Rifleman* at the very least would get an open shot at her back with its large lasers and heavy autocannons. Sure, she'd be able to return fire with the light laser mounted in the back of the *Sas-*

quatch's head as she ran, but she knew all too well how little good that would do—*Sweet bugger all, basically,* she thought grimly. She'd take damage—perhaps *serious* damage—but at least she'd be able to prolong the fight a little further. She ground her teeth. What the hell *else* could she do? Nothing. Unless. . . .

Frak it, it's worth a try. Carefully, she bent the 'Mech's knees, crouching the giant vehicle down. The *Sasquatch* simply wasn't engineered for this kind of move, she knew; she had to pay close attention to keep the center of gravity firmly over the 'Mech's clawed feet. Sweat rolled down her temples from under the neurohelmet as she counted slowly down from five.

Two . . . one . . . zero! She gripped the controls, forced the twin joysticks forward.

Still in a crouch, the *Sasquatch* lunged forward, out from behind the hangar, torso pivoting to the left as it did so.

There was the *Rifleman,* a huge shape looming in Sam's view port. Instinctively, the *Rifleman* pilot triggered all his weapons . . . and, just as Sam had hoped, the laser beams and autocannon rounds split the air a couple of meters over the head of the crouching *Sasquatch. Eat this!* she thought as she lit off all her own weapons: Gauss rifle, lasers, even the machine guns (for what little good they'd do). She didn't even wait to see what damage she'd inflicted. Before the fireballs and smoke had even cleared, she was sprinting into the darkness, away from the hangar area. A spread of missiles from the second *Griffin* bracketed her, but only a couple actually impacted on the back of her BattleMech's legs. The *Sasquatch* staggered, but she managed to recover, to keep the massive war machine on its feet and moving.

On her rear IR sensors, she could easily pick out the heat source that was the *Rifleman.* She hadn't killed the machine, but she'd certainly hurt it badly. The display showed secondary explosions licking across the right torso and arm, and the place on the left leg where there was no armor whatsoever left to protect the 'Mech's internal structure. Slowly, clumsily, it turned away, withdrawing from the battle. *And that's as good as a kill,* she realized. *Three down. . . .*

The administration building was to her right. A salvo of missiles had struck around it, and part of the ground floor was already burning. Lights were on in one room on the fifth floor. *Mandelbaum's office?* She couldn't be sure.

Her *Sasquatch* jerked violently as another spread of missiles slammed home, this time detonating in a great curtain of fire across the 'Mech's broad back. Warning tones stabbed at her ears, and this time she couldn't take the time to silence them. On reflex, she loosed a couple of shots from the *Sasquatch*'s rear-firing laser—suppression fire to distract her opponents, more than an actual attack with any hope of inflicting damage—and pivoted into the shelter of the ferroconcrete admin building.

And now *what?* There was still a *Griffin* out there, and what the computer had now provisionally tagged as a *Warhammer,* both more or less undamaged. (Great, *Dooley. You always find your way into the deepest pile of shit.*) The *Rifleman* wouldn't be coming after her, she didn't expect . . . but if she made the mistake of blundering into its field of fire, it could still ruin her whole day. Even worse, *she didn't know where the goddamn things were!*

Why didn't we cover this kind of thing in the simulations? she asked herself fiercely. In all the scenarios she'd played out in the can, her sensors had been able to localize her enemies within a couple of meters. Now? For all she knew, there could be a *Griffin* coming around one side of the building this instant, with the *Warhammer* coming around the other. The first warning she'd have would be when the point-blank shots breached her *Sasquatch*'s armor. *God* damn *it, there's got to be* something *I can do.*

Of *course* there was. None of her simulation sessions had included cooperative tactics, but as part of her training the technicians had taught her how to use the BattleMech's encrypted short-range commlink. With a silent curse, she brought the comm suite on-line, selecting the base frequency and encryption algorithm for Saber Stable communications. "This is Dooley One," she grated into the microphone. "Anyone on this freq? Anyone reading me?"

The speaker behind her head roared with static. *Nothing. . . .* Then, suddenly, "Dooley!" She jumped in her harness at Silver's voice. "Sam, are you okay?"

She struggled to keep her irrational relief out of her voice—*I'm still in deep shit, here, remember that!*—as she replied, "For the moment. Two bandits down, one badly damaged.

"Sterling, I need you to spot for me. I've got a *Griffin* and a *Warhammer* out there, and I don't know where the frak they are."

"Got it, Sam," he came back crisply. "You've got them cautious. I can see them moving in slowly—the *Griffin* to the west, the *'Hammer* coming around to the east. Standard flanking maneuver."

Sam nodded—that's basically what she'd expected. "Distance from the admin building?"

"So *that*'s where you are." She could hear the grim smile in Silver's voice. "Like I say, they're cautious. *Griffin*'s maybe 75 meters out, the *'Hammer* another 25 past that."

"Any infantry support?" For the first time, Sam realized she could hear gunshots—laser and slug-thrower—in the background of Silver's transmission.

The blond-haired man chuckled. "Afraid somebody's planning a game of kick the can? Good thinking, but we've got that end of things pretty well tied up."

"What kind of casualties?" Guilt twinged at Sam's gut; she hadn't even thought of that until now.

"Heavy," Silver replied grimly. "We've lost good people. Now the trick's not to lose any more before . . .

"Hold it!" he cut himself off sharply. "We've got . . . yep, the *Griffin*'s moving. . . .

"Ah, holy shit . . . Dooley, he's jumping. Heads up!"

Holy shit's right, Sam thought grimly. She searched her brain for any details she'd learned about the *Griffin*'s jump capability. *Pretty good, I think,* she recalled. *Better than mine, at least.* In her mind's eye, she saw flame belching from the *Griffin*'s jump jet exhaust ports, hurling the 'Mech's 55-ton mass into the air.

Her mind seemed to shift into overdrive, the seconds digit on the console-mounted clock seeming to slow to a crawl. What was the *Griffin* pilot thinking? What was his plan? Just to close with her *fast,* before she could get into a good defensive position? Or was he planning a devastating "death-from-above" attack, intending to land right on top of her *Sasquatch*? What was her best move, in either case? Bug out . . . or . . .

Before she could talk herself out of it, she triggered her

own jump jets. The sudden acceleration drove her deep into the padding of her couch. She spread the *Sasquatch*'s arms out to the side to improve the BattleMech's balance as it rose on a boiling totem of flame.

Yes, there was the *Griffin,* still climbing, jets still firing at full power. Sam cut her own jets immediately. They'd done their job, vaulting the 85-ton *Sasquatch* onto the flat roof of the administration building. She absorbed the landing shock in the knees of the 'Mech, imagining rather than hearing the knee actuators groan under the stress. Again she crouched the 'Mech, both decreasing her size as a potential target and bringing her multiple weapons to bear more quickly.

The *Griffin*'s jockey recognized his mistake, cutting his own jets. Much too late—the light BattleMech was just a ballistic object now, no longer under its pilot's control, in the iron grip of the laws of physics. Sam saw blue-white light lash out from the *Griffin*'s right arm, but the particle projection cannon bolt came nowhere near her *Sasquatch,* instead blowing a gaping crater a good twenty meters away in the roof of the admin building. On her HUD, multiple targeting cursors superimposed themselves over the *Griffin,* falling free in its parabolic arc. With a growl deep in her throat, Sam triggered all her TICs, spiking the *Sasquatch*'s heat well into the red. A piercing siren sounded. Deep down in the guts of the machine, she knew, some key component had been overloaded by the heat.

It didn't matter at the moment. Four laser beams tore into the torso of the *Griffin,* as the Gauss rifle shell blew its right leg clear off at the knee. Sam crouched even lower as the enemy 'Mech hurtled by overhead, smashing to the ground behind the admin building, where she'd been standing seconds earlier. Instinctively she triggered a shot from the light laser mounted in the back of the *Sasquatch*'s head. She might as well not have bothered, she saw in her rear-facing monitors. The *Griffin* was down—crippled, incapable of moving. *Splash three!*

A furious fusillade of fire ripped out of the darkness to her left—laser beams, actinic-blue PPC bolts, followed by a salvo of missiles. Her *Sasquatch* staggered under the impact. Sam screamed as she was flung hard against her harness, her neurohelmet slamming against the side of the canopy. Whole panels on the console went black as the salvo flayed away entire sensor subsystems. Below her, in the chest of her 'Mech, she heard a high-pitched grinding sound, like a chunk of metal held against a high-speed flywheel. *Gyro damage,* she knew. She hit the jump jet controls again, but nothing happened. The actuators must have been shredded by the last attack. Clumsily, she pivoted her torso, searching for the *Warhammer* that was still out there . . . *somewhere.*

Her IR scanners would have been able to pinpoint the heavy BattleMech easily. With that last salvo, the *Warhammer* jockey must have racked his 'Mech, spiking his heat way into the danger zone. In her IR subsystem, the overheated 'Mech would be a giant, glowing target. *Too bad the goddamn thing's been blown to kingdom come. . . .*

"Where is it, Sterling?" she yelled into the microphone. *"Where?"*

Silver replied immediately . . . but not with the answer she wanted. "Wait one," he snapped.

She glared at the commlink. *Wait one . . . ?!?* What the hell did he think was going *on* here?

Another salvo of missiles arced out of the darkness toward her. Before they could actually strike, she squeezed off another Gauss rifle shot at their point of origin.

The *Warhammer* jockey had rushed his shot. Instead of taking the entire salvo in the chest, Sam's *Sasquatch* caught only two of the missiles.

That was almost enough. Shredded armor flew like shrapnel, rattling off the reinforced canopy. The *Sasquatch*'s left arm with its four medium pulse lasers hung uselessly, its upper arm actuator blown to splinters. Below her, in the 'Mech's torso, she heard a sharp crackling, almost like popcorn popping. *Machine gun ammo cooking off,* she realized with a chill. *I'm on fire down there.* Blindly, still dazzled by the fireballs of the impacting missiles, she slapped at the switches for the fire suppression system. *Please, God, let* that *still be intact!*

The *Sasquatch* was dying, she knew, and with it, the hopes of Saber Stable. "Sterling!" she almost screamed. "Spot me a target, damn it!"

But it was too late, she knew with sudden and stunning certainty. All her forward sensors were gone, but her rear image-enhancement units were still intact. A small screen showed clearly—Too *clearly,* she thought numbly—the three BattleMechs emerging from the darkness behind her. She recognized them at once—*Phoenix Hawks*, relatively lightly armed and armored as BattleMechs went, but more than enough to slag her damaged *Sasquatch* down to molten metal.

It's over. The realization was like a cold, empty void in the pit of her stomach. She slumped against the harness.

"Sam." It was Sterling's voice sounding from the speaker. "Sam, incoming 'Mechs."

It was almost too much effort to talk. "I see them," she said dully. "Sorry, Sterling, I tried."

The commlink went silent. Then, "Sam," he said, "they're friends, Sam."

And a new voice—cool, confident—rang from the speaker. It took a couple of seconds for her to place it. Then a smile of total and utter relief spread across her face. "Dooley One," said Will Zdebiak, the leader of Team Alpha from the VGL. "The cavalry's here—a little late, but better late than never. Why don't you just hang back and let us do the mopping up, hm?"

27

G*od, the casualties—on* both *sides.*

There were more than twenty dead, laid out in rows in the compound's central square. Most of them were Saber personnel, but more than half a dozen were from among the attackers. (*How many did I kill myself?* she asked herself, feeling suddenly sick. *I don't want to think about that.*) And then there were the prisoners: a dozen or more of them, most wounded more or less seriously. By the time the sun was coming up, Bloch—somehow he'd managed to make it through unscathed—was still questioning the captives, trying to make sense of the attack. She should have been interested, she knew, but she couldn't bring herself to focus on it. The attackers had come from some other stable—Frost Lynx, or something like that—but it was going to take time and effort to figure out who'd *really* been behind the whole thing. One of the Successor States? Probably . . . but *which? Leave that to Bloch and to Silver,* she figured. *I've got other things on my mind.*

Not the obvious things, either. She didn't think Will Zdebiak understood at first when she ignored him, walking right past him to where the casualties were laid out on the hard, cold ground. Luke Trent and Meg Richardson, the two MechWarriors Silver had introduced her to in the commissary, were among them. Luke, of course, had been killed by the booby trap on the 'Mech hangar; Meg had been cut down by shrapnel from a missile burst. Beside them was Renard Gilbert, one side of his skull a charred ruin from a laser shot. Jonas Clay was there, too, cold eyes open, his hands still clenched around the stock of his laser rifle. Machine gun rounds had blown him nearly in two as he'd tried to distract the *Warhammer* to prevent it from finishing off Samantha's *Sasquatch.*

The person she was *really* looking for, she found no sign of, neither among the dead nor among the survivors. Colonel Mandelbaum. Jared Bloch had seen him in the thick of the fighting, he'd claimed, a laser pistol clenched in his fist. Lethal enough against flesh-and-blood opponents, of course . . . but Bloch had seen Mandelbaum firing on one of the assaulting *Griffins. Like taking on a tank with a peashooter,* Sam knew. And then the tide of the battle had separated them. No surviving member of Saber Stables had seen him after that.

What happened to him? Sam wondered dully. *Did he die a warrior's death, alone and unremarked? Was he blown to shreds by a missile, or charred to ash by a laser?*

Did he finally find, in death, the peace that he'd rarely known in life?

She felt a stinging behind her eyes, and wiped at them impatiently with her fingers. *What if he* is *dead, anyway?* she asked herself. *I didn't know him for long—well, hell, if you get right down to it, I didn't know him at all.* Still she felt . . .

What *was* it she felt? Kinship, and loss. Echoes of other emotions. Echoes of Pop-Pop's death, of course, but more than that. A sense of . . . *Well, I guess "lost opportunities" is one way of describing it,* she decided. *I sensed it in Mandelbaum's office, and I still feel it now—that the aging warrior was a kindred spirit, that we had something profound in common. That he'd learned lessons I have yet to learn, that he'd made mistakes I have yet to make . . . and that I've lost a chance to avoid making those mistakes, to learn from his example.* She turned away from the silent dead and focused her attention on the living.

There was some strange dynamic between Sterling Silver and Will Zdebiak, she sensed at once. The Saber MechWarrior was obviously bursting with questions he just as obviously wasn't going to ask. (*Why?* Sam wondered. *Because he knows the answers he'll get are too disturbing?*) Samantha saw him shooting strange looks at the *Phoenix Hawk* from which Will had dismounted, frowning over details of the light 'Mech's construction. *What's he noticing?* she asked herself. Finally she saw his face clear as if he'd come to some conclusion, or some decision.

And Will . . . well, he was doing much the same thing. He had his own questions that he wanted to ask Silver, that he'd never be able to ask for his own, very different reasons.

The two men *did* talk, finally. Sam couldn't overhear them, but—judging by their expressions—they didn't overstep the mental bounds they'd set for themselves. From the way they kept glancing in her direction, she knew they were talking about her.

Finally, Zdebiak strode across the square to join her. Silver wanted to watch the conversation—Sam could read that clearly from his body language—but he forced himself to look away, to watch the cleanup process.

The gray-eyed pilot gave her a lopsided grin. "I guess your ride home's arrived, Ms. Dooley." He gestured toward his *Phoenix Hawk.* "My machine's a two-seater, so if you're looking to hitch a ride. . . ."

She fixed him with a steady, speculative look. "I don't know," she told him honestly. "I don't know if I am."

He blinked, nonplussed. "Huh?" His mouth worked wordlessly for a moment, then, "I can take you *home,*" he said.

"Oh?" she asked coolly. She shrugged. "I guess I'm traditionally supposed to jump at that offer." She gave him a crooked half-smile. " 'There's no place like home' and all that crap.

"But what's waiting for me at home, Will, huh? Tell me that. The VGL's equivalent of a summary court martial? Or maybe I just vanish—Amy said that's happened in the past. Or maybe I just get cut loose, and I'm allowed to live as long as I don't breathe a word about this to anyone."

She gestured with empty palms. "Either way, where's the attraction? I go home, and nothing changes. I stay here . . . and I *belong.* I get to do something I'm *good* at." She knew she was echoing Mandelbaum's thoughts, just in different words. "There's no room for lone wolves back home," she concluded simply.

Will didn't answer at once, she was glad to see—no knee-jerk repudiation of her concerns. He actually seemed to listen to her words and consider their meaning. At last, he said musingly, "I always thought *I* was a lone wolf. It took me awhile to find it, but there's room enough for *me.* Anyway," he shrugged, "set that aside for the moment. I hear what you're saying, Dooley. You've found a place you feel you belong. That's important. Most people go through their whole lives without feeling that. And you've found something you're good at. I can't argue with that, either.

"But what is it that you're good at, Dooley?" he asked. There was a strange earnestness in his eyes she hadn't seen before—as if he'd set aside the cooler-than-thou fighter-jock persona, and was talking to her as a real person. "Wrangling a BattleMech? Maybe. Maybe that *is* what you're good at, maybe that *is* what you were born to do. But I don't think so."

Sam gestured around her. "*What,* then?"

"*Adapting,*" he said firmly. He chuckled. "You know that old homily, 'When your life turns out to be a lemon, make lemonade'?" He looked around him pointedly. "You made lemonade, lemon chicken, lemon meringue pie—a whole goddamned meal. You got yourself dropped down in U–N–V one-thirty-seven"—he grinned like a bandit—"and you grabbed it by the nuts, and you shook it until you got what you wanted out of it.

"And you know what?" he went on forcefully. "You might have ended up in U–N-V one-oh-five, or U–N–V sixty-three . . . and the same thing would have happened.

You'd have grabbed *that* universe by the nuts too. Okay, sure," he gestured deprecatingly, "this time the adaptation meant you had to learn to jockey a 'Mech. *Fine.*

"But that's just the *packaging,* Dooley. Don't you get it? If it hadn't been BattleMechs, it could have been submarines, or spaceships . . . or horse-drawn *chariots,* for chrissake.

"Has there ever been any situation you've been dropped into—*any* situation—where you haven't made it through? No," he corrected, "*not* just 'made it through'—*excelled*?" He laughed. "You can ride a motorbike, can't you?"

Caught off-guard by the question, Sam nodded.

"And it was a boyfriend who taught you, right? Didn't he stop letting you ride his bike after about the sixth time, when you could ride it better than he could?"

Sam blinked . . . then she laughed out loud. "He broke up with me, too," she admitted.

"Idiot that he was. And it was the same with every other new situation, wasn't it?" Will gestured. "So I rest my case. You're not a born 'Mech jockey, Dooley. You're a born *survivor.*

"And that makes you a born member of the VGL. That's what the League needs. *Geez,* Dooley, if Burton and Bell were alive today, they'd rip the balls off anyone who got in the way of your membership."

Samantha shook her head slowly. *Too fast,* she thought. *Too much, too fast.* "I don't know, Will."

"Hey, it's your choice," Zdebiak said simply. He gestured around him. "Solaris Seven—now, this place is an adventure.

"*An* adventure. As in *one.* If that's what you're up for . . . I say, hey, go for it. *Any* virtual world is going to be an adventure." He changed mental gears sharply, disorienting her for a moment. "How many virtual worlds do you think there are, Dooley?"

"Huh?" She blinked. "How the hell would I know?"

"An infinite number," he shot back firmly. "An *infinite* number. Think about it. Each one different, each one a new challenge. And the League needs *survivors*—people who can adapt to anything—to explore them. I figure you're one of those people." He shot her another of his pirate smiles. "And *I'll* rip the balls off anyone who says otherwise.

"So it's your choice, Dooley," he said, sobering suddenly.

"I can't guarantee anything. When it comes to policy, I'm low man on the totem pole. I'm no policy wonk—I just *do* the stuff that other people debate about."

Sam nodded. "I know the name of *that* tune," she admitted.

"It's your call," Will went on quietly. "Where *is* home, anyway?"

Samantha looked at him for a long moment. What Will had said . . . she knew it was true. All the things she'd done just to satisfy her own curiosity about the relatively minor mystery surrounding her grandfather's death, the way she'd survived—no, more than that, she'd overcome and bested the challenges of Solaris Seven—she could have figured out the answer for herself, but Will's words struck a chord in her soul that told her he was right on the money. She felt her face crease in a smile. "I've made my decision," she said quietly.

"It's been a pleasure and an honor working with you, MechWarrior Samantha Dooley."

She smiled, not a little sadly, at Sterling Silver. "What are you going to do?" she asked.

He shrugged. "What else? Get the stable up and running again. *Keep* it running until Mandelbaum decides he wants to come back and take over." He glanced away, as if afraid she'd see the emotion in his expression. Firmly, he stuck out his hand toward her. "There's always a billet for you at the Saber Stable if you ever decide you want to take it."

For a moment Sam didn't know what to say. Then she realized that maybe she didn't have to say anything. She took his hand and shook it . . . then pulled him in close, and wrapped her arms around him. His answering hug almost squeezed the air from her lungs. Then he released her and held her at arm's length. There was something strange in his expression—some wry, knowing edge that she hadn't seen there before. "Who knows?" he said. He was trying to keep the words light, but there was that strange undertone to his voice, as well. "Maybe I'll see you in the badlands sometime."

And with that, he pivoted on his heel and walked away.

Epilogue

He knows, doesn't he? Sam lay back on the bed, staring up at the acoustic-tile ceiling. *Silver—he knows, or at least he's guessed.*

She sighed. Well, that was okay, wasn't it? He wouldn't tell anyone else about it; she was sure of that. Her secret—the VGL's secret—was safe.

After everything, the return to the Generro Aerospace compound—the return *home*—was pretty anticlimactic. Will's wingmen had climbed aboard their 'Mechs, while the mission leader had helped her up the chain ladder into the specially modified two-seater cockpit of the lead *Phoenix Hawk.* Somehow Sam had managed to suppress her smile when she saw the interior of the UFT cockpit again, saw how woefully primitive and simplistic it was in comparison to the real thing. Beyond checking that she was comfortable in the jerry-rigged backseat, Will had held his peace as he led the three *Phoenix Hawks* out of Roland Fields into the hills that surrounded this part of Solaris City. As soon as he was confident the 'Mechs were out of sight of any locals, he'd contacted Macintyre. A couple of seconds later, Sam had felt the falling sensation as they'd translocated back.

And here I am, she thought wryly. There'd been security guards waiting for her, flanking the gantry where Will's cockpit—*Gemini,* the two-seater prototype was called, "The Twins"—had reappeared in the control room at Generro. Ernest Macintyre had watched wordlessly as the guards escorted Samantha away, taking her to the room where she'd spent the last few hours.

For the dozenth time, she looked around the room to which they'd taken her. It was surprisingly comfortable, she had to admit. From the moment she'd decided to leave Solaris Seven, she'd expected that her next stop would be a cell of some kind. She'd accepted that thought with a kind of fatalism that had surprised her at the time. *It was worth it,* she'd told herself—worth it for what she'd learned, what she'd experienced. Worth it for the possibilities that the VGL represented.

So the room had come as a pleasant surprise. No bars, no metal-framed bunk. All in all, the decor had reminded her more of Slumber Lodge than San Quentin—like a motel room, comfortable enough, totally unremarkable.

Except that the door wouldn't open when she turned the handle. *And a locked door makes a cell, doesn't it, no matter what the decor . . . ?* She sighed again, and she closed her eyes to wait.

The click of the door lock roused her from a shallow, dream-filled sleep. She sat up quickly, swinging her feet to the floor and running her fingers through her hair.

"Ms. Dooley."

She smiled when she saw the two men in the doorway. "Mr. Macintyre," she said, echoing the young engineer's tone. "And Mr. Warner." She gestured to the two straight-backed chairs against the wall. "Please."

The young engineer blinked and nodded. Warner preceded him in. Carefully shutting the door behind him—Sam smiled as she heard the lock click shut—Macintyre crossed to the chair and sat, placing his briefcase (an incongruous element, Sam thought) at his feet. Warner just leaned against the wall by the door, an unconscious "visual echo" of Silver's posture.

Macintyre just regarded her for a long moment, his expression a complex mix of curiosity, chagrin, and other emotions. Finally, "How are you, Ms. Dooley?" he asked.

"Well enough," she said with a shrug. "And please call me Sam; you did before." She leaned forward, resting her arms on her knees, looking from one to the other. "What now?" she said simply.

Macintyre glanced away, apparently unable to meet her eyes. *And that's a clear enough answer, isn't it?* Sam asked herself sadly. Still, she managed—she thought—to keep her feelings out of her own expression.

"That . . . represents a problem," Macintyre admitted slowly. "The Virtual Geographic League has always had to take its security seriously." He shrugged, still unable to meet her gaze. "You understand that, I'm sure, Samantha," he said. "The technology we've developed . . . if it got into the wrong hands. . . ." He shrugged, letting the sentence trail off.

He didn't have to go on. *The Soviets advancing on Western Europe in BattleMechs? Terrorists armed with laser rifles? Point taken,* Sam thought. But, "Are there any *right* hands?" she asked rhetorically.

It was Warner who replied. "It's been argued that there aren't," he admitted. "I don't necessarily agree . . ."—he smiled self-consciously—". . . but then, I'm biased."

"I could promise you that I'd never talk about what I've learned," Sam said quietly. She traced an X on the breast of her jumpsuit. "Cross my heart and hope to die."

Ernest Macintyre chuckled softly, but didn't answer. *Not that he* has *to,* Sam knew. "I ask again, gentlemen," she said—her voice surprisingly calm in her own ears. "What now?"

The engineer turned to exchange glances with the aging pilot. After a few moments, Macintyre said, "You've broken every rule of security by which I've lived my life." He turned his pale eyes on her for the first time since entering the room. "*And* some that the security personnel had to explain to me," he added ironically. "You're a maverick, Samantha. A loose cannon. You're dangerous."

"Yet Mandelbaum's report praises you," Warner put in, "in the most glowing terms possible."

"Wait." Sam raised a hand. "Wait," she said again. " 'Mandelbaum's report'?"

Macintyre chuckled softly. "You didn't think Will and the others *just happened* to show up, did you?" he asked. "Granted, their timing was . . . *fortuitous,*" he noted carefully, "but they wouldn't have been there at all if Mandelbaum's message hadn't made it through some channels that hadn't been activated in years."

Sam nodded slowly. *Too much to think about now,* she told herself. "Go on."

"His report used terms like 'tactical genius,' " the engineer said. "Like 'enormous potential,' 'natural-born warrior.' Do I have to go on?"

She shook her head wordlessly.

Warner continued, "From anyone else, the report wouldn't have carried nearly the weight. But Mandelbaum . . ."—he shrugged—". . . is *Mandelbaum.*"

"And so that's where it stands," Macintyre said. "In certain quarters, there are objections. . . ." He chuckled suddenly. "I'm surprised you haven't heard the grinding of teeth. But I've been officially requested to offer you membership in the Virtual Geographic League."

Sam stared at the two of them, the young engineer and the test pilot. She realized her mouth was hanging open; she shut it. "I . . ."

Sid Warner cut her off. "Don't answer right away," he advised. "Give it some thought. It's not something to be taken on lightly."

His mouth twisted in a wry smile. "Take some time," he went on. "Anyway, I thought you'd like some reading material that might help you make your decision." He gestured to Macintyre.

The engineer opened the briefcase at his feet, and took out a leatherbound book, which he handed to Sam. She took it, staring at the name on the cover.

"When you're ready to talk, I'll be available. We *both* will." Warner rose to his feet, Macintyre following a moment later. They both turned toward the door.

Warner hesitated, glancing back. "I know it's premature," he said, "but . . . welcome aboard, Samantha Dooley." And with that the two of them left, closing the door but not locking it behind them.

For almost half a minute, Sam just sat on the bed, staring at the door. Finally she shook her head and opened the book to the first page. She smiled as she read the handwritten inscription: "PERSONAL JOURNAL OF JAMES R. DOOLEY, SR."

She leaned back on the bed and began to read.

. . . We therefore pledge our energies and our honor to the creation of the Virtual Geographic League for the purpose of exploring Elsewhen. . . .

The Virtual Geographic League: Our First Fifty Years, a reconstruction by Bruce Bayer and Nigel Findley, recounts the disappointments and triumphs of the men and women who devoted their lives to reaching Elsewhen. The accomplishments made possible by the theoretical foundation laid in the work of Alexander Graham Bell and Nikola Tesla and furthered through the pioneering achievements of Einstein, Westinghouse, McDonnell, Ford, and others have pushed the League far beyond the hopes and dreams of its founders.

An excerpt from *Our First Fifty Years: Legend's End* offers first-person accounts of the exhilaration and devastation of the first manned mission to Elsewhen. That mission cost the League—and the world—the life of Amelia Earhart. And though hers would not be the last sacrifice made in the name of progress, it may have been the most valuable. The Virtual Geographic League has always asked much of its members, but gives immense rewards in return.

The history of the Virtual Geographic League is available at Virtual World sites worldwide.

0902 EST, May 24, 1937
From the journal of George Putnam

She's gone. My wife, Amelia Earhart, just left on her great adventure.

Her *last* great adventure; she promised me this as the team made its final preparations for the mission. "I have a feeling there's just about one more good flight left in my system," she said quietly, with a tired smile, "and I think this is it."

I just squeezed her hand. She knows, I think, how I feel about her work—that she's paid her dues, she's done more than her fair share of pushing the limits and tweaked the nose of the Grim Reaper more times than is perhaps wise.

Everything was ready. Her cockpit was in place on the gantry, loaded with food, a sextant and other mapping instruments, the experimental underwater breathing apparatus (which we all hoped she wouldn't need), and a leather-bound journal with gold letters on the cover: GP TO AE, MAY 1937. The final briefing began at 0830, conducted by Otis Barton and William Beebe. When the briefing ended and the two men walked away from her, I could see even at that distance that her eyes were alive with the challenge.

I knew the mission was going to be dangerous. We all knew there was a chance she wouldn't return. We'd talked about that in the days and weeks leading up to the mission, and A.E. steadfastly insisted that she must go—there was no reason to talk about it again. As the clock ticked off the last few minutes before the flight, we slipped away to be alone together.

The two of us settled on the concrete steps outside the building. What do you say to someone you love at a time like this? I didn't know then, I don't know now, and I'll probably never know. So neither of us said anything. We just sat there, silent, appreciating the other's presence.

Too soon, Barton stuck his head out to quietly announce that it was time to get underway.

"The camera pod's come back," he said, "and everything checks out. That's fourteen for fourteen. We're stable." A.E. just nodded, and a few minutes later she, and the cockpit, disappeared.

0908 EST, May 24, 1937
From the journal of George Putnam

Now I know why Tesla was so doggedly set on redundancy. When he'd quietly insisted on *three* of those damned expensive stepper things for the first manned mission I'd tried to talk him out of it. But that damned European stood firm. As I berated and barked and bellowed, he quietly continued to reiterate all the sound, scientific reasons why we needed three of the big instruments: in case one (or even two) failed. I will forever remember his final comment, the one that stopped me in my tracks and shut me up for good. "So, this cost is the value which you apply to a human life, yes? Even your lovely wife's?"

The clock read only two minutes into the ten-minute mission when the stepper failed. Even I knew something was wrong, and I realized it almost as soon as the technicians and scientists. The smooth, high-pitched hum of the electricity took on a harsh, rough edge, becoming more of a burr. Before I could determine the source of the problem, however, the technician Cameron was already yelling up to the control room to cut over to the second stepper.

As he yelled for the cutover, he leaped from his panel of dials and gauges to do something inexplicable to the thick power conduit that led into the stepper. That put him right next to the massive machine when the white sheet of electrical flame lashed out from inside the casing.

Cameron screamed and jumped back, as any man would. But an instant later he threw himself back into that sheet of flame, to finish the task he'd started.

Other technicians now ran forward, most carrying buckets of sand to smother the flames. Before they reached him, though, Cameron did something that quenched the fire. He stood there for a moment, half his hair gone, his white lab coat blackened and smoldering, his exposed skin the color of a boiled lobster. Then he collapsed into the arms of his colleagues, moaning with the pain of his burns.

Once I saw the man was alive, I sprinted up the stairs to the control room and flung open the door. "What happened?" I shouted.

Tesla turned to me, his expression calm as ever, as if one of his complex devices hadn't damn near exploded in front of him. "A short circuit, perhaps," he said evenly. "Such things happen, I fear."

I looked over to where the cockpit had rested. What effect had this had on my wife? My throat was too tight with fear to ask the question.

I didn't have to ask it. Tesla laid a reassuring hand on my shoulder. "Mrs. Putnam will have suffered no ill effects," he told me quietly. "Thanks to Mr. Cameron, the cutover to the second frequency-rectifier coil was so smooth that the cockpit would not have even 'noticed' the transition, if I may use such imprecise words." He looked over at the still-smoking hulk of Stepper 1, then back at the dials and gauges in front of him. "The second rectifier unit is operating acceptably within every parameter," he pronounced.

1018 EST, May 24, 1937
From the journal of Fred Noonan

It's happened! We all knew it might, but we all convinced ourselves it *wouldn't.* We all knew the risk. But *how* it happened . . .

If the system had failed when Stepper 1 failed—if the control crew hadn't been able to cut over to Stepper 2, for example—the harmonic field that translocated the cockpit to the other world (or wherever) would have collapsed, and the cockpit would have simply reappeared. The fact that it hadn't come back proved that nothing had gone wrong. That's what I thought at the time. That's the way we *all* thought it worked.

At 0910 precisely, I looked at the glass-fronted control room and watched Tesla open the large knife-switch that controlled the components creating the harmonic field. Without so much as a flicker, the cockpit reappeared on the gantry, just as if it had never left. All the hums and whines faded as the techs cut the power to the systems.

Right away I *knew* something was wrong. I didn't need to see the expression on the face of the tech standing ready with the wooden stepladder. His face went pale like he was bleeding to death, and I *knew.*

0019 EST, May 25, 1937
From the journal of George Putnam

The seat was empty.

What happened? Every moment since, my mind has turned back to that question. Where was A.E.? Where was my wife?

We'd decided early in the planning for this first manned mission that only the occupant of the cockpit could open it once it was closed. Better to risk needing to break an unconscious pilot out of the cockpit with crowbars than give some hostile inhabitant of the destination world easy access to the traveler. So A.E. must have undogged the hatch voluntarily.

But *why*? We'd deliberately decided—all of us on the planning team, *including* A.E. herself—that the traveler would remain in the cockpit *no matter what happened.* No matter how fascinating or innocuous or *whatever* the destination world turned out to be. What had happened to convince A.E. to disregard that decision?

As soon as I regained some modicum of control over myself I demanded we make some kind of rescue attempt. Even though I knew no more about how the cockpit functioned than I did about flying A.E.'s beloved Vega, I'd have climbed into it willingly myself and dogged down the canopy.

But I would have had to join the end of a very long line to get into that cockpit—following every man jack who knew how the mechanism functioned.

0054 EST, May 25, 1937
From the journal of Fred Noonan

Finally, and for the first time, I really *believe*. All my doubts, all my delusions—they've been swept away forever. I know the truth. I've seen another world.

When the cockpit carrying Millie disappeared, I'd felt the transition like a kind of internal shift. Now, inside the cockpit myself, the shift was infinitely more intense—almost like a plane dropping when it loses lift, except that this "drop" was in a direction I never knew existed. For an instant, there was nothingness outside the canopy.

Not just blackness. Blackness is a property of *something*. *Nothingness.*

Then light came crashing in, brilliant, blinding light, coming from all around. I cringed, and I think I yelled from the shock.

A few seconds later I opened my eyes just a crack, shading them with one hand. I looked around, trying to make sense of my surroundings.

The cockpit was in a desert, resting at an angle on sands of so pale a yellow that they looked almost silver. Rolling dunes marched away in serried rows into the distance. The sun beat down from almost directly overhead, and that's why I'd been confused at first: the sand reflected the light and made the ground almost as bright as the sky. The desertscape was beautiful, in a brutal, stark away. There was nothing to break the mathematical regularity of the terrain—nothing but the cockpit, of course. There were no trees, no oases—no sign of life, no hint of water.

Where was the ocean? The cockpit should be sinking in

a dark, cold ocean. Was this desert part of the same world? Or was it a different world entirely? Whichever, this obviously wasn't where I was supposed to be. Much as we thought we knew, this proved we really were exploring the unknown.

My first reconnaissance mission would last only five minutes, time enough for me to check out the landscape, maybe even sketch out a simple map—and, most importantly, to determine if Millie could survive outside the cockpit.

I looked around again. This harsh, forbidding desert wasn't the kind of place where you wanted to be stranded for long, but a person wouldn't necessarily die right away, either. I reached for a compass to take bearings on the nearest dunes.

Just then, something that was nagging at my mind became obvious. At first I thought it was something I'd seen but hadn't paid attention to. But then I realized it was something I *hadn't* seen.

Footprints.

If Millie had set down here and left the cockpit, the fine, pale sand should show her footprints. There was no trace that anyone or anything had ever set foot on these sands. Had the cockpit even brought her to this wasteland? Wasn't it possible that the machines had sent Millie somewhere *else*?

From the corner of my eye I saw a redoubling of light on the horizon to my left. When I looked in that direction I saw what could be a second sun—a tiny point of blue-white, electric brilliance that seemed to shine tens of times brighter than the red disk overhead—climbing slowly into the sky.

Before I could be sure, the internal shift racked me again, and I was back in the New Jersey hangar.

0101 EST, May 26, 1937
From the journal of Fred Noonan

Christ, the sights we've seen! The stories are simply amazing. A burning desert that might have two suns in its sky. A dense, primeval forest under heavy clouds of midnight purple. An ocean of some milky, viscous fluid, rather than water. Far beneath the ramparts of a huge mountain wall, miles high, where fire falls from the sky like rain. A featureless plain of black rock under a sky so filled with stars it was bright as day. A valley between two volcanoes that belched black smoke into a pink sky. And pure and empty space, like between the planets, with stars burning in the infinite distance and no air whatsoever.

The repeated translocations are harrowing for everyone involved, but at least we see wonders to offset the danger and fear. It's much harder on the people forced to sit and wait for the outcome of each mission.

God, Millie, I'm starting to believe you're truly lost. Where in the infinite universe—or *universes*—are you?

I have to go. Another mission, my fourth.

0306 EST, May 28, 1937
From the journal of George Putnam

Three brave men dead of the twelve who've ridden the cockpits. That's 25 percent attrition, a figure more fitting to a combat battalion than a scientific research team.

Virgil Atkinson was the first to lose his life.

No more than three hours later, the second fatality. This man was dead when the cockpit arrived. As the technicians ran for crowbars to jimmy the canopy open, we could all see the body of young Derek Halsey, his unseeing eyes wide open and a smile of transcendent wonder fixed on his face.

And now the third. At least we assume it is a fatality. The cockpit containing Fred Noonan simply did not return. When the power to the system was cut, the harmonic field collapsed as usual, yet the gantry remained empty.

We terminated the rescue missions then. We simply had to accept that there was no chance of finding A.E., not this way. Each translocation took the cockpit to a different location, apparently at random (or according to some law or principle we do not understand, which is effectively the same thing).

I'm not giving up hope. A.E. could still be alive, that's the hope and the belief that must sustain me during the years while the theoreticians try to understand the random factor in manned translocation, and while the engineers build a new transporter that will compensate for that randomness. While we create the technology that will allow us to reach wherever it is that A.E. is now.

I'll be busy too. They'll need money, and raising money is one of the things I do best.

But first I must stage-manage the disappearance of Amelia Earhart. Though others in the League have realized this too, only Richard Byrd has mentioned it . . . and then, kindly, in only the vaguest terms. A.E. was—*is*—a public figure, the world's most famous aviatrix. She can't simply fade from public view. Snoops from the press, well-wishers, and her "camp followers" wouldn't accept that. They'd dig into her "disappearance" and eventually put the secrets of the League at serious risk. Some kind of cover-up is required.

The trick will be to balance fact with mystery. I know how reporters think. Give them too many neatly connected facts and they'll suspect a set-up. Give them too few facts, and they won't buy the cover story. A fine line to walk—and possibly the most difficult public-relations campaign I've ever undertaken. But I can do it. I *have* to do it.

We *will* find you someday, Amelia Earhart. I dedicate everything I am—every fiber of my being, every breath, every dream—to finding you, and bringing you back to me. And perhaps that questing will help fill the emptiness you left behind.